SECOND SIGHT

Clapping her hands to her ears, she moaned, looked up at the mirror, saw her hair like a crimson Medusa leaping with fire . . . saw him reach out toward her, pounding on the glass as if he were locked behind the mirror, screaming words she could not hear. She felt the stinging in her back, over and over, sharp jabs of the knife, his voice roaring, counting as he stabbed.

"Not me, not me!" she cried. "Not my death, only a dream, a bad, bad dream."

Theresa fell forward against the sink as the vision snapped off and the mirror reflected only her own terrified face. She couldn't stay there waiting like the good girl everyone wanted her to be. She had to see him, handcuffed, gun at his back, led to a squad car with grilled windows. To know they had him. Otherwise she'd never feel safe. She could not stay here a minute longer in this broken house with its smashed window, shattered moon. . . .

SHATTERED MOON

KATE GREEN

A DELL BOOK

Published by
Dell Publishing
a division of
Bantam Doubleday Dell Publishing Group, Inc.
666 Fifth Avenue
New York, New York 10103

The trademark Dell® is registered in the U.S. Patent and Trademark Office.

ISBN: 0-440-17593-3

Printed in the United States of America

Published simultaneously in Canada

January 1986

10   9   8   7   6   5   4   3   2

RAD

For Burton, again

Acknowledgments

Many thanks to an old friend from a past life; to Mary Jo Berendt; to Jean-Yves Pitoun and Lynn S. Baker, M.D., for offering insights and information regarding detectives and psychiatry; and I'd especially like to thank Jonathon Lazear.

Chapter 1

"Can you find her?" The woman's voice sounded far away, though she was just across the room. She looked down at her tightened fist and opened it to finger the ring. "We were told to bring something that belonged to Bonnie, some jewelry or clothing, something Bonnie had felt attached to. You know, I told my husband on the flight down to L.A. that I wished we hadn't come. I hope you'll pardon me for saying it all seems like a lot of hocus-pocus crap." Mrs. Humphrey laughed nervously.

"But she also said she'd try anything," said the woman's husband.

"I just don't believe in it."

"Nobody's asking you to."

"It scares me," Mrs. Humphrey whispered.

"Do you want to find her?"

Mrs. Humphrey paused, set the ring down on the end table, and settled back into the couch, crossing her legs. "I guess I'm relieved now that I'm in the same room with you. You look too young to be a psychic, Miss Fortunato."

"Please call me Theresa." The psychic leaned back against a table, nearly sitting. She waited calmly while Mrs. Humphrey expressed her doubts. Let them talk it out, she had learned. Take it slow. They'll relax. Theresa Fortunato turned and toyed with an arrangement of white flowers in a glass vase before a mirror.

"I expected a craggy old gypsy with a turban and a crystal ball or a crone with a pointed hat," said Mrs. Humphrey. "Why, you could be one of Bonnie's college friends home for a weekend visit." Her voice broke and

11

she pressed her hand to her lips. "She's simply disappeared."

Theresa Fortunato glanced at herself in the mirror. It was the early streak of gray at her left temple that gave her age away. Otherwise, no one would guess she was twenty-nine. Her thick black hair was pulled back into a loose braid, her eyes dark, penetrating, taking in the reflection of the Humphreys behind her. She noticed that she looked tired, circles under her eyes. With her thin hands she broke off a flower that had wilted and turned back to face the couple.

"Please," said Mrs. Humphrey, "we don't know what else to do."

Dr. Humphrey spoke. "As you know, a colleague of mine at the university referred us to you. Frank Brandon. He gave Bonnie some work last summer cataloguing some of his research."

Theresa smiled and nodded.

"I've known him for years," the doctor went on. "Met him when he was first setting up his psychiatric practice. He was interested in parapsychology even back then. He told us you were the real thing, very reputable. Even said you were 'miraculously accurate.' "

"No miracles," Theresa said. "Just intuitions. Perceptions." She could tell they were more at ease now. At first it had seemed odd seeing clients in her own house instead of an office, but Theresa had come to view it as an advantage. When she let people into her personal life in this way, they seemed more comfortable about opening up. That was important.

Theresa watched as Mrs. Humphrey studied the room. It was a tiny bungalow off a patio court, pale green stucco flaking. Number Three Jasmine Court, Venice. Inside, it was like a dollhouse, but it didn't feel cramped. It was impeccably ordered. Neat rows of books lined the shelves, pillows were stacked on the wood floor next to the couch, a collection of rocks and crystals was spread out on a table, and thick plants hung in a small sunroom off the

12

living room where they were sitting. Everything in the rooms was beige and white—furniture, rugs, curtains—everything but a framed collection of fortune-telling cards on the wall beside the couch.

"I don't usually do this kind of work," Theresa Fortunato said. "Frank—Dr. Brandon—asked me to help you out as a personal favor. I'll see what I can do, but my practice is mainly healing and personal consultation. I've never worked with the police before. Frank and I have worked together with cancer patients up at Berkeley. Did he mention it?"

"Not in detail," said Mrs. Humphrey. "He just told us that you had a great gift. He thinks very highly of you—and he said that you were recommended by his sister, Elizabeth. Isn't she a medium, too?"

"One of the best," said Theresa.

Dr. Humphrey sat forward on the couch. "Brandon mentioned that you'd studied with her."

"You could say that I'm her apprentice." Theresa Fortunato pulled up a straight-backed chair and sat opposite the Humphreys. She knew that clients would not guess that she, too, was nervous during the initial consultation. Theresa watched them studying her, questioning why they were there, doubting in some way. She had trained herself to move gracefully, circling her hands with a fluid motion as she spoke. She knew that her voice, soothing and low, would reassure them. "How long has your daughter been missing?" she asked.

"Two months," said Dr. Humphrey, "and the police haven't turned up a trace of her. They don't want anything to do with the case. They say no crime has been committed. No stolen car, no forged checks. Claim she's a runaway. Say they can't go chasing after every missing nineteen-year-old girl. The last time we saw her was May. May twenty-sixth, to be exact. She was home over Memorial Day weekend and came back down here to register for summer school. After we put her on the plane, we never saw or heard from her again."

"No phone calls? Letters?"

13

"Not a word."

Mrs. Humphrey raised her hand to rub her forehead, picked up the ring from the table, and handed it to Theresa. "She almost always wore this. I found it by the bathroom sink after she left. I was going to send it back to her. She got it for her sixteenth birthday."

Theresa turned the gold ring over in her palm. There was a small opal set into it. Then she opened a leather bag, pulled out a tiny white pouch, and slipped the ring carefully into it.

"Maybe we should have gone to a private detective," said Dr. Humphrey. "We thought about it."

"You might still want to," said Theresa. "But I'll see what I can do. As I said, I don't do this kind of work much, but I might be able to pick up something that could be useful." Theresa glanced at her watch. "You'll be in town a few days, then?"

Dr. Humphrey rose and cleared his throat. "Through Sunday, I think. We're going to talk to some friends of Bonnie's again. And we'll be cleaning her things out of her apartment. We kept putting it off, hoping that . . ." He paused, then went on. "Let me give you the number where you can reach us. And also"—he took a white calling card from his wallet and gave it to Theresa—"this is the police detective we've spoken with a few times—the one who can't handle the case until there's a crime."

Theresa looked at the card. In black print at the card's center it read SHERIFF'S DEPARTMENT, CITY OF LOS ANGELES, PETER J. PITCHESS, SHERIFF. Then down in the corner: O. T. JARDINE, HOMICIDE BUREAU, DETECTIVE DIVISION.

"You went through the Homicide Bureau?" She lifted her eyes toward Dr. Humphrey.

"He's a friend of a friend, this Jardine. Our only contact with the police besides the main number where they always put you on hold. He seems like a pretty good man, actually. But not much help."

14

"Well," said Theresa, standing. "I'll get on this as soon as I can. I'll start tonight."

"What will you do?" asked Mrs. Humphrey.

Theresa Fortunato sensed the woman was nervous again and she tried not to look directly at her. People always thought she was reading their minds, staring right through them to something hidden at the back of their skulls.

"I'll just open myself to her," said the psychic softly.

After the Humphreys had gone, Theresa walked down the several blocks to the ocean. It was mid-August, but the evenings were cool by the water, and she pulled her sweater up around her neck as she stepped onto the boardwalk. The wind carried the familiar salt smell and swept her hair back from her face. She stood for a moment watching the last groups of people leaving the beach, a family gathering children, wrapping them in plaid car blankets as the sun hung low, a flat orange disc, over the palm trees.

The small silk bag holding Bonnie Humphrey's ring was in Theresa's pocket. She didn't want to open it yet, but it kept pulling at her. She didn't like what she felt.

She tried to clear her mind. The sky was white with thin low clouds, and a haze obliterated the mountains. Yesterday, her friend Camille had told her not to do this, even before she met with the Humphreys. "You don't know what you're messing with, girl."

"Frank almost begged me," Theresa had answered.

"Because Elizabeth won't touch it, am I right? Elizabeth won't have nothing to do with no police."

"You know Elizabeth doesn't do readings at all anymore."

"Honey," Camille had said, "just you be careful, that's all I got to say."

Theresa sat for a few minutes on the cool sand, listening to the rush of waves. She was always drawn to the beach at sunset. A wash of late light played across the swelling water out beyond the breakers and a familiar shudder went through her. She'd felt it before, an anxious fear she'd never been able to name. For some reason the sea, reddened, made her think of flames.

The streetlights came on behind her, fluorescent in the dusk. She rose and headed back up the boardwalk. A few lone skaters cruised by her with their headphones on and a middle-aged black couple pushed a shopping cart in which a huge radio played a soft scat trumpet. Her mind was ready.

The images seemed to hover just below the surface of her thoughts, a dream she couldn't quite remember. She tried to hold them off until she got back to the house.

Jasmine Court was more of a sidewalk than a street. Each pastel cottage had its own wooden fence. A cat hunched on the steps of Number One and Theresa had to duck under the thick bougainvillea that leaned out over the fence of the second house.

Number Three was at the end on the left. Theresa noticed that the red plastic FOR RENT sign in the house across from hers had fallen down and someone had propped it up in a rusty birdbath next to the crumbling steps.

Inside, she drank some tea and watered the plants, then couldn't put it off any longer. In fact, she almost felt it calling her.

Dusk was a good time to read. The spirit world was near. Theresa called it reading, though she wouldn't actually use the cards. She didn't need them anymore, she only used them as props. Still, it was rather like opening a book, seeing the story appear inside her like a tiny movie dreamt in some deep part of her mind.

A candle flame swayed on the table before her. Theresa breathed deeply, cleared her mind to darkness, and held the girl's ring in her open palm. The images came quickly like a camera jolting suddenly to telescopic close-up. Theresa steadied herself to slow the images down.

She saw a road: gravel, high. Lights far below her like a field of stars. A car beside her. It was dark out, empty. No houses near. A steep hill rose up on one side, sudden ravine plunging down on the other. Dry chaparral and tall brush, low twisted trees. Another presence. Hot liquid fear inside. *Not mine—hers. Her fear.* Stay out of it, she told herself.

The night was black around her. *Slow down, back it up. Where?* Riding in the car on the desolate road, high over the city. *Over the valley,* it came to her. A tall power line supported by huge metal girders crossed over the road once, twice. Pavement, houses, street signs: ENCINO HILLS DRIVE. She saw it clearly, then felt herself thrown back to the first scene she'd gotten, felt herself dragged, struggling, from the car. No breath, no air. *No.* She lay still then with her hands at her sides. No fear now. No breathing. There was nothing.

The other presence was trembling, gasping. It was male. It placed her hands on either side of her body, then something in her hands, sharp. And now he was leaving, scrambling down the hillside.

Theresa could see all of this in her mind. But where am I? she thought. Where? She floated in the windy dark down the embankment to the road. Were there any other signs? *I need to know. Tell me where I am.*

She opened her eyes. The candle threw huge shadows of plants on white walls. As she pushed the window shut, the leaf shadows went still.

Theresa took a deep breath. No fear, she thought. This is not my life, but yours. Where are you? She let herself sink back into the dream. The girl was blindfolded and her hands, something about her hands. Pierced like Christ on the cross. Theresa tried to clear her mind. *Don't let the Jesus stuff interfere. I need to see clearly now.* The body on dry earth, her hands at her sides. And cut. But where? Float down dark tangled brush, Theresa. Emerge on the road. *Where am I?*

Lieutenant Oliver Jardine took the call in his office just past nine P.M. The air conditioner in his office was out of order and would only wheeze stale air on low. His shirt stuck to his back. He was in his early forties, slightly

17

balding. Sleeves pushed up on his arms, he hunched over an old file, wiped his large forehead with a paper napkin, smoothing down the thin hairs he combed over his bald spot. Then he crumpled an empty Styrofoam cup.

"Psychic *what*?" He scowled. "What is this shit?"

"I told you," said Cooper. "Man, it's stuffy in here." The younger detective fingered the end of his mustache. His pale brown face was dotted with sweat. He tucked his blue shirt into his pants, hitching his belt up around his thick waist. "Remember that doctor from Berkeley? You know, that friend of your old golf buddy you owed one to? Their missing daughter. They went and hired a psychic who says she knows where the girl is. This is the psychic calling to tell you where. Line three."

Jesus Christ. Why hadn't he stayed in Milwaukee where the cases were simple? So he liked the goddamn weather and the palm trees. Drugs and weirdos, crazies and warlocks. "Jardine here," he snapped.

"My name is Theresa Fortunato. I was given your name by a Dr. Richard Humphrey—"

"I know. What can I do for you?"

"I'm a psychic. I have a practice here in Venice. The Humphreys hired me to locate their daughter, Bonnie. I've found her. I'd like the police to come with me to the site."

The woman's voice was deceiving. She did not sound like a weirdo. She spoke clearly and with authority as if calling to say he was overdrawn on his bank account.

"The site?" he asked, rubbing the bridge of his nose. He had a headache. Damn sludge coffee, bottom of the pot. He ought to give it up. He flipped off the desk light.

"The site of the body," said the psychic.

"Are you reporting a murder, miss?"

She paused. "A death. I'm reporting someone dead."

Jardine took out a pen and tapped it on the desk blotter that was scribbled with phone numbers and curlicues. Why did people have to go and do something crazy? That doctor had sounded fairly intelligent on the phone the few times he'd talked to him.

Cooper slipped the Humphrey file onto Jardine's desk and opened it to the girl's picture. The case was coming back to him. Runaway. Hundreds of them. Fools hitchhiking all over the damn country. Never heard from again. He should have gone into insurance with his brother in Wisconsin.

"Okay. Go ahead," said Jardine. "The address."

"I have to show you. It's outside. It would be hard to explain."

"Have you actually seen the body?" he asked.

"Yes. Not in person. Lieutenant, look, I haven't worked with the police like this before. I'm sorry if I'm not aware of the proper procedure. I know where this body is and I'd like someone in an official capacity to—"

"Listen, Miss Fortune—"

"Fortunato. Italian. Boston, North End."

"I don't care about your family tree," he said, irritated. "If this family hired you, why don't you show them the body and then call us? It might save everybody a lot of time."

"I don't think they would want to see the body. I want police there."

Oliver Jardine swiveled his chair toward the window and peered out through the dusty blinds. He should send a squad car to check it out; it was probably a humbug. But it was true he owed one. Shit, it was late. He could go himself and cut out after that, get something to eat. Clear his debt. *I went all the way out there myself,* he could tell them.

He sighed. "Where?" was all he said. He peered out at the lights of the city as the woman on the phone calmly explained where she would meet him to show him where a dead girl was.

Her car was pulled off to the side of the road, past the last house with its yellow windows lit in the darkness. "Take Havenhurst all the way to the top of Encino Hills Drive," she'd said. "We can ride together from there."

19

Jardine lit a cigarette as he approached her car, dragged on it, then stubbed it out, remembering the warnings against brush fires in the hills. The San Fernando Valley glittered below him in a haze.

As she got out of her car, he saw that she was a handsome woman, stern-looking. She was small-boned and moved easily, like an athlete. Could be pretty if she'd fix herself up a little. Put on some lipstick. Her black hair was pulled up in a loose bun and strands fell down over her forehead, tangled in long earrings that jingled softly as she walked toward him. She kept her eyes focused directly ahead. Odd, he thought. She looked carved. Like a statue. Cold.

She even felt cold to the touch as she shook his hand firmly and gave him her card: THERESA FORTUNATO, PSYCHIC CONSULTANT, BY APPOINTMENT ONLY.

"Thank you for coming." She didn't smile. "I just wanted this all on the up and up. I don't usually do this kind of work. I just didn't think it would be good for the family to be present."

He wanted to say, *I don't usually do this kind of work either. When a murder is reported, there's usually a real body, not just a ghost in a trance.*

"Okay," he said. "So where's the body?"

"Not far," she said.

As he opened his car door for her, the squad car he'd requested pulled up behind them. He gestured for them to follow. The woman directed him up the road, which was gutted with deep ruts and potholes. They rode along the top of the mountains overlooking the valley. Strange there was a place so desolate so close to the buzz of the city below. Then he realized this was an undeveloped section of Mulholland Drive.

"Could you turn your brights on?" she asked. "I'm looking for some power lines. Here." The car bounced over a deep hole next to the metal structure that towered beside the road. "Up here," she said. There was a second tower. "Stop." Her voice was low, a monotone. She

20

thrust herself out of the car and the other patrol car halted behind them. When Jardine looked up, the woman was moving smoothly across the road, her legs bent in an odd way as if she were in a place with a low ceiling and had to bend her knees. She disappeared up the edge of the embankment into the chaparral. One of the officers from the patrol car hooked a large German shepherd onto a leash.

"Don't you want a light?" Jardine yelled into the darkness, but the woman was way up ahead of him. He ran to catch up with her, scrambling up the rocky cliff, stumbling, his black shoes slipping. There was no path. Dry branches snapped in his face.

The dog behind him began whining frantically. Jardine could smell the body before he got to it.

The photographer finished his last shot and a stretcher was brought up for the remains. Jardine checked his watch as he slid, catching himself, down the cliffside toward the road, lined now with police cars. Radios crackled on the officers' belts. Jesus, it was nearly two. He was hungry.

Fortunato would have to be looked into. She was sitting back in his car. Her thick, wavy hair had come down and she was combing it out with her fingers. She reached in her pocket as Jardine stepped toward her.

"The family will want this back," she said, handing him the ring. "They gave it to me to help find her."

Fortunato seemed relaxed now, her shoulders loose. "I'm exhausted. Can I get someone to take me back to my car?"

"I'm afraid not. We'll have to take you downtown for questioning."

"*Take* me?"

"Manner of speaking," he mumbled. "Routine. It's a homicide. You understand, miss. Anyhow, you'll want to see the Humphreys. They'll be coming down to identify the body."

Theresa winced. "Do they have to?"

The body, covered in plastic, was carried down the

21

hillside and placed in the back of an ambulance. The red lights were turned off. There was no hurry now.

"They were taking pictures, weren't they?" asked Theresa.

Jardine remembered the picture of the girl in the file. Pretty high-school portrait. Teeth straightened by expensive dental work. Long blond California hair. It was a shame.

"The way she was laid out," said Theresa. "She wasn't just dumped there." The girl's body had been found under a stand of bushes. She was blindfolded. That was not strange in these cases.

"You suggesting a cult or something?"

"Maybe," said Theresa. It was the knives they were speaking of. An initial examination revealed the girl had been stabbed. There was a deep slash across what was left of the side of her face. But the hands. There was a single knife stuck through each of her open palms, holding the body onto the earth.

Cooper strode over to them as Theresa leaned against the car. "Lieutenant!" he yelled. "Hold up a minute!" Cooper opened his handkerchief and showed it to Jardine. "Fell out of the pocket when they lifted her," he said.

Jardine motioned to Theresa and Cooper held out to her two small plastic swords, the kind they put in club sandwiches in hotels, the kind stuck through olives in bars all over Los Angeles.

"Do these mean anything to you, ma'am?" he asked.

Chapter 2

I've seen her a couple times. I go in for breakfast and her hair, it's sometimes wet like she just got out of the shower. I like to think of her at home in the morning before she puts on her uniform and goes to work. She calls me by name, though I gave her the wrong name. I like having a lot of different names. One for each day of the week. She smiles and pours me coffee. Her uniform is pink. She's so clean in the morning in her white shoes. Like a nurse. She could take good care of somebody.

I noticed her about two weeks ago. She wears this little cross around her neck. I like that. I asked her if she went to church. She said, "Yeah, sometimes." Then she said, "You aren't one of them evangelical types, are you?" I said, no, I didn't even go to church myself, but I like the music. She looked at me kind of strange so I didn't say anything else except, "You know, those big organs, like that." But she was busy and had to go down to the other end of the counter and pour coffee.

I don't go in every day because I don't want anyone to think they know me, know my pattern. Don't want to do anything the same, day in, day out. Had enough of that prison feeling, that locked-in, shut-up-in-a-dark-hole, crouched-down-in-the-shadows-with-the-insects feeling. But when I go there again, she recognizes me and nods and smiles, and I decide it's all right. It might be all right if one person really knew me. Really deep inside the place no one has ever touched.

I like her because she's full of light. This morning I asked her about the light. I laughed like it was a joke to see what she'd say. "Have you seen the light?"

She said, "You're not giving me some more of that religious bullshit, are you?"

Then I noticed she wasn't wearing the cross around her neck anymore. And she looked different too. Her shoes were kind of scuffed up and some grease or ketchup was on her apron. She was always so clean before. Her name is Carolyn. It's on her plastic name tag. I don't like dirty people. Don't like dirt. I like things wiped up and scrubbed with Lysol. No germs, no fingerprints. They can't find you then. But I don't talk about this stuff to anyone because I've learned how to be quiet so I can move around in the world without being noticed. If you don't say anything they just think you're shy or dumb. Quiet and good and no trouble. Just sit all day and watch the TV. I've learned that.

So I watched her wiping the counter and she smiled and flipped her hair back. It was dark and frizzy. In the sunlight it looked red. I asked her if she'd like to go to the beach together sometime, how about tonight. Just go for a walk or something. I was thinking how full of light she was and glowing and then she said she couldn't, she had to go to her yoga class.

I said, "You aren't following some guru, are you?" and she said, "Yeah, you should check him out." His name is Shrii Shrii something or other and my heart was sinking because then I knew she was lost too. Like everyone else around here.

"What about your cross, you never wear it anymore."

"No," she said. "I don't know about Christ, to tell you the truth. I just want to check everything out. You should really come to this place. You sit and meditate. It makes you real calm. Why don't you come?" she said.

And I don't know why but I got scared and looked away so she wouldn't see my eyes because I knew she wasn't at all who she thought she was. She was dark and tempting me and calling out to me to set her right. There was something false about her like a windup doll that only just pretended to be real. Her face got all smiley. The devil's *always glad to get you off your path. Always watching and waiting for you. So I said, "Yeah, I'll go. I'll even drive."*

It makes me sad, all the darkness surrounding. I'm almost crying when I'm getting ready for her tonight. But I never cry, I can't. It just sticks in my throat like a fist is jammed down there clenching onto something in my chest. Oh, God. When I think of her white shoes.

Theresa often wore white when she did readings for people. It put her in the right frame of mind. She used to think that maybe it was too much, it would put people off. What was she trying to prove, acting so pure and angelic? Now she did what she felt like. Buttoning the white blouse over her tan skin, she tucked it into her skirt.

She still felt so tired. It had been five days since the Humphrey girl had been found and she could not erase from her mind the terrible image of the girl's swollen body in the underbrush, that gray-black face that was no face, flashlights streaking over her, frantic striations of shadows, the dog shuddering taut on its leash. Early dawn, downtown L.A., thick white smog. The top floor of a gray building. Inside, lines of plastic chairs, smell of smoke and questions, questions. Mrs. Humphrey's red eyes, swollen from crying, her face distorted. She'd thrown her arms around Theresa and wept.

Yesterday Frank Brandon had called from Berkeley to thank Theresa. That had helped. He told her how much the Humphreys had appreciated it. He said the anxiety and uncertainty had been awful for them. Theresa almost wished it hadn't been so easy picking up on the dead girl's vibrations, entering her last minutes on earth.

So this morning she'd sat for several hours on the beach, burying her feet in sand and watching old men, Asian and Hispanic, carry long fishing poles and pails out onto the Venice pier. Every seventh wave rolled in high, swirling up the sand and sucking it back with great force into the sea. Fat seagulls squawked overhead. The rhythmic sway of the water usually calmed her, but today she felt again that old anxiety the sea brought on. She closed her eyes. Burning, quick orange flames racing over the sand. That's what she saw: water and fire. For a moment her hands felt hot as if she were holding them in that imagined fire.

Her client was due at four for her weekly reading. Theresa prepared for the reading in the sunroom off the tiny living room, remembering what Elizabeth Brandon had once told her—"The preparation for the ritual *is* the ritual." She set out the Tarot cards, watered the ferns in the window, and lit a white candle on a small wooden table at the center of the room.

Evelyn was a regular, a divorced woman who told Theresa that the money she spent on her readings was the money she used to spend on a shrink, only the readings made her feel a whole lot better. Theresa had tried once to wean her from the weekly sessions, "You just don't need them this often, Evelyn."

"Look," Evelyn had said, "maybe I don't, but they lift me up. They take me out of the ordinary. They remind me that this isn't all there is to life, credit cards and what's for supper. I think of you as a teacher."

Theresa counted among her clients doctors, musicians, professors, housewives, students, waitresses, and car mechanics, people in workaday lives who were hungry for some connection to the universe. She knew that because she, too, had felt the emptiness of days ruled only by routine, money, or the lack of it. Some people leaned toward religion or politics, seeking a sense of order in their lives, but Theresa thought both church and state attracted those who craved answers. Priests and politicians were ready to provide them with belief systems that could satisfy. But those who preferred the questions themselves came to people like her, psychics, astrologers, numerologists, Tarot readers, mediums. The ancient occult traditions held out to them not pat explanations to life's dilemmas but the query itself. It was the seekers who came, the ones who wanted a journey, a secret path. Even while they sat at large gray desks or stood before hot stoves, they wanted to know they were indeed traveling, that being human was something magical, a puzzle, a mysterious game.

After a while Theresa had come to realize that Evelyn scheduled her weekly sessions just to get a hit of some consciousness beyond the mundane, and while Evelyn had perhaps become a little addicted to the sessions, well, there were worse things to crave. Theresa could hardly criticize it. After all, she'd been so drawn to that realm that she'd become a psychic. She had wanted to be on the journey all the time, not only visit it now and then.

Theresa straightened the chairs on either side of the table. The bell rang exactly at four. Evelyn was never late.

"Theresa, I love your new sign! When did you get it?" Theresa stepped out the front door to admire again the small circular sign she had painted and hung in the front window. FORTUNATO, it read. And then underneath:

PSYCHIC CONSULTANT
READER / ADVISOR

But the part of the sign she liked best was the logo—a circle with a half-moon crescent inside it. Across from the crescent was a T-cross, each of the lines of equal length.

"It's real nice," said Evelyn. "Did you design it yourself?"

"No," said Theresa, "it was given to me by my teacher."

"I like it." Evelyn brushed past Theresa into the reading room. The women each took chairs and sat opposite each other, the table between them. Theresa unwrapped the Tarot cards from a square of silk and began shuffling them.

"Now take a deep breath, Evelyn, and let all thoughts and worries of the day leave your mind."

Theresa had done this so often, she didn't have to think. As usual, the reading began coming to her before she even saw the cards, as if a channel had been turned on in her mind. The cards just helped to make the reading visual for

27

the client. There was no problem opening to the images. The problem was to quiet the flood of information so that she could not only give a clear reading for the client, but try to lead something of a normal life herself, go about day-to-day business without drowning in the voices and intimate thoughts of every stranger that passed her on the street.

As soon as Theresa spread out the cards, she began speaking in a quiet, almost monotone voice, trying not to think about what she was saying, but letting the words spill out from some dreamlike place inside her. She spoke quickly in a rush without breathing, her eyes on the colorful cards on the table. The simple pictures with their symbols invited meaning as she nearly whispered, "First of all, Evelyn, I see that you're still worried about your health, this heart thing. I want to tell you right away that you're holding on to the idea of your illness because it gives you a sense of identity. You have a purpose now: to be sick. In this Ten of Pentacles there is almost a sense of greed about the illness. It gives you reason to feel important to yourself."

The cards were turned up one after the other on the table and Evelyn listened quietly. It was then that the feeling of dread began just up under Theresa's breastbone. Theresa stopped, leaned back in the chair, slightly nauseated and light-headed as it spilled into her mind—the girl's body, hands puffed up like fat rubber gloves filled with water, the black jackknives jammed through the open palms.

Theresa squeezed her eyes shut, then opened them, flipped over the next card, and gasped. Evelyn looked up in alarm. "Is it that bad?"

The overturned card was the Ace of Swords, which pictured a hand reaching out of a cloud. The hand was holding a golden blade.

Theresa shook her head, rubbing her temple. "I haven't been feeling right today. Maybe I'm getting a little flu bug or something." The image of the girl's body crowded in again, pounding in Theresa's skull. The hands, Christ hands, nailed right through. Bonnie's hands. Knifed into the ground. She couldn't concentrate. She heard the rustling of branches, dry scrape of gravel beneath her. A man's voice coming at her whispering, "Don't you? Don't you believe?"

"Theresa." Evelyn was beside her, holding on to her arm. "Are you all right?"

The room seemed to blur for a moment, Evelyn only a vague shape, a thick, slurred voice from far away. She felt as if she were moving underwater, slowly and with great resistance.

"I must have felt faint. I'm sorry, Evelyn."

"Don't apologize. Here, you should lie down. You've been working too hard. I know you. You ought to take a few days off. Take a vacation or something. Eat more protein."

Theresa nodded blankly. "I think I'm okay now." She promised Evelyn she would read for her next week and showed her to the door. In the sunroom she placed the cards back into a neat pile and wrapped them again in silk. She drew the shades in her bedroom at the back of the house and lay down. The day was too bright and she couldn't get the girl out of her head. Forget it, she thought. *Erase, gone*—but still the hands floated inside her. It was not just the memory of the scene. This was something else. It was like entering the exact moment of Bonnie's death, just before it happened. She could see it all through her eyes and relive her terrible unrest and fear.

This was the fourth appointment this week that had gone badly. She'd canceled one reading because of a headache. In two others the images that came to her had been vague, and once she'd dropped the deck to the floor, cards scattering beneath the table. The day before, she'd given a confused reading full of violent images, the card of Death, the Tower. The man she'd been reading for, Josh, was another regular client. He was her car mechanic and they often worked out exchanges, a lube job for a reading, his future for a fixed carburetor. Fortunately, he'd been understanding and had said it wasn't urgent, he could wait a week to reschedule. But this had to stop.

Theresa had been sleeping restlessly as well, waking several times each night with disconnected dreams she could not quite remember except all of them were about Michael. She'd waked with one last night, and had gotten up to splash cold water on her face. In the dream she had seen a car accident. The car rolled in slow motion down the side of a canyon and she ran to save the driver, pulling open the crushed door of the car. It was Michael Ballard and he was cut open and laughing at her.

Theresa sat now at the edge of the bed, gathered a shawl around her shoulders, and went back into the sunroom. She unwound the cards from the silk scarf, shuffled them, then flipped over the top card to see the picture of a man lying face down in darkness with swords stuck in his back. "No," Theresa whispered, and slammed the card face down on the table.

Camille glanced at Theresa in the dressing-table mirror and carefully applied deep brown lipstick to her already brown lips. "I told you not to mess with no cops, Resa. You only asking for trouble. Why you go looking for a mess anyway? Ain't life complicated enough?" Camille fingered the ends of her hundreds of thin braids, touched the tiny diamond at the side of her nose, and checked over her long violet fingernails. It was early evening and the room was darkening except for the intense spot of light from the lamp before the mirror.

In the four years that Theresa had known Camille, she had never once seen her look scruffy or unkempt. When they'd lived together at Elizabeth's they would often rise early, Camille elegant in a black Egyptian gown, her hair braided down, her eyelids dusted with gold powder even before dawn. They had been Elizabeth's favorite students, Theresa with her ear for the voices of the cards, Camille's ability to perceive past lives in people as if the stories were engraved across their foreheads. "Hey," Camille would say, "see that man? He had a life once as the wife of a fisherman whose boat went down in a storm. That's how come he always be hanging out at the beach and can't do nothing but stare out to sea like he's waiting for somebody to come back."

"Sarene!" Camille called out, still facing the mirror.

"What, Mama?" The child yelled back from the living room where the TV was blasting.

"Turn that thing down!" Camille spun around on the dressing table stool and began smoothing Vaseline onto her long black legs.

"The police were okay, really." Theresa sat on the unmade bed. "They were no trouble."

"You can't expect to deal in no violence and it ain't going to touch you."

"But I wanted to help. They were friends of Frank's. What could I do?"

"Just stay out of it from now on or you're a damned fool, that's what. Sarene!" she hollered. "Bring Mama her purse!"

The six-year-old girl ran into the bedroom, tossed the bag to her mother, and dived into Theresa's lap. "I didn't know you was here!"

Theresa hugged her. "I came on my broom."

"Abracadabra," said Sarene, and she grinned widely, showing off a space where a tooth was missing.

"Hey, did the tooth fairy bring you a dime?"

"Brung me five whole dollars."

"Even the tooth fairy's hit by inflation." Camille winked at Theresa and said to Sarene, "Go on, now, Resa and Mama's talking business." The girl leapt out of the bed, hesitated briefly at the door, then disappeared down the hallway.

Camille hooked the ankle straps on her high heels and sat down next to Theresa. "What exactly is going on?" she asked.

"The image of that girl's death is bleeding through onto every reading I do. I hear her voice. It's like she's calling

31

out to me. I can't make out what she's saying. I can't get her hands out of my head, and those knives—whenever I lay out the cards, half of them are swords. It's taken over everything.''

"Are you afraid?"

"A little."

"Why? It ain't you who died. You got to detach, Theresa. Let that spirit go. She was ready to travel on. Do some protective prayers, cleanse yourself, do a fast.''

"And Michael—"

Camille frowned. "Not him."

"He's in all my dreams with this girl, and they're so familiar. Nightmares, really. I can't even sleep.''

"It ain't nothing to get all in a state about. You know what the connection is between your ex-husband and that poor dead girl? You got yourself in trouble when you married an undertaker in the first place, I swear.''

"He wasn't an undertaker when I married him."

"He always did give me the creeps," said Camille.

"It's just a job. Somebody's got to bury the dead."

"Uh-uh. Just burn my ass and throw me in the Pacific, honey. I want you to promise you'll do that when I die. I know my family will want to put me in the ground in Watts and then my bones will have to spend eternity where I grew up and that would be a damn shame. I got no intention of hanging around the physical plane when I could be out cruising the spheres. Listen, girl, I got to go to work. Almost nine now.''

Camille stood before the round mirror and smiled at herself. "Don't I look good," she said, smoothing her hands down over her wide, angular hips and muscular thighs. "Just relax, baby. And don't mess anymore with no cops. It ain't your business.''

Theresa turned in the sheets, shivered, tangling. She knew it was a dream but could not wake up. The girl was young, her dark hair curled around her face. Not the dry mountains like before, but an open road, an irrigated field,

32

three red shacks in a row. She couldn't see, her eyes were covered, and the knife was at her throat. "You're not going to kill me, are you? Please don't kill me. I'll do whatever you say. Please," she said, and spun suddenly, breaking his hold, tearing off the blindfold. It was Michael and his neck was slit open like a mouth screaming. He was dancing like a tap dancer wearing white shoes.

Theresa woke sweating, grabbed the clock radio. Three forty-five glowed in red numerals. It was too real, her hands were shaking, she was breathing hard. She stumbled barefoot into the dark living room. Wind blew the curtains in and she pressed the window shut. Wake up, she told herself, but it was no dream. It was happening, somewhere, now. Her throat was thick, she couldn't swallow. The bougainvillea outside thrashed in the ocean wind and the FOR RENT sign across the way rattled down the sidewalk, lodging next to the picket fence.

Michael will come soon, she thought. And then: Jardine. I have to call him in the morning.

She woke tired, feeling as if she'd been walking all night in her sleep. The backs of her thighs ached and she was tense and restless. Watching the morning window rustle with green shadows, she lay awake awhile before rising, then wrapped herself in her robe, put the tea on the stove, and went to the front door to pick up the paper.

Paging through the *L.A. Times* at the breakfast table, her eyes were drawn to a photograph of a young woman whose face was bordered by thick, dark curls. I know this woman, Theresa thought. One of my clients? She yawned and read the headline:

WOMAN MISSING AFTER
STREET SCUFFLE

A woman has been reported missing following a possible abduction in Venice last Friday. Twenty-year-old Carolyn Svedrup was last seen leaving the Seaside Café, where she is employed as a waitress. Witnesses reported that a woman who fit Svedrup's description attempted to get out of a tan car near the restaurant. There appeared to be a struggle between the driver and the woman. Her roommate reported Svedrup missing yesterday. She had not returned home in three days, which was unlike her. "She's very regular," said the roommate. "Always on time." Police have no suspects at this time.

Chapter 3

Lieutenant Jardine would think she was crazy, calling in to report a dream she'd had. What would she say? "Oh, Officer, I had a nightmare. I dreamt my ex-husband was tap-dancing with a dead girl."

Theresa spent the morning in the small strip of garden along the back of her house, weeding between the zinnias and the two zucchini plants, picking up shreds of eucalyptus that had fallen from the great tree next door. It calmed her to kneel on the dirt and feel the dry earth in her hands. The ground smelled of salt and evergreen. She liked the neat ordering of the plants, the meticulous rows, the round pots of tomato plants. She liked plucking off the old dried nasturtium blossoms so that new blooms would come.

This attraction to order was what had first drawn her to the Tarot. She loved the old symbols and their hidden meanings handed down from medieval times. Some said the images on the cards went even farther back than that to schools of initiation in Egyptian pyramids. There was clarity and precision in the numbered system of cards and the various patterns she could place them out in—the Celtic Cross, the Wish Spread, the Tree of Life. She was part of a long line of Tarot readers and sometimes she imagined them all as an ancient society spanning centuries, all the alchemists, sorcerers, and querents of the Kabbalah standing behind her as she read. The cards, with their colorful stories and rich history, provided a framework for perceptions that could be confusing to her or even frightening, and as she snapped withered leaves from her plants, she longed for that feeling of order.

Last night's dream still bothered her. It hung in fragmented images around the edges of her thoughts—the three shacks, the sensation of being blindfolded yet still able to see. And Michael Ballard grinning, clacking his shoes—what did it add up to? She felt a slight fear in her stomach, an acid feeling as of drinking too much coffee. Kneeling in the early sun, Theresa was aware that the voices were near and could speak to her if she would only open to them. "Go away," she whispered aloud. "Go away."

When the voices had first started, it felt just like this. Sometimes there was a cacophony of voices, whole choruses of them swarming and hissing like insects. She lay in bed for hours, her ears stuffed with cotton, but it only kept the voices in and she hadn't known how to control them or make any sense of what they were saying. Her mind was too open. It made her think of a woman she'd heard of who kept picking up radio signals in her new fillings, sure she could hear angels singing Beautiful Music and reporting the weather and evening news.

It was Elizabeth Brandon who had helped her, taught her to focus on a single voice, to quiet the others, shut down the waves of images that flooded through her like nausea or dread. Without Elizabeth's techniques she might have gone mad, become one of those crazy ladies on street corners in New York, talking to no one in a loud voice. *All in her head, all in her head.* Elizabeth had taught her to visualize one voice coming through a single band on a radio. "You are in control," Elizabeth had instructed. Theresa did not feel at all in control now. Maybe she did need the vacation Evelyn had suggested. She could go up to Big Sur, sleep in a tent. Get away from all this noise.

Even the morning mail had brought unwanted voices—an off-the-wall fundamentalist tract featuring a collage of newspaper headlines about astrology, prayer in the schools, the number of abortions performed in Orange County, and a woman convicted of murdering her mother after Satan told her to do it. Lettered in large red felt-tip pen across the bottom of the page was the phrase *Witches Get Burned.*

That was the part of the legacy of psychics she would like not to think about. If this were Salem in the seventeenth century, she certainly wouldn't hang out a sign in her window advertising her services. Thousands and thousands of women had been burned throughout history, midwives, healers, witches, and pagans. The Church had not liked the notion of spirit voices. During the Inquisition those who owned Tarot decks kept them well hidden or disguised as a simple game of playing cards. As Theresa stood holding the menacing letter, it occurred to her that even in the twentieth century, it was not totally safe to practice her powers. She crumpled the letter and threw it into the wastebasket.

She was not surprised when she opened the card from Michael Ballard; she had felt the dreams bringing him close. Strange sense of déjà vu about them, as if she'd dreamt them all before. The card was large and ornate with silver bells on it. HAPPY ANNIVERSARY, it read. Inside he'd scrawled, *Five years. Now we've been divorced for as long as we were married. We ought to celebrate. I'm taking you out to dinner whether you like it or not.*

Why don't you stay away? she thought. Why can't you just let go and leave me alone?

After lunch she held two readings in the sunroom, and the calm feeling induced by the trance states was welcome and familiar. Both had been simple Tarot readings—love in question, when should I have a baby, should I change my job? A sword card had turned up in the second reading, but it had not seemed odd and no brutal scenes forced their way through the cards.

Theresa was relieved as she put the cards away for the day, wrapping them in their square of silk. This was how most of her readings made her feel—graceful and loving, with a mild elation that came from being of help to others. Camille had once told her, "Every reading I give to someone is for me too. It's my own kind of high, and there ain't no crash."

It was only three when Theresa finished, and the day

37

was hot, the sky brilliant, cloudless. She decided to walk to the bookstore where she taught classes in psychic development, Tarot, beginning and advanced. She would check through the appointment book to see if she'd been scheduled for any readings and find out how many people had signed up for her class. After tacking a note to her door that told prospective clients they could find her at the shop, she started out.

The hot sun made the top of her head hurt as she walked the angled streets away from the ocean toward Washington Boulevard. She tried to keep to the shady side of the street, but there was none. Venice was one of the few places she'd lived in Los Angeles where it was possible to walk everywhere—only a few blocks to the beach, eight blocks to the shop past funny little houses painted crummy pastel colors, thick ivy on high fences, oleander and fuchsia shading a sleeping dog on a fake zebra-skin pillow in front of an apartment building. A poster on a telephone pole announced a Latin gospel concert, fire dancers Friday at a vegetarian restaurant, jazz harp Saturday. Theresa walked slowly up Washington, peering in the dark window of a secondhand store, past the bar where Camille worked, a plant shop, a sailboat supply store, and an aikido school, before coming to the bookstore.

Inside, the shop was cool. The lights were turned off and a single green candle in a brass candlestick burned on the counter next to the cash register. The smell of piñon incense drifted through the air. The clerk stood behind the counter talking to a man about a small purple bag. She paused as Theresa entered. "Hi! Couple more readings," she said, shoving the leather-bound appointment book down the glass counter.

"Silk," the clerk said to the man. "You put your cards in it. They say silk protects the vibrations of the cards."

"Okay," he said, "but what deck would you suggest?" He was a short man, both slender and well-built. His long beard looked slightly out of place on his youthful face, more red and scraggly than his smooth chestnut hair. He studied the embroidery on the silk bag and peered earnestly into the case filled with Tarot decks wrapped in cellophane.

"You know, the person you should ask is Theresa," said the clerk, motioning up the counter. "Theresa Fortunato. She's the Tarot reader."

The man looked up, his eyebrows raised. "You're the psychic?"

"One of them." Theresa smiled. "You're looking for a deck for yourself?"

"Yeah. I was given a deck as a present but I lost them," he said. "I'd like to know more about them but I'm not sure where to start. I was thinking about taking a class. You teach one, don't you?" He held up the flyer that listed the current classes.

"Have you ever had a reading?" Theresa asked. "Sometimes that's the best introduction."

"Can you tell about other people in a reading? Besides yourself, I mean. Relationships, family stuff."

"Oh, yes," said Theresa. "Families—that's one of my specialties."

"Which deck do you use?" he asked.

"I collect them, actually. I read with them all, it depends on the client, the day, my mood."

"Yeah," said the man. "All right. A reading, that's cool." He kept tucking his silky hair back behind one ear. Up close she could see that beneath the beard, his face was pocked with acne scars. His eyes were amber-brown and he looked serious and impressionable. As she looked at him closely, she saw that he was actually quite beautiful, his face delicate as a young boy's, but it seemed as if he were trying to hide himself behind his scruffy beard and his mottled skin. She felt that there was something in his life that he feared, that he'd witnessed something he couldn't forget, and was stuck there watching it over and over again in his mind, unable to move on, haunted by, yet drawn to, some awful recollection of childhood terror. Oh, stop, she thought. Wait until you're really reading for him. But it was amazing how much she could tell about a person sometimes before the cards were even set out. The only trouble was that she didn't always trust her intuitions, her images, until the pictures on the cards validated them. And she couldn't read correctly if it had to do with herself. Trying to read for herself was like looking in a window that had been painted black.

Maybe it was just that she was too subjective, too close to both the query and the source of the reply. Whenever she tried reading the cards for herself, the psychic part of her mind seemed to close down. Nothing came to her.

Elizabeth had seen this as a weakness. She'd suggested getting a special deck to be used only in readings for herself, and although she'd followed Elizabeth's instructions, the problem had gotten worse. The readings had been jumbled, disconnected, and made no sense to her at all. "You've got a block," Elizabeth had said, and then she told Theresa to go through the deck card by card, asking her subconscious for a dream about each card until she had "made friends with the deck." Finally, Theresa had come to accept her limitation. After all, doctors were advised not to diagnose themselves, and if she wanted or needed a clear reading for herself, she could always go to another psychic.

Theresa opened the leather-bound book and explained to the bearded man that she made appointments at the bookstore but held the readings at her home. She gave him directions and penciled his name in the appointment book. When she looked up, she saw Michael stalking into the bookstore, causing unicorn mobiles and Chinese paper kites to go fluttering in the stillness.

Oh, God, she thought. Not here. "What are you doing here?" she said aloud in spite of herself.

"Some greeting," said Michael. "Saw the message that I could find you here." He stood in the center of an aisle grinning at the wind chimes, the rainbows, the posters of Buddha and Isis on the walls. He shook his head. "You kill me," he said. Then, "Did you get my card?"

"Today."

"And?"

"I suppose."

"You're so thrilled, Terry."

"Don't call me 'Terry,' " she whispered.

"And we're not going to some avocado-and-brown-rice dump," he said.

"I don't eat steak, Ballard."

"Can't we be on a first-name basis?" He leaned over the glass counter and kissed her lightly on the mouth. Theresa pulled back, looking down. "How about seafood?" he asked.

Theresa opened a glass case on the counter and began straightening a line of pendants and rings. Michael, what am I ever going to do with you? she thought. She hadn't seen him in four or five months. They'd danced together at a party last spring and she hadn't let him take her for a drink afterward and he'd kissed her anyway. She'd cried as she'd driven home. Now he'd lost weight and was wearing a silly Hawaiian shirt with flamingos perched all over it, crazy pinks and greens. Standing that close to him in the shop, she caught his familiar smell of English Leather, Right Guard, and cigarette smoke. She wished she could simply be indifferent to him after all this time instead of feeling that adrenaline rush in her heart that meant both longing and despair. As unhappy as she'd been with him, there had been no one since who'd gotten as close.

Michael Ballard was a tall man in his early thirties. He had the body of an all-around high-school athlete who'd given up sports. His legs were long, arms thick and muscular, his chest was broad and his waist still lean, but there was a softness about him, a slackness. He'd tried jogging but was easily winded and wouldn't quit smoking. He carried himself stiffly. Standing before her in the store, he toyed with his dark mustache. His hairline was thinning slightly, but Theresa noticed he was growing his hair long

41

again. It flipped out to one side at the neckline. That had always made him mad.

When they were married, people sometimes mistook them for brother and sister; their coarse black hair, thin noses, and thick eyebrows nearly matched.

"I wasn't surprised to get your card, Michael. Actually, you have been on my mind lately." Theresa closed the leather appointment book. "I've been dreaming about you."

"That's nice." He smiled.

"It's not what you think."

"Well, dream on, Terry. Theresa," he added quickly, then glanced at the young man who stood next to Theresa, peering into the glass case and listening in on the entire conversation. Michael glared at him and made large bug eyes. "Excuse us," he said, and the man looked up.

"No problem," said the bearded man. "Don't worry about it." He slipped the bright orange knapsack over his shoulder and walked out of the bookstore.

"Who was that?" asked Michael Ballard.

"His name is Raymond"—she opened the appointment book—"Mead. He's worried about his family, he had a traumatic childhood, there's been an illness in one near to him, lots of doctors—why am I telling you this?"

"You love me madly, you tell me everything."

"Cut it out, Michael." Theresa turned to the shelf behind her, silently lining up all the candles in a neat row.

"So. When will we have dinner?" he asked.

She shook her head no.

"Come on, you just said yes," he insisted. "It's our yearly date."

"It won't be a date, Michael."

"How about Thursday, then? Day after tomorrow. Besides, you've got to listen to your dreams. You witches have got to follow up on your premonitions, don't you? Hey, Thursday," he repeated. "I'll call you." He turned and walked out into the brittle sunlight.

Michael had always been persistent and thick about things, hard to hurt in small ways. She used to think he was indestructible. Nothing ever got through to him. She once thought that if only she could hurt him, it would mean that he cared. Maybe then she might have stayed in the marriage. But for so long he just seemed oblivious to her, and being invisible to him was more than Theresa could bear.

Walking home from the bookstore, she felt first drowsy, then sick, just as she had when she'd been reading for Evelyn. Theresa leaned her head against the side of a brick building and felt her skin cool with sweat. There it was again, that familiar smell of smoke and English Leather, Michael's body smell, his slight growth of beard, his gentle hands that had once become so terrifying and fierce.

The fumes of bus exhaust and afternoon smog filled her breathing. Hovering voices pressed in on her to receive them. "Please," she whispered, clenching her teeth. If she could keep her own mouth shut, maybe the voices would not come.

Theresa felt faint and knelt beside the sidewalk, thinking she might be sick. Last night's knife dream blinked in her mind, glittering razor-edged blades rushed past her head in slow motion, one, two, three to the heart. "God," she whispered. And here was Michael poking around in her life again. The nightmares familiar as her own face in the mirror. Of course, she'd dreamt them before. How could she have failed to remember? She'd blanked them out, the memory too painful, the old dreams of Michael killing someone over and over again. Theresa, the witness. It was years ago, when things were so bad in the marriage, when it all felt tragic and doomed. Stress, the doctor had said. Symbolic of some part of her that was dying inside, she'd said. Theresa was just beginning to learn how to control her psychic powers then and was afraid even to lie down, knowing the killing dreams would return, eat up her sleep, cut their way through her pure darkness, and she'd wake sweating in damp sheets, shivering, alone, the clock glowing three forty-five exactly every night.

Even the drugs they'd given her in the clinic hadn't

stopped the nightmares, and she'd lain on the hard bed in the white box room with the bars on the windows to keep her from getting to the glass. *You can leave anytime you want to, Theresa.* But she couldn't leave her own head, could she, Doctor? She'd watched the car lights make stripes flap across the ceiling through the bars as she forced herself to stay awake, her eyes grainy and dry, but the Dalmane and the dreams had always won out. But that was years ago and she'd survived.

Maybe she should walk back to the cool bookstore, relax, and drink some more tea until this passed, but she felt so dizzy. Theresa put her hand on the ground to feel it there. Earth. Safe. Ground. God help me. But they came anyway, the voices calling from a great distance, then becoming shrill—*It's so dark, so very dark, get me out*—until she was not just seeing the dream but in it. Living it.

She reeled against the cement and let it wash over her, through her—the dusk lit the inside of a small wooden building with strange orange light. She was wearing white shoes. "Why don't you wear this?" said the man. His hands on her neck, fastening the chain around her, delicately, like a lover. Then he turned to her, but his face was gone, a blank hole. He jerked the necklace off her, dragged her down on the dry ground, no breath, no air, blade to throat, and then it was over. She did not even cry out. She could not cry out of her silent closed throat.

She, not me, not me, thought Theresa.

Hands. Chipped nails. Theresa knew the dream was leaving. She lay dizzy on a patch of dry grass. But before it was over she pulled back, absorbing the image of the girl's hands being tied, the blindfold wrapped over her eyes. He wound a long white cloth around and around her body, binding her arms tightly to her sides. He pulled the small black jackknives out of a brown paper bag. Then he stuck all eight of them into the ground, circling her still body.

Chapter 4

Lieutenant Oliver Jardine just missed being an attractive man. He was wiry and thin and stood nearly six feet in his black detective shoes. Over the years he had tried gaining weight, drinking protein supplements, lifting barbells, finally buying an isometric pulley machine because he'd heard it developed the inner muscles. The back of his closet was crammed with old sports equipment. He'd given up on the protective shin and kneepads, the helmets and plastic mouth guards. They'd never done much good anyway and his face was lined with a variety of small scars in odd places, on the upper lip, under the left eye, a deeper one drawn through his eyebrow.

At forty-two he resigned himself to his face. He had an easy smile, brown eyes that slanted thin and glinted when he laughed. He kept his pale curly hair clipped short so it wouldn't spring out of control in humid weather, and he'd nearly stopped trying to comb the remaining hairs down over the bald spot at the crown of his head. It was his nose, though, that did it. "Ruined by the Jardine nose," his brother always said. Bulbous and red, even when he hadn't been drinking, it was pushed to one side as if he'd pressed his face lightly against a window. He'd broken it twice, once in an intramural hockey game at the University of Wisconsin and once in a fight in the army. *Boxing,* he lied to friends when drinking. Over the years Oliver Jardine had decided the smashing of the nose had improved it.

Still, he did not like mirrors, he dressed plainly, stood up tall, and had trained himself to look away from his own face to the details of others', to become not merely a good listener, but a watcher of people, an observer, immersed in the minutiae of the world around him. He wondered once if it wasn't all because of his nose that he'd become a detective.

Jardine scratched the scalp at the back of his neck. It was nearly five and he was hungry. He wanted to go home to his apartment, where the air conditioner blasted fresh, cold air, and finish the leftover potato salad in the plastic bowl in his refrigerator. Instead, he sat in his stuffy office at a desk buried in papers, the Humphrey file open before him.

After eleven years in the Detective Division it was his maxim that if you did not find anything substantial within forty-eight hours of the discovery of the crime, you weren't going to find it. He had found very little. No fingerprints. Body left too long for there to be any footprints or car tracks. The search for threads, hairs, pieces of cloth, had revealed nothing of significance. The body had been out in the weather for approximately three months. The medical examiner fixed the date of death between the twenty-sixth and the twenty-ninth of May.

Furthermore, while the victim had been stabbed in the face and hands, she had not died of knife wounds. It was strangulation, probably manual, not by rope or scarf or wire, and it was done from the front. Little sign of struggle. The woman had not been sexually molested.

Jardine concluded, along with Cooper, that the murder had taken place somewhere else, the body carried up the embankment and left there. The jackknives through the palms had occurred after the death.

Bizarre. Jardine glanced at the photos of the hillside where the girl had been found, shoved them back in the envelope, and lit a cigarette. Nothing. Nothing. The girl had just moved out of the dorm at UCLA and into an apartment. Her new roommate had called the Humphreys on June second. Registration was supposed to start the next day. Where was Bonnie?

Good question. Missing Person. No clues; no case. Until one night some woman claiming to be a psychic calls up and tells you the girl is dead and she'll take you to the body. Sure, lady.

Shit. His stomach growled. He stood, opened his office door onto the large chaotic room where the younger detectives' desks were in constant disarray. It reminded him of a high-school classroom after Teacher stepped out. Men with feet propped up on wastebaskets played catch with a piece of crunched-up paper, dealt out poker hands, slept head down on a typewriter. "Cooper," Jardine said loudly over the clamor, and motioned for the man to come in.

"Did you get hold of this Elizabeth Brandon?" he asked.

"Tape recorder answers the phone, sir," said Cooper. "Might have to drive up there. She lives in Malibu."

"What else?"

"Not much that you didn't get from Frank Brandon. Fortunato is not her real name. It was Ballard when she was married. DeVito is the family name. She had it legally changed. Let's see . . ." Cooper flipped through a hardbound notebook, peering closely at the pages.

"Quit squinting," said Jardine. "You need glasses or something?"

"Oh, yeah," added Cooper. "The ex-husband is a mortician."

"Bizarre," Jardine said, aloud this time. "An undertaker and a goddamn witch. Did you talk to him?"

Cooper shook his head. "Not yet, sir, I—"

"What the fuck have you been doing?" Jardine tossed the file to the young black man, who let it fall to the floor beside him. "Christ, I'm hungry," said Jardine.

"Well, what did the psychic have to say?" asked Cooper.

"Nothing new. I haven't talked to her since last Thursday. Why?"

"Didn't you get the message?" Cooper began shuffling through papers on top of Jardine's desk, fumbling with the open file and producing a small pink slip from beneath a photograph. "Urgent," he read. " 'Call as soon as possible.' I left it right on top."

47

"Christ," growled Jardine, glancing at his watch and dialing Theresa Fortunato's number with a jabbing motion. "Now what?"

She sounded breathless, as if she'd run to the phone. "Lieutenant, thank God. I've been waiting for you to call."

Jardine opened his notebook and lifted a ball-point pen out of his shirt pocket. "Sorry. I just got the message. What's up?" he asked her.

"I think there's been another murder, that woman in the paper, Carolyn, Carolyn . . ."

Over the phone Jardine heard the rattling of a newspaper. "What do you mean, 'you think'?" he asked.

"I saw it"—she hesitated, then went on—"in a vision. That is, in my mind's eye, like I saw the other one."

"Let me get this straight," he said. "Another family hired you to find somebody?"

Theresa Fortunato sighed deeply. He could tell she was trying to compose herself. "No, no. Nobody hired me. I just know. The information came to me. I thought I should report it to the proper authorities. I didn't know who else to call." She was trying to sound official, her bank-officer voice again, but he could tell she was shaken. She went on. "Here's the article. The woman's name is Carolyn Svedrup. It was in this morning's paper, she was reported missing."

Svedrup, he jotted. Now, who the hell had that case? "Look," he said "you think you know where this woman is, correct?"

"Yes. She's dead."

"I got that. Where?"

Again Fortunato sighed. "Can I take you there? Look, Lieutenant, when I get this information I don't get a street map with it and an address book. I get numbers, some sense of direction, landmarks like the towers crossing twice over Mulholland Drive. I have to *be* there. I have to show you."

"All right, all right." Again he glanced at his watch. At

least this would get him out of the office. Normally, he'd never do this—he'd send a squad car instead—but this way he could talk to her, watch her at work. In action, he thought. Anyway, he could stop at Arby's on the way over.

The drive to Venice from downtown was slow, the freeways clogged with rush-hour traffic. It had been a clear day and the smog alert signs were turned off. Jardine wanted to make a note of Fortunato's voice in his notebook. It was not the authoritative, professional voice of last week. She'd sounded strained, her voice scratchy, as if she had a sore throat.

He had no real reason to suspect her of anything. The Humphrey family hadn't known her before and her credentials checked out. No apparent motivation. Still, who went around seeing murders in visions and reporting them to the police? Jardine had seen too much to discount anything.

Especially in Venice. He'd had enough cases originate or end in Venice, that tacky neighborhood shoved in beachfront squalor between Marina Del Rey and Santa Monica. Venice with its dealing and junkies, winos, old hippies who'd never gone into real estate and psychotherapy the way their peers had. Sure, he guessed there was some charm to the place on a weekend visit—street vendors and musicians along the boardwalk, the roller-skaters and the sidewalk café. He'd come with friends once in a while to gawk. Show some visiting cousin from Eau Claire the remnants of the old canals and the swarms of ducks in the postage-stamp yards.

"Just like Italy! Geez, Ollie, quite a town. And you living right in Hollywood. Wait'll I tell Uncle Vern."

Theresa Fortunato's house was set back from the street behind a tall stand of flowering trees—he could never remember their names. Before going up to her door he circled the court with its small cottages. No alley. He didn't know if it would be necessary, but it would be a difficult house to secure, no good view from the street.

Hard to see the back because of the shrubbery. High fence running along back and more bushes.

He noticed the sign in her window as he knocked at the front door. Presto chango, he thought. You will soon take a journey by water.

A silent wind chime hung above the door. There was no wind. Through an open window he heard an old Billie Holiday tune being played on the radio, and he hummed along. The chain bolt was unlocked from the inside and Theresa Fortunato opened the door.

"Hi. Come on in," she said. "I'm just about ready."

She stood before a mirror, wrapping a scarf around her head. Jardine was struck again by her almost harsh beauty. He studied her profile, thick eyebrows, strong chin, as she finished tying the white scarf at the back of her neck.

"I really want to get this over with." She sighed.

"It's not a pleasant business."

"I'm not used to it. I've never done this before, except for the Humphreys' daughter."

"No?" he asked, holding the door open for her, following her across the open courtyard. Leave her room to talk. Good listener. People loved to tell you the story of their lives.

As he slid into his car, he noticed that she was wearing all white like an orderly in a hospital, white jeans and shirt. Even the scarf was white. The car rattled as he started it up.

"The valley," she said quietly. "Old San Fernando Road. You know it?"

He nodded.

"Thanks for coming alone," she said. "That was probably a weird request. It's just that it's hard for me to concentrate with lots of people around."

"If we find something, I'll be calling in others," he told her.

"That's okay. It's just finding the place that's hard."

"I'd like to ask you some questions," said Jardine, once on the freeway. The traffic had eased up; he judged

50

that it would take them at least forty-five minutes to get out there. "Can we talk as we drive?"

Fortunato looked straight ahead without speaking. Finally, she said, "What? What do you need to know?"

"Everything." He laughed, then saw she didn't think it was funny. She was nervous, twirling a strand of hair in a ringlet around her finger. He went on. "How does one get to be a psychic? How does it work? How did you know you were one? How do you know if you're right? You know, everything. Mind if I smoke?" He opened the car window a crack and lit up, rubbing his chin.

So she wasn't chatty. He could wait her out. After a silence she spoke. "I guess I've always been open to people, situations. I pick up on things. Some call it intuition. Some call it crazy. I just don't believe that the mind is enclosed in its own little skull. Thoughts, mind pictures, images—they have power, they radiate out beyond a single person. Psychics can pick those images up. It's up to the individual to interpret them." She cleared her throat, her voice raspy.

He wanted to ask her if this was her introductory speech to a class she taught, then thought better of it. Just let her talk. The sun was low over the mountains. It would be dark soon.

"Myself," she continued, "I had a certain ability, but I didn't know how to channel it. Like someone with an ear for music that has never had a lesson. I studied with someone, a medium who lives up the coast. Elizabeth Brandon, maybe you've heard of her. I learned how to focus my mind, how to be open to everything. How to be a vehicle for other people's thoughts."

"Even dead people?"

"In this case, I guess so."

"Doesn't sound too scientific."

"It isn't. Not at all. Maybe that's why I've never done this type of psychic work before. I'm not usually good with hard facts like numbers, specific times. Information comes to me more as a feeling-tone, an emotional wave-

51

length. That's why I couldn't give you an exact location, I have to feel it."

"Are you ever wrong?"

"Hardly ever. But then, I don't give out information I'm not sure of. If I believe it, if it comes through with a feeling of truth, it will usually come to pass. But like I told you, most of my work is with people who want help figuring out their lives. Their marriage is messed up, they need to make a change in their jobs, or their health is bad—that kind of thing. I try to help them see where their choices might lead.

"But I'm not trying to make a correct prediction. I've never really approved of psychics predicting assassinations and earthquakes, whether or not Princess Di will have a girl or a boy, that kind of thing. When I read for people, I'm reading possibilities. They have to use free will to make their own choices. But that's when I'm reading for someone who's alive."

"Why do people believe what you tell them?" Jardine asked. "Doesn't what you say affect their decision making?"

"I hope so!" Theresa laughed. "Lieutenant, I guess they believe me because I appear to know so much about them. It's funny—the more specific you are in telling personal details about someone, the more they trust you—but that's not always the sign of a good psychic.

"For instance, if I tell you that"—she closed her eyes and her eyelids seemed to quiver as if she were moving her eyes quickly back and forth—"that you're from the Midwest, the north, maybe Michigan—no, Wisconsin. I see cold water, very large, very high up, better than everything. Superior, that's it. Lake Superior. The town is also called Superior, right? Where you lived as a boy. You have . . . an older brother, close in age to you, your father died when you were a teenager—" She broke off.

"That's uncanny." Suddenly Jardine felt nervous. Could she just go around reading minds, then? "How did you do that?" he asked.

"I picture you as a circle of light in a dark field. Like a

52

star. Then I visualize other stars, they swim around for a moment, then come to rest. A slightly larger light near yours would be an older brother. The large light on the left—the left is always a female for some reason—that's your mom. The father light was there for a while, then it faded.''

"What about Wisconsin, how did you know that?"

"It came to me like wordplay, free association.''

Jardine stubbed out the cigarette in the ashtray. "Now I'll have to believe everything you tell me."

"Not really," she said quietly. "It's important to believe only what feels true based on your own experience."

They drove in silence and the sun dipped behind a bank of clouds, the sky glowing peach; dark, dark blue above. They exited off the freeway, drove out the old road past fields, low buildings, a flatbed truck by a billboard.

"Can I ask you how you know where the body is? How do you know she's dead?"

"When I read for Bonnie Humphrey," she said, "I projected myself into her energy looking for a feeling-tone of fear or trouble to see if anything was wrong. Then I experienced her death. All the elements of the scene were there, the dirt road, the view of the valley. I read her deliberately, the way I might read the cards for someone. But this one, Carolyn, just took me over. I didn't ask for the vision. It swept through me. I had no control over it."

"So you didn't locate the body on purpose."

She shook her head. "I had no choice."

"I want to let you know that I had you checked out," he said. "It's standard procedure."

"Did I pass?"

He picked up his notebook from the seat beside him and read, "Referred to Humphreys by Dr. Franklin Brandon, Berkeley. Research in parapsychology, Kirlian photography. Worked with several psychic experiments involving clairvoyance, mind control, and so-called healing of cancer patients."

"Did Frank say 'so-called healing'?"

Jardine grinned. "No. I did."

"Go on."

"Raised in Boston, Italian—you told me that. One year college, NYU. Married at nineteen to Michael Ballard, divorced five years ago at age twenty-four. No children. Studied with noted medium Elizabeth Brandon, the good doctor's sister."

"You knew that already," she said.

"You've had your own practice for two years. Excellent character references. Professional people, actors and musicians. Good health. No criminal record."

"I could have told you all that."

"I had a nice chat with Frank Brandon. Is there anything else I should know, anything I've left out, injuries, illnesses?"

She shook her head. "No, I've always been pretty healthy. Why?"

"Just routine questions." He shrugged. "What about the name Fortunato?"

Theresa smiled. "My grandmother's maiden name. How could I not use it? I had it changed after my divorce. Wait," she said suddenly. "Slow down." She closed her eyes and put her hands out in front of her. "I'm going to have to be quiet now."

"Just one more thing, Theresa," said Jardine, ignoring her request. "If you can find the victims, can you find the person who is killing them?"

Theresa looked down at her hands and cleared her throat. "I don't know. I'm not sure that I want to. To be honest with you, I don't like it, any of it. What I try to do is spiritual consultation. Healing. 'So-called.' I try to affirm life in my readings. This kind of thing is so"—she paused and closed her eyes—"it's so sickening. It's just that . . ." She seemed distracted, glancing behind her out of the back window of the car. "I don't know why this information is coming to me, Lieutenant. It's a responsibility, being psychic. I mean, what if I hadn't told you where Bonnie was? I don't particularly *want* to do police

54

work, but this feels almost like, well, an obligation, if that doesn't sound too high flown.'' Then she inhaled sharply. ''Up here up here up here,'' she chanted in a low voice. She was panting, her breath shallow and quick.

As Jardine pulled off into a small run-down ranch, the car skidded slightly on the dirt driveway, dust spinning up behind them. A for-sale sign tilted over in the front yard. Before Theresa got out of the car, Jardine noticed that her pupils were dilated. She walked in that odd way, her legs slightly bent. She ran or almost flowed toward several small red outbuildings, her hands extended before her, palms down, as if she were feeling for something in the dark.

Jardine slid from the car, grabbing a flashlight from the glove compartment. As he ran up behind her, the dusk light was eerie. The fields on either side seemed to glow as if lit from within, an orange radiance not only in the sky but in the air around them.

''In there,'' she shouted, pointing to the last of the shacks. Then she covered her face with her hands and her knees buckled. She collapsed on the gravel road.

''Hey! Are you all right?'' Jardine bent over her. Her eyes were rolled back in her head. Christ, was she epileptic? She was shaking. Hyperventilating. ''Theresa,'' he said. Then under his breath, ''Damn, I knew I should have brought Cooper.'' He held her head from the ground and she seemed to come to.

''Don't feel so good.'' She panted. ''I just don't—too much—headache—''

''Slow down, slow down,'' he said. She looked dazed and frightened. He lifted her to her feet, steadied her, then guided her back to the car. ''Just stay here,'' he ordered, and he walked to the shabby house, peering in the windows. It was vacant, windows broken and boarded up. Then he headed back to the three shacks. One appeared to be a tool shed, another a chicken coop. The third one was larger, possibly a machine shed.

Its wooden door was unlocked and slightly ajar. He

55

shoved it open with his foot, flicking his flashlight on. The floor of the shed was dirt. The body lay face up in the exact center of the floor. Her entire body was tightly wound in white strips of cloth like a mummy and she was blindfolded. Small black jackknives were stuck in the ground around her in a circle like the numbers on a clock dial.

He stood for several minutes at the door, taking in the details of the shed—tools moved out of the way, neatly stacked against the back wall. The dirt floor had been raked over—no discernible prints. The body was arranged in a perfect line in the center and the knives—eight—he counted them.

He'd better call Cooper. He should drive to a phone. Better to have a secure line. If he called this in on the radio, the place would be a madhouse. Jardine spotted a ranch house about a quarter mile up the road. He trotted back to the car, flashlight still lit though it was not fully dark yet.

Back at the car Jardine found Theresa face down on the back seat, the door open. "Was she there?" she asked, raising her head to look at Jardine.

"Yes. You need some water or something?"

"I just need to get away from here. It's too loud. In my head," she added.

"I'll call for an extra car to drive you home."

Theresa rolled over and Jardine extended his hand, pulling her to a sitting position. The white scarf had come off and her hair was matted, pressed flat to her head. Mascara was smeared under her eyes.

"What about the knives?" she whispered.

"Yeah. Jackknives. Same ones. There's definitely some connection." Then he realized that she had not even gone into the shed. She had never seen the body or the knives.

"And she was all wrapped up, wasn't she?" Theresa grimaced. "She was swaddled up like a baby."

Jardine nodded, watching her face. *Go on.*

"And blindfolded, right? How many? How many knives?

56

Did you count them? There were eight, right? I saw them, I saw them in my mind. Just that way. Exactly eight of them all around her." Her voice was quiet and slightly hysterical. He was afraid she would begin to cry or scream.

"Why don't you just lie back down," he said, "until I can get somebody out here to take you back. I'm going to drive us to that house up there so I can call in."

Her eyes were very wide and she was shivering. She curled up tightly on the seat. He pulled a dirty wool blanket from the trunk, shook it out, and covered her gently.

He fumbled in his pocket for a cigarette and rubbed the dust from his eyes. His mouth tasted dry and chalky. He could never live out this far in the valley. There was nothing here. Nothing for miles. He looked back at the open door of the shed as he got in behind the wheel. Damn, he should have shut the shed door. Even from this distance he could make out the white bundled body arranged like an altar on the earthen floor.

Chapter 5

And Jesus shall bring a sword among us. It will be the division of man, it says right here in Matthew. The Jehovah's Witnesses came to my door and told me straight out.

Today, I floated around the beach watching people, feeling like I added something to the world. I felt invisible, clear. No one knew me, no one knew anything about me. I was out in the world like any normal person, eating a blue Popsicle and watching some guys lifting weights on the sand in front of Annie's Chili Dogs.

Sword among us, sword inside you. Inside her. Cut away the sickness like a surgeon. That's what I did. She was better after that. The next world, Mother always used to say. Better in the next world. I was too young to understand. I thought she meant next door. Next time. Next to nothing. There is no next time. No use praying for a future that isn't even there.

You know, I can't pray like I used to when I was little. I'd put my hands together and raise my face up to the sky that was blank. And black. I'd say, "Jesus?" But I can't do that now. When I'm quiet, I hear too many things in my head. It hurts and I take Excedrin and cold pills, the time-release ones that leak out little by little and keep me sleepy and slow it all down, slow it all down.

Jesus might make me say I'm sorry, and I'm not. No one who sins should wear the cross. She knew that. She should have known. That gold cross bouncing on her throat. I tore it off her so she'd know. I had it in my pocket at the beach today. I dropped it into the sand so it was lost. Buried.

She didn't need to be buried. It was enough to wrap her

up like that just like it showed on the picture. Even dead, she knew she was better off. Not dead, maybe. Just asleep. Just like a baby. The knives they told me to bring along, I put them in the dirt all the way around her. She was very quiet and very good like a good baby. No more crying, no more tears. The jackknives in the ground were like a bouquet. Because it was night and the knives were black. Flowers don't grow in the dark.

The color didn't come in well on the TV and the newscaster's face was green. Michael Ballard put his feet up on the coffee table piled with magazines and dirty dishes. He lit the joint he'd just rolled, drew in hard, then let it out, watching it trail up slowly to the ceiling of the apartment where he lived above the funeral home.

The place was a mess. He should have someone come in to clean it up, but he didn't care. Maybe if it were a real apartment in a real building with a swimming pool and a sauna. He'd buy new furniture, a leather couch, maybe.

He'd only lived in one other place in the five years since he and Terry had split up, an apartment near Westwood. He'd moved in with a girl he was seeing not so much because he cared about the girl as because he hadn't been able to stay in this place with the memory of Terry so crowded in with everything. *Theresa*, he thought. Excuse *me*. Terry DeVito. Terry Ballard. He knew *that* girl. Or he had. Past now. All over. Five years. Hard to believe it had been that long. Now she was Theresa Fortunato, Psychic in Residence. He laughed to himself, relaxing back into the sofa, looking forward to having dinner with her tomorrow night.

Ballard thought of Terry more often than he wanted to. Her memory came and went in waves, images all stirred up, spiraling around this place with the rest of the ghosts. He could picture her lying naked in the lumpy bed next to the window with a cold washcloth over her forehead for the headaches. How she always used to sneak out down the back stairs to avoid going through the funeral home.

Said the people were still floating around near their bodies and bumping into her as she passed. Sometimes, he'd play tricks on her, turn pictures upside down on walls, change flower arrangements from room to room in the middle of the night, and tell her it must be the spooks at work. Michael chuckled. Crazy Terry. Crazy Terry, gray puffy face in the clinic in a dirty white sweater, bone thin, eyes dilated, the one time he ever saw her smoke. "Give me a cigarette, Michael," her hands trembling as she held it to her lips to be lit.

No. Reprogram. Erase. He didn't want to remember those times. Maybe that's why he got in touch with her every now and then, to remind himself that she was okay, to see how she was doing, have a drink with an old friend, old girlfriend. Old wife.

And also just because he couldn't seem to forget her in this apartment where they'd lived together above the funeral home, where he still lived, where his parents had lived when they were first married right after the war. And it looked much the same as it had in 1954 too—faded melon-colored walls in the dining-room alcove, speckled cracked linoleum in the kitchen, the kind with little black and turquoise boomerangs. He'd gotten lost in the pattern one night on an acid trip. This same gold-flecked couch, frayed down to wood at the arms.

But it was convenient. Didn't have to drive to work. Just jump down the stairs, past the cold-storage room where the flowers were kept, into the office where his father had sat for twenty years.

Ballard could already hear voices downstairs. Chapel would begin in a few minutes. Three of them today, all old men laid out for inspection, waxy and serene, surrounded by carnations. One visitation and two wakes tonight. The families had just barely brought the clothes in for the one old guy. Fighting over what to have him wear. Who the fuck cared if Gramps wore the black pinstripe or the plaid sportcoat? Uncle Sid sobbing, "He would have liked the sportcoat.'' Maybe he wanted to wear his golf shoes to heaven too. There was no dress code.

Ballard looked up as the newscaster's voice came back from the dish-detergent commercial that promised your hands would look years younger, and the green-faced man droned on.

"Last night police found the body of a Venice woman reported missing three days ago. The woman has been identified as twenty-year-old Carolyn Svedrup. She had last been seen Friday leaving the Seaside Café, where she was employed as a waitress.''

Damn, another one, thought Ballard. Really starting to turn them up now. Crazy town. If I were a woman, I'd get a black belt. Why do they go out alone?

Ballard watched as the camera cut to an on-the-scene reporter standing in front of an old shed. "The body was found here late yesterday at the site of this abandoned ranch in the San Fernando Valley. There is some evidence that the death may be connected to another homicide discovered last week. Police once again enlisted the aid of psychic Theresa Fortunato, who was instrumental in locating the missing Humphrey woman, found shot last week. Ms. Fortunato was not available for comment. We'll have more on that story on our late-night report.''

Ballard sat straight up on the couch and buckled his belt. He snapped off the TV with the remote control. Jesus H. Christ, what was she getting herself into now? She hadn't mentioned that at the bookstore yesterday. Since when was she into finding dead bodies, hanging around with cops? That was just dandy, just what he needed. Terry and her visions.

She messed with things that were none of her business. That's how all the trouble had started in the first place. Witchcraft. Dreams. Crazy shit. That's all he needed was for her to start finding bodies for the goddamn police. Wait'll Lowell heard about this.

Downstairs, the voices of families coming in for the

61

wakes mumbled beneath the floor. He'd have to put on his suit coat, straighten his tie, put some Visine in his red eyes.

The voice on Theresa's phone was shrill. "Are you that one on TV? That psychic that found them girls?"

Theresa hesitated. "Are you calling for an appointment?" She ran a finger over the buttons of the answering machine that took her phone messages. Late-afternoon light brightened the kitchen.

"Yes," said the voice. "I got to talk to you in person."

"Fine," said Theresa. "Why don't we arrange an appointment?"

"I got some questions I got to ask you. If you died in the next hour, do you think that God would let you into heaven? Do you truly feel that you would be saved?"

"Who is this?" Theresa demanded.

"Have you accepted Christ into your heart?" wheezed the voice, now even higher.

Theresa bit into the pencil she was holding and made tiny teethmarks all the way down to the eraser. "Go to hell," she whispered, and pressed the receiver down onto the white phone. That was the second strange call tonight. The first had been some pervert wanting to know if she was into psychic sex.

Theresa sat down at the kitchen table and braided her long hair, then unwound it strand by strand. She hadn't told Jardine he could release her name to the press. She supposed it was standard practice. It could be good for business, but not this kind of business. Maybe she'd have to get an office away from her house after all. Keep regular hours. But that just wasn't like her.

Theresa picked up the phone again and dialed Camille's number. Sarene answered, "Yeah, she's here. She's getting ready for work. She's putting silver polish on her toes."

Camille picked up the extension in the other room and

Theresa heard the child hang up. "Say, girl, how you doin'? You feeling better?"

Theresa was relieved to hear her friend's cheerful voice. "Silver toenails?" she asked.

"You ought to try it. Make you light on your feet."

"Have you seen the news, Camille?"

"You know I don't care about no TV version of history."

"I found another girl. For the police. Her body, I mean."

"What, you joining the force or something? They going to give you a badge?"

"Camille, I couldn't help it. It came on me like a dream, a nightmare. It knocked me right off my feet. I'm not exaggerating. It was awful. Now they're reporting it on TV and all sorts of weird people are calling me."

"Told you."

"You're so sympathetic."

"Theresa, it just don't mix. You supposed to be dealing with spirit."

"Don't you think these women have spirits? Don't their families have spirits?"

"Hey, you want me to clap for you, baby? Tell you what a dynamite job you doin'?"

"I need some support, Camille."

"Ain't getting none from me. I told you not to mess with it and I meant it. Leave the dead be. You can't help them now, can you? What good will it do, going around digging up graves?"

"They aren't in graves. That's the whole point. They're missing people."

"Listen, Resa. Why don't you come down to the bar tonight? After I'm done dancing, we could go out and get a bite to eat. Get your mind off this stuff."

"They found another little plastic sword on this girl, Camille. It's like the signature of the killer, whoever he is."

"What makes you think it's a he?" asked Camille.

Theresa stopped. "I don't know. I just saw him."

She clicked the phone down softly and watched out the back window the play of dusk light in the tall eucalyptus. She was not sorry. She'd done nothing wrong and could not repent for something that came to her as a gift. She had no control over it; she simply *saw*. That was all.

People always thought that being psychic was a mutant trait; you were an oddball, a weirdo, even evil. Maybe that was why she'd wanted so much to use her gift to help others, to show that being psychic was not a sickness or a sin. Her mother had always laid that on her—she was damned. She lied, she made up stories. She was possessed. "Mary Theresa, you read too much, you make up tales in your head and then you go around believing in them." Once at the dinner table when she was sixteen, she'd announced out of the blue that Mrs. Paglucci, who had been in the store that morning, was cheating on her husband and had been for several years. Her father slapped her so hard with the back of his hand that she'd flown out of her chair against the kitchen wall.

To Michael being psychic meant you were insane. He'd almost convinced her: "The voices are a chemical imbalance in your metabolism, Terry. The visions are acid flashbacks. Your mind's not right. You'll feel better under this doctor's care. She's trained to deal with this. *You're sick.*"

Theresa thought Camille, of all people, understood that she did not ask for the visions. She did not decide to be psychic.

She had no intimation of the gift as a young child, only the usual invisible friends, fantasies of fairies, and fears of ghosts. The oldest of five girls, she spent her playtime helping her mother upstairs, dusting the living room, rolling out dough for bread, or downstairs in her father's small grocery store staring into the glass cases of olives, cheeses, and long tubes of sausages. He was a short, fierce man with a huge belly under his white apron, and a loud laugh that went on too long. Sometimes he would sing to her like an opera star as he sliced up meat for a customer.

There was nothing unusual about her days at Our Lady of Peace School fidgeting during morning Mass, playing with the hem of her blue plaid skirt instead of saying her rosary. It wasn't until she was fourteen that the visions began. At the time it seemed part of coming of age. She became a teenager, got pimples, grew breasts, and began hearing voices in her head.

Theresa remembered the first time so clearly. It was the fall of 1967. She and her mother had gone down to New York on the train to visit her grandmother. Theresa slept on the couch, listening to her mother and grandmother argue in Italian in the small kitchen, slamming pots and pans around as they dried them. Grandma Anna Marisa Fortunato Scarpelli was thin-boned as a bird. Her white hair was pulled into braids and wound into a tight bun. She always wore black and had a deep voice that seemed to come from some other woman's body, buxom and large.

Theresa couldn't speak the language well, but she could make out what they were saying. "You can't stop me!" Grandma Anna shoved a cupboard door shut. She wanted to go see a gypsy woman who could talk to the dead. Grandpa had been dead seven years now and she could feel him near as if he were sitting in that very chair. "He wants to talk to me! I know it! But I can't hear him by myself. He's on the other side of a wall."

Her mother yelled. "That's the devil's work, Mama. I won't take you. Go see Father. You want to talk to Grandpa, you talk to God first. You getting crazy senile in the head with this crazy talk. I put you in a nursing home, you don't do as I say."

In the morning they fought again over breakfast. Theresa's tiny grandmother stood in her black dress shouting and her mother shouted back, throwing her hands in the air and finally screaming, "Who's to stop you? But don't drag me into it!" The grandmother narrowed her eyes and muttered as she lifted the doily off the top of the radio,

65

pulling out crisp green bills and stuffing them into her purse. She stormed out of the apartment, stomping down the dark stairs to the street.

Theresa caught up with her at the corner. They walked shoulder to shoulder past the busy shops and storefronts before descending into the subway. Grandma Anna was quiet on the train, her mouth drawn in. Theresa held tightly to her bony hand.

The gypsy lived three flights up a narrow stairway. The apartment door was slightly ajar, and inside, Theresa could see the small living room crammed with furniture, an old powder-blue velvet couch, several oversized recliners, every tabletop crowded with photographs of weddings, graduations, babies, and several large gold trophies of high-school wrestling matches.

The gypsy answered the door wearing tight black stretch pants and a lime-green mohair sweater. Her daughter was an exact replica of her, except that her sweater was coral pink, and she sprawled on the couch watching Saturday-morning cartoons on TV and chewing a large wad of gum. Both had stiff bouffant hairdos that stood out from their heads like helmets, both wore thick black eyeliner, and their lips seemed to disappear under flesh-colored make-up.

She led Grandma Anna and Theresa into the dining room, shut the door to the kitchen, and shooed two small children out from under the table. Theresa huddled next to her grandmother and leaned over the table toward the gypsy, close enough to inhale the scent of garlic and menthol cigarettes. Large rings with different-colored stones glittered on her hands as she shuffled a deck of tattered cards with her eyes closed.

One by one she flipped over the cards and laid them out on the lace tablecloth. "Just a minute," the gypsy whispered. "I think I hear him."

Theresa heard him, too. But not Grandpa. Just a soothing low voice, comforting, like someone telling a child a story. It was so familiar. Whose voice was it? No matter.

She just began to speak, repeating what the card's voices said, telling the story of the images laid out upon the table.

"Your heart is still aching from the past," said Theresa in a lilting voice. "You're holding on too tight to your husband's death and he has other work to do now. He wants to travel on but you won't let him go. So he feels that he has to carry you like a burden in a boat over the endless waters."

She felt a strange elation that she'd only experienced before in church on high holy days, watching the candles on the altar being lit, evening fading behind stained-glass angels and saints. Her heart swelled with longing and she almost wanted to cry, she loved the voice so much. It wasn't at all frightening. Theresa intuitively trusted it as if it were an old friend whispering in her ear.

The gypsy opened her eyes. "You know these cards?"

"No," said Theresa. "I can just hear them."

"You hear them?" Then to Grandma Anna she said, "You don't need to come to me. This girl knows the cards, she can tell you what to do. She has the gift."

The gypsy woman stood motioning wildly with her hands. She called her daughter in from the other room and they whispered excitedly. "This girl, she knows. Watch." She laid card after card down and Theresa again felt compelled to repeat the sounds of the voices inside her. They came in a singsong voice. Grandpa had given a lot of money to his family in the old country and it had never been returned. But that was no reason for anger. After all, it was done and he was gone. Uncle Frankie had always resented her, this was true—and so the voice came, calmly, musically, while Grandma Anna and the two gypsies listened. Theresa could have gone on and on. The voice was in control now. She had moved her own self out of the way and someone else had stepped in behind her mouth. Light-headed, dreamily, she let the voice take over.

Suddenly Grandma Anna slammed her hand down on the table and drew Theresa close with her other arm.

"What are you doing to her?" she said in her deep voice. "You stay away from this child!"

"I have done nothing, madame," said the gypsy, indignantly.

"I never should bring her, my daughter was right."

The gypsy's daughter grabbed Theresa's palm, blowing a bubble from a cheekful of pink gum. "Well, just look at it," she said to her mother. "Just look at that split in destiny."

The older woman peered down at the palm which the daughter held open. She put her hand to her white mouth. "Oh, God, child, what a life you're going to have!" Suddenly, she reached into a drawer behind her and set a new pack of the fortune-telling cards on the table.

"I am at your service," she whispered to Theresa in a gravelly voice. "However I can help you, teach you—you come to me. I will guide you. You will need so much help!"

Grandma Anna said, "She wants nothing from you. We go."

"But, Grandma," Theresa protested.

Grandmother stood, pulling Theresa to her feet. She tried to give the gypsy woman some money, but the woman waved it away. "No, it's all been decided. It's too late. Her destiny is split and her death is forked."

It was the first time since they'd arrived at the gypsy's that Theresa was afraid. What was a split in destiny? The voice had stopped completely, startled away. Theresa wanted it back. What if it never came again?

Grandma placed her hat on her thick white hair. As she turned to leave, one of the small children scurried over to Theresa and hugged her legs. The child reached up to her, pulling Theresa's sweater. She felt the child's hand in her sweater pocket and understood.

The gypsy woman folded her arms and shook her head as Theresa and her grandmother left the apartment. All the way home on the subway, Theresa fingered the cool surface of the new deck of cards hidden in her dark pocket.

The cards would have to be kept from her parents. She wanted to rush back to her grandmother's, open the deck in private, finger the beautiful pictures, call the voice in. If only that presence would move through her again! She'd never wanted anything so badly. It burned in her, her discovery, her power, and it was clear that no one must know about it. They would only respond as Grandma Anna had, with fear and anger. No, the cards and voices would be her secret.

Grandma Anna died the next spring, and Theresa did not return to New York until she was in college. Once she looked for the building the gypsy had lived in four years earlier, walking the Manhattan streets searching for a familiar landmark. But the woman had moved on. Theresa was disappointed. She'd hoped to study with the gypsy. Her life had changed after she'd been given the cards. She had a sense of mission about her powers but had no idea what to do about it, and even though she could clearly hear the voices of the cards, at times they overwhelmed her, chanting and whining inside, sweeping through her at inappropriate times, a ringing in her ears like a fainting spell. She'd thought the gypsy could have helped her understand why she was different. Chosen—that's how she felt. This, too, she kept secret. Her father would have beaten her if he'd known that's what she thought. Only God knew past and future. But if that was true, why had the voices come to her with their messages and visions?

When the doorbell rang, Theresa was startled from her memories. At the door she recognized the bearded man from the bookstore. She'd nearly forgotten she had a reading tonight and she didn't feel up to it. She was tired of other people's lives, their tangled images and blurry questions. Why couldn't anyone come to her clean, transparent, like the old gypsy's crystal ball?

"Hello," said Theresa. "You're Raymond, right?"

"Raymond Mead," he said. He tossed his car keys from one hand to the other.

"Come on in." She showed him to the reading room and seated him at the table, while she lit a candle and shut the glass doors to the living room. It was early evening and dusk light filled the small sunroom, a Mediterranean light, Theresa thought, as she turned back to Raymond Mead. Her eyes blurred for a moment and she rubbed them, blinked. There: it was gone. For an instant it had been like seeing double, a second man superimposed over him. A shadow, like the second image in a camera lens that must be brought into focus with the first. As she sat down opposite him at the table, she remembered her first impression—a person hiding within himself. "Now," she asked, "what are you interested in? Any specific questions?"

"Well, like I told you over at the bookstore, it's a family thing." He cleared his throat, folding and unfolding his hands nervously on the table. Theresa saw that he was trembling slightly.

"See, it's about my brother." He paused. "I'm not sure how much to say before you do the reading."

"Whatever you feel comfortable with."

"Well, we've never gotten along at all and he's been sick a lot." Theresa remembered her initial reaction to Raymond in the bookstore: an illness in one near to him. Hospitals, doctors. "Now, see, he's come to stay with me for a while. To recuperate. But I don't know if it's going to work out. What I really want is for him to split. See, whenever he's in my life, it's awful. He fucks everything up. But then again, I don't know—he's the only brother I've got, and where else is he supposed to go? Maybe I'm just being selfish." He was still jingling his keys in his open palm.

"Could you put those down?" Theresa asked.

"Oh, sure, sure."

Theresa reminded herself to relax, to empty her mind of herself, to open to this being before her. She hesitated as she unwrapped the cards, feeling slightly faint. Not again, she thought, but then it passed. She willed herself to go on, handing the deck to Raymond to shuffle. Even as he held the cards, the reading began to form itself inside her—two men crossing each other, opposition. Patriarch reversed. The energy of the reading was coming on so strong that Theresa shut her eyes from what appeared to be rays of heat coming off his hands like ripples off a black-top road on a hot day. Her ears were ringing and she felt the suck of a vacuum in her head. She put her hands over her ears.

"Am I doing it wrong?" asked Raymond.

"No, no," said Theresa. "It's just me. I haven't been too well lately." She gazed as his face blinked from one face to another like a man changing masks. He hadn't said he wanted a past-life reading. What were all these faces doing melting from one to another?

She forced herself to deal out the cards, even though the cards seemed hot to the touch: Knight of Swords, Page of Swords crossing—just as she'd seen them. Five of Swords, Queen of Swords, King of Swords reversed. Raymond looked up at Theresa. He did not look down at the cards.

The urge to cry hurt her throat and she sensed a terrible loneliness in him, a sad energy locked into his body, a dark knot of fear. It filled her with remorse. Detach, she told herself.

Closing her eyes, she visualized Raymond as a small globe of light and tried to bring the brother's light into the dark field of her mind. The light moved in slowly, then merged with Raymond's, swelled to a larger size, and separated again, leaving Raymond's light diminished.

"I see what you mean," said Theresa. "His presence swallows you, drains you. You're half a person around him. But—yes—I can see you're also very close, deeply bonded in some way and—" Again, the lights joined, then divided like cells under a microscope. "I'm getting a definite sense of your inability to detach from him, almost a double presence, an interdependence."

Raymond leaned forward. "That's exactly the way we are," he said, and then he added, quickly, "but we hate each other."

Quickly, she laid out the remaining cards, all of them swords except for one, the Ten of Cups, the rainbow card of love placed in the postion of Fears. She shook her head as the tears came, but no sound welled out of her throat. Theresa swept the cards off the table, the voices droning quietly inside her like an engine.

"Get out," she whispered.

"What?" said Raymond, surprised.

The voices inside her grew louder, whining, *Get out get out get out*. Theresa realized the voices were speaking to her, not him. "I have to get some air," she said, staggering out of the room to the front door.

It was a beautiful evening, the sky lavender. She leaned against the house, her hands at her throat as if something sharp were caught there and she couldn't breathe. The wind rustled the huge bougainvillea next door. The flowers seemed to swim before her.

"Did I do something wrong?" Raymond put his hand on her shoulder.

"It's not you," Theresa gasped. "I'm sick, I can't do it anymore, whenever I do a reading, all I get is swords, swords."

"I'll get you some water, here, sit down."

"Just go!" she shouted, startled by the strength of her voice. A man across the courtyard was carrying boxes into the house for rent. He stopped to look at them, started toward them.

"Okay, Okay," said Raymond. "I now when I'm not wanted."

"It's not you," cried Theresa. "It has nothing to do with you. There's something wrong with *me*. I'm sorry—"

"You need some help?" called the man across the courtyard.

Theresa felt a tremendous pressure in her chest, a black grief filling her lungs until she could not hold it in. Raymond Mead stalked down the courtyard, the sound of his tennis shoes muffled on the gray stones. When she heard his car door slam and the engine start up, she sucked her breath in hard, gulping like a drowning woman surfacing for air, and gave in to the violent sobbing that shook her chest. She slumped against the side of the open door, covering her face with her hands.

Chapter 6

In her dream she was in bed with Michael. He nuzzled up
behind her, slid his hand over her hip, but his hand felt
cold and thin like a hook. He drew the metallic hand
against her thigh, tracing the inside of her leg, slowly
drawing it up to her belly, between her breasts, then
holding the rigid hand against her throat. "Did you say
your prayers before you went to sleep, Terry?" he whispered. She saw then that it was not his finger against her
neck but a razor, the one he had always used to cut the
cocaine into slender rows on the gold-edged mirror. "Now
I lay me down to sleep," she whispered. "I pray the Lord
my soul to keep, and if I die before I wake . . ." Michael
pressed the razor cleanly into her neck and she accepted it
like a kiss.

Theresa threw the blankets off and scrambled out of the
covers, clutching at her throat. She sat, hunched over on
the edge of the bed, the sheet crumpled in her fist. The
luminous clock dial read ten forty-five. Still reeling from
the dream, she rose and went barefoot into the dark living
room. Out of the window she caught a glimpse of the man
who'd been moving that afternoon into the house across
the way. He was standing at his kitchen sink opening a
beer. Theresa tried to slow her breathing and shake the
dream. In the bathroom she washed her face. "Get out of
my head," she whispered to the mirror. "Get your voices
out!"

This was too much, there was no rest. She could hardly
do a reading anymore without feeling sick, and the stabbed
women's deaths leaked into her sleep, knives crowded into
the cards, nausea flooded her waking hours. She would

have to do something. She would have to call Elizabeth and ask her advice, even though she knew she shouldn't.

But it was still early. She didn't want to be alone. Camille would be at work. She pulled the nightgown off over her head and dressed quickly in jeans and a lace blouse.

Though it was close, she decided against walking and drove the few blocks to the bar on Washington, passing the bookstore on the way. The car made an odd scraping sound when she braked to pull into a parking space. She knew it needed a tune-up. The street was dark, the shops closed, only the lights from the bar blinked blue shadows onto the sidewalk and, farther up, the twinkling white Christmas tree lights that year-round decorated the front of a vegetarian restaurant. She realized that some people would consider this dangerous, a woman alone on a dark street not far from the boardwalk where even now winos, junkies, and solitary figures dressed in ragged clothes leaned back on the benches that faced the sea. But she felt safer here in the open city than home alone with the door locked where she was closed in with her own thoughts.

Inside, the NightTime was dark and smoky. It was a Wednesday night, not too crowded. The bar had been open only a few months. Rock and New Wave dance tunes blasted from large ceiling speakers during the week and sometimes the owner brought in a jazz band on weekends hoping to draw the more affluent clientele from Marina Del Rey. Gleaming in chrome, mirrors, and glass, the bar seemed out of place on the shabby Venice street. Violet neon scrawled THE NIGHTTIME IS THE RIGHT TIME across a Plexiglas wall and two cylindrical platforms rose up from the center of the bar, outlined with tubes of blue lights. On top of one of them Camille danced alone in a silver leotard, her beaded hair whirling, catching the diamond light points from the mirrored ball that spun from the ceiling.

"Hey, beautiful." The bartender smiled. Theresa nodded at Spider and he bent over the bar. "Haven't you got a smile for your old pal?'' he said. "Or have I become a stranger? You haven't been in for a while.''

"I haven't been feeling too good,'' Theresa shouted over the loud music.

Spider reached to her face and touched one finger to her chin. "Camille says you've been down about those killings. I saw it on the tube. Man, it's too close to home. Makes me want to get a bolt lock on my door. Let me get you a drink. Pretty heavy work, huh?''

"Just wine, Spider,'' said Theresa, nodding.

He filled a stemmed glass with pale wine. Spider's blond hair, frizzed out in a halo around his head, looked blue in the neon glow of the bar. He wore a white satin cowboy shirt, the sleeves rolled up over thick freckled arms. "On the house,'' he said. "Now, you take it easy, pretty lady, hear me?'' Placing the glass before her, he turned back to his other customers, who were gazing up at the dancing woman above them.

Only Camille could pull this off—go to a meditation temple in Santa Monica in the morning, practice her yoga exercises on the orange shag carpet in her living room, drink papaya juice for dinner, then come down to The NightTime and dance from nine to midnight in the lunar disco light.

"I got to move!'' she told Theresa when she first got the job. "I can't type, can't add, and can't spell. I can't sleep nights. This job is made for me. Everybody else pays to work out—I get paid. That's the only thing I can't accept about the meditation temple—they say the body is unclean. They say, 'You are not the body.' But we are, we're immaculate, the body on fire with life. We born human, why not love it? My dance is one of praise. Yeah, we bleed and sweat and shit. We human. But 'hide it under a bushel, no, I'm going to let it shine!' ''

Shine, she did. When the song ended, Camille climbed down the chrome ladder at the side of the platform, toweled the sweat off her face and arms, and pulled on a purple sweatshirt that said THE NIGHTTIME across the chest.

She came over to Theresa. "Thought I saw you hulkin' down here."

"Couldn't sleep. Bad dreams."

Towering over Theresa in her high heels, Camille reached down to brush her friend's hair out of her eyes. "I'm glad you came. I was going to call you," she sighed. "Girl, we got to talk. I mean it. Not here—I got one more short set. Then let's go jump in the ocean, okay? We got things to discuss."

Theresa sipped her wine as Camille finished dancing. Her muscular body looked almost iridescent in the glowing darkness. She supposed it was a good job for Camille; she seemed able to piece together three or four part-time jobs and still raise Sarene by herself. An aspiring dancer, Camille took class several times a week, waitressed at a Hollywood club, did past-life readings in her apartment while Sarene played in the next room, and worked out on her platform at The NightTime as the lights swirled around her. Theresa wished she had half Camille's clarity and resolve, her sense of joy about life. Maybe it was having a child around, not being so alone in the world.

It was after midnight when the two women drove away from the bar. "Want to go over to the pier in Santa Monica?" asked Camille. "I just feel like walking."

The wind in the open car window made Theresa shiver slightly.

"Theresa," said Camille at the stoplight, "listen—that last girl you found—Carolyn?"

"Thought you were above the news."

"Didn't hear about it on the news. I know her. Knew her."

Theresa glanced at Camille. "Why didn't you tell me?"

"I just found out. Spider told me. She came to meditation. She was taking a beginning yoga class. Resa"— Camille reached over and touched Theresa's shoulder— "it's real bad vibes. Don't do it anymore," she pleaded. "Please. I'm getting real strong feelings, baby. I could

77

sense it in the streets, walking to the bar tonight. People be all nervous and jumpy, looking at you funny. When something like this happens, a whole town gets sucked in. Don't you get pulled in too close, girl."

"I know. Every reading I do seems to get more and more violent. I read for a guy today and totally blew it."

"It's the pull of negative energy," said Camille. "It wants to put out any sunshine it sees. I'm just scared for you, Resa. Dark forces be bouncing back like a boomerang, circling back to get you."

"But I'm not the one who's into the dark force. Look, I've been thinking really hard about this because this kind of work is so new to me and I'm not sure how to protect myself. But I also know something is calling me to do this. They're real people with real problems, Camille. How would you like to be left lying out on top of a mountain with knives in your hands? These are human spirits."

"Elizabeth always told us not to work with no cops."

"I've been thinking about that too," said Theresa. "I know that's her position, but in a way she closes herself off from reality. She's got her ivory tower on that cliff in Malibu, she's not in the world. But I am. I can have a positive effect on these people's lives."

"And fuck up yours."

"Come on," Theresa protested.

"I never saw any good come from working with cops. I saw my whole community go up in flames over that kind of trouble. I won't never forget Watts burning that summer and my people beaten down."

"This isn't the same, Camille. These are individual people who need my help."

Camille just shook her head.

Theresa parked the car on the lot under the pier and climbed the wooden steps while the black ocean rushed in waves below them. Though it was late, the pier was still busy, the midway games and bumper cars blinking lights, country music amplified from the front of a small bar. The

78

space-age twitter of video games from an arcade dotted the sound of the ocean around them. Only Madame Nina's Gypsy Fortune Teller booth was closed. Theresa always smiled when she saw it. Now, that would be the place for an office. She rested against the wooden rail of the pier, looking down into the swirling water. A sliver of moon hung in the sky looking fake, an ornament tacked to a black wall.

Camille leaned next to Theresa, looking out over the water. "So what else is new, besides all this weirdness?"

"I'm going out with Michael Ballard," Theresa blurted, though she'd meant to keep it to herself. She knew Camille would disapprove.

"Girl? For a smart woman you real dumb, you know that?"

"I know, I know."

"You sure hold on to old shit, Resa. Like no one I ever knew. You got to learn to release."

"It's not really a date, Camille. I don't know why I still get together with him. It's just that there's still something between us."

"I've been watching you sorrow over that man for four years."

"We have some kind of unfinished business. I can feel it."

"Well, you best finish it up or you be carrying it around with you into your next life." Camille shook her head. "He's good-looking, but there's other fish in the sea, baby. How you going to get with somebody new, you keep going out with your ex-husband? Hey, I'm going to take a little dip."

Theresa watched as Camille descended the steps and walked up the dark beach. She followed her into the night and sat on the cool sand, waiting.

She supposed it was strange to go out with Michael, even if it was just a friendly gesture, but there was nothing really wrong with keeping in touch through the years. After all, they would see each other often if they had children. They wouldn't simply disappear from each other's lives. Maybe it was some misplaced longing for intimacy and family. She was so cut off from her family back East, and bad as things had once been, Michael was the only relative she had on the Coast. No one else had known her as long or as well, even Camille. Maybe too well. Michael knew things about her that would probably best be forgotten. He knew where her fault lines were, where she would crack if the pressure grew too great.

When she first met Michael, Theresa had not been a practicing psychic. At nineteen she'd come out West to get as far away as possible from the East, from her family and all that seemed to close in on her, telling her there was something wrong with what she thought of as her gypsy blood. After all, hadn't Grandma Anna's maiden name been Fortunato?

She met Michael Ballard her first month in California, and married him only a few months later. Michael knew a little about her voices, but he didn't take them seriously. He admired her quickness with the fortune-telling cards at parties and he called it her "magic act."

It was 1972. Theresa was nearly twenty, working as a waitress. Michael Ballard drove an old MG, always had money in his wallet, worked sporadically at a record shop, and did some dealing now and then. He bought her an antique sapphire ring that seemed outrageous in those days. A long-haired priest married them on the beach while a friend played the dulcimer. Everyone wore flowers in their hair, patchouli oil, and India print dresses. In spite of herself she'd called her parents and told them, and her mother had cried and shrieked in Italian, "What do you mean, he's not Catholic! You want to put your poor mother in her grave?"

They found a small house to rent in North Hollywood and Theresa kept her first garden. Weeding the rows of flowers and herbs, she let the voices come to her slowly. She studied the well-worn deck of cards the gypsy had given her, reading for friends by candlelight. They told their friends and others sought her out in turn. *She's really good. She knows what she's doing. She's magical.* Theresa liked the feeling of importance that reading the cards gave her. She felt wanted, her psychic gift had some real function, it wasn't merely a self-indulgent flexing of personal power. It didn't bother her that she could hear other people's thoughts, but some days they were too loud and she couldn't sort out her own thoughts from the other voices. She'd drive over to the beach then and let the voices drown in the rolling waves.

Once she fell asleep on the beach and dreamed that she was floating high over the sand, bobbing on the end of a string like a helium balloon. She saw herself below, a curve of pink on the blanket. It came to her that maybe this was not a dream at all—she'd been reading about out-of-body experiences; this must be what they meant, this pleasant sensation of having two bodies, one physical, sleeping on the beach, one spacious as a cloud and located nowhere in particular but up in the waving wind, almost flapping like a piece of cloth hung out on a line to dry. How can I see myself, though, she thought, if I don't have eyes? And as if the thought itself had waked her, she was jolted violently back to the ground, where she lay still for a long time wondering how she had ever managed to leave her body. Was it only an accident? Could she ever do it again on purpose? She understood that if she ever left her body again, she should avoid thinking about it too much. That was what had brought her back, analyzing it. Again, as she had many times before, she wished she had someone like the gypsy in her life, to answer all her questions.

Those were happy years, high parties with plenty of Orange Sunshine and Windowpane, good sex, Michael tender and funny, his dark hair down to his shoulders like an imitation rock star's. But after they'd been married two years, Michael's father developed emphysema and asked Michael to come into the business. Theresa objected. She'd moved out West to escape the cloistered pressures of family, not to get embroiled in Michael's. Besides, Michael would have to cut his hair, wear a suit, be around death all the time. But he insisted. They'd have money, he told her. She'd never have to work a day in her life. Besides, he had to. It was family. He was the only child.

She quit her waitressing job and they moved to the apartment above the funeral home. Even if it was a free place to live, she hated climbing up the back steps looking in the window at the people standing nervous and silent by the body in the coffin. She hated coming in through the storage garage past the new coffins stacked to the ceiling, the fleet of limousines and hearses shining gray in a row. She hated the thought of the plasticized bodies lying below her as she slept and the new dead, not yet embalmed, lying on stretchers in the basement. Once, going down to look for Michael in the embalming room, she'd come across a dead woman curled uncovered on a metal stretcher, her hands hardened into a claw shape, mouth gaping open, her skin ashen and blue. Theresa screamed and ran past. She'd never seen death like that without make-up. Michael had laughed at her as he sat drinking a Coke in the embalming room, loud tape of Jimi Hendrix blaring while he and the other assistants hooked a body up to the embalming machine. Theresa didn't go down in the basement after that.

It was there, though, in the funeral home, that her powers began to grow. Maybe it was the influence of all the spirits passing from one world to another. She sensed presences there, confused and full of loss, as if they were clutching at their loved ones in human form, floating around the mortuary, over the gladiolas and wreaths of carnations. Sometimes Theresa felt sure the place was thick with ghosts—when she came down in the morning flowers would be in different arrangements, pictures found upside down on the walls. She'd tell Michael about these things but he'd only laugh. After a few months there Theresa began having trouble sleeping. She grew despondent. This was not the pastoral cosmic life she'd imagined for them.

Michael seemed unhappy too. He fought with his father,

who came, emaciated, to the office to do the books, coughing and wheezing, growing more and more skeletal by the day, slowly growing toward the death he had served all his life. At night Michael drove around picking up bodies from frantic families and hospital morgues. Once or twice a month he would disappear for a few days—"Just a little deal on the side," he always said—flying cocaine back from Miami for his old canyon friend, Lowell. Theresa would drive Michael to the airport, feeling distant from him and lonely.

"Can't we just leave all this?" she begged once. "Just go away, go down to Mexico for a couple of months or move up to Oregon and get a cabin in some mountains?" Michael would return from Florida bearing expensive presents for Theresa, handcrafted amethyst rings and tortoiseshell combs for her nearly waist-length hair.

When he was out of town, her powers seemed stronger. She'd lie in the sun at the beach and slip away out of her skin. As she became more accomplished, it was easy as taking off a glove. At first she only floated above the sand; then she began practicing going higher into the blue, farther and farther away from where her sleeping form lay. She called it sleep, but it was more like a light trance. She simply held two locations in her mind and widened the distance between them.

Once she saw a hang glider loop in the wind off a hill, hover, and turn in a circle, soaring with the grace and abandon of a large hawk, and she wondered if she could do that. Letting herself relax, she breathed into the wind and found that she was able to ride the dipping currents like a surfer in waves. Ecstatic, she'd stayed out-of-body longer than she ever had before.

As she grew confident in her ability to go out-of-body, she realized that she should do more with it than simply play in the wind. Maybe, she thought, I could actually enter someone else's body, go into their thoughts.

Again, she practiced at the beach, inducing a light trance state. Just before the drop-off into sleep, she'd ease out, seeking a person who felt very relaxed and receptive and come in behind them, a shadow superimposing on their bodies. Theresa was amazed how easy it was, how little seemed to separate people, how the boundaries of skin were such an illusion.

Once, though, she had gone inside a young woman who was sunning in a chaise longue and an odd thing happened. On entering her, Theresa felt there was something wrong with the woman's ankles, an old injury, a wound of some kind. Instead of just hearing the woman's thoughts or seeing things from her point of view, Theresa felt herself fall more deeply into her. At first she thought she must be experiencing the woman's dream and then she realized it was the woman's childhood, her memory—and she was not just observing but felt she had become the woman's child-self waiting in a bed in a dark room, holding her arms tightly around her feet as if protecting them.

Theresa did not like the emotional atmosphere of dread and fear. She knew she should leave the woman, return to the white wind, but she was unable to. The scene became less dreamlike and more vivid: clutching sheets over her small body, a door opening, slant of light falling across a wood floor and large shoes. *Stare at them—brown holes in them, only the shoes. Don't look at the face, hands as they pull the sheets down, pull at your ankles, drag you down toward the end of the bed, hold you down, hold you down while—*

Theresa tried to flee the scene but felt like a bird trapped in a room, and she could only flap madly between closed-in walls, unable to find a way out, now banging against the edges of something, room or body or time, until finally she felt herself fall out into a swaying darkness.

She panicked. The beach was not there, no girl, no sand, only blackness surrounding her, moving rhythmically. She sensed she'd gone too far from the physical plane, stayed too long out-of-body. She could feel the rocking presence of the ocean all around her but she had no idea how to get back.

Then she remembered that time she'd begun to analyze the experience, think too much about it, how that had tugged her back to herself. *Eyes*, she thought. *How can I see inside that girl if I am not in my body and I have no eyes? How can I possibly go into someone else's memory if I am me? If I am not anywhere, then how can my body still be there on a blanket on the beach? And if time has no boundaries, then how can there be a present?*

Suddenly, she felt a painful yank on her stomach and she was thrown hard, hurtled back into her body. She lay on the cool sand, her legs and arms numb, breath coming hard in short gasps. The beach was dark, nearly empty. It took a long time before she was strong enough to walk back to her car.

Realizing it was dangerous to try these things on her own, Theresa vowed to renew her search for a teacher. Her powers were growing beyond what she could handle.

After that she was sometimes afraid at the beach at sunset, as if she would be drawn back into that crack between night and day, present and past, unable to find her way home.

One afternoon, picking Michael up from the airport after one of his runs, Theresa nearly fainted from a migraine headache that bored into her skull like screws. Michael had to drive back to the funeral home. She was sick for two days, churning with hot, sweaty fever dreams.

That was the beginning of the knife dreams. Repetitive nightmares destroyed her sleep—Michael with a knife coming at her, chasing her. Or hiding somewhere, she would watch him stab some woman over and over in a house empty of furniture. One dream she still remembered clearly: Michael was a magician and Theresa was his assistant. He was throwing knives, outlining her body against a board. She feared that he would throw a knife right into her heart.

For days she had a severe headache, and voices needled inside her, at first far away, then growing louder. Sometimes it sounded like the buzz of a crowd of people in an auditorium all talking at once, but one voice kept breaking out of the din, a high, whining singsong, someone almost crying, *Let me out. Please. I want to get out. I can't open the door, can't find the door. Want out, Mama. Help me. Can't anybody find me?*

One night Michael came in late from a party. Theresa lay exhausted from the headache and the sad voice inside her. He sat next to her on the bed, smoothing her hair back. "Are you sick again?" he asked.

"It's this headache," she said. "Maybe I'm getting migraines or something."

"Want something for it?"

"I don't want to get high, if that's what you mean. It only makes it louder."

"What do you mean louder?"

She could tell he'd been drinking and was probably tripping too. His pupils looked large and black as pools and he was tapping his foot endlessly, unable to sit still. Finally, she told him about the voice and its insistent message. "It just keeps coming over and over, saying stuff like 'Help me,' and 'Let me out!' It's like somebody locked in a room or trapped or hidden away. She's so sad, Michael, and it makes *me* sad. Just the other day she started saying things like 'I don't have it. This is all I've got. This is all there ever was.' It's weird. I just can't stop it."

"It's probably nothing," he said. "You're just imagining things."

"Michael, I'm not. The dreams are so real. And the voice comes when I'm awake, not asleep. It comes right in the middle of the day. It's like someone's calling out to me from under a grave saying, 'Let me out, let me out.' Sometimes the voice is right here in this room and—"

Without warning he slapped her across the mouth, bringing blood to her lips. "Shut up!" he yelled. Theresa was too shocked to cry. She touched her bleeding mouth and cringed away from him. He shook her by the shoulders.

"It's just your imagination, you're making it all up. You're nuts, Terry!" He was shouting. "I have to deal with dead people all day and now I've got a lunatic for a wife. I'm sick of this. I've had it with your ghosts and your gypsies and your goddamn visions!"

Theresa kept the voices to herself after that, but she knew he was keeping something from her. He worked long hours, spending time down in the embalming room in the basement. He went out late to parties without her, while she stayed home, growing used to the incessant, whining voice inside her. She laid the cards out night after night, silently seeking for some explanation, and, oddly, the same cards kept coming up no matter how much she shuffled them. They were telling her a story, but she didn't have all the clues, only the sad, locked-in voice and the card's pictures: Seven of Wands, someone trying to ward off attack with a large staff; Nine of Cups, a greedy miser hoarding his wealth; the Moon, some hidden secret, not yet revealed; the thief, Seven of Swords, stealing away from the tent; Judgment, gray-blue bodies rising out of open graves, angel sounding the golden horn above them. Theresa couldn't put it together, but one thing she felt sure of: The thief represented Michael.

She became obsessed with the cards and wouldn't leave the house without them. Several times a day she'd shuffle them and lay them out, knowing already the same cards would turn up. One evening she went to the beach to calm herself, to drift off into a trance state, float on the wind. It had occurred to her to "enter" Michael the way she had gone inside others' minds, but she was afraid. As she lay in the orange dusk light at the beach, trying to relax, to slip out-of-body as she had so often before, she couldn't do it. Instead, she felt physically sick, her stomach cramped. She doubled over on the blanket.

Maybe that was the first time she had seen the water burning, that blue burst into red, then off again, the sand, too, glowing like white ashes. The illusion haunted her. She'd rushed home, held the cards in her lap all night, not

87

wanting to let them go. Something was wrong with her, she knew, and it frightened her to think how strangely she was acting.

One night Michael came home very high on cocaine. They hadn't made love in several weeks and had hardly spoken to each other, but that night he seemed forgiving. It was the old Michael that knelt beside her, slipping the nightgown off over her head, kissing her breasts and her neck. She fingered his coarse hair, kissed him hard, her tongue in his mouth, eager for his affection. "Baby," she whispered, "let's not fight anymore, okay?"

Afterward they lay awake, and Michael smoked a cigarette in the dark. She sensed an open space between them and it seemed as if he wanted to talk.

"So are your voices all gone?" he asked.

She shook her head. "No, they're still here and I'm really tired of them, Michael. They won't go away. It's like a ringing in my ears. I don't know what to do."

"Maybe you should see a doctor." He sighed out a breath of smoke.

"Yeah," she agreed. "I guess you're right. But there's something else now too. Whenever I lay out my cards, these same ones always turn up. Every day. One of them is the Seven of Swords, the thief. I know this sounds funny, but—I mean, you are in trouble or anything? The cards are telling me this thief has something to do with you."

"Give me a break. Let me see it," he said. She opened the deck and pulled out the card. "It's just a dumb picture, for Christ's sake. Terry, I mean it, you should go to a doctor. Get some Valium or something."

"But, Michael, something is going on with you, I know it. Let me show you." She reshuffled the deck and laid out the cards on the pillow. There they were, too familiar. "Look," she said, "the Moon, a secret, something hidden. And this wand card is a person being attacked because of greed. See this fat guy hoarding all the cups? Then Judgment, *death*, bodies in graves, and this thief

88

stealing away from the scene with all the swords. Michael, he is always there. Always!''

"Let me try it," he said, grabbing the deck. He shuffled them for a moment and then ran out of the room.

Theresa yanked her nightgown back on over her head and chased after him down the stairs. "Michael!" she yelled. "Give them back!" She tore from room to dark room, frightened by the large shadows of open coffins, the muffled sounds of her own feet. *"Michael!"*

Then she heard him in the basement, slam of metal— and she raced down the cement stairs past the embalming room to find him standing in front of the incinerator, his arms folded, sound of the gas jet rushing into flames.

"No!" she shouted. "That was the deck the gypsy gave me!''—and she ran to him, clawing, pounding her fists against his chest. He tried to take her in his arms, but she dug her fingers at his eyes and he cried out, pushing her back against some stacked boxes. She fell into them, scrambling upward, her nightgown tangled around her knees.

"Get away from me," she screamed. "Back off!" Grabbing an old cast-iron fireplace poker used for stirring ashes in the incinerator, she raised it over her head and brought it down against his forehead. As she lunged at him again, he kicked her full force in the stomach, knocking her back to the wall, where she fell, the wind knocked out of her.

He threw himself on top of her, holding her arms to the cold floor as Theresa gasped for air.

"Terry, Terry!" he was yelling. "Something's wrong with you. We'll get you checked out. You've got to get away from all this occult shit. It's making you crazy."

He waited until she seemed to calm, then carried her upstairs and set her on the couch, her eyes black with fear, voices wailing inside her. He paced the small living room, then disappeared.

She thought of running down the back stairs out into the night. She didn't know where she could go, but the voices were like endless music, *Get out get out,* they chimed. *Get out, Theresa!*

Taking the car keys, she tiptoed barefoot down the rickety steps to the parking lot behind the funeral home. As she opened the car door, he grabbed her from behind, his hand over her mouth, his arm so tight across her throat that she couldn't breathe.

"No, you ain't," he whispered, pulling his arms tighter. Then he dragged her to the other side of the car, threw her in, and drove off through the early hours, the streets empty and eerie. Every few minutes he reached up to his head with a dirty rag and wiped at where she'd hit him with the poker, blood on his hair and cheek.

"Where are we going?" she cried, huddling against the door.

"Someplace where you'll feel better," he said. "Just do what I say and everything is going to be okay." It was his mortician tone—there, there—the one he used to comfort the grieving.

Soon he pulled the car into the circular driveway of a small clinic on private grounds. "Terry," he said quietly. "It's best you stay here for a while. You know it's for the best too."

"But, Michael, there is nothing wrong with me."

"How can you say that, Ter? You've been hearing voices. You're hallucinating."

Theresa started screaming, "You know it's my powers, you son of a bitch. You know I'm right! Don't tell me I'm crazy!"

As she struggled, Michael hauled her from the car into the paneled lobby of the clinic, where orderlies helped to restrain her, finally shoving a hypo into her arm. Theresa had no idea how much time elapsed as the voices and dreams stirred inside her where she lay cold and afraid in the white room.

After a few days she felt safer at the clinic. She was glad for the drugs they gave her, first the Dalmane, then the Haldol to stop the sensation of visions in her mind. She felt a quiet inside her for the first time in months, but it was not a peaceful quiet. It was the eye of the storm, a deadly stillness. She knew the voices were still there, that the drugs were just repressing them. After a week the doctor asked her if she wanted to go home. "No," she had said. "I just can't." How could she go back to that house of ghosts where her mind swarmed with voices humming like bees in her ears? "I'm afraid," she told her doctor.

"Of what?" the doctor asked in her pleasant, even tone.

"Myself," said Theresa.

She stayed three months. The voices and the visions stopped. The clinic routine was ordered and clean and there was no death. No blue bodies. Only silence. She'd never felt so alone. Michael came only once to see her. She'd asked that he stay away so she could sort things out, but she knew he'd won. He'd succeeded in making her doubt herself. Maybe she *had* gone too far. Her psychic gift, which had once mysteriously inspired and uplifted her, had become a sickness. Now her mind was calm, but it was also dulled. She was placid and blank as the TV static in the second-floor lounge.

Toward the end of her third month at the clinic the doctor asked Theresa if she would like to go along on an outing of patients to the beach.

"Because I've been a good girl?" asked Theresa.

"What do you think it has to do with being good?" asked the doctor.

I'm normal. Everyday mind, Theresa thought bitterly. *No crazy psychic babble.* "I mean, because I've been feeling better, I guess," she said quietly. "I haven't felt so out of control."

The doctor nodded.

They drove in a van to a quiet stretch of beach. A picnic had been packed and the other patients, all under medication like Theresa, sat in folding chairs eating tuna fish sandwiches and drinking Pepsi. They chatted about the beautiful weather, other fine days at the beach. Theresa was tired from the strain of having to act nice. Being at the water made her want to weep. All she really wanted was to wander down the shore by herself, feel her mind alive again, not just with her old wild thoughts and celestial visions, but with even the simplest joy. The ocean had always brought out in her an intense awareness of all her possibilities, vital and creative. There on the sand, sedated along with her companions, she felt merely empty. She had turned away from something as essential to her life as breathing, and some part of her was dying.

That night the nurse forgot to take back the pen she'd been given to write in her diary, the one the doctor would ask her about in their weekly session. Theresa slipped the ball-point pen into her pocket and took it back to her room. They were so careful to keep the patients from violence; anything sharp or hard was confiscated so they couldn't hurt themselves or attack someone else. In the dark that night Theresa lay with the pen in her hand. Mindlessly, she twirled the point against her palm. She could see the blue dot of ink in the slant of light that fell through the slightly open door. She lay quiet, spinning the sharp point, pressing harder, digging deep, wondering how much pain she could tolerate inflicting on herself. Could she jam it into her jugular vein? Could she just let her body die as her mind was dying? Why not hurt? At least it was something. She'd given up the best part of her life, the only thing that had ever held any meaning. Yes, Michael had betrayed her, the gypsy's cards were ashes, but she'd also betrayed herself. She'd probably never hear the voice again, it had left her forever because she didn't deserve its presence. She was worthless.

That's not true. The voice, long silent, came to her. Theresa stopped pushing the pen into her hand, and listened. *Again.* She wanted to hear it again. Had she only made it up? Her palm burned, there was blood there. She licked it, salty and warm. Then, for the first time, she realized the voice was not someone whispering inside her head, something other than herself. *You are worthy,* said the voice, and Theresa had to acknowledge that it was her own.

"Oh, God, help me," she whispered. "I don't want to

die here. I want to go home. I want to get out of here and go home," she sobbed into the stiff sheets, letting the tears come, forcing them out with relief, washing her clean.

The next morning in her session Dr. White asked her, "So you do feel better now, without these voices?"

Theresa sat in a wicker chair, smoking a cigarette the doctor had given her, staring out at the beautiful Los Angeles summer behind the barred window. "Without that one voice, yes, the trapped one," she said. "But I miss the other ones."

"The other ones?"

She sat still for a long time. *The other ones.* The doctor was waiting for her to speak. If she talked honestly about being psychic, she would be thought crazy. Mentally disturbed. Chemical imbalance. Subject to delusions. Treatable with drugs. If she told the truth, she was crazy. If she lied, she was sane. Yes, she feared that one voice and was glad it was gone, but she didn't like this empty sane mind they'd given her. It was false and blurred, plain and predictable. It was quiet as an idling engine and it was not her. She knew that in the normal view of the world it *was* insane to be psychic. Yet she knew that it was part of her, that it would always be with her. That voice was real, and while she was confused and afraid, she was not mad.

That afternoon, walking the quiet, well-kept lawn, knowing she was walled in there even if it was her choice, Theresa came to a decision. If she was crazy, she wanted to stay that way. It was true that she must be half crazy to have the powers she did, but that was part of the bargain.

From now on she would dedicate herself to her psychic gift and see it as a responsibility, not a disease. She remembered the gypsy's warning: "You will need so much help!" Well, she needed it now, but it wasn't going to come from taking a blue pill or staying in the safe prison of the clinic. It wasn't going to come from Michael. Maybe it was just as well the cards were gone too. She would have to find someone who could help her, another psychic, a medium. She wasn't the only one in the world.

Theresa vowed that no one would ever again convince her she was crazy, no one could make her turn away from herself in doubt like that again.

Theresa was released home on a probationary stay, and Michael watched her closely. She was careful to act normal. Everything was fine. She knew then that she would have to leave Michael. She knew that he could never accept her and that he was somehow dangerous to her. She lifted money from his pockets and his stashes of dealing cash and stored it in a safe deposit box in Santa Monica. After a year had passed, she moved out and filed for divorce. She was twenty-four. Michael didn't fight it. He was afraid of her. And she was afraid of him.

He'd come once to her new apartment bringing the last of her things from the funeral home. Michael had seemed relieved the marriage was over and for a few hours some old feeling of friendliness and honesty had returned to them. They'd made love slowly and tenderly on the mattress on the floor and afterward he'd let his guard down, apologizing for what had happened. Theresa lied and said, "Forget it. It's over."

Michael had said, "I don't think so. We're not finished with each other, Terry."

Theresa was cold, waiting on the beach for Camille, who had walked up the shore. Now she spotted her running back through the darkness. Together they strolled to the car, and drove home quietly. "Did you ever think you were crazy for being psychic?" Theresa asked as she pulled up in front of Camille's building.

"Think? I *know* I am! But I just got the secret of craziness. Everybody's a little magic but they just ain't dealing with it."

"Sometimes I just wish I could control it better."

Camille looked at her sternly. "You know what Elizabeth said about trying to stop it."

"I'm not saying I want to stop it. I know you can't turn

it off once it's been opened up and I don't want to. I just wish I could talk to her about this.''

"No way, Resa. You know her rules.''

"Yeah," said Theresa. "More like her commandments.''

Driving home alone, Theresa felt the headache sear suddenly up her neck and burn across her temples. She veered the car wildly to the side of the road, held her head, and rocked back and forth in the seat. This time there were no voices, only a silence so vast she thought her whole mind would be sucked into it. The image was clear and sickeningly familiar. It was as she had always seen it in the periphery of her vision, a shadow that had been with her for years, but she'd never opened to it. Now she let the image come toward her: the huge orange globe of the sun magnified in a haze against the horizon, sky bloodred, fiery clouds. Not just clouds but earth as well. A cliff overlooking the ocean, the entire hill burning beneath her. Hands of fire, coal-red, searing inside her. Turning in the flames, she saw him reaching toward her, pleading, then falling, both of them falling into the rising fire. Knowing it was Michael, that he was dying, that there was nothing that she could do. That it was her fault. Looking up, she saw the red light from the flames flick mechanically across the rocks. The sea was calm far below.

We're not finished with each other, Terry.

Theresa knew in the clear and silent vision of what was to come that she would somehow destroy them both and that she had always known this was true.

Chapter 7

It was against the rules, but Theresa had to see Elizabeth. Wasn't Elizabeth always saying, "Opening your mind to the possible is knowing there are exceptions to every rule"? Certainly, this was one.

It was early Thursday morning when Theresa set out for Malibu. The sky hung low and cloudy over the city, the air smudged with yellow smog. Whenever she put her foot on the brakes, there was that odd scraping sound. Reminding herself again to bring the car in for a tune-up, she drove up the coast past the still, empty beaches, rows of houses perched closely together along the shore or precariously balanced on hills that jutted up from the sea.

It had been over a year since she'd been with Elizabeth. Just seeing her might solve everything. Elizabeth: clear, sharp, as cut glass, a brilliant mirror. She would tell Theresa what to do.

But as Theresa neared the house on the cliff, she wasn't so sure it was right. Elizabeth could refuse to see her. She could be terrifying at times, harsh and cold.

The image of death hung in her mind like a sad, haunting song. Theresa opened the car window, smelling sea salt and dust, trying to erase the repetitive scene that seemed part dream and, strangely, part memory. For years she'd seen the fragments, vague, partially formed—the burning, the ocean, always at sunset—but never had the scene played out so precisely, Michael falling toward her, pleading. Theresa shuddered. Not everything she envisioned actually came to pass, and it had taken her years to learn how to decipher a true vision from a false one, a glimpse of a possible future from a phantom, a fear.

Usually, it was clear to her which images to believe, but ever since she'd discovered Bonnie Humphrey's body, she'd felt her powers running out of control, her psyche spinning out violent pictures, and she couldn't tell anymore which were valid, which were distortions.

Elizabeth's teachings kept churning through her as she drove. "You can't afford to ignore the messages your mind gives forth, Theresa. If you don't live by the words of your spirit guides, they will abandon you. They may even destroy you."

It was said that when a person was ready for a teacher, the teacher would appear. There was no need to go to the banks of the Ganges searching for a guru. Sincere desire was enough to draw the student to the source of knowledge. One night during the spring Theresa had separated from Michael, she'd looked in the paper to check on the time of a movie and had come across a small advertisement for a lecture to be given at UCLA that evening by Elizabeth Brandon, "Noted Medium, Author of *The Psychic Within You.*" It was a book Theresa had read over and over, its pages lined with red ink marking paragraphs she wanted to remember, notes scribbled in the margins. A short article stated that Brandon sometimes taught classes in psychic development and Theresa prayed that this woman might be the mentor she so desperately needed.

There were only about twenty people in the lecture hall. Theresa was surprised by the tall, gangly woman who stalked up to the podium in an elegant black suit and stared out at the audience, examining each of their faces. Elizabeth Brandon's eyes finally stopped in Theresa's gaze and she nodded as if she knew her. Then she lit a Camel with a silver lighter, clicked the lighter shut, and began speaking.

"The human mind is a great and powerful and mysterious thing, and we use such a small portion of it. There's a vast intelligence within each of us we don't even know how to touch. The rational mind has been developed and valued above all else in our culture, but the unconscious, the dream life, the intuition, the psychic within you, are there latent, waiting to be brought to life just as Sleeping Beauty was awakened by the Prince's kiss. Most people, even if they do get a glimmer of their own psychic intelligence, hardly know what to do with it. They deny it, they laugh at it, they repress it, or they don't even notice it at all. Others, whose abilities are more highly developed, must come to terms with that intelligence. They must recognize who they are and why they were born with this powerful and sometimes difficult gift."

Following the lecture Brandon asked for questions from the audience and there was a long silence during which Theresa's whole mind ached. There were so many things she wanted to ask, she didn't know where to begin, couldn't even form the words. Elizabeth Brandon took off her glasses, tapped them gently in her open palm, waiting for the audience to respond. She stepped awkwardly to the side of the podium and pointed at Theresa with her glasses.

"Yes?" she said. "Could you repeat your question for the rest of the group?"

Theresa stuttered, "But I—I didn't say anything."

Elizabeth squinted, then put on her glasses and regarded Theresa closely, brow creased in thought. "No, I don't suppose you did."

There were no questions from the audience at all, but people clustered around Brandon afterward, hovering at her side, asking her to autograph her books. Theresa waited in her seat until the group had dispersed, waited with her question formed finally in her mind, the one she knew Elizabeth had already silently heard her ask: *May I be your student?* As Theresa approached, Elizabeth again removed her glasses, looking at Theresa as if she recognized her from someplace.

"Aren't you one of my students?" she asked.

"I would very much like to be."

"Yes," said Elizabeth, and she began rummaging through papers till she found a pamphlet which she handed to Theresa. "Clearing Your Mind" was the title, and Theresa

wanted to laugh out loud in relief. "You see," said Elizabeth, "I've been waiting for you to free yourself up so you
could begin your formal study unencumbered by emotional
blocks. Mary, is it?"

"Terry. Theresa."

"Ah, but it is Mary. Mary Theresa, it must be. I have
been looking for a Mary."

Theresa closed her eyes, feeling faint for a moment.

Elizabeth went on. "Your grandmother has sent you to
me. She tells me"—Elizabeth paused as if receiving some
inner information—"that she's not angry with you for
using her name and she knows that the Divine Mother will
watch over you."

"Her name?" asked Theresa.

"You'll be using her name, dear. Was *her* name Mary?
No, it is her *last* name—she wants you to have it. Now,
Mary, Terry, Theresa—whatever—here is my phone num-
ber. You'll call me when you're ready."

With that she swept her books and papers into a briefcase, and stalked out of the lecture hall.

Theresa called the number the next day and Elizabeth
told her that the class would begin the following week, an
intensive seminar for advanced students to be held at her
home in Malibu. Theresa arrived early for class and waited
in the spacious living room with another student, a tall
black woman who introduced herself as Camille Taylor
and who kept saying, "Where is everybody else? Are we
the only ones? I thought I came on the wrong day or
something."

Before long Elizabeth joined them, perching on the edge
of a leather couch, wearing old khaki pants and gray sweater,
quite different dress from the elegant suit she'd worn for
her lecture.

"I'm so glad you could finally make it." She smiled.

"We were waiting for the others," Camille said
nervously.

"There are no others," said Elizabeth, and she in-
formed them that when particularly gifted students pre-

sented themselves to her, that is when she chose to teach. The class could begin that day, and it would be better if they both lived up here with her at the cliff house. She told them to quit their jobs, that they'd be given room and board as well as a small salary in exchange for help with the unkeep of the house and for assistance with her writing and psychic sessions. Theresa felt a slight reservation. The woman was overpowering, and something about it all reminded Theresa of joining some religious cult where she'd have to give up everything to find God's true way. Nevertheless, she knew she had been waiting for this woman ever since her visit to the gypsy, that she must take the risk. She could not hold back. Elizabeth Brandon was her teacher. Of that Theresa had no doubt.

The advanced seminar began that morning, and as far as Theresa knew, it was still in session even though she hadn't seen Elizabeth for over a year. As she sped up the coastal highway, she pictured the remarkable woman who had so altered the course of her life.

Though Elizabeth was in her seventies, she carried herself as if she were twenty years younger, her walk wide-gaited and energetic. Her large feet nearly stomped, long-fingered hands whirled the air as she spoke. Her hair was white, thinning, coiled into a neat bun at her nape, bangs cut short. Sometimes, though, when she'd been out standing in the ocean wind, her hair unraveled from the bun and hung scraggly to the middle of her back. Burning an icy, disturbing gray, her eyes were wide, almost bulging with some inner vision. Her arched eyebrows affected a look of permanent surprise.

Over the years Elizabeth Brandon had refined her diet "to develop her psychic side," she claimed, eating mostly raw foods and drinking an herbal tea friends sent her from New Delhi. It filled the house with the scent of rose petals and oranges as it steeped. But in the lower left-hand drawer of the mahogony desk in her study, she hid a cache of Snickers, which she ate while she worked, and she'd given up years ago trying to quit smoking the unfiltered

Camels that her husband had also smoked until his death in 1963. Her husband, a German Jew who'd emigrated to Switzerland before the war, had been a psychiatrist who'd studied with Jung. He and Elizabeth had traveled widely in Indonesia, the Orient, and India, and it was there in the early fifties that Elizabeth had begun meditating and honing her own psychic powers.

She claimed always to have been psychic, to have known that her gift was directly related to physical healing. Disease appeared to her as a darkness in the body, and in that darkness she could feel the wronged past lives of the patient like a scene in a snowy paperweight. She could enter that scene with her powers and dispel the darkness. While she'd accept money for lecturing and the sales of her books, she never took payment for the actual healing sessions conducted with the two or three patients a year who came to live with her in Malibu at the modern redwood house with its curved walls and huge picture windows that faced out over the water. Her patients stayed several months, and she hired students to live with her to cook, tend the garden and the ill. That was how Theresa had come to live down the hall from Camille and her infant daughter.

During the two years that Theresa lived at the cliff house, she came to have immense respect for the way in which Elizabeth regarded her psychic powers. While she was brilliantly intuitive, anticipating questions that had never been asked, knowing where lost objects could be found, prying unspoken doubts from Theresa's mind, she maintained that all that was mere play, "easy psychic stuff," and not the core to which they should dedicate themselves.

She told them never to cheapen their gift by brandishing it about, predicting things in a public way for gossipy tabloids or using their powers to gain celebrity status. There were periods of time during which Elizabeth seemed almost to hide her powers, and one might never have guessed that Elizabeth was a true psychic except that the people who came to her unable to breathe because of asthma or twisted by arthritis went home after a few months healthy, vital, and changed.

Once Theresa saw Elizabeth come out of a healing session with a woman who was dying of lung cancer. She was very pale, leaning against the wall. "Theresa," she said, "make me a fish soup with lots of kelp in it and bring it to me immediately." Theresa found Elizabeth in bed, sweating, feverish, her eyes red and watering, nose running. The old woman was barely able to speak. Alarmed, Theresa asked if she should call a doctor. "No, don't worry," Elizabeth had instructed. "We've had an excellent transference of energy and I've just got to burn it off." Later that evening Elizabeth emerged from her room, completely well. She nodded to Camille and Theresa and told them that the patient would be leaving very shortly, that she'd finally released years of grieving from her sick lungs and she'd be healthy in a few weeks.

Elizabeth had come from a wealthy Hartford family, and when she lectured she wore elegant clothes, old Chanels and Balenciagas she'd bought in Paris twenty, thirty years ago, but she loved to wander the grounds of the Malibu ranch in old khaki pants and a cardigan that had belonged to her husband, Kleenex and candy wrappers stuffed in the deep pockets. She wrote her lectures and books pacing the deck outside her study, dictating into a small tape machine, chain-smoking her Camels, then huddling over a typewriter in her study, her large cat Madame curled in her lap.

As Theresa neared the cliff house in Malibu, she remembered the way Elizabeth's loud laugh would turn suddenly to harsh silence, her unpredictable mood swings. Theresa would have to be careful, conduct herself properly, try to be honest about what was happening. Elizabeth wouldn't tolerate falseness in people, and if she disliked someone's talk or actions she wouldn't say anything but would merely stare until the person felt the silent heat of her disapproval.

Theresa loved and feared this woman who seemed to know her every thought before she even spoke, and as she pulled in past the white brick pillars on either side of the road and up the gravel driveway darkly shadowed by eucalyptus and pine, she tried to tell herself it was all right to break "the rule."

Camille always called it that. After completing the apprenticeship with Elizabeth, the two women had begun their own practices and Elizabeth had told them that during the initial stage of working on their own, they were not to contact her for two years. "Wean yourselves from me," she'd told them. "You can't be truly powerful and honest in your work if you are always looking to me for help. Become your own teachers."

Theresa parked the car at the side of the road and walked up to the house, listening to the crunch of pine needles beneath her feet. A comforting stillness permeated the empty yard. A glass wind chime tinkled in a window somewhere. Lifting the brass knocker, she hesitated before letting it clunk down on the carved wooden door. "Please," she whispered, "please see me."

Elizabeth swung the huge door open and stood before Theresa in her uniform of old khaki pants and cardigan sweater. Her hair was pinned neatly back and she wore a string of amber beads. She didn't smile and Theresa finally had to look away from her gray gaze that never faltered. She knew she should never have come.

"If my timing is correct, Theresa, I should be meeting you in about eight months. I've been looking forward to it. I thought I'd have you and Camille out for the spring equinox."

"Please, Elizabeth, I know I'm not supposed to be here, but I have to talk to you. I wouldn't have come if I wasn't desperate."

"Don't gush. It doesn't become you." Elizabeth let the heavy door slide open, then turned to walk into the spacious tiled entryway, where shoes were lined in a neat row against the wall. Theresa followed her past the kitchen,

103

where a woman and a teenaged girl were doing the dishes. They turned to smile at Theresa. Elizabeth's new apprentices. Suddenly, being back, Theresa felt homesick.

Elizabeth was always saying that you've got to have your own—love, strength, clarity, health. You couldn't get it from outside yourself. Why, then, just being here did she feel as if everything was all right?

Elizabeth led Theresa to her study, down a long hall past rooms that were still dark in the morning shadows. The house was cool. Theresa thought of menthol, mint. In the study Elizabeth poured a cup of tea from a brown pot and motioned for Theresa to sit down in the worn, overstuffed chair. Elizabeth sat across the room at her desk. "I've got a session in about twenty minutes, Theresa, so I don't have much time. You're here about this, this murder business, isn't that correct? Frank told me about it."

Theresa didn't know where to begin and felt flushed and nervous. Elizabeth would expect her to be direct, truthful, perceptive. All she felt was a tangle of confused emotions. She took a deep breath. "I feel like I'm in danger."

"From within or without?"

"I'm not sure." *It's all within*, Elizabeth always told her. "Within?" Theresa answered with a question.

"Theresa, I'm going to be honest with you. I don't want to see you, but it's not because I don't want to see you. You know it's part of the apprenticeship, this separation. But I can see that you're anxious and frightened so I'm letting you in. But don't play guessing games with me or try to please me. Be clear. What exactly is going on with you? Is there some problem?"

Theresa let out a loud sigh. She felt like a young girl. Was she still so uncertain and hungry for Elizabeth's approval?

"I'm not sure, Elizabeth. I guess that's why I'm here. We never covered murders in our sessions."

"With good reason."

"Why not?"

"You know I don't approve of that celebrity sort of

work, police investigations, publicity. You've already been in the papers several times, haven't you?''

Theresa nodded.

"My concern is healing. I told Frank I wouldn't do it and he said he was calling you. It's your business if you want to get involved in that sort of thing.''

"I'm not asking you to help me find the murderer or anything, Elizabeth. It's something else, but it seems related.''

Elizabeth looked at her watch.

"It's just that, well, I found this body for the police. The woman had been killed, stabbed. It was much easier to find her than I thought it would be. I took the police right to the spot as if I'd been there before." Theresa sipped from the small brown cup and looked back at Elizabeth. "Well, I can't shake it now—the image of it, the violence. It was a week ago and I've been having terrible dreams, visions of stabbings. The image of knives keeps interfering in every reading I do until nothing but sword cards will come up. The nightmares all involve Michael, my ex-husband. Then I found another body. The image just took me over, I didn't ask for it. I nearly fainted, it was like having a fit or something. Last night, the same thing—I had to pull over to the side of the road and I had this terrible vision, like a death vision. It was of Michael and me. I just had this overwhelming sense that I would destroy both of us.''

Theresa felt cold, she shivered.

"Tell me something about what you saw," said Elizabeth, and as Theresa repeated the fragments of her vision, the old woman closed her eyes, put her hand to her forehead, eyelids fluttering slightly, open then closed. Then she took the top off her fountain pen and wrote in a notebook. "What advice did you expect me to give you?" she asked without looking up.

"What should I do? I mean, I don't know if I'm receiving real images or if I'm just making it all up. Maybe I'm

105

seeing it wrong, I've gotten so upset over these murders, it's affecting my mind.''

"And what should you do, Theresa?" Elizabeth was still writing.

Theresa thought for a moment, turning the ring on her finger. Camille's words came back to her and she repeated them. "Do some protective prayers. Cleanse myself. Fast.''

"Camille is wise," said Elizabeth. "Why didn't you listen to her? What else?''

She thought for a moment, then continued. "I guess I have to clear my mind, right? Like stop doing readings for a little while? Take a break. Put the cards away, do a fast like Camille said. Maybe I should get a past-life reading from Camille to see if my vision is correct.''

"See, Theresa? You already know what to do. This is what I want you to experience. I want you to find the teacher in yourself, the one inside you, that *is* you, who is wise and knows what to do.''

Theresa felt small, silly. Was it all just stress, then? *Take two aspirin and call me in the morning.* Did Elizabeth think she was just a weakling, dependent and whiny?

Elizabeth rose and walked over to the window, staring out at the flat clouds that lay over the water. Theresa looked down at her hands, waiting in what seemed an endless silence. Finally, after several minutes, she blurted out, "But what about the vision with Michael? I mean, did I really see my own death, Elizabeth? Or will it all just go away if I am a good girl and drink my carrot juice and go to bed early?''

Elizabeth turned to face Theresa, shaking her head. Theresa was startled by her face, grave and sad.

"Don't put that on me, Theresa. That Oh-mighty-Elizabeth-save-me tone. Poor, helpless Theresa. You want me to make it all better, right? Put my hand over your third eye and divine the correct interpretation of all of this, wave my magic wand and make it all go away.'' Elizabeth smoothed her white bangs over her forehead and fingered the amber beads. Theresa found herself nearly in tears, and she struggled to hold back the emotion in her throat.

Elizabeth pulled her chair up to Theresa's and looked directly into her face. "I can't help you with this, Theresa. And I resent your making me feel responsible for solving it. You know why I insist on this separation, the two years of no contact with Big Mama Teacher? I'm not some swami guru. But I will tell you that you don't need a past-life reading about this because you've already had one. Don't you remember the final session we did before you moved out? The tunnel?"

Theresa thought for a moment and shook her head—not because she didn't remember but because she didn't want to.

"As soon as you mentioned fire, Theresa, well . . . you are Pisces, but you've got three fire signs in your chart. You're going to be tested in fire, I've always seen that. But whether or not you'll rise like a phoenix from the flames, purified, I don't know."

"What do you mean, you don't know?" Theresa almost shouted.

"I do not know all the answers, Theresa! And I'm going to be very honest with you—this one is too big for me. I've seen it over and over in readings for you. We've discussed this before, so don't pretend you don't know what I'm talking about."

Theresa felt shocked, sick to her stomach. She *did* want Elizabeth to make it all better. Make the bad dream go away. For an instant Theresa felt herself burning, a sudden fever concentrating in her hands, then fading.

Elizabeth took a deep breath, adjusted her glasses. "I have warned you of a time in your development when you must confront a lack of clarity in yourself. There is a time when no other person, psychic or not, can confirm your visions for you. Not me, not Camille. I have seen a time when you'll be tested, Theresa, and I gather now that the test is upon you. Very few psychics can read their own

107

deaths. It is better that way. It is like a veil of protection. So much is up to the will, there is always a crack in fate.

"But you, you can see elements of your death, though you may not know if your vision is correct. With you there is that flaw we worked so hard on. You have great difficulty the moment you begin trying to read for yourself. My God, you are a genius when it comes to someone else's life, but your own—it is your blind spot. Stay away from reading for yourself, especially if it is an image of death. It is utter confusion for you."

Elizabeth reached over and touched Theresa's knee. Theresa put her hand over Elizabeth's, wanted to embrace her, to be held in the old woman's arms, *take care of me, yes, mother me*.

"Understand, Theresa? It's beyond me. It's up to you alone. This is a great challenge for you, a test. Maybe a sort of initiation. If you are clear in your mind, you will take the correct course of action. Otherwise . . ." Elizabeth's black pupils seemed mirrors into Theresa's mind. Suddenly Elizabeth whispered in a very quiet voice, "Go to the mountains, Theresa. Leave the sphere of confusion. Get away from the ocean. Draw power from the earth."

Taking Theresa's hand in hers, she rose and led her down the hallway, back to the front door. "Until the equinox, then?" Elizabeth's face was serious. She had let her hair down as they'd walked and the wind blew it back from her face. Then she pushed the large door shut.

So. She'd given Theresa advice after all. Theresa stood before the closed door looking at the intricate designs, hoping to find one last clue or teaching in the detailed carved symbols. Then she walked down the driveway back to her car.

Chapter 8

In the five years since their divorce Theresa and Michael had made love three times. She kept track of such things. One of the times had been friendly and sweet, an impulse after they'd attended the party of a mutual friend. The other times made Theresa feel even more lonely than if she'd never seen him at all.

Sitting in a white wicker chair in her sunroom, Theresa brushed out her long hair, still damp from washing, smelling of lavender bath salts. She'd changed clothes several times in preparation for this evening, deciding finally on a sea-green sundress that left her tan shoulders bare. Several silver chains hung around her neck and she was careful to remove the amethyst pendant she almost always wore, the one that Michael had given her. She chose a gold coin-shaped charm that Elizabeth had given her, inscribed with the crescent-moon-and-cross insignia. No, not right. He'd ask what it meant. She wore coral instead.

The night was warm, the air soft around her. A peculiar, radiant peach-colored light hovered in the southern California sky. As she drove to the restaurant to meet Michael, she wondered about Elizabeth's advice to leave the ocean—had she meant now, today? And where should she go? Maybe she ought to be driving to Colorado or New Mexico this very minute instead of up La Cienega Boulevard. She'd have to call her clients, cancel readings, make an appointment with Josh to get her car tuned for mountain driving so she could travel comfortably. She didn't just want to fly off somewhere and be stuck with no car, and she couldn't afford to rent one. Then there was Lieutenant Jardine, she'd have to let him know she'd be going. A week from tomorrow was Labor Day weekend—maybe that would be a good time to leave. It had been a while since she'd taken a real vacation, and Evelyn had been right—she needed it.

At a stoplight she gazed in the rearview mirror at the long row of cars behind her, each driver lost in his own private thoughts. A man wearing mirrored sunglasses stared into the side mirror of his blue car; behind him a red Fiat, a doughnut delivery truck. After getting on the freeway and off again, she glanced again in the mirror. How strange—she was sure she spotted the blue car that had been at the light near her house. She slowed but the car hung back, letting a van come between them.

Theresa arrived early at the restaurant, parked her car, and strolled up the street, peering into shop windows. There it was again, she was sure of it, the blue car. A man sat in the driver's seat looking at a map or a newspaper. He was dark, deeply tanned, and wore mirrored sunglasses. He was bent over and she couldn't see his face clearly. The chrome of his car shone, highly polished.

Returning to the restaurant, Theresa spotted Michael through the plate glass window. He was sitting at a small table under a large potted tree. Smoking a cigarette, he stared blankly toward her, not seeing her. She could see her own reflection in the window, standing over him, her face warped, her body rippled and slanted to one side. Again, she experienced the dizzy sensation of a double image as in the reading she'd given the other day. As she entered the restaurant, Theresa vowed to tell Michael about the recurrence of the stabbing dreams. The last time they'd discussed it—the knives, the voices, the card of the thief—Michael had told her she was insane. She didn't know how he'd respond now, but she had to ask him.

He rose as she approached and kissed her on the cheek like an old friend, his dark hair grazing her shoulder, lips cool, fingers on her neck. "Hey, hey," he said, "good to see you, Ter. You really look good."

"You don't look bad yourself, Michael. Since when do you wear suits on your off hours?"

"Oh, this? This is my *GQ* special," he said. "Well, hell, it's our yearly date, right?"

"Yeah. Big fun."

"That's what I like about you, Terry, you're so excitable, so enthusiastic."

"I'm here, am I not?" She tried to call some subtle truce in the teasing or it would escalate into old unpleasantries. Amazing how quickly they could get down to hurting one another.

Over salad they exchanged small talk, comments about the economy, news of their families, and then there was a long silence between them, not uncomfortable. Michael touched her hand with the top of the gimlet straw, tracing the line of her knuckles. "You're so quiet, Ter."

"Got a lot on my mind."

"You usually do!" He laughed. "Hey, what's with this police work? You starting a new line of business? You could refer a few clients my way!"

"I suppose you saw it in the paper."

"Nope. Caught it on the tube. Haven't read the paper in a couple of days. Next thing you know you'll be on talk shows."

"Not a bad idea."

"How do you do it, anyway?" he asked, leaning toward her.

She glanced up at him. "You know, Michael. Don't you remember?"

"I mean, do you go off into a trance?" he asked. "Do you use those cards?"

"A little of each. I just see things, I know things."

"How do you know that you're not just making it all up?"

Theresa circled a finger around the rim of her glass. Good question, she thought. "Since when are you so interested?"

"Hey, you're a celebrity, Ter. Give me a break, I'm curious. I'm your average Mr. Joe-on-the-street, okay?"

"It's just—you weren't always so hot on the subject."

He looked out the window. "Can't we ever just forget the past?"

"No. At least, I can't."

"Well, let's just change the goddamn subject to something nice and safe. Who are you sleeping with?" He grinned mischievously, pouring wine into her glass from the green bottle on the table.

Peering over Michael's shoulder out the large picture window, Theresa saw the man, the one she'd seen in the blue car. He was standing in the doorway of a record shop. When he saw her looking at him, he ducked quickly into the store.

"Michael, that man"—she rose from her chair and put her face to the glass—"I think he's following me. He's watching me, I swear."

"Who?"

"He's gone now, he looks Persian or something. I saw him behind me twice in a car on the freeway and now he's in that store."

"Ah, he probably just recognizes you from the news. You're big time now."

"What do you mean, the news? They used my picture on the news?"

Michael thought for a minute, then said, "I'm not sure. I think maybe they did."

She'd have to ask Jardine about that when she talked to him about her trip. She didn't want people staring at her on the street.

Their meal came and they ate quietly. It was an odd dance they did with each other. There was so much to say, so much to avoid saying. Theresa wished suddenly that she could break through it all, laugh easily, enjoy his dark glances, the curl of hair above his shirt collar. She realized she was afraid to bring up the knife dreams. She took a deep breath. *Let go, Theresa. Old burden.*

112

"Michael, can I ask you a personal question?"

"Shoot," he said.

"When you were dealing, doing the Miami trips, were you ever roughed up?"

"I thought we weren't going to discuss the past."

"But did anything violent ever happen?"

He sighed and crumpled his napkin. "I told you a hundred times, I was never in any kind of trouble dealing. Nothing violent ever happened, okay?"

"You know, Michael, we have all these dangerous topics with each other, marked *No discussion allowed.* Whenever I see you, I just keep wondering, what's left for us to say? Why do we get together?" He looked away from her. "I really want to talk to you about something," she said. "I just don't know how to bring it up."

"Well, what do you want to say, then? Really."

"I guess it's just these women, these stabbings. I keep having bad dreams about them. It's as if they're talking to me. It's spooky."

"I guess," he said.

"Michael. What I'm trying to say is that they're very familiar to me, these dreams. They're the same ones I had when we were married. Remember?"

"You were always having crazy dreams."

"Well, I'm having them again. I'm trying to figure out why."

Michael shrugged. "You're saying I give you nightmares?"

Theresa rubbed her eyes. "I don't know what I'm saying. Maybe back then, I was dreaming about now, these dead girls calling out to me. Maybe I was just seeing the future in those dreams, and now it's here. At the time I thought it was you. I couldn't interpret them. Remember how I always thought you were in trouble? Remember the thief card?"

"You're one of a kind," he said. "You live more in a dream than you do in reality."

"You wanted to know how I work—things come to me

113

and I have to pay attention to them. It's like a message is trying to get through. Like a name appearing in invisible ink. Like the name *Bonnie,*" she blurted out suddenly.

"What?" he said. He stopped eating and slowly removed the piece of steak he'd been chewing and put it in a napkin.

"Bonnie," she said. "You know, the dead girl."

Ballard put down his fork.

"It's like she's calling out to me from under the earth. She's crying out from the grave."

Ballard grabbed Theresa's wrist and the people at the next table stopped talking and looked over at them. "What do you mean, *Bonnie.* Bonnie who?" he whispered. He looked shocked, the color gone out of his face.

"*Michael.* Let go. She's the girl I found in the hills. Bonnie Humphrey. And the dreams I have of her are the same ones I had right before . . . the hospital and everything. Don't you see?"

"No, I don't see." He let go of her wrist and she pulled back her hand. Holding back tears, she wanted to scream, "Don't touch me like that." At the same time—*old burden, old hurt*—she wanted to call out to him, "Michael, what is it we are both so afraid of?" She rubbed her wrist, red where his fingers had pressed into her. "Spirits speak," she said. "They do. You see death as so final, don't you? Death is just business for you. For me it's part of life."

"You're still nuts, Ter. You're still a goddamn flako."

"Well, that's not really your concern anymore, is it?" Theresa lifted her glass to Michael in a toast. "To five years apart," she said.

He looked back at her a long while, then slowly he brought his glass to hers, clinked it. "Five years," he said. Tipping the glass to his mouth, he drank.

Chapter 9

Ballard stopped at a phone booth in Westwood on his way home from the restaurant and waited while a woman in nylon jogging shorts finished her call. He leaned against the hood of his car, suit coat over his shoulder, sleeves rolled up. Terry had looked beautiful, damn her. Something about her fragile wrists, thin waist, that mass of black hair and pouting mouth, made her seem like a bratty, insolent kid. It made him want to shake her, shout *No* at her, *No! No!* until she got some sense back in her, until she would just listen to him and do what he said.

But it was more than just her size, it was the power contained in that small body, her power to see into him, through him. He hated it, hated having to lie to her. And it seemed that she brought that out in him no matter how nice he tried to be, how friendly, how warm and sincere. He supposed he kept wanting to convince her that he really was a good guy after all. He wanted her to forgive him for all that he'd put her through, but within fifteen minutes of seeing her, his front broke down and he was revealed as who he really was: the betrayer, the liar.

But it was her fault too—their inability to come clean with each other. It was that damned psychic bullshit: her mind was too quick, too open, and half the time she didn't even realize what it was that she saw. She was so naive. She stuck her nose in places she had no business being. If she'd been a normal woman, they would probably still be together.

When the phone booth was empty, Ballard eased in and shut the door. It was hot in the closed-in square of Plexiglas. He dropped in the coin and dialed Lowell's number.

A woman answered. "Who?" she asked, and he repeated his name.

When Lowell answered, his voice was slightly nasal and high-pitched. "What's up?"

"I have to talk to you," Ballard said. "In person. Not over the phone."

"We're getting together Saturday, right? Can't it wait? Jenny's here."

"It's urgent, Lowell. Important business."

The man paused and sighed loudly. "Hold on, then. I'm going to take this in my office."

Ballard heard him call to Jenny to hang up the phone, then a splash. They must be out by the pool. As he stood by his car watching the mindless traffic wheel by in the darkness, he thought how strange it was that he'd known Lowell all these years and they still weren't really friends. How many times had he flown to Florida for him, how many suitcases of money or dope had he delivered to hotel rooms and empty rented apartments? Their partnership lacked the social graces that most associates would have. He never saw Lowell outside of business. They never went and shot some pool or met for a game of racquetball. As often as they were in contact, he had no idea who the hell Jenny was or how long Lowell had been with her. Lowell was a strange one, secretive, cerebral, with a dark-eyed stare that could scare you though he stood nearly half a foot under Ballard's six feet and was more scrawny than lean in his expensive clothes.

"This better be good," said Lowell, coming back on the line. "I was right in the middle of something."

"It's about that girl," said Ballard. "That girl."

"What girl, Mike? Come on."

"That girl from Miami. You know." Ballard lit a cigarette, breathed out hard.

"What about her?"

"Look, the agreement was that if either of us ever got questioned about that—that situation—if anybody ever came

116

even close to it, we'd let each other know immediately, right? So somebody's nosing around and I'm edgy."

"Man, that was five, six years ago. Who the hell is asking questions now?"

Ballard pulled his necktie off with a hooked finger and stuffed it in his pocket. He could hardly breathe in the stuffy booth.

"Terry. My ex-wife. I thought she might have suspected something at the time. Now she keeps bringing it up, dreaming about stabbings and hearing voices from the grave."

"Voices from the goddamn grave? Mike, you get me out here to tell me Terry is having bad dreams? I mean, she hasn't got any real information, does she? You never told her anything—"

"Listen, Lowell, you know those two murders that have been on TV this last week?"

"The ones found by that psychic?"

"Well, that's her, that's Terry. She changed her name to Theresa Fortunato and now she's a psychic in Venice and working for the cops."

Lowell was silent. Finally he whistled and nearly whispered, "You've got to be kidding. You're saying you think she's on to you psychically?" He drew the last word out slowly in disbelief.

Ballard stared at the taillights of a white Mercedes idling at the intersection. "I'm not sure what she knows. She makes these sudden connections when she sees me. It's like she can read my mind"—and he tried to tell Lowell about the argument in the restaurant.

"This whole thing happened once before," he said. "I never told you about it, but she started getting into all this occult shit, these Tarot cards and having psychic dreams and voices and every other thing, and damn if she didn't have the whole thing practically figured out. That's when I had her committed, remember?"

"I thought she was in for a drug freak-out or an OD or something," muttered Lowell.

"It was, in a way. I kept slipping her a little of this and a little of that, bits of acid or downers in her morning orange juice. I tried different things. I thought if she was a little bit buzzed, it might clear her head or convince her that it was too scary to mess with and finally I just had to have her hospitalized, she got so strung out." He'd spoken all in a nervous rush and felt out of breath. His stomach was sour and he wished he had a drink or a good joint.

"So did it work?"

"Well, it depends what you mean by 'work.' She backed off it, if that's what you mean. She never mentioned it again, until tonight."

"But what does she really know?" Lowell asked. "A first name, voices in her head, a picture on a fortune-telling card? Bits and pieces. She won't put it together. And who'd believe her if she did?"

"She's putting it together pretty well on these other murders, Lowell, and the cops seem to be eating it up. And the thing is these murders—they're stabbings just like, just like—" He found himself flustered and stuttering, took a deep breath, and began again. "I just don't want her making any connections," he said.

"Well, Mike, what are you going to do about it? I mean, she's your old lady."

"And it's not just *my* problem, Lowell, don't give me that."

"But if she's picking up on information from you psychically, then it's up to you to shut her down, right? It's you she's hooked into. It's that simple. She simply can't be given any more facts. The files must be made unavailable to her. *Comprende*?"

Lowell hung up and the dial tone buzzed on. Ballard stood with the receiver in his hand for a moment, then clicked it down into place very slowly as if it would break.

The funeral home was dark. Ballard parked the car in the large garage behind the limousines and shiny hearses and went up the back stairs. In the upstairs apartment he poured himself a glass of Scotch and turned on the TV, staring at Johnny Carson with the sound turned down. The cat purred against his leg and he lifted it with his foot, thrusting it across the room. It cowered, then ran under the couch.

"Damn it, Terry," he said aloud. He knew she couldn't really help it. She was an innocent, a receiver, an amplifier. She didn't try to fuck up his life, she did it automatically just by getting near to him. She didn't read his mind on purpose, but being married to her had been like living with a goddamn spy. He'd had to stop her and the only way he could think of was to convince her she was nuts. He thought a couple of days in a psych ward would bring her around, plus maybe they'd give her something real strong that would stop her mind from working that way. He'd never intended that she stay that long. He'd had her committed for three days on the grounds that she was dangerous to herself and to him. After all, she had attacked him. She could have come back home after that and continued treatment as an outpatient, but she chose to stay on. Three months in that place. Yeah, she'd stopped the crazy talk about voices and that card about the thief, she'd stopped wearing white and having visions, but she'd also been drugged into a personal Twilight Zone. All the light went out of her and whatever love they'd had was rubbed out. She'd never been open to him after that and he'd always been afraid she would know what he was thinking. Even tonight at dinner he'd had to watch his every thought, but he hadn't been able to stop himself from thinking that girl's name. It had rung in his head as if he were just begging her to pry into his mind and know everything.

The connection had been made through his old fraternity brother from UCLA, Travis Reslow, now an attorney in Miami. Old straight Travis with his family money and his good looks. Once when Travis was back visiting in L.A., he'd introduced Ballard to Lowell at a party. After that it was easy, even fun.

Every month or two he'd get a postcard from Travis—

palm trees, flamingos, the Keys. On the postcard there was a phone number disguised as a fictitious address and a date. He'd fly to Miami on the given date, call the number at the stated time, be given instructions as to where to pick up the package. He'd often fly back the same day. Most of the time he wasn't even sure exactly what he was carrying.

Sometimes, he'd stay a few days to visit Travis in Coconut Grove or just relax at the beach. For a few years the flights, as he called them, were carried out with no problems at all. He wasn't even paranoid. He felt that he was somehow protected; it all seemed casual as a visit home. On one of his trips he picked up a small package wrapped in brown paper, locked it in his suitcase, stashed it in the closet of his motel room, and went to have dinner at Travis's.

They were out back by the pool when Travis told him Lowell had just called from L.A. ''Something really strange is going on,'' he said. ''Honey, hand me a smoke, will you?'' His girlfriend tossed him a pack of cigarettes and leaned back in her chaise longue. ''Lowell says something's up. Somebody's got wind of the arrangement and you can't fly out of the Miami airport.''

''Feds?'' Ballard asked.

''I don't think so. He didn't say. Just said to fly out of Tampa or Orlando or something. And instead of bringing the goods to L.A., go to San Diego. And bring it to this address.'' Travis handed him a scrap of paper with the address scribbled on it and a date and time.

''What's this?'' he asked.

Travis shrugged. ''I guess you're supposed to meet him there.''

''So I'm being watched,'' Ballard said. And he looked around him at the pool, the palm trees, the aqua patio furniture.

It was Travis's girlfriend who came up with the plan. She was from San Diego and was planning on going home to see her parents anyway. Why couldn't she pick up the package from the motel and take it to San Diego? They (whoever *they* were) would be busy following Ballard. She could even deliver the package for him. Lowell knew her, he'd known her for years. He trusted her, didn't he?

So it was. That night he'd left Travis's and gone to a bar in the Grove while Travis's girlfriend drove to the motel and got the package. She flew to San Diego the following day while he and Travis flew to New Orleans to catch the last days of Mardi Gras.

Back in Los Angeles the night of the rendezvous date, Ballard got the call from Lowell. He remembered standing in shorts in the kitchen in the apartment upstairs from the funeral home, and Lowell's voice, usually crisp and businesslike, sounded hollow and shaken.

"Where the fuck are *you?*" he asked.

"Here. I'm right here," said Ballard.

"That's what I'm saying. You're supposed to be here, right? Didn't Travis give you the message?"

"Yeah, but—"

"Mike, look, I can't talk on the phone, dig? Just get your ass down here, immediately. Right now. And drive a hearse, okay?"

"A hearse?"

"Drive a goddamn hearse, Ballard. As a cover. I want you to deliver something for me."

"What?"

And Lowell hung up.

On the drive to San Diego he smoked a joint, watching the quarter moon shift over the ocean sky. It was very late when he pulled up in front of the large Spanish-style house. An electric door lifted for the hearse and he glided in. Lowell was waiting for him in the darkness.

"Christ, Lowell, you're acting like this is some B movie. Where's your trenchcoat?"

"Shut up, Mike. Give me a cigarette." The tiny burst of flame lit Lowell's face for an instant and he blew the smoke out in the dark.

"I've got a special job for you, Mike," he said. "It's a job only you with your unique talents can perform."

121

For a moment Ballard was flattered. "What can I do for you?" he asked.

"I want you to bury somebody for me."

Ballard was stunned. He felt the thrill of fear inside him.

Lowell went on, "We've got a body that needs to be disposed of and I want you to give it a proper burial."

Ballard thought for a moment and lit a cigarette himself. "Hey, man, this is a bit much. I mean, carrying goods is one thing. Besides," he continued, shaking his head, "the funeral home and our dealings have got to stay completely separate. The funeral home has got to stay clean, it's a family business—"

"Mike," said Lowell through his teeth, grabbing Ballard's arm. "You have no choice, *comprende*?"

"Give me a break, Lowell."

With that Lowell bent in the dark to what appeared to be a small woodpile covered with a green tarp. He pulled the tarp back and Ballard felt the blood drain out of his head as he saw the ashen face of Travis's girlfriend.

"Yeah, fuck head," said Lowell. "What was she doing delivering, goddamn it?" and he pushed at Ballard, shoving him against the shiny door of the hearse.

"What happened, what happened, my God—" Ballard felt sick and dizzy.

"You tell me, motherfucker."

"You said I was being followed, we thought it would be better if she delivered the package, we didn't think—"

"I don't pay you to think!" Lowell rubbed the bridge of his nose and for the first time since knowing him, Ballard realized that Lowell did not know what to do. That he was even afraid.

Lowell rested back against the cement wall and slid to the floor, sitting hunched over for a minute as if to rest. Ballard listened to a small dog barking up the street.

"Who killed her, Lowell?" asked Ballard.

Lowell put his head on his knees. Ballard had never seen him like this, his bravado and cool efficiency drained away, leaving a small nervous man crouched on the floor of an empty garage.

"I got here a little late," said Lowell, his voice exhausted. "About twenty minutes late, and she was, she was in the kitchen and she was dead. Her throat slit. It was a real mess, let me tell you. There was no package, of course. I called you, I cleaned everthing up, and brought her out here and now it's now. And you're here. Mike, can you do it? Can you get rid of her?"

Ballard felt both numb and clearheaded, as if he were watching himself on an old rerun. "I can't," he said. "I can't get dragged into this. It wouldn't be right."

"What the fuck *would* be right, then, Ballard?" Lowell stood and tugged at his windbreaker. Ballard saw that he was wearing sailing clothes, red and white, his pants dusty at the knees, spotted with dried blood. "Going to prison? Would that be the right thing to do?"

"We could call the police," said Ballard, "or we could just leave her here or something, we could—"

"Would it be right to die, Ballard? How about dying, motherfucker? Would that be the moral thing to do?"

Lowell was pointing a small handgun at him. Ballard just stared at it, feeling that he was watching it all from a great distance, two shrunken figures huddled together on a black-and-white set with the sound turned down low. He looked at the gun and then at Lowell. "Did you kill her, Lowell?"

Lowell stood dumbly in his white deck shoes, still pointing the gun at Ballard. "Somebody found out about this, Mike. I don't know who. And someone was here waiting when she got here and someone killed her and intercepted the package. Now, I own this house, so we can't just leave her here. And we can't call the police, because if you remember this is a fucking drug deal and we can't put in an insurance claim for stolen dope. Now, I don't know who did this, I don't know how they found out about the meeting place, and I don't know why you sent her instead of coming yourself, but I do know we're going to load her into your hearse and I do know that somehow you're going to get rid of her and I do know that you will receive a good deal of money for carrying out this transaction and if you should choose not to do this, you will be in danger. In fact, you will most likely be dead. Not now, not here, but the chances are very good that your life span will be considerably shortened. *Comprende*?''

Ballard reached toward Lowell and pushed the gun down. ''Don't threaten me, Lowell. I could just walk out of here right now and go straight to the police.''

''Who do you think I work for, Mike? The board of education? Disneyland? The organization that employs me is very smooth, Mike, very clean. And it's got to stay that way.'' His voice was becoming shrill.

They stood staring at each other and a sick heat spread through Ballard's chest, black fear in his throat. Ballard shoved past Lowell and muttered, ''Give me a hand,'' and together they lifted the body into the back of the hearse. Ballard covered it with a dark cloth and got in behind the wheel.

''Don't talk to anybody, Mike. Don't call Travis until we've had a chance to figure out what's going down here. I'll come over tomorrow morning. Early. We'll talk then. Mike,'' he said, gripping Ballard's shoulder. ''Thanks, man. Thanks.''

Ballard drove back up the coast. His mind was strangely blank and he was cold. He couldn't get over the unreality of this whole thing, the feeling that he was watching it all on TV, that he was merely going along with a plot that had already been decided on. It was quarter to four when he pulled into the funeral-home garage, loaded the girl onto a metal stretcher, and wheeled her into the embalming room. Upstairs, Terry slept soundly.

As he worked on the body, a dirty dawn light seeped through the thick glass of the basement windows. Ballard's mouth felt dry as he lit another cigarette. He felt that he must call Travis and yet he was afraid. Lowell's arrangements had always been flawless. There had never been any trouble before. Who had leaked information? And just who had been watching him? It certainly was not the *federales*.

Ballard carried the girl's body to the storage area where the new caskets were kept and locked her in a coffin in the back corner, not sure what to do next. He couldn't cremate her. The funeral home didn't have its own crematorium and there was too much paperwork involved in cremations anyway. Could he bury her in a grave that had been opened for another burial, down deeper with the second casket going in on top of hers? But that would entail going to a cemetery and digging holes by the light of the moon. There had to be a simpler way.

Lowell did not come early the next day as he'd promised but he came the following evening dressed in a pinstripe suit, composed and cool. They talked downstairs in the office, Ballard behind the rosewood desk as if he were talking Lowell into a prearranged funeral on the installment plan.

"No, I haven't disposed of the remains yet," he said. "I will when I figure out how."

"It shouldn't be that hard, should it?" asked Lowell.

"Want a shovel, man?" Ballard tilted back in his chair. He felt intuitively that Lowell was not telling him something. "I need to know what happened, Lowell. I need to be able to process all the information. *Comprende*?"

"Back off, Ballard, if I knew what happened and why, she wouldn't be dead, now, would she?" Lowell looked uncomfortable in the brocade chair. He rubbed at the toe of his shoe with a piece of Kleenex. "I told you everything I know, which is nothing. Let's be cool with each other, okay? Just be cool," he repeated.

"But what about Travis?" Ballard asked. "What am I going to tell him?"

"Mike, I'm going to ask you never to mention anything about any of this to a soul. Including Travis. I just don't know the source of the information and I—"

"Travis wouldn't set up his old lady, man."

"I don't know, I don't know. All I can tell you is that I've gotten word that the girl didn't have all the goods."

"Goods? Word from who? What are you saying?"

"It was only a partial delivery. You figure it out. As for the source, let's just say it's inside the company. Now, I only want us to have one more conversation about this situation and all I want to know is that she's safely—that she is safe. Is that clear?" Lowell handed Ballard an envelope with bills in it. "For your trouble," he said solemnly.

Ballard could not sleep that night and he was exhausted, his mind spinning as he sat in the living room, listening to Terry breathe heavily in the next room. He went over and over it in his mind, and he counted the enormous sum of money in the envelope. He dialed Travis's number in Miami and there was no answer.

Had Travis and his girlfriend tried to rip Lowell off by delivering only part of the cocaine? Had Lowell killed the girl and kept some of the shipment for himself? Had Lowell intended to have Ballard killed in the first place? He couldn't sort it out and he still did not know what to do with the body hidden in the expensive coffin in the back of the storage room.

Several days later the solution came to him: he would bury her in someone else's coffin. The man whose coffin she would share had died in a fire. The funeral would be "closed casket." The man was obese and the family had had to purchase an oversized coffin. Late the night before the funeral, Ballard carried the girl to the coffin and placed her alongside the man's remains, draping the satin over her small body. There was more than enough room. The interment went well, and by the following morning the coffin was covered with fresh earth, the new lawn heaped with wreaths of roses.

It was then that Terry started in with her dreams. Up until that time he'd been intrigued by her growing psychic abilities, but the dreams were too much. They pointed straight to him and he could not have it. Morning after

126

morning she repeated her awful nightmares to him and then began telling him she knew he was in trouble. He drank to forget the horror of the girl's body lying for eternity inside a fat man's coffin.

But Terry would not let him forget. He had to silence her mind. It was her mind that got her in trouble, her crazy mind.

He visited her in the clinic after she'd been there a month. One look at her face told him more than he ever wanted to know. Her eyes were blank, the skin around them blue and sunken. Her lovely hair hung stringy and oily past her shoulders. She wore baggy pants and an old sweater. She'd lost weight and looked like a prisoner of war. He knew she would never forgive him and he knew she would never understand.

He could not bring himself to confess to her. Somehow through all of this she had become the enemy, the one to fear, the cause of his guilt and shame, the source of his sense of worthlessness. It was her presence in his life that pointed a finger at him day and night. As the marriage wore down into a silent war, he drank heavily and Lowell's endless supply of fine white snow numbed him to the pain and loss. When Terry finally moved out and filed for divorce, he was relieved and broken.

Now here she was, years later, back at it. Ballard took off his clothes and lay on the bed, smoking a cigarette in the waving blue lights of the silent television. *The Tonight Show* had given way to a movie. He must have dozed off. Half asleep, he walked to the bathroom, swallowed two aspirin, and returned to bed.

Those other murders must have jarred something loose in the recesses of Terry's mind. He was afraid it would all open up and come clearly to her. She would know everything. This time he couldn't convince her or anyone else that she was crazy. She even knew Travis's girlfriend's name, even if it was a coincidence. *Poor Travis. Poor Bonnie.* He didn't know how, but he had to stop Terry from knowing any more.

Chapter 10

It had been three days since Carolyn Svedrup's body had been discovered bound in strips of white cloth and circled by jackknives in the dark shed. It was a Friday in late August and the city outside Oliver Jardine's smudged window was sheeted in gray-white smog that hung still in the inland air. He squeaked his desk chair back and forth in a rocking motion and wished he'd eaten a real breakfast. A piece of white toast just didn't make it. He should go out for breakfast. He should take off early and play a round of golf. He should drive out to Venice and see Theresa Fortunato because a girl had been murdered three days ago and he had no real lead to follow.

Jardine regarded again the two files open on his desk and his own scratchy writing on a yellow sheet of legal paper beside them. Both young women. Both found with plastic cocktail swords in their pockets and black jackknives used in some pattern: through the hands, surrounding the body. Neither woman had been sexually assaulted. One had died of knife wounds, the other of strangulation. Giving the news media the false information that they'd both been shot had only been useful at turning up nothing. True, it gave them a method of screening out the thirty to forty odd calls a day from people claiming to know or be the killer or to have some urgent clue to divulge. All the detective on duty had to do was ask what kind of gun they thought had been used or in what part of the body the woman had been shot. If they answered, it proved they knew nothing.

The killer had left few signs behind except for the deliberate ones. There were no fingerprints. The lab reported that the murderer might have been wearing rubber cleaning gloves when he'd killed Svedrup. Traces of a commercial cleaning fluid had been found in her hair. Out at the ranch he'd been careful to rake over his footprints all the way out to the car. He even appeared to have pulled the car out onto the road, going back to rake over the tire tracks behind him. Two fabric samples had been taken. The torn sheets he'd wrapped Carolyn Svedrup in had recently been washed and may have been used in some sort of an institution, a hospital or boarding school. Specks of lint from a gray sweatshirt were found on the sheets.

What else? Jardine whistled quietly, trying to open the avenues of his thinking, to see beyond the obvious, or at least see the obvious for what it was. He wondered if Theresa Fortunato did the same thing when she was having her visions.

All ten of the jackknives were alike and might have been purchased in bulk. A search of local hardware stores and camping-supply outlets had not turned up any large knife orders except those for camps and scout troops. At any rate a case of knives could have been lifted from any loading dock or warehouse, and plastic swords were used commonly enough in hundreds of bars and restaurants throughout the city. He'd asked Cooper to compile a list of places that used that particular type, the semitransparent ones with handles like little fencing swords. Jardine doodled on the legal pad as he thought, sketching a pirate with a dagger in his teeth, a patch over one eye. The way the knives had been used definitely suggested ceremony. Ritual. At the library last night Jardine had read about the use of knives in witchcraft, black magic. Knives were used to inscribe a ritual circle and, in ancient times, were used in the sacrificial killing of animals, but nowhere in his reading could he find an indication that knives were arranged in some pattern at a death.

Jardine took a red pen out of his desk drawer, licked the tip, and wrote KNIVES * RITUAL * WITCHCRAFT in large block letters across the page. He pictured Bonnie

Humphrey's hands impaled by jackknives and one last thought occurred to him. He added to his list the words CRUCIFIXION * CHRIST * SAINTS * STIGMATA. Under this he wrote, almost as if in automatic writing, SAINT THERESA. Beneath that he drew a cross, sketching lightly with the red pen and lighting the cigarette he held in his dry lips.

There was only one obvious way to go. The victims had four things in common: plastic swords, jackknives, they were dead, and Theresa Fortunato had found them. He'd go out to Venice this morning again and talk to her.

Jardine shut the two files gently, patted the edges of papers and photographs back inside, and slipped on his suit coat. His stomach grumbled. No time to eat. He glanced down at his drawing of the cross and the lily and was pleased with the way his mind had come up with that idea independently of his conscious thought. It must be like that for her, only more so. But impressive as her skills appeared, it was very difficult for Jardine to believe she could know so precisely where the bodies were without, at least, some kind of subliminal knowledge. Maybe he was just too well trained in doubt. There was certainly much more to her visions than to his hunches—it was uncanny how she'd picked up on the name of his hometown—but if he thought too much about her globes of light and her trance states, it all seemed implausible. Still, the trouble was that she did check out. She was as legitimate as a psychic could be, he supposed. She'd worked with doctors and professors at two prestigious universities, assisted in studies of psychic phenomena involving others, and had also been the subject of extensive studies herself—EEG measurements, galvanic skin response in trance states, observation of her sleep and dream patterns. Her references were excellent, she had no criminal record.

Maybe it would help if he could get a look at those medical records. Who would have them—Frank Brandon? It wasn't that he didn't trust her, but whenever he thought about the murders, his mind went back to her again and again. There was some connection, there had to be. The intuition was strong and he couldn't ignore it. Fortunato would be the key to solving these murders, but it would not be because of information she gave to him directly, though that had already been substantial. No, it would come through observing her, he was sure of it. Some revelation would surface through watching her closely, just talking to her, understanding how her psychic powers worked.

Jardine checked his suit coat pockets for his keys and made a mental note to talk personally to the detectives who'd been following her for the last forty-eight hours to see what they had turned up. Then he walked out through the front office and waited for the slow elevator down.

The day was bright out near the ocean. Wind blew stiffly off the water and the air smelled clean and salty after the clogged downtown streets. Jardine took his suit coat off as he walked up the patio court to Number Three. He rang the bell and waited for several minutes, noting that Theresa's shades were drawn. He'd better tell her to stick around. Just as he was about to turn and leave, he heard her voice behind the thin wooden door. "Who is it?"

"Jardine," he said, clearing his throat.

He heard the rattle of bolt lock and chain and the door opened. She must have been sleeping. Her eyes looked puffy. She had a blue robe on, her hair was tangled in wild curls around her face. The robe was tied loosely, open at the chest, and a gold pendant dangled on a chain between her small breasts. She pulled the robe closer with one hand and pushed her hair behind one ear with the other.

"I hope I didn't wake you."

"You did. That's okay. Come on in. I haven't been feeling too well."

Theresa disappeared into her bedroom and called out to Jardine, "Sit down, I'm just getting dressed."

Don't bother, he thought. It was true she didn't look too

131

good. He wondered if she smoked dope or drank a lot. And she ought to see a doctor about that seizure or blackout at the ranch on Tuesday, but still, she was pretty in an odd way. He wouldn't have minded talking to her in her silk robe, legs curled under her on the couch. *Dream on, Jardine. That's what happened when you didn't eat breakfast. She wouldn't look twice at your smashed-in face.* Unconsciously, he sucked in his stomach and stood up straight as Theresa reappeared in white jeans and a loose T-shirt.

She sat on the couch under the framed card collections and he took out his notebook. He wanted to look more closely at those cards.

"You got a touch of that flu that's going around?" he asked.

She sighed, wiped a finger beneath one eye. "No. Maybe it's mental exhaustion. I didn't think that working on these murders would wipe me out like this. How do you do it year after year?"

"You get used to it after a while. What about that blackout you had out at the ranch—has that happened again?"

"It wasn't really a blackout," she protested. "I just felt dizzy."

"It was more than a dizzy spell, Theresa. You passed out cold. You haven't ever had any kind of seizures before? Epilepsy?"

She shook her head.

"Diabetes?"

"No, my health has always been pretty good."

"By the way . . ." Jardine pulled a folded piece of paper from his suit coat pocket and handed it to her. "Standard form authorizing a doctor to release your medical records."

"But what for?" she asked.

"If you don't mind, I'd like to take a look at the results of some of the medical tests you've had done up at

Berkeley—the EEGs, that sort of thing. It might help me understand what exactly it is that you do."

"If you find out, why don't you let me know, okay?" As she smiled for the first time, her face relaxed and suddenly she looked quite young, vulnerable. At the same time there was something about her that Jardine had sensed only in women much older than she, a raw sorrow they'd given up trying to heal. Strange mixture in this woman of innocence and sad wisdom.

Theresa shrugged, taking a ball-point pen from Jardine and signing her name.

"I probably just need a rest," she said. "I know it's all related to seeing those bodies. To tell you the truth, I'm scared."

Jardine stood up. "Why is that?"

"For one thing, I'm getting threatening mail and weird phone calls from people who've seen me on the news. Stuff like 'You're in league with the devil,' and 'Witches get burned.' You didn't give a picture of me to anyone from the TV stations, did you? I want to help you out, but I don't know if I want my involvement to be so public."

"As far as I know there's been no picture used on the news reports, no. But I'll check on it. What about the mail—can I take a look at it?"

"Threw it out. It's all stuff from religious nuts. Guess I'm getting paranoid. I even felt like somebody was following me last night."

Quick, she was, he thought.

"I went out to eat and I kept seeing this blue car. The driver was wearing mirrored glasses. He was dark, Middle Eastern, maybe. But more than that, it was just a feeling. You aren't having me watched or anything, are you?"

He didn't really want to tell her about the detectives. There was no use telling people any more than they needed to know—they acted funny when they knew they were being followed even if it was for their own protection. They stopped their normal activities and started acting like television spies, glancing over their shoulders.

"If I told you no, would you know psychically that I was lying?" he asked.

Theresa rolled her eyes. "Come on. I don't go around reading people every waking hour. I turn it off, okay? You *are* having me followed?"

He admitted, "We've had a detective covering you for a day or so, yes."

She clicked the ball-point pen hard with her thumb. "Well, at least I'm not just going crazy or getting paranoid or something. But why didn't you tell me?"

"We didn't want you to worry. We thought you should have some protection, we wanted to watch who came and went from your place. If for any reason the murderer is connected to you in some way—"

"Connected to me!" She seemed sincerely shocked. "But that's ridiculous! How could it be somebody I know? I never even met the Humphreys before last week!"

"Calm down, calm down. I've got to check out a lot of different possibilities even if they seem incongruous or out of place. Anyway, you said yourself you felt paranoid. We thought it would be good if somebody was keeping an eye on your place, and we didn't want it to be obvious like a squad car outside your front door, okay?"

"Well, I don't want anybody's eye on me. That's an invasion of privacy, especially if I don't know about it. If I'm going to work with you, it has got to be a private thing. Take them off my case or whatever you call it. God—no wonder I've been feeling so strange." Theresa held her arms across her chest as if she were cold.

"Lieutenant, this whole thing has been so awful. My readings have been going badly, I can't sleep, I'm having a lot of bad dreams. And I feel like I can't talk to anybody about this stuff. Nobody except you, really. Who else would understand? My friends think it's totally bizarre, that I never should have gotten involved in the first place. Maybe I'm just letting it get to me. Do you ever have trouble detaching from your cases?"

As she leaned forward to put the pen on the coffee table,

her long hair fell over her shoulders, black curls on the white shirt. *Yes,* he thought. *Yes.* Aloud, he said. "If I'm too detached, I can't get anywhere. I've got to be a little hung up on a case, know what I mean?"

There was a subtle boundary in detective work between objectivity and empathy, and Jardine recognized that in Theresa's case the boundary was in danger of disappearing. He put his hands in his pockets and walked over to the framed collection of cards on the wall by the couch. She was near enough to touch. *Pull back,* he thought. *Remember the J-O-B.* Peering closely at one of the frames, he asked, "What do they call these again?"

"Tarot cards," she said.

"You collect them?"

She stood next to him, pointing. "These ones are Egyptian. These over here are French. They're from the seventeenth century. They were a gift from Frank Brandon."

"And you use them when you do your consultations?" He remembered the business card she'd given him.

"Not these particular ones. I have some working decks I use."

"May I see them?"

Theresa hesitated, flicking her thumbnail and fingernail together. "I put them all away," she said, looking down. "The ones I read with. I just couldn't concentrate with all this other stuff going on. I'm taking a little break."

"Would you mind showing the other decks to me?" he asked.

"Not at all." Walking across the room, she pushed open the glass doors to the tiny sunroom. Jardine followed, watching as she took two keys from a silver dish on the bureau and unlocked the bottom drawer. She squatted, lifting out a carved wooden box. With a second key she unlocked the box, revealing a small bundle wrapped in a white scarf, which she set on the table at the center of the room.

"There's a lot of ceremony involved in this, isn't there?" he asked.

135

"I guess so. You get into a pattern. It's not a rigid thing." She sat down at the table and motioned for Jardine to take a seat. He noted that as she began to handle the cards, her demeanor changed. Her voice deepened and she spoke more formally. She seemed in control, centered, her posture straightened. It was subtle, this transformation from the tired young woman who'd been seated in the living room a few moments before to this woman who seemed both secretive and powerful, the cards held loosely in her hands.

"You feel differently when you read the cards?" he asked.

"When I read, I'm on duty," she said, unwrapping the scarf and setting the deck on the table between them. "Like you, you're on duty now. This is research, correct?"

"I'd like to think it's a little more than just research, Theresa. If we're going to work together on this, I hope we can be friendly. It's pretty hard to get to know someone when you only see them at murder sites."

"I'm sorry, it's just that this is all new to me." Then she smiled at him. "I'd feel friendlier if you would promise not to have me followed anymore. Please?"

He hesitated. "If that's what you want. But if you change your mind and you want somebody around, let me know. Now, I really *would* like to know how you do this, these Tarot cards, your readings. Would you tell me about them?" he asked.

She explained that the Tarot was an ancient set of symbols used to represent life situations, that when the cards were laid out in a pattern to tell a story, the series of images revealed things about the person's life.

"You just lay them out at random?" asked Jardine. "How can that mean anything?"

"It seems like it's random, but it's not. Some say that it's a person's unconscious that shuffles the cards, but I like this explanation—at all times everything is correct in the universe. So if you spread out the cards in the proper form, the order is correct."

Jardine cleared his throat. "A bit cosmic for my taste, but go ahead."

"The modern playing cards," she continued, "were descended from the four minor suits of the Tarot. The ancient wands, long sticks sprouting buds, evolved into the suit of clubs. The pentacles, a circle enclosing a five-pointed star, had become diamonds, the suit of money and the material world. The traditional suit of cups became hearts, the realm of relationships and love. The final suit," Theresa said, "had to do with change, challenge, clash, the necessity to cut away all that was not needed, to see through veils of illusion. And that is the suit of swords," she said.

"Swords?" He stopped her. *Jesus Christ,* he thought. "I'd like to see that suit, all of them, may I?"

"Sure," she said. "Of course, these are the ones that have been giving me so much trouble. Whenever they come up in a reading, all I can see is that girl's hands." Theresa put the deck down and Jardine saw her shudder, swallow hard. She put her hands to her ears as if she were hearing a loud siren. "That's why I put them away, Lieutenant. I feel just terrible whenever I see the swords. I can't get those murders out of my head."

She covered her eyes briefly with her hands, then looked at him, almost pleading. "I get sick when I see them," she whispered. "I know that sounds dumb."

"Why didn't you say something about this before?"

"I thought you'd think"—she stopped, shrugged, shook her head—"that it was silly. I thought you were having a hard enough time taking me seriously as it was." She was shaking her head back and forth now, wagging it rhythmically from one side to another. "Whenever I see them, I hear voices." She patted her ears, rose, and paced about the room, turning back to look at him. "Nuts, huh? Voices?"

"Like what? What voices?"

"I don't want to channel them now," she said, rubbing her forehead. "I don't want them to come."

"Sit down, Theresa. Are you okay?" Don't pass out, he thought.

Theresa pressed her hands over her eyes as she scraped out the words. Wrong. It wasn't her voice at all. Low, raspy, like someone with a bad cold who'd been screaming. *"Please,"* she whispered, *"let me out of here. Get me out. I don't have it, I swear. It is so dark here. Mama? Come get me, please, someone. Can't anyone hear me?"*

She drew her breath in with a gasp and reached for the cards, scrambling them into a pile. "I just can't have these around anymore. They're driving me—I mean—God!" Her voice broke and she half fell into the chair, struggling to keep from crying. "You see why I put them away, Lieutenant?"

Jardine took the messed pile of cards from her hands and sorted out the sword cards, placing them face up on the table, fourteen of them in all, ace through king. He studied them for several minutes. The ace pictured a hand coming out of a cloud holding a golden sword. No, he thought, *knife*. The Three of Swords was a large red heart, three knives piercing its center, and the Two of Swords, a blindfolded woman with her arms crossed over her chest, sword gripped in each hand.

"Please, Lieutenant," she begged. "Let me put them away."

He looked at them again. Blindfold, sword in each hand. Knife in each hand. The Eight of Swords showed a woman blindfolded, bound with white cloth, eight knives in the ground around her. Holy Christ, it was all right there.

"Theresa," he said quietly, "these two sword cards are perfect representations of the murders."

She came slowly around to his side of the table, peering over his shoulder, holding her hands over the cards as if they radiated heat and she were warming her palms after being out ice skating. When he turned up to look at her, her pupils were wide, black, her breathing shallow. Skin ⁓e pale. Head shaking in disbelief.

"You never noticed this before, Theresa?"

"I just kept thinking there was something wrong with me, that I was overreacting because of the murders. That's why I put the cards away and stopped reading. But the cards were speaking to me and I didn't listen. I didn't trust them. I can't believe I didn't see this."

She turned from the table, pacing back and forth in the small room. "Two and eight, two and eight," she muttered. "Well, whoever is doing this isn't using them in any numerical order."

"It's a goddamn blueprint," he said. So he had been right about Theresa—it wasn't always going to be what she told him that would help. Answers would come through her, through her. He didn't know what to make of it. She was so familiar with the cards. How could she not have seen this pattern in them?

He tensed for a moment when she spoke. It was exactly as if she'd heard his silent doubt.

"It's because sometimes I have trouble reading the cards when it has to do with me." Her voice was very quiet. "I get too close, I can't see things. Doesn't that ever happen to you, Lieutenant? You doubt your own intuitions?"

Yes, he thought, still staring down at the cards. He was doubting now. Maybe pulling the detectives off would be the wrong thing to do. And there was another doubt, some unformed question that nagged at him from under his thoughts.

"Theresa, are you very sure you don't want one of my men to keep an eye on your place?"

"Yes, I'm sure. I need to be left alone. I need to think through if I want to have anything more to do with this at all."

"Theresa, you must know how important you are to this case. I need your help in any way you can think of. I want you to tell me anything that comes to mind that seems even vaguely related to these murders, will you?"

She turned away from him, rubbing her arms as if she were trying to keep warm.

"I'll try," she whispered, but he sensed she was not telling the truth, not completely. She was holding something back. Maybe she didn't even know what it was she was avoiding telling him. He wished to Christ she'd not picked up on the tail. Now more than ever he needed to know about her life, to keep a professional distance from her, much as he liked her.

Suddenly she spun to face him, her dark eyes intense, face white against the thick black hair. "Trust me, will you please?" she whispered.

Chapter 11

*I came down here to the ocean to clear out my head but
it's no use, there are too many people even on a weekday
and I start to realize they're all in on it in some way. I sit
on the benches, watch them lifting weights in a fenced-in
yard. It reminds me of that place. Lockup. The grilled
windows I used to cut my fingers on, I used to just sit there
and squeeze the wires until I bled, just to feel something.
Now I feel plenty. It's these people that can't feel. Robots.
Computers on roller skates. None of them even see that
they're surrounded by eternity. But they will. They'll find
out.*

*I walk up toward that pier and buy some sunglasses
from a little Chinese man. They have blue mirrors on the
lenses. I like that. No one can see me, I'm invisible again.
I'm a bee with a million eyes. I have to prepare myself to
be fully and truly invisible. A ghost. Leaving nothing
behind.*

*There is only one person who can see me and if he
wasn't always looking over my shoulder, I'd feel better.
He watches me all day, he sees everything I do. Even more
than God, because he's so much who I am that we have
the same face in the mirror. I wish I could just escape, but
where would I go? I can't even pray without him listening
in. But if it wasn't for him, I wouldn't have been able to
sacrifice her and God would be angry. Slap me down. Me
under the ground, buried alive in the world. That's how I
feel.*

*Part of me feels bad for what I've done, but then I've
always felt bad, not only for things I've done but for just
who I am. I was always the bad one, the one who didn't*

turn out right, the one they never expected. She always hated me. That much I know. Good and evil cancel each other out. If I cancel you out, I win. I'm still alive.

I get confused out here in the world. Too many people. Streets go every which way and the houses all have windows like eyes eyes eyes and the people walk after you. They're spies. They know and they know. Like the nurses white and good, they always seemed to know. Aren't we feeling good today? Aren't we bad? Let's settle down now in our bed. It's only your head, my dear. You're dead. Oh, dying could be so quiet and white.

So anyway I followed him the other day to that place. I stood outside the door and I knew it was a hole where some of the evil was leaking into the world. I could feel it. I'd like to put my hands on the very spot like that little boy who stuck his finger in the dike. But there are so many holes! Every star might be a needle prick where the darkness runs in like black blood ruining the perfect plan of the universe.

And I saw her standing there in all her foul beauty. She even reminded me of Carolyn with her dark halo. Then, outside the door, I saw the poster and I knew that was the only way to stop it. Get the teachers and the preachers of darkness. Not just the students. Thinks she's a purple goddess, rays of light coming off her head. Make ye no idols. Especially not the Self. Obliterate Self. Kill it. Or someone else will have to.

I walk up to the edge of the ocean to breathe and even though it's hot I feel cold and afraid about what I'm being called upon to do. I follow the directions given in ancient times because the struggle is that old. And my destiny is part of it all. If only he doesn't stop me. If only he would quit watching everything I do and listening to everything I think.

After Jardine left, Theresa sat at the sunroom table cleared of cards, hands in her lap. She was almost glad he had taken that deck, the loud one, the one that seemed to

142

amplify the voices in her mind. She'd been so stupid not to have seen the pattern of the images screaming out at her. Elizabeth had told her over and over, "Trust in the voice within. Don't push it away." But how could she trust? The voices and visions always came so clear when they were for somebody else, but when they were for her, they were loud and awful, the visions hallucinogenic, surreal, the ocean in flames. They didn't make sense. Elizabeth was right about her flaw—she couldn't interpret correctly when it came to herself.

Even so, she felt relieved: at least she wasn't crazy. There had been something to those sword cards after all.

Theresa changed into a swimsuit and T-shirt and walked the crooked blocks to the beach, down the boardwalk, past the sidewalk café. The day glittered bright, the sun intense, sand white, air full of salt smell spraying up from waves that rushed and belted at the shore. She spread out a blanket and lay face up in the sun.

This morning Jardine and last night Michael. That had been another act of stupidity, thinking there could ever be any honest human contact with him. The way he'd grabbed her wrist, the old violence. He could never be honest with her. She didn't know why she kept seeing him. She ought to cut it off for good. Closing her eyes briefly, she remembered the vision of Michael falling toward her, mouth open. Calling out to her. What was he saying? What was the use of it? *Stay away from visions about your own life*, Elizabeth had warned. Then: *Trust, trust in your mind's eye*. But Theresa hadn't trusted those sword cards, those murders spelled out before her. She'd been blind to them, just as if her eyes had been covered, just like Bonnie. Just like Carolyn.

Stop, she told herself. "Just stop it," she whispered aloud. Fear rattled through her like a fever. *Clear yourself, cleanse yourself*.

Through her closed eyelids Theresa perceived the sun's radiance, bloodred, brilliant, baking her. She appeared to be sleeping on the blanket, but she was not. This was the technique Elizabeth had given her to shield herself from outside forces. She visualized a circle of light surrounding her still body. Then she brightened it, using the energy from the sun, transmuting light directly into her skin until she imagined her whole body glowing—teeth, hair, lungs. She was a being of light. She was powerful, loving, and protected.

As Theresa floated in her self-made halo, Frisbees sailed over her. A small girl running away from her mother sprayed sand on her. People strolled by laughing, carrying loud radios. Once, a big dog curled up beside her on the blanket and licked her hand. Theresa didn't move. She knew that animals were often drawn to those deep in trance states. The world was there and she was in it, but it seemed far away like some childhood event dimly remembered.

When she came out of her meditation, she curled and uncurled her fingers, opened her eyes, and sat up on the blanket. The sun had slanted down close to the horizon. Her skin was a deep brown-red. She rose and walked toward the waves.

All right, then, that is what it would take—rest, concentration, inner balance. Her powers could overcome outward chaos. Hadn't they before when not even one person had believed in her? Now, in spite of her present confusion, she had helped two families find their missing daughters. Tragic as the deaths had been, those people could move on in their lives toward some eventual peace. Jardine was counting on her continued assistance. It was important to keep in mind that she was doing this for others, for the families, for Jardine, and if they found the murderer, she could even be saving lives. Maybe there was a hidden gift in this dilemma: Focus on the lives of others and you will be all right. Don't be so self-centered. Give more.

Theresa strolled along the wet sand, letting the tide push over her bare feet. She made up her mind that she would stay to help Jardine for one week. Then she'd go to New Mexico to the mountains as Elizabeth had advised, camp on the mesa near Taos, visit friends in Santa Fe. Three or four weeks in the high, clean air would clear her head. She'd get out of this two-bit beehive of a city. Feel the earth again.

Theresa turned and walked back to her blanket, and as she bent to pick up her things, she felt light-headed. Her ears rang, closing out sounds of shouting, seagulls, and waves. Watched, she thought. I am being watched. Someone is looking at me. She was afraid to look up but did anyway, scanning the beach crowd. No blue car. No binoculars. No one staring, at least no one that she could see. And anyway, they were all wearing mirrored sunglasses, silver, blue lenses, pink and green, reflecting the late sun like windshields. Theresa felt chilled by the sunburn. She shivered and began to walk up the boardwalk back to her house.

At home she was nervous, jumpy. When a dog barked out in the courtyard, she dropped a glass on the floor. It shattered into pieces around her. She wished she had curtains on all her windows. As the sky darkened into evening, she glanced out often to the courtyard. No one on the steps. The sidewalk along the street was hidden by a wall of bougainvillea. She wanted company. Camille was working tonight. Maybe she'd go down to The NightTime and have a glass of wine, watch Camille in the blue lights, try to relax.

It was Friday and The NightTime was crowded early. Theresa huddled in a corner chair, rolling and unrolling a cocktail napkin into a tight little tube. Spider, the bartender, had told Theresa that Camille had taken the night off, and she felt strange sitting by herself with no one even to wait for. She'd finish her wine and go home, leave the crowd to the music and the loud talk, though sometimes, when she felt strained like this, it was better to be in a crowd. The sheer number of minds blocked out any individual voice and she was comforted by the din around her. But tonight, instead of comfort, a wave of dark silence passed through her like a tremor and she looked up quickly, searching for someone staring. She watched as the man approached her and stood over her table.

"Dance?" he asked.

"No, thanks." The man looked familiar, but then she always thought that. She and Camille often laughed, saying they'd known everyone in Los Angeles in a past life. They'd all been together before in Atlantis when the ocean rose up and all good souls sank into the sea.

"Then can I buy you a drink?" he asked, smiling openly, hands in his pockets.

She tried to scan him with some inner radar, but she couldn't focus. Was the tremor she'd felt just some guy noticing her? Slender and lean, the stranger had well-developed arm and shoulder muscles and wore loose brown trousers with pleats in the front, a thin belt, pale-green shirt. A jacket was draped over his shoulder. His sandy hair was cut short, it spiked up from his forehead in a cowlick. A large handlebar mustache covered his upper lip and he grinned with his mouth closed, blue eyes brightening at her.

"If you're waiting for someone . . ."

"No," she said. The man was good-looking and seemed pleasant. Theresa hesitated, wondering if she should talk to him. She couldn't go running from every person she met, demanding to see their sunglasses or asking if they collected jackknives.

"Look, I don't mean to bother you," he said, bending down toward her. "I live across from you. Just moved in."

Theresa smiled, relieved. "I thought I recognized you." She motioned for him to sit down, glad there was some reason to act friendly, thinking how paranoid and suspicious she'd become.

"You sure?"

She pulled the chair out from the small round table. "I didn't mean to be standoffish," she said. "It's just—"

"What are you drinking?"

"Chablis. Thanks." He was attractive in a rough way, but he seemed out of place in The NightTime's cheap splendor. His clothes suggested a quiet Beverly Hills bar, a private club, but his shaggy mustache didn't quite fit. He'd have looked more comfortable in faded jeans and a cowboy shirt.

"So, did that guy ever leave you alone?" he asked, flagging the waitress. He spoke loudly over the music.

"Who?" she said. "What guy?"

He folded his arms on the table. "The day I was moving in, you were yelling at some guy. Crying. I was a little worried. I've got a friend who works at a shelter for battered women. After listening to her I get to thinking I've got to take care of everybody. But I saw he left. What was it, lovers' quarrel or something?"

"No, nothing like that. He's a client. I was reading for him. I do—" She stopped, wishing for a moment that she were a lifeguard, an actress, something normal in the world. "I'm a psychic."

"Saw the sign in your window. Don't believe in the future myself." He laughed.

"Well, it's coming anyway."

"Nope. This is it." He waved around him. "The present in 3-D Technicolor reality. The future is just a dream that never comes."

"Very profound."

"Yeah? I think it's a line from a country-western song. So that guy, he wouldn't pay you or something? I thought I saw him here."

"Raymond Mead? Where?" She glanced over her shoulder.

"Back that way. Other room. What did he do, anyway? You were pretty upset."

When he opened his hands, she saw that there were calluses on the ends of his fingers. He must play the guitar. He wore a silver chain around his neck with a small piece of turquoise on it. Boulder, she thought. Aspen.

"Nothing, really. A misunderstanding. I was sick that day."

"Hey, I almost forgot," he smiled. "I'm Arthur. Arthur Holton."

"Theresa Fortunato."

"I know. The sign." He picked up her hand and shook it, then held it for a minute before letting go. Theresa's face felt warm from the wine and his touch. But why was the name Neal in her mind?

"Want to dance?" asked Arthur.

She smiled. "Yes, I'd like that." As they approached the dance floor, the music slowed suddenly and the blue lights glowed to magenta. They both stopped and Arthur Holton pulled her politely close to him, swaying her on the silver floor. His body felt healthy and strong, his hand pressed against the cloth of her dress. She leaned comfortably into him, thinking it had been months since someone had held her like this, even a friend. She was tired. The long day in the sun had made her feel light-headed. She yawned, wanted to rest her head on the soft green of his shirt. Arthur swung her gently, his cheek against her hair.

"It's nice to meet a neighbor," he spoke above the music. "Does this mean I can come over and borrow a cup of sugar?"

"Honey," she laughed. "I mean, I'm above sugar." Theresa closed her eyes, and as Arthur pulled her closer, she could smell that his hair had been freshly washed. How long had it been since she'd even gone out with a man? Almost seven months since she'd stopped seeing Stan, and that had been short and disastrous like all her relationships. Like Michael. Not that it had been serious with Stan. Or Carlos. Or the man before him. She didn't let things go that far. "You're chicken," Camille had once told her. "I'm not always the one that's backing out," Theresa had answered.

She hadn't realized how much she'd missed this pleasure and ease of a man's cheek against her hair, warm breath on her forehead, or how lonely she must be to feel such longing for someone she didn't even know. Better that way. When you really knew them it all blew up in your face. Better this casual electricity of a stranger, his hips close to hers in the music. Theresa pressed her head to Arthur Holton's shoulder in the false intimacy of the dance floor and when the song ended, Arthur held her a moment longer.

"Nice," he whispered. "Thanks," and they made their way back to the table. Finishing their drinks, they watched the dancers jerk to the fast song, arms twisting and jabbing in reflections of the mirrored partitions and walls. The music was too loud for talk and Arthur fingered her hand on the table almost absentmindedly, as if they'd long been lovers, comfortable and without much to say.

Theresa knew she was getting a little drunk, and in the haze of wine-blur she imagined going home with Arthur from the bar, taking him without need for words to her white lace bed, lying down with him in the moonlight, glad to be faceless and unfamiliar in the darkness, his strong thighs rocking against hers. But it was never like that except in magazines, soft-lit photographs of nude women with no blemish, odd hair, or stretch mark. No, it was always more messy than that. Sober, by daylight, he'd seem too young or too old, talk too much or be withdrawn and sulky. Even if he did become a lover, he'd back off soon enough. They all did. Tell her to quit analyzing them, quit watching, invading their minds, because she could never keep her powers turned off for long and it only screwed things up. Fascinated and repelled by her, they all moved on, adoring but keeping their good distance from the witch in white, the Terrible Theresa. Temptress. Trap. Theresa downed the last of her wine. She wanted this boy next door. This cup of honey.

As if reading her thoughts, he kissed the ends of her fingers and smiled. No, she thought. The relationship had already begun and ended in her mind, played out. Over. Why bother to act on it? Besides, a bar pickup was always

149

tacky and she'd have to face him across the courtyard. Her face stretched into a small yawn.

"That bored?" asked Arthur.

"No, just sleepier than I thought," she lied. "What time is it?" As he looked at his watch, she stood beside the table and picked up her purse. Arthur put his hand on her arm.

"It's about eleven. You aren't going yet, are you?"

"I thought I would," she said, hesitating, not sure if she wanted to or not.

"Come on," he said, "we haven't even danced a fast one yet. At least let me give you a ride home."

"Thanks, but I drove. I'm sure we'll see each other across the way."

"I'm sure we will," he said. "Hey, there he is. That guy."

"Where?" Theresa turned, spotting Raymond Mead across the sea of dancers. He was leaning against a Plexiglas partition and the lights made his eyes look sunken, his forehead blue. "Well," she said, "thanks for the drink, Arthur. And the dance."

"My pleasure, neighbor," he said, bowing.

On her way out Theresa made her way over to Raymond Mead. She wanted to apologize for the reading that had gone so crazy, she wanted to explain that any reading she would do now would be all wrong as long as she was involved with this violence.

Theresa raised her hand to wave to Raymond Mead but a swarm of dancers pushed between them and she lost sight of him before realizing she'd been looking at a mirrored wall. She spun to see him behind her, staring with a dull look at the bobbing dancers. "Raymond," she called out, but he regarded her blankly as if he didn't see her. Easing past a tall woman with pink hair, she tapped his shoulder. "Raymond, I want to apologize for the other day. I've been under a lot of stress and what happened that day had nothing to do with you."

He backed away from her, looking her up and down.

"I really am sorry."

Surely, he must recognize her, or was he pretending not to? She wouldn't blame him if he was. It's true she had been terribly rude to him, yelling at him to get out of her house. He turned away from her and stood watching the dancers. She touched his arm.

"Look, the day I read for you I was sick. I lost it, I know, but—you do know who I am, don't you? Theresa Fortunato—"

Suddenly, he bolted past her, snaking his way along the edge of the dance floor, his back to her, and Theresa felt the strength drain out of her legs. She steadied herself against the wall feeling dizzy, claustrophobic. *Got to get air,* she thought, shouldering her way toward the door. Too much wine.

Out on the street the dark glowed blue in nervous flicking neon. And there he was standing next to a white car She touched her fingers lightly to the stucco wall to gain her balance, her vision blurring. Her mind ached with a searing light that shattered into dots and swam, light pricks coalescing into two globes. As she opened her eyes, he nodded at her, crossing and uncrossing his arms in front of his chest, tucking his long hair behind his ear. So he did want to see her after all. Maybe he'd just wanted to talk to her alone.

The light-headed sensation stopped abruptly and she took a step toward him. The blue neon of the bar sign blinked on and off, throwing changing shadows on his face, making it appear as if he had two different faces, one smooth and blue, one hidden in black shadow.

"I'm glad you didn't leave, Raymond."

"No, I ain't leaving, just out here waiting for somebody."

"I thought you were trying to avoid me, running out like that."

"Running out?"

"Just now, in the bar. You acted like I was a complete stranger. I thought that—"

"I haven't even gone in there yet," he said. "I'm

151

waiting out here for somebody to meet me; they're late, as usual. You probably just made a mistake. It's pretty dark in there."

But Theresa was sure that had been him. Maybe he was just embarrassed, trying to cover up.

"I did run out the other day, though," Raymond continued. "I'm sorry I left like that. I guess I was scared. I never went to a psychic before."

"It's me who should be sorry." She moved toward him again, and he backed away off the curb into the street. "Please," she said, "don't be afraid of me. I really am sorry about what happened. Like I said, it was all my fault. I just haven't been well. To tell you the truth, I've been sick. Migraines or something. I've felt pretty awful."

"Yeah, I saw you on TV, about the police and everything. I guess I wouldn't feel too good, either, if I was in the middle of all that."

"Raymond, I'd like to reschedule your reading. I won't charge you or anything, all right? It'll have to be at the end of September, though—I'm going out of town for a couple weeks."

"That'd be cool, I guess," he said. That was better. He had moved out of the blue flashing of the sign and looked like a normal person again. "I really could use it. I'm still having a hard time," he added. "Fuckin' relatives . . ."

Suddenly she snapped her head around, looking over her shoulder, sure there had been someone standing directly behind her, but the sidewalk was empty. "I know you are," she said. "I'll be back in a couple of weeks, then. You'll call me?"

"Yeah, I probably will. Maybe things will have cooled out by then."

"I hope so. For all of us."

Theresa walked quickly to her car and drove the few blocks back to Jasmine Court, thinking of Raymond. She really had to get hold of herself. She couldn't afford to go around losing it in front of clients. It wasn't professional. So much depended on word of mouth in this business. And

152

Raymond seemed sweet, nothing more than a kid. Evelyn and Josh were her regulars. She couldn't go around acting crazed. She'd be an old crone before her time, dried up and broke and alone.

At home she changed into her kimono and sat in the living room drinking another glass of wine. She lit a candle and placed it on the table in front of the couch. The room was dark except for the pale flicker of flame. She felt slightly feverish from the sunburn and her head was starting to ache. Through her own reflection in the window she saw Arthur Holton stride across the patio, carrying a brown bag in his arms. He must have stopped for groceries or a six-pack on his way home. She found herself visualizing the contents of the bag—Fritos, eggs, doughnuts, Velveeta. He opened the door and went in. Lights blinked on in the window and a curtain was drawn.

He had offered to drive her home. She could have been with him now like any ordinary woman who had just danced with an attractive man at a bar. She could be sitting in his living room on the couch, drinking a beer and asking him about his life. She could be with someone instead of always here alone with her decks of cards, her incense, her empty bed, and the swaying flame of a single white candle burning in the darkness.

Her dream began beautifully. Cruising slow-motion over bright hills to Malibu to see Elizabeth. The colors stood out as if she'd never seen them before, hills glowing with spring, sky indigo, and the ocean striated with aqua, emerald, and gray where the tide shifted and sand rolled in the waving water. Theresa felt she was floating over the road, not driving on it. Then she realized that was true. She was flying high, sailing in the blue air outside of her body.

At Topanga Canyon she turned inland, away from the coastal road that led to Elizabeth's. Still, she felt elated, knew she would hear her teacher soon. Had Elizabeth moved? she wondered.

She found herself in a bookstore and was disconcerted.

The man at the cash register asked if she had an appointment with Her Grace. She was afraid she'd gotten lost and ended up at the bookstore on Washington. "Her Grace," said the man, "can not see you now."

Theresa drifted out above the road that wound up the hillside through thick trees. She was lonely, suddenly, and afraid, standing at the edge of the road where there was a thin sandy spot for a car to pull over. She thought of hiding, then realized she was invisible. Still, she squatted behind a large rock across the road.

The car pulled up to the sandy spot and an old woman got out on the passenger's side. Theresa's heart sped but she saw that it was not Elizabeth. Though short, the woman was large, heavy in her flowing dress, and she glowed purple, a halo radiating out from her head. At first Theresa thought it was a headdress or a tiara but then she saw it was real. The woman was no angel but she did glow. It was night now and the dream colors faded, the scene lit oddly like the negative of a photograph. The woman's short gray hair riffled in the wind as she stood gazing out over the cliff at the stars. The city glowed dusty behind the foothills.

The shock wave slammed into the center of Theresa's belly and she was blown backward out of her hiding place, straight up into the air above the woman. She tried to scream, to warn the woman, but she did not know what to warn her of. Her throat was filled with a thickness as if she were underwater, and she could only hover mutely over the purple woman, flapping her arms like helpless wings.

A small man dressed in a doctor's white coat got out of the car, walked quickly up behind the woman, reached around in front of her, slid the razor cleanly across her throat, and pushed her effortlessly forward over the cliff, where she rolled like a spiraling doll through the weeds and did not stop rolling until she was resting in a dry creek bed far below with her hands covering her face.

Chapter 12

Dawn filtered in through the slat blinds and the birds were starting up in the early light. Theresa sat naked in bed, blankets pulled up around her. If she could have cried, she would have felt better. It was too pleasant, the promise of another gorgeous California day. Suddenly, she longed for dull gray rain, a thunderstorm along the Atlantic.

She closed her eyes, leaned back against the pillows, and covered her face with her hands, then pulled them away, afraid to mirror too closely the deathly image of last night's dream. A week and a half ago she would not have believed the confusion she now felt lost in. Was there a third body to be found or was it just another one of her bad dreams? She took a deep breath and tried to decide if she should call Jardine. She'd promised to tell him about any images she received that had anything to do with the murders. If she called, she could let him know about her plans for leaving next Friday. Besides, even if she'd wanted to, she couldn't ignore the picture in her mind of a woman lying dead at the bottom of a ravine. Why were these people calling out to *her*? Feeling that she had no choice but to find the woman, Theresa dialed Jardine's home number, vowing to stay calm as she asked him to meet her in Topanga Canyon.

There was a gas station near the turnoff into the canyon and Theresa parked there, watching the morning spread up over the hills into another hot blue day. She glanced often into her rearview mirror, watching for Jardine's car. Tilting her head back against the cracked vinyl of the car seat, she thought of getting a cup of coffee from the row of machines near the ladies' room. Her head still ached from last night's wine. Maybe if she'd gone home with Arthur she'd never have had the nightmare at all. She'd have waked up with him on this clear Saturday, laughed over coffee, and they'd have walked arm in arm up to the sidewalk café for breakfast, watching the water catch the morning light. But, no, she held steadfast to bad dreams, memories of lousy affairs and a failed marriage. She thought of Michael grabbing her wrist at the restaurant, their years of misunderstandings. She'd tried so hard to sort it out, let go of the past, and arrive at some feeling of clarity and forgiveness with him. Camille had told her she'd never be able to love again until she released the hatred she felt for him. Theresa had cringed when she'd spoken the word "hatred." Who, me? she'd thought, with my white gowns, my mystical visions, the celestial music of the sea only blocks from my doorstep? But she knew there was truth in what Camille said. She knew, too, that she had seen her own death and Michael's, that they were irrevocably bound by some destiny that tangled around them like a net. A noose.

The scene bloomed into her mind with its old melancholy now mixed with fear. Not now, she thought, recalling Elizabeth's admonition not to focus on visions about herself, but the image was persistent, brightly visual, aching just back of her eyes. She held her breath like someone trying to stay on top of water, little gasps to keep from drowning in it, and then she sank down. There was the cliff, sea below, sun-oval blazing into blue. A shimmer of heat waved off the flames as the whole hillside spread with fire. Cyclic red lights zipped across the cliff rocks, around, around again like a child playing a flashlight over the roof of a tent. Near the edge of the precipice a tan-colored car, not moving, door locked. Inside the car Theresa saw herself screaming, pounding on glass, inaudible words, Michael stumbling toward her, open-mouthed, his face rippled by heat.

As the image faded, Theresa gulped for air, coming up

out of the dread and heat of it, back into the cool morning. Holding back tears, she could not shake the feeling that it was her fault, her fault. *But nothing has happened*, she told herself. Why then was that burning so familiar, like a memory at the root of everything upon which all else had been based? She'd never been in a fire, never been badly burned. Elizabeth's words: Past lives leak through to the present. All time is happening now, there is no past, no future.

Theresa tried to bathe herself in the imagined white light that could heal her, quiet her heart.

"Astral inclinant, non necessitant," an ancient teacher of the Tarot had written. *The astral inclines, it does not necessitate.*

Was she bound by her own thoughts, her own terrible visions? Surely if she knew there was a possibility of an event taking place, she could avoid it. She was always telling her clients that the future was merely a possibility. They were in charge of creating their lives with their thoughts. Besides, the vision had to be wrong. It was flawed, incorrect, because it was all about her. Theresa rubbed her eyes. Where was Lieutenant Jardine? She did not want to be alone.

As Theresa heard the car halt behind her, she opened the door and stepped out. Jardine loped toward her, smoothing his thin hair down. He was dressed in jeans, black T-shirt, a blue sweatshirt, unzipped. She realized she'd never seen him dressed in anything other than a suit. He looked younger, less intimidating. He raised his hand to her in greeting, then stopped to write something in his notebook pressed against the hood of his car. They could have been friends meeting for a morning jog along the beach instead of a detective and a psychic going to look for a murder victim seen in a dream.

Theresa slammed her car door shut, put her hands in her back pockets. "So," she said, "we meet again." He nodded without looking up, held up his hand to silence her, and finished writing.

157

"Hi, Theresa." He clicked his pen closed. "Why don't we go in my car?" He took her elbow and guided her to his car, opened the door. As he walked around the front of the car, she felt her breathing quicken, that little adrenaline speed of fear at the thought of finding another body. In the car they sat quietly for a moment before he finally asked, "How are you doing today? You look bad."

"Thanks a lot." She tried to make her voice sound light. "I guess it's true, though. I am bad."

"Because of the dream? Did you have another blackout?"

She pointed to her head. "It's like everything is amplified in here. Any stray thought becomes huge, out of control. I'm too open. But I have to tell you that in spite of how weird I've been feeling, last night I made up my mind to stay with you on this."

"I'm glad," he said. He looked as if he might put his hand on her shoulder, touch her hair. Instead, he pulled out a cigarette, lit it, filling the car with wafts of smoke which he waved away with his hand.

"Until Friday" she went on, "and then I'm going out of town. One week, okay? I'll do what I can for one week but then I'm going to have to rest from this for a while."

"Can't you rest here in town?"

"I've already made plans to leave."

"You should have told me. I don't want you to leave town without telling me. Where are you going?"

"I *am* telling you. What, do I need your permission to leave?" She raised her voice. "I'm going to the mountains, all right? I'm thinking of Colorado, Boulder. I've got friends there." It was a half-lie. Why should he know her every move? Theresa blew out a sigh. "You know, Lieutenant, sometimes I get the feeling you just don't trust me. You have me followed without telling me, and yesterday at the beach I got the feeling you were still having me followed even after I asked you not to. Now, when I'm going on a simple vacation, you question me like I'm skipping town or something."

"I didn't say you were skipping town. Don't get so upset."

"I'm sorry. I think I have a right to get upset."

The Saturday-morning traffic to Malibu was already busy. Jardine sat silent in the seat for several minutes holding on to the steering wheel. Theresa was uncomfortable. *Holding back,* she thought. Image of a dam in her mind, river leaking slowly through, pressure of blocked water building behind it. *He thinks I'm holding something back from him.*

"Lieutenant," she said, "yesterday with that pattern in the sword cards—you didn't think I knew that all along, did you?"

Jardine tapped his fingers on the steering wheel. "I'll admit it seems odd that you didn't make the connection. You know those cards so well."

"You think I'm lying, then?"

"Of course not. Don't be ridiculous."

"Lieutenant, it's just that I need to know that you trust me. I can't work with you on this if I don't feel clear with you. I need to know that there is one person who is on my side in all of this."

He looked directly at her. "Theresa, first of all, please keep in mind that I am a detective. I have to come to a case, like you, with an open mind. I'm looking for connections, possibilities, things that don't quite match, and I've got to check out everything. It's my business to question. You, everybody. It doesn't mean I don't trust you. And I did pull the detective, like I said I would. He's not following you, you have my word.

"The other thing you have to remember is that I have never worked with a psychic before. I've never even met one. I know some other departments have worked with psychics—I have not. I'll be honest with you: I'm not a true believer. Maybe it's just not my nature. But I'm very impressed by what you've come up with and I think you are essential to my finding out who is doing these killings. If you're picking up feelings of doubt from me, you're absolutely correct, but I don't think I'm any more doubtful of your powers than the average person would be. Anyway, you said yourself that it wasn't necessary for me to believe in you. You said I should just let my experience prove you right, remember?''

Theresa picked up the small tape recorder that had been sitting on the seat between them. It distressed her that she needed so much approval—from Jardine, from Elizabeth. Even Camille. She did want them all to believe in her. Theresa, Queen Seer, Source of Information from the Hall of Records, oh, Infallible One. Jardine was right—what difference did it make if he had his doubts? It was only human. The people who came to her for personal consultations were already convinced. They wanted to believe a psychic could divine some inner truth about them. But if she was going to take her work out to the world, beyond the small circle of her clients, she would have to learn to ignore skepticism, move beyond it.

"Well, then, are we clear with each other?" Jardine broke the silence and extended his hand to her.

"We're trying." She tried to smile, then took his hand, and after a moment they shook.

"Would you mind recounting your dream again on tape?" Jardine asked. "I'd like to know everything you remember, even insignificant details."

"Sure," she agreed, and Jardine clicked on the machine, turned the volume up, while Theresa repeated the dream, trying to visualize its disjointed elements, the location of the turnoff, the description of the woman, the small doctor-man whose face she could never see.

"There was one thing that was very different about this dream," she added when she was through. "All the other times, with Carolyn and with Bonnie, I was inside them. I became them as if it was all happening to me. But this time I was just watching. I was invisible. I was a witness."

Jardine clicked the tape off, adjusted his glasses, turned the key in the ignition. "Okay," he said. "Ready?" They drove slowly up the canyon road under dry trees. Dust swirled up behind them. As they swung around a slow turn past a tiny bookstore perched at the roadside, Theresa said, "I'd forgotten that was there. The bookstore. In my dream I thought that I was back at the shop in Venice. Keep going," she added. "It's up from here."

There was little morning traffic on the canyon road and the sky above the hills was pale yellow. Theresa tried to keep her mind empty, open to signals that they were nearing the spot. As they rounded a curve she saw it, right side of the road, not even enough room to turn around, just a wide spot near the edge of a steep hill. "Here it is."

Jardine pulled over and Theresa slid out, listening to the quiet hush of the trees. Tinderbox, she thought. The late summer hills looked ready to crackle into flames. She stood for a long while, waiting for that instinct that had guided her before, the sensation of being propelled forcibly forward, hurtled to the site of the bodies. She stared down the rocky hillside where she knew the woman had rolled, but she didn't move.

"Well?" said Jardine. "Is this it?"

"It is, but something's wrong. I don't know what. I can't feel where she is the way I could with the others." Theresa approached the rocky cliff that dropped down to the dry stream bed a hundred feet below.

"Let's have a look," he said.

They slid sideways down the gravel incline, grabbing hold of spindly scrub trees as they went. In the dry sunlit creek bed Theresa listened to the quiet birds, the stillness of the canyon. Hills jutted up high above her.

"I'm sorry," she whispered. "She's not here."

"Maybe we should drive farther up the road."

"Let me be quiet here for a little while. I just need to feel the space here." She sat down in the dirt in the center of the creek bed while Jardine turned and walked up over the small ruts and stones.

Theresa closed her eyes and put her hands out in front of her like a divining rod. When she'd found Bonnie and Carolyn, she'd reacted to a tremendous pull toward the bodies. This time she felt nothing. She was certain she'd come to the right place but all she picked up was a shadow. That was it—not the body, but the shadow of a body. The image of a dead woman, not an actual woman. She didn't understand and she regretted having brought Jardine here.

It must have been ten minutes before she heard stones rolling above her and saw Jardine scramble over a large rock, extending his hand to help her to her feet. "Nothing up that way. Should have brought the dogs."

"It's not working, Lieutenant. Something's not right." Theresa tried to explain about the shadow image, her sense of expectancy.

"So you think that the body could have been moved?" he asked.

She shook her head, ran her hands through her hair. "I guess I blew it. I was off. I didn't have it right." Jardine was tossing gravel from palm to palm. "I'm really sorry."

"Maybe Monday you could come downtown and look through some photographs. A face might stand out for you—this person from your dream."

"In the dreams I can never see his face," she said quietly, "but I could try."

Jardine looked around one last time at the rocky creek bed, then started back up the hillside while Theresa remained in the silent dappled shadows listening hard for a voice she felt sure was about to call her.

Through the hot midday Theresa slept dreamlessly and hard as if her head were being pressed down against the pillow. In late afternoon she woke sweating. The air was thick. She could go to the beach, sit in the salt wind off the surf, but she needed to focus her mind on something, not just wander aimlessly by the sea, so she dressed and went out shopping. In spite of her long sleep she did not feel rested.

As she drove, she found herself glancing around often, and she could not help sensing that, in spite of what

162

Jardine said, she was being watched by someone. She tried not to think about the odd dream, the search for an absent murder victim, the image inside her of an open mouth about to scream or cry out, but waiting—waiting for something. She tried not to think about Michael.

As she went from hardware store to drugstore, she hoped that making preparations for the trip would calm her. Concentrate on the mountains, she told herself, crossing items off her list: farmer matches, nylon rope, dried fruit, boot polish. At home tonight she planned to go through her camping equipment and see what else she needed. When she got to the mountains, she'd take a long hike by a rushing stream, stare into perfectly blue sky, lucid, empty, and open. Once she got to Taos, all this would heal, but even visualizing that wide sky didn't help. She kept feeling an almost physical presence press against her back, and once, in the drugstore, she'd stalked back down an aisle to make sure no one was lurking just around a corner. Driving to her house, she'd deliberately stopped over and parked, watching the traffic behind her to see if anyone would pull over.

After staring into the rearview mirror intensely for several minutes, Theresa rested her forehead on the steering wheel and a shudder went through her neck and shoulders. *"You idiot,"* she breathed. *If somebody is following you, it's not going to be a cop. They are the least of your worries. It could be him you're picking up on*. Watching, blank-faced. Waiting. He'd seen the news, too. Heard her name, where she lived. Certainly he would find her. Certainly he would not want her to find him. She'd been a fool to have turned down Jardine's offer of protection.

Returning to Number Three Jasmine Court, her arms full of paper sacks, Theresa was struck by the terrible impermanence of her life. Any life. It all used to seem so solid, so daily and expected. She had the feeling that her life as she'd known it these past few years was nothing more than a fragile illusion about to be blasted away like a mirror shattered into a million pieces. She could not go on

163

here anymore. It was too loud, too violent, too fast. Maybe it was just L.A. The earth shook here, it wasn't solid. The sea rose up and fell back in time with the moon, and it pulled everyone with it. She couldn't hear her own thoughts in the swarming din of the city.

As soon as she'd set down the paper bags on the kitchen table, she put in a call to Jardine.

"Hold, please," the nasal voice snapped, and she waited awhile before hanging up and dialing again.

"I was holding for Lieutenant Jardine and I was cut off," she lied.

"The lines are all still busy, can you hold please?" repeated the operator.

"Oh, all right." Theresa traced a pen in a tight black circle on a piece of paper until the point had torn through the sheet, and again she hung up. She tried Jardine's home number. No answer. It was six-thirty; she'd just have to try again later. Maybe he's stepped out to get something to eat.

As afternoon darkened into evening Theresa changed into her nightgown and began pulling camping equipment out of the back of several closets, stockpiling the gear in a corner of the living room. There: sleeping bag, cookstove. Tarp, poncho, mess kit, tent. She found old maps from previous trips to Big Sur with Camille and Sarene, to Colorado with Stan. Even a map of Oregon left from an early trip with Michael.

It was nearly eight before she felt hungry, and she didn't want to stop to eat. She washed a nectarine in the sink, bit into it, and then, glancing at the phone, she dialed downtown again. "Hold, please," the same robot voice intoned. Slamming the phone down, Theresa muttered, "What would you do if you really needed help?" It wasn't until then that she remembered to flip off her answering machine. She pushed the rewind button, licked the juice off her fingers, and tossed the nectarine pit into the wastebasket. The recorded voices played back, sounding scratchy and warbly. A new tape was needed. Evelyn had called twice about the fall seminar in advanced Tarot. Josh wanted to reschedule his reading. Camille had called: "Baby, I'm craving guacamole enchiladas. Can you sit for Sarene tomorrow night?" There were two inquiries about readings and then a low voice she didn't recognize. The speaker had a sore throat. It was a woman's alto voice or a man's guttural whisper, she couldn't be sure. As she listened, her shoulders tightened and she sat slowly on the kitchen chair.

"Stay away from him," the voice said. "Leave him alone or you'll be next. Get out of his mind, I'm telling you. Now he wants to see you. Because he thinks you have things to say. He doesn't know it's all lies. He thinks you're wise. What do you know about God or the leak in the world or those stabbed girls? They're dead and you're in the way. You're blocking the—" The loud dial tone snapped on, cutting the message off.

Theresa put her hand to her chest and her heart clapped blood loudly to her head. *He*. Who was *he*? Who was he talking about?

Her ears rang with the voice and she pressed her hands over them. Deep breath. Steady now. She rewound the tape and played it again, the throaty voice, the threatening, frightened tone. *You'll be next*.

Oh, God, she thought, and, trembling, dialed Jardine's home number. There was no answer at his apartment, and for the fourth time she dialed the department office. "Operator," she said loudly, "it is very urgent that I speak with Lieutenant Jardine. What do I have to do to get through to him, dial 911?"

"One moment, please."

But when the call was put through, Theresa got only a tired clerk who grumbled that neither the lieutenant nor Cooper could be reached at the moment—they'd return the call on Monday during regular business hours.

"But this is very important," she insisted. "It's about the Humphrey and Svedrup killings."

"Yes, ma'am," said the somnolent voice. "I'll leave

the message, and if they call in, I'll have them contact you.''

"Right away," she insisted.

"Yes, ma'am, right away."

Theresa pressed the phone down and clenched her teeth, trying to keep the fear and anger down in her belly. Trying to keep it from rising darkly into her mind.

She reached over the sink and yanked the kitchen curtains closed. Fishbowl. She lived in a damned fishbowl. She felt suddenly that there were no walls on her house. She'd never been afraid here before. People were following her, someone behind her driving, someone on her phone, someone in the darkness behind the garden.

Give me my life back. Yes, protection. It would be much better that way. And she would ask Jardine to make them stop it—the news coverage, the use of her name on TV and in the papers. Her involvement from now on must be private, confidential.

Quickly, Theresa jerked at the curtains in the other windows and then hurried to the bedroom, snatching closed curtains and blinds. Bathroom. Living room. Shut them out. She hesitated at the sunroom door before going in. That room had no curtains at all. Anyone could see in. She felt vulnerable, naked to the night that surrounded her. Tomorrow she'd hang a curtain over the door. For now, she draped a sheet across the glass square. Yes, that would do it.

Theresa stood in the sunroom she'd once loved, the wooden table where she'd laid out the cards, the tiny crystals hung in the window that caught the morning sun and sprayed prismatic rainbows on the white walls. Over the tiled roof outside, the moon was rising, a pale crescent above the dark leaves.

Wrapping her shawl around her shoulders, she stepped out onto the sidewalk, looking around carefully to make sure the courtyard was empty. She breathed in the sweet salt air and was filled with a longing to cry, to sleep, to get

166

away and see the moon from somewhere else, see her life from another angle.

"Pretty, huh?"

Startled, Theresa turned to face the shadowed source of the voice. "God, you scared me," she said. "I didn't see you there."

Arthur Holton sat on a plastic lawn chair in front of his cottage, his head tilted back against the stucco wall.

"When it's full, does it make you crazy?" he asked.

Crazy. That word still hurt. Crazy, crazy lady. Woman in the moon. "All the time," she said. "What about you?"

"Yeah," he said. "I get all hairy and I howl. You might hear me tonight if you leave your windows open. Want to sit down?" He motioned to the empty chair beside him.

The cement patio stones were still warm from the hot day. The metal chair creaked as she sat on it. Theresa gathered her white nightgown around her ankles. Suddenly, she felt shy and glad to see him. Her long hair fell in waves over her shoulders. "I don't always sit around out here in my nightgown," she apologized.

Looking down at the eyelet lace of her hem, he laughed. "Thought it was a prom dress." He gulped beer from a can, then held it up to her, eyebrows raised.

"No, thanks," she said. The moon looked as if it were stuck in the branches of a dry eucalyptus. Arthur leaned toward her. He smelled of soap and lime. His hair was wet. He looked handsome and relaxed in old faded jeans and white shirt, sleeves rolled up over sunburned arms.

"Tell me," he said. "Did psychics in your high school go to the prom?"

"I wasn't a psychic in high school."

"No? You majored in it in college?"

She laughed. "Sure. I did graduate work in chants and cauldrons. Now, if you'll excuse me, my broom is waiting."

"No," he said, putting his hand on her arm. "Don't go."

167

"I wasn't, I was just kidding."

Through the open window of the next cottage Theresa saw a gray-haired woman ironing, watching a color TV, the screen blurred in fluorescent greens and corals.

"What's it like, then?" asked Arthur.

"What? Being a psychic? It's pretty weird, actually." She tried to smile.

"How so?"

"Oh, I don't know. It used to be better. It's like being that TV over there. I've got a lot of channels. Sometimes they all come in at the same time and there's a lot of static."

"Could you read my mind?"

"I'm not keeping business hours tonight."

"But could you? What am I thinking of right now?" He squinted his eyes shut.

"Another beer."

"Nope," he said, still squinting.

Please, she thought. Don't ask me to do this. Let me be ordinary tonight. But her mind flicked like the buzzing television snow. Another picture superimposed on Arthur's face like a mask. She saw him typing, taking notes. "You're thinking of writing this down," she said.

He opened his eyes, nodding. "Very good, very good. I did write about you in my journal," he offered.

"Please don't do that."

"Write about you?"

"Not that. Don't make me read for you," she pleaded.

"A Turkish woman read my coffee grounds once. She said I'd be a sailor and have many children."

"And?"

"I'm a rotten swimmer and so far no babies. That I know of. So much for the future. I don't think I'd really want to know my destiny anyway. It would scare me."

"You know, that's refreshing."

"You think so?"

"Everybody always wants it all laid out for them so they don't have to figure anything out. They want me to

168

solve all their dilemmas for them and tell them it's going to be all right.''

"And do you?"

"No because it's not going to be all right. I mean, it is really a maze, isn't it? A labyrinth? And we're always having to make up our minds—should I take this little corridor, or that one? I guess I just have the ability to rise up over the maze and see some of the possible corridors. The future as it happens is only one chosen path, but we all know the end of the story, right? We die. It's the present that's the real mystery, isn't it?"

"You tell me, you're the mystic."

She groaned. "Don't say that. It's all just a bad habit. Have you got another beer?"

"Sure." He grinned. "Hey, you hungry?"

She was. She realized she hadn't eaten a meal all day.

"I've got some shrimp salad. Made it myself." He hopped up from his chair and crunched the beer can in his hand. "Why don't you come in? I'll fix you a plate. I've even got some good French bread and some Brie. Come see how I fixed my place up."

So much for the Velveeta, she thought, following him into his cottage. "A fat woman lived here with her son," she said as she entered the front room. "She had two cats. Her kid played the Police all day long." .

"You can tell that from just coming in here?" he called from the kitchen.

"No, I *knew* her, Arthur. I'm not *that* good!"

She could hear Arthur open the refrigerator, clank of spoon on glass. The living room was quite bare. An old rust-colored couch was pushed against the wall, an over-stuffed chair beside it. The brass pharmacy lamp arched over the chair appeared to be the only new thing in the place. There were no paintings or posters on the walls, only a small family photograph on a tippy dresser that also held a stereo speaker. On the bare wood floor in front of the couch was a Navajo blanket that looked authentic.

The place had a strange feel to it. In spite of herself

Theresa felt her mind open like the lens of a camera. A shelf on the wall was stacked with books and notebooks. Peeking around the corner into the bedroom, she saw a typewriter on an old card table. There was something unreal, dreamlike, about this place. She judged Arthur to be thirty-one, thirty-two, not much older than she. Did he own so little? His vibrations were not in this room. He did not own these things. They were recently purchased, but not his. Garage sale, maybe. Secondhand. Owned by other people. But he'd only just moved in. Maybe he had just bought all this stuff. She walked over and stood on the Navajo rug. Better. This was his. He owned this rug. She closed her eyes and saw a red pickup truck and a bar with pink neon that said JACK'S.

"*Voilà*," said Arthur, appearing from the kitchen with a plate of food. "Are you okay?"

"I'm fine," she said quietly, opening her eyes. "A little tired."

"Here you go." He held the plate out to her, and a glass of cold beer. Theresa sat cross-legged on the rug while Arthur put a jazz record on the stereo, a husky saxophone breathing mournfully into the night. Then he fell back into the overstuffed chair and smiled at her.

She was sorry that she felt this distance from him just now. She wanted to like this man, this Arthur Holton with his long fingers, his soft sandy hair and sunburned forehead. She wanted to sit in this man's living room, eating his leftovers, wearing her white nightgown and listening to a saxophone. Not see past every moment into another. Just be in this one place. Not feel distrust, just relax. Taste the cool beer, watch the moon rise over the red-tiled roofs.

Arthur fingered his scruffy mustache. He looked boyish when he smiled. Tan crow's-feet crinkled around his eyes. He crossed his legs. "How is it?" he asked. "Is it good?"

"Yes," she said, nodding, looking deeply into his face. She tasted the salad and washed it down with a sip of beer. Arthur leaned back in the chair and closed his eyes, taking in the bluesy music. *Who was he, anyway?* "Yes," whispered Theresa. "It's really very good."

Chapter 13

It was Sunday morning. She'd be home. He'd find her there and talk to her, maybe take her out for breakfast. Calmly, he would ask her questions. He wouldn't threaten her or call her crazy. He had to convince her this was wrong. Finding these missing women was wrong.

Ballard knew the way her mind worked. Yes, she saw things, she made connections, but she got things all mixed up. Saw too much for her own good. Like that Tarot card the thief that she always said stood for him. He wasn't a thief. He'd never stolen the package and he hadn't killed Bonnie. If anyone was a thief it was probably Lowell himself. But all that was past. Literally buried. Why unearth it again?

Ballard sat at the linoleum table in the small kitchen in his apartment above the funeral home. There were no funerals today, just two visitations this afternoon, and everything was ready, the flowers arranged in huge bouquets around the open caskets, the deceased resting peacefully under satin covers. He had some paperwork to do but that could wait. He needed time to think about how he was going to stop Terry from delving any further into Bonnie's murder. Six years had gone by and nothing had happened. It was behind him. He wanted it to stay that way.

Last night Lowell had called, saying that he'd read about Terry in the paper again, demanding to know what else she'd found out about the murder.

"I'm very concerned that your wife is going to find out something regarding the case we discussed," he'd said in his phony office jargon. "Have you spoken with her since you called me?"

"My ex-wife," said Ballard. "No, I haven't." Come off it, he thought, rolling his eyes at Lowell's executive code-talk. "I think she'll stay out of it if I don't see her."

"I do not want information on this case coming to light under any circumstances, Mike. I think you ought to arrange a meeting with her to ascertain the extent of her knowledge on the subject. Don't you agree? Then we would know how to proceed."

"Maybe it's better to lie low. I might have just overreacted, blown it all out of proportion. There's probably no chance that—"

"Find out how much the woman knows," Lowell interrupted. "Specifics, Mike. I want to know if she's getting any specifics so that, if necessary, a plan of action can be formulated."

"What kind of plan of action?"

"Termination of her position."

"Will you speak English?" Ballard had said. "What exactly are you trying to say?"

"I'm saying—exactly—that it would be dangerous for you if she comes anywhere near the case in question and that it is your responsibility to see that it doesn't happen."

"Dangerous for me?"

"For both of you. *Comprende?*"

"Look, I don't want her in the file, either, Lowell, but until she figures out something, I—"

"I'm not interested in taking that risk, Mike."

"But how am I supposed to find out what she knows without arousing some curiosity on her part?"

"I know you'll think of a way, Mike. You're creative. I'm counting on you." Lowell had hung up without saying goodbye.

Even after all the years they'd worked together, Lowell never asked or requested, he always demanded. Ballard wondered if Lowell didn't keep using him as a way of securing his loyalty. He was so deeply involved in the "business" that he could never extricate himself. After Bonnie had been killed, Ballard had stopped transporting

172

plain brown packages and had handled finances, laundering money through the funeral-home books and investments, and sometimes he kept "shipments" in the storage room where the caskets were stacked. Lowell set it up so that the more guilty Ballard was, the more money he made.

He'd spoken with Travis a few times after Bonnie disappeared and Travis told him he'd hired a private detective to find her, but nothing was ever turned up. Ballard let Travis believe his girlfriend had split for Brazil or Argentina with a fat purse and a Swiss bank account. Though he'd agonized over his secret knowledge, he'd never trusted his old friend enough to tell him what had really happened. Besides, he wasn't sure what really *had* happened. It was only after several years that he'd come to believe Travis was innocent of trying to set him up. Travis's concern for Bonnie had been too real, too deep. That only left Bonnie. And Lowell.

Ballard's theory was that Lowell had gotten wind of a plot to ambush the deal and had tried to ward it off by having Ballard come to the house in San Diego. When Bonnie showed up instead of Ballard, Lowell thought she was part of some planned conspiracy. And she might have been, who was to know? Maybe it was something even Travis had been ignorant of.

In hindsight Ballard knew he should have refused Lowell's request—demand—to get rid of the body. He should have simply left. But he'd feared Lowell's threat of using his connections to have him silenced, and though he didn't want to admit it, he was still afraid.

Now and then he'd asked himself why he continued working for Lowell. There was something about that fear that he liked. He also liked the nontaxable income and the contact with life other than the business, that endless parade of corpses through brocade rooms. Lowell's was a mysterious world, part Hollywood, part danger, part cash. It troubled him when he realized that if it weren't for his dealings with Lowell, his marriage to Terry might have

173

worked out. Might have. But probably not. Maybe they'd always been doomed.

Some nights lying awake above the funeral home, zipped on coke, smoking endless cigarettes in the dim light, he'd feel the old ache for her. One woman he'd dated accused him of being obsessed with her. "I don't want to hear another word about your ex-wife. Terry this and Terry that." He hadn't even realized he talked that much about her. They were better off divorced, he knew that much, though it had always made him mad that *she'd* left *him*. He was the one who'd wanted out, but he thought he had to take care of her. Poor unstable Terry. Poor sicko Ter.

Sometimes when he hadn't seen her for a while, he'd imagine they could get back together. She had looked damn good at that party where he'd run into her last spring and she'd been flirtatious out by the pool in a white strapless sundress, her long hair curled darkly around her shoulders. They'd started laughing about funerals and he'd realized he could hardly talk to anyone else about that.

He'd asked her to dance and it was strange how familiar her body felt after all that time, thin waist, coarse hair against his face. He'd leaned down to kiss her—yeah, he was a little drunk, so what?—and they'd kissed pretty hot for a while, taste of some forbidden dessert he'd sworn off, until she'd pulled back with her "No, no." What harm would there have been in a friendly fuck? After that she'd gotten all huffy and cool the way she did when she thought she was so superior and cosmic and psychic and he was just a lowly mortician. It was useless with her and it always had been. Well, maybe not always. They'd had good times. Maybe it was just her body he still loved. Mostly, though, Terry was less an ache to him than a distant memory, an old love perfect because it wasn't real anymore. And now here she was in his life again, stirring up old dust. Damn her.

Ballard put on a T-shirt and tucked it into his jeans. He made a cup of instant coffee in the plastic mug he kept for driving. Outside, the morning air was cool and fresh. He set the cup down carefully between the car seats, hoping it wouldn't spill, and drove to Venice with the windows down.

When Ballard pulled up in front of Theresa's courtyard, it was still early, only a little after nine. He sat in the car and finished the greasy doughnut he'd bought along the way, slurping the last of the lukewarm coffee. She'd be up. She always got up early. She'd be sitting there wearing a Japanese kimono, drinking peppermint tea and burning jasmine incense. He knew her.

He knocked at the front door but there was no answer. There was a sign in her window, a moon and a cross in a circle. Was she going back to the Church or something? She'd hated all that stuff when they were married. After waiting for several minutes and knocking again, he decided to look out back in her garden.

Around the side of the cottage he spotted her kneeling in the dirt, picking weeds and putting them in a pile. She didn't hear him as he came up behind her.

"Terry?" he said quietly. She fell forward, scrambling to her feet, stumbling over a line of lettuce, and stepping in a patch of marigolds.

"What are *you* doing here?" she spat.

"Cool down, Ter. I came to take you out for breakfast."

She backed away from him, holding the spade out in front of her. "Right there, Michael, stay right there. Don't come any closer."

"Jesus, don't get paranoid, Terry."

"You scared the hell out of me," she said sharply. "Don't go sneaking up on people like that. What are you doing here first thing in the goddamn morning, anyway?"

"I wanted to talk to you about something. I thought we could go out and get some coffee."

She stepped over the flowers back onto the sidewalk, brushing the dirt from her knees. "You thought you'd take me out for breakfast. Out of the blue you show up at dawn and you want to buy me a cup of coffee. That's swell, Michael. Just swell."

175

Ballard took a deep breath and sighed loudly, inscribing an arc in the dirt with the heel of his sneaker. It was all going wrong. It always did. He'd never find anything out from her at this rate.

Theresa walked up the steps to the open back door. She was wearing running shorts, her thighs were muscular and lean. Her long hair was tangled, tied up into a ponytail. Ringlets fell out, curled over her neck and shoulders.

"Ter, look. I'm sorry I startled you. I apologize, okay? There are just a few things I want to discuss with you."

She stood with her back to him, then pushed open the screen door and went into the kitchen. He followed her.

"I'm not really in the mood for one of our little talks, Michael. If you have something on your mind, just get it out."

Ballard sat down at her table, fiddling with the chain of the tea ball that hung over the edge of the pot. This was not what he wanted. It was too stiff, too obvious. He should have phoned her first, planned this out better. What was he supposed to say to her, "By the way, Ter, how much do you know about that dead girl I buried, huh? How 'bout it?"

Then he could feel it, that itching sensation, uncomfortable in his skin. She was reaching into his mind and he did not want her there.

"What is it, Michael? It's about my work, isn't it?" Theresa turned the flame on under a pan of water.

"Well, yeah," he admitted. "I did want to talk to you about that. We seemed to get off the track the other night."

"What track, Michael?"

"I was just curious. I just wondered maybe"—he stuttered, slowed himself, and went on—"that woman you found, her name was Bonnie, right? I wanted to ask you about her."

"At eight in the morning?"

"Nine. It's after nine."

"What's up, Michael? What is the point?"

He had to lie. Would she know? "Well, the reason I acted so surprised the other night—it didn't hit me when I heard it on the news, but I thought maybe I knew that woman you found. She wasn't from around here, was she?"

"No, she was not," Theresa muttered.

"Was she from San Diego?"

"Michael, she was from Berkeley." Theresa sounded exasperated, as if she were addressing a naughty child. He looked down and was silent.

"Is that all?" she asked loudly.

"All right. Look, I used to date this girl named Bonnie, okay? She was from San Diego. I lost touch with her and I heard from some friends that she'd completely disappeared. I wondered if it was the same person."

"That's ridiculous, Michael."

"It was you who suggested some connection between us, Terry. You said you were having all these terrible dreams about me and this girl you found, and frankly, I was seeing this Bonnie around the time you had all that dream stuff when we were married, so I thought, maybe it was her. I just wondered what you thought the connection was."

Ballard cringed at how easy it was to lie to her. Their whole relationship was founded on it.

Theresa reached for the teapot on the table, gave a little whimper, and looked up at Ballard in alarm, then down at her hands. Turning quickly to the sink, she thrust her hands under cold running water.

"Burn yourself?" he asked.

Holding a dish towel, she turned back to him, her face drained, yellow-gray. She looked sick. "What do you really want, Michael?" she whispered.

"Just what I said."

"You're lying."

"I'm not. Why should I lie?"

"You are lying. You're lying to me and you're lying to

177

yourself. You think I can't feel it? How dumb do you think I am?"

"I swear I'm telling the truth, Terry!"

"Don't shout at me. Look. Look at this." She held out her hands to him. They were bright red. She must have burned them. "You don't believe in such things," she continued. "Signs, omens. You're lying, Michael. You've always lied to me."

"What omen? You burn your hands and it's *my* fault?"

She lifted the pan of boiling water off the stove with a potholder and poured it into a teacup. "Michael, I can't see you. No contact at all. I want you to leave me alone, do you understand? Because if you don't, if you ever come here again, I'm calling the police."

"No!" he yelled, rising toward her, grabbing her wrist. She knocked the teacup over and the water spilled over her, burning her already red hand.

"Get out, Michael!" She pulled away from him.

What was the use of trying to talk to her? God, he should never have called Lowell in the first place. *Dangerous for both of you.* "Terry!" he shouted. "Listen to me!"

He reached toward her, taking hold of her thin shoulder. She yanked away from him and he clutched a handful of thick black hair. As she swiped at him with a claw hand, he threw her against the kitchen wall, where she cowered, covering her face, crying.

He didn't want her dead. *Just shut off your mind, would you?* he wanted to scream. Lowell had killed once before when things had gone badly. He was only interested in his own protection. *And so,* thought Ballard, *am I.*

Theresa edged away from him to the counter. Tears slid from her sharp, slit-eyes. She spoke through her teeth. "You don't know, Michael. If you knew you'd stay away from me. If you knew what's good for you, you'd never come near me again."

"Oh, now you're threatening me, huh?"

She stood there in a rumpled T-shirt, her hair snarled,

dirt on her knees. She looked gorgeous, wild-eyed, a caught animal.

"You know, Ter? You're just a stupid, crazy bitch," said Ballard. He stalked out, slamming the screen door behind him, but a rug was caught on the threshold and the door only made a muffled thump, bouncing back open again.

Chapter 14

"I could kill him!" she hissed as she thrust her hands under the cold running water at the sink. Then she pressed her lips together tightly. Trembling, light-headed, she lowered herself to the kitchen chair. *No, no, don't say that, don't even think it. Astral inclinant.* Elizabeth had taught her that events always began in thinking, thought forms in the astral. That's how we chose our lives. So shut it down. She bit her teeth together. *Cancel. Erase it from your mind. Non necessitant.* What business did he have barging in like—

The doorbell jangled, followed by a loud pounding. Theresa's body tightened. She clamped her fingers into fists and screamed from the kitchen, "Go away, will you!"

The banging continued, and a male voice, not Michael's called out, "Theresa. Police. It's Jardine."

Thank God, she thought. Briefly, she put her hand to her forehead. With a kitchen towel she wiped her face, then went to the door. Behind Jardine stood Detective Cooper and two uniformed officers.

"Sorry I yelled." Her voice came out in a tense whisper. "I thought you were someone else."

"Who?" asked Jardine.

She hesitated, not wanting to go into detail about Michael. "Just some neighbor kids," she said. "They ring the bell and then run away."

"May we come in?" As Jardine stepped into the living room, Theresa backed away from the open door. Though it was still early, Jardine's dark suit was rumpled and dusty, the thin hairs on his head blown out in odd directions, his cheeks flushed. She saw that he was looking her over too: dirt on her knees and hands, eyes red from crying. He noted the flowered sheet hung over the sunroom door.

"I was out back." She sniffed. "Gardening."

Holding his notebook open in his palms, Jardine stood squarely at the center of the small room. He nodded at the uniformed patrolmen and they exited to the courtyard, shutting the thin door behind them.

"I'm so glad you're here," she said, trying to compose herself. She pulled her hair back from her eyes. "I tried calling you all afternoon yesterday, but they kept putting me on hold. Don't you have a special number I can use if I need to get in touch with you?"

"I got the message and called you back last night," he said. "Several times. You weren't home." He was silent, as if waiting for an explanation.

Theresa sat down on the couch, rubbed at the dirt on her knees. "I was at my neighbor's, Arthur Holton. He lives across the way." Then she told Jardine about the answering machine, the rasping, halting voice on the tape.

Jardine quickly closed his notebook, handed it to Cooper. "Let's hear it," he muttered.

He followed her into the kitchen, where she fumbled with the buttons on the answering machine, rewinding to the spot where the dial tone ended abruptly and the scratchy voice filled the sunny kitchen. "Stay away from him. Leave him alone or you'll be next. Get out of his mind, I'm telling you—"

"You recognize this voice?" asked Jardine.

She shook her head, leaned forward against the sink. Cooper gazed out the back door.

"Lieutenant, I don't think this is just another weirdo. Is this the murderer? He knows the women weren't shot, right? Didn't you tell me that's how you screen out calls coming in downtown? Hear where he says 'stabbed girls'? Lieutenant," she went on, "I've decided I want protection after all."

"Good," he said.

181

"I mean, this guy knows I'm working with the police. It's been in all the papers, on the tube. What if he just decides to come after me? Maybe I should leave before Friday. I'm goddamned scared. That's why I hung that sheet up over the French doors last night. I get the feeling this guy could be watching me, following me." Her voice was growing more and more tense, high-pitched. Finally, she nearly shouted, "What am I going to do?"

Jardine snapped open the lid of the answering machine and ejected the tape. "Can I take this?" He handed it to Cooper. "Why don't you sit down." Jardine motioned toward the table.

"We found the body, Theresa." He was watching her face closely for a reaction, and her stomach dropped in an instant of dizziness.

"You did?" she whispered. "Where?"

"Where do you think?"

"I don't know."

"Of course you know"—his voice was stern and official—"because you took me there yesterday."

"But there was nothing there."

"Yet. There was no body there yesterday morning because the murder hadn't happened yet."

Don't scream, she told herself. *Calm*. She placed her trembling hands under her bare thighs and waited for him to continue.

"The call came in this morning. A couple taking an early-Sunday stroll up the canyon found blood along the roadside and streaked down the hill in the dirt. They hiked down to the creek bed. The body was there, Theresa, exactly where you took me."

She felt faint and closed her eyes. She could see it all and did not need to be told, the image filled her.

"Just as you described her. Female, about sixty years old, short gray hair. Heavyset. Dressed in purple. Hands arranged over her face. Wired there, Theresa, so they'd stay in place. Nine knives, this time all in a line over her head. Her throat slit once by a razor."

182

Theresa's eyes burned, she couldn't swallow. She held tight to the knot in her throat so it would not open. Jardine took a Tarot card from his pocket and handed it to her.

She shrank back in her chair as she had as a child when her father approached her with his belt, tapping the buckle softly, so softly, in his open palm. She took the card, but already knew what it was. "Nine of Swords," she whispered. "Woman with her hands over her face. Two, eight, nine. He's still not using them in any kind of order."

"There's more," he went on. "She worked at that bookstore we passed on the way up Topanga Canyon. In fact, she taught classes in subjects that should be familiar to you—out-of-body travel, healing the human aura." He held out to her a piece of paper and she unfolded it carefully, a poster, the woman she'd seen in the dream, smiling radiantly. Rays of purple light off her head. The halo.

"Her first class met last night from seven to nine. She was killed sometime after midnight. The coroner will know the exact time by this afternoon."

Theresa stared at the shining woman on the poster. She thought she'd heard of her before. Maybe Elizabeth knew her. Her name was hand-lettered across the page in neat calligraphy. Just the first name, no last. GRACE, read the curling letters.

Theresa slumped, stunned, her head against the high-backed chair. The feeling of expectancy, of the voice about to call out to her. So she'd seen the murder correctly after all. Before it ever happened.

Jardine rubbed the bridge of his nose and slipped his suit coat off, hanging it over the back of the chair opposite her.

Theresa felt blank inside, fear numbing to a cold hard point. In some odd way she was relieved that her dream had been correct. She wasn't just having crazy nightmares after all.

Jardine sat down next to her at the table and motioned to Cooper to hand him the file he was holding. "I have to tell you, Theresa, I was really angry when I came here." He

183

lit a cigarette, opened the file, and flipped through several papers. "Why couldn't you have known your dream was about the future? Or why was I so stupid I didn't have that canyon road staked out?"

"I'm sorry," she said, concentrating on the papers that Jardine was spreading out on the table. *Don't cry.* "I just didn't know."

"I'm at a loss, Theresa. I don't know how to use you. You give me this information and I just don't know what to do with it. Maybe we're coming at this all wrong, waiting for the murders to happen. There's got to be other ways we can make use of your powers. I don't know what else to call them.

"I already asked you to come down and look at some photographs. Could you try to picture this guy's face psychically and describe him to a sketch artist? Could you hold on to one of the jackknives or plastic swords and read it the way you read Bonnie Humphrey's ring? We just can't go trailing around after bodies, we've got to get something more concrete." Now he was shouting. He stood up, flicked ashes into the sink, yanked at his tie, twisting it until it came off.

"Sorry," he said quietly. "It's been a tough morning. It's hard to accept I could have prevented that murder somehow."

Jardine reached down and fingered the edge of the file, riffling the papers like a deck of cards. He seemed to be thinking hard about what he was going to say.

Theresa looked at the picture clipped to the file: Polaroid snapshot of Carolyn Svedrup. She was sitting by a pool with an older woman, probably her mother, smiling bright smiles in the sun. Drinking a can of pop. Alive on a summer's day.

"The three women who have been killed have all been involved in occult activities," said Jardine. "This Grace— Girard was her last name—that's obvious. She was a psychic, like you, Theresa. A teacher. Like you," he repeated. "Carolyn Svedrup, the yoga classes. I talked to

184

her parents in Cincinnati. They didn't know anything about their daughter's interest in yoga. Said she was a confirmed Episcopalian, wore a gold cross. She belonged to some Christian youth group after high school. But we checked with the meditation center and she'd been attending classes there for about two months.

"Bonnie Humphrey? Called her folks up in Berkeley. They said she had a strong interest in astrology. She read all about it, talked about it all the time. Drew up charts for her friends. Even wore a necklace with her zodiac sign on it, the whole shot. She was a Gemini."

"You think that's how the victims were chosen?" Theresa whispered.

"The thing is that this person or persons, whoever they are—"

"Person. One," said Theresa firmly. "One man. That's his voice right there!"

"That hasn't been established, but say it is one man. He knows the occult. He knows the Tarot cards, right? He's using the sword cards as his map, so to speak. His directions. He probably hangs around occult circles, goes to yoga classes himself, goes to psychics."

Theresa felt cold suddenly, as if she could not breathe, something pressing in on her lungs.

"So what we're looking for is a pattern. We're checking out everyone who signed up for Grace Girard's class. Everyone who takes yoga at the center. People who've taken classes in astrology."

Theresa shook her head. "That's the whole West Coast," she said. "There are too many."

"You have a list of clients? A mailing list? I'd like to check those out too. Anybody who's ever studied with you or had a reading."

Theresa rested her head in her hands, trying hard to keep from crying or screaming. She shuddered. "But maybe that's why I should leave town before Friday. I don't want to sit around waiting for him to . . ."

Jardine pulled his chair around by hers, put his hand on

185

her arm. "I know you can help us find him, Theresa. Your abilities could affect a whole community of people. If we can get a description of him or if you can anticipate the next murder, we can stop him. I promise you we'll have somebody watching your place every minute. And when you leave, we'll have a second car assigned to follow you."

She shook her head. "I just don't know."

"Think of the potential victims, Theresa."

Theresa broke then, put her head down on the table, and let out one sob, then held her breath—*Pull it together, don't breathe, don't cry,*—and when she looked up she saw again the smiling summer snapshot of Carolyn and her mother. She pulled another photograph out from under some papers in the file, the girl's corpse ashen white on a metal table in the morgue with a tag wired to her foot.

She thought back to the day she walked the grounds of Hillview Clinic, her mind dulled of vibrancy, dead to intuition and imagination. Vowing then to remain alive to her psychic gift, to serve it, she hadn't backed down from that responsibility. Besides, this was all part of the test Elizabeth had spoken of, to separate her personal subjectivity from her visions, to cut away confusing emotions and see clearly, not just for herself but for the world somehow. Wasn't that what Elizabeth had meant?

"All right," she said. "I'll try to work with your artist. I'll try to read the knives. But on Friday I'm leaving. I'll give it this week if you promise to protect me. Then I've got to get out of here."

Jardine left Cooper waiting in an unmarked car outside Jasmine Court until the undercover detectives arrived. Theresa locked her doors and kept the shades drawn. As the afternoon heat grew intense, she sat in her dark bedroom, fan blowing at the lace curtains.

To see correctly. That was the test, she thought. Separate personal emotions from this case, believe in her visions and not doubt. But that's what frightened her. What was she to do with that constant replay of the burning

186

image, building in intensity and clarity, Michael at its center? Trust or doubt?

Even though she was hot, she pulled the white blanket up over her, perhaps to hide under covers like a scared kid. Michael, with his questions about the murder and his old violence—there was some connection, there had to be. As she curled, head on pillow, eyes closed, Theresa rubbed her hand where it had been burned that morning by the steaming water.

Chapter 15

"Let's begin with his eyes. How do you see his eyes?"
The artist held her hand over the blank sketch pad. It was
Monday morning and the small room in the downtown
Detective Division office smelled of stale cigarette ashes.
The artist was a plump woman in her late forties, her face
kind and patient. She wore a bright flowered blouse and
tight green pants. Theresa thought she might just as well
be consulting a decorator in a department store about a
shade of Levolor blinds.

"I've always seen them as holes," she said quietly.
"Just dark holes."

"Deep-set?"

"I don't know. Holes. Skull holes."

"Let's say deep-set, dark eyes," said the artist, and
swiftly she swept her hand over the paper, sketching lightly.
Theresa's mind felt stiff. She tried to relax, to open to the
face she'd never seen in the dreams she could not forget.

"How about his nose?"

No picture. The face was a hole, a mask. That's how
she saw him. "Small," said Theresa, without thinking. "Pointed at the end, hair coming out of the nostrils.
His eyebrows, they're thick, they almost meet in the
middle."

*It was coming, good. Like a reading, just open. Trust in
the truth under the conscious mind.* Theresa closed her
eyes and went on. "Deep-set, Okay. Dark circles, and the
eyes are dull, vacant. Close together. Partly open, that's it.
Tired eyes."

Theresa could hear the swish of pencil and chalk across
the smooth paper, and the softer sound of fingers smearing

black to gray as she continued describing round cheeks, receding hair, black and thick. Open lips. She had no face in mind, only fragments. She was only going with the words that seemed to well up, unformed, from beneath her thoughts.

"How about this?" asked the artist, and Theresa opened her eyes, horrified to see a face she'd always known peering out from the page, only younger, much younger, her father's face. The sketch was an uncanny likeness of that World War II portrait her parents kept on top of the television set, her young soldier-father already broken and menacing in sepia-brown.

"No, no" she stammered. "That's not right. I don't think this is going to work." She closed her eyes again. "Beard. He's got to have a beard, and his hair is longer. Down to his shoulders. His nose, make it bigger. Almost hooked. Curved."

The pencil jabbed at the paper, altering the face. Don't just remember any old face from the past, she told herself. *Concentrate. Visualize.* Agitated, afraid of what she might see, she sipped lukewarm coffee, twirled the hair behind her ear into a tight ringlet around her finger.

"Like this?" asked the woman, her voice high and cheerful.

Theresa's throat felt sore. She didn't want to talk anymore, give any more information away. Just be silent, lose her voice. She looked sadly at the new portrait, the Christlike face she'd described. He was a Jesus without light, a dead Jesus, a sleeping one. When had she felt like this before, this need to escape, to get up and pace the small room, open windows, get out? Just like that reading last week, claustrophobic, no air. Raymond Mead running from her house, afraid. And even farther back than that. Doctor's office, was that it? Dr. White, her psychiatrist at the clinic: *"What's on your mind today, Terry?"* *"Nothing. Nothing."* *Keep it back, shove it back down, don't say, don't see.* "I'm fine," Theresa whispered, "just fine."

"What's that?" asked the artist.

"I don't know," said Theresa. "I'm getting descriptions, images, but this isn't the killer's face. I can't see his face at all. That's the problem, his face is hidden."

Then, searing up the back of her skull, a burning migraine blindness. That face in the dark, a face she could not see: blank, hole-face, features eaten away. Where? Where had she seen it before?

"Was he masked, Theresa? Is that why you don't see his face?" The artist waited for her response.

The face hung in the back of her mind, just out of view. Old childhood monster-in-the-closet. She did not want to look at it, did not want to see. It flashed in her mind, huge, dog face. Blink. She covered her eyes. Waiting for her. Blink. End of the hallway, end of the dark tunnel. Smell of fire, smoke in her hair.

Theresa whispered, coughing, "Make his beard thicker, all over his face. You can hardly see his face, his hair hangs down. It's in his eyes, it's always in his eyes."

The woman pressed down hard, stabbing hair strokes across the penciled face. There—that was him, whoever he was. Not some memory of daddy or daddy-god. That really was him, the face at the end of the tunnel—what tunnel?—waiting for her to give it to him. *What? Theresa, give him what?*

Theresa stood and came around the side of the table, grimacing at the hair-mask figure on the sketch pad, canine features nearly hidden. She wondered where she had met this person. In what dream or real-life street had they passed each other, and where would she meet him again?

"Well, what do you think?" asked the artist, striking a match to light the long cigarette she held in her chalk-smeared fingers. Theresa jumped back in terror at the pinpoint flame flickering at the match top, her pulse wild as she waited tensely for the woman to puff the small fire out.

"I guess so," Theresa whispered. "That's as close as I can come to him."

*   *   *

Sarene sat on the floor in front of the couch as her mother braided her hair into neat corn-rows. Camille's slender fingers, her magenta nails, flipped each tiny strand deftly into place. The girl sat quietly watching *Scooby Doo* on the giant television set.

"Resa, I can't believe you're letting yourself get so sucked into this thing. It don't have nothing to do with you."

Theresa hunched in the corner of the couch as if she were cold, her arms wrapped about her knees. "But it does. Why else am I receiving this information? Why is that face haunting me?"

"Don't get your ego all in it, girl. This stuff is happening and you got your face stuck in it like a fool. It ain't marked 'Vision, Special Delivery, Theresa Fortunato,' is it? If you keep working with the police, you're going to get yourself wasted."

"Maybe this is my test, Camille. Maybe this is my initiation."

"You don't need to prove yourself like that."

"Elizabeth said I do. I saw her."

"You *what*?" Camille stopped braiding, her hands still for an instant in the air above her daughter's head.

"Last Thursday. I went up and saw her at the house."

Camille pursed her lips, shook her head, and her beaded plaits clacked softly together. "Okay, little girl," she said to Sarene, putting her arms around the child and kissing her hair. "You all set, baby."

Sarene stared contentedly at the TV. Camille motioned for Theresa to come into the kitchen, where she pulled the door shut behind her.

"Tell me this again, because I know you're losing it now. You saw Elizabeth?"

"I had to. She said all this was my test, my challenge. 'The fire that purifies.' "

Camille stood at the sink and again she shook her head slowly from side to side. Theresa went on, "My bridge to cross, Camille. It's like I have to do it and come out clean, I—"

"*Wrong,*" said Camille. It was a whisper but its intensity filled the small, bright kitchen. "No, that ain't right. I never knew Elizabeth to set you up like that. It may be a challenge but it ain't your big karmic cross to bear, your purification baptism ritual. That's just cosmic melodrama, girl. You want to come clean about something, you go straight to God, Goddess, Jesus, Mary, Buddha, Krishna, Isis, whoever you want, and you come clean, but you ain't got to do it by catching a killer for no pigs and getting yourself ripped off in the process. This ain't no game, Theresa!" She raised her voice. "There's some maniac out there real as you and me, and he ain't far away. This is happening here in Venice, girl. I know I got my doors locked. I know I'm not letting my little girl out to play in the yard without me watching. You think this is your little private crisis? No, baby. Besides, you sucking in everybody around you. That cop even come here this morning talking about how long did I know you and when did I start going to the meditation center and how did I meet Carolyn."

"Oh, God, I'm sorry, Camille. I never meant for anyone else to get involved in this." Theresa looked up at her friend. "Part of me wants to get out of it, but I almost feel like I have no choice. I'm trying to tell you—"

"You ain't telling me shit that I can't see, and I don't need my powers to do it! You messing with a man you s'posed to left five years ago. You digging around in dead people's lives you ain't got no business being in. You prostituting your powers—"

"I'm *not,*" Theresa interrupted. "I can't believe you'd say that."

"You're lucky you know me, Resa." Camille shouted. "I'm the only one mean enough to be honest with you."

"I'm not even taking money for this, I'm doing it for free!"

"No you ain't. You paying. What's the price? Your

life, that's what. Now, you listen to me. You get out of it, and you cleanse yourself, and that's it. I don't want to hear no more about it till you promise me you will.''

Theresa poured salt into the palm of her hand and swirled it around in a small circle. ''It's more than just this police thing, Camille. It's bigger than just these killings. I can't explain, but there's something I've got to figure out about my life, about my past, and all this is connected.''

''You're damn right you better figure out your life.''

Theresa stared at the salt in her palm and her hand began to burn as if the salt itself were a coal. Heat throbbed through her palm. She dumped the salt on the table. A voice behind her whispered mockingly, *''See me? Can't you see me? I'm right here. . . .''* And she spun to see nothing but the refrigerator full of taped-up pictures Sarene had drawn in school. Wind, she thought. Just refrigerator buzz.

''Camille, I just can't go backward in life. You said the other day you can't try to turn the stuff off once it comes.'' Theresa opened her palms, looked at the familiar pattern of lines and creases in pink skin. ''I'm open to two kinds of psychic channels—one has information about other people, past and future, and the other is personal. My fate, my destiny. The trouble is that they bleed into each other, and if I don't learn how to separate the two, I'm not going to be able to grow as a psychic.'' Theresa paused for a moment, considered whether or not to tell Camille about the fire death image. No, she thought, not now. I'm not even sure what it means and Camille is opposed to all this enough as it is.

Slowly, she went on. ''I've been given a challenge, a test of some kind, so I can expand my powers, enlarge them. I just don't want to spend the rest of my life doing nice little readings for people about their love lives. I want to be of some use in a larger way, Camille. Helping Lieutenant Jardine with this—it affects the whole city.''

Camille regarded her silently, black eyes narrowed.

''I promised the lieutenant I'd help him for one week

and then I'm going to Taos for a while. I'm leaving Friday. This isn't just cosmic melodrama, Camille. It's scary and it's painful, but I can't run away from it."

"Maybe it's a past life," said Camille. "Maybe that's what Elizabeth meant by a test—some past life's come to haunt you. If you look and confront it head on, maybe it'll go away and leave you alone. Longer you don't look, more it be ghostin' around."

"Maybe you're right," whispered Theresa.

Camille sat down next to Theresa at the table. "Baby, I'm scared for you. That's why I'm shouting and fussing like this. I wouldn't be so upset if I didn't love you and want you to do the right thing."

"I'm just in too deep to stop, Camille. I've gone too far with it."

"I know. That's what scares me."

The phone rang and Theresa could tell by the sound of Camille's voice that it was her mother, Hattie, on the other end. Theresa went down the narrow hall to a back porch that tilted out over an overgrown lawn, and moving a stack of newspapers out of the way, she sat down on the faded velvet couch. Maybe when all of this was over, she and Camille could live together again just as they had up at Elizabeth's. Life could be slow and calm again. Ordered. No ghosts or demons cramming into her head. They could get a big house together, plant an herb garden. All this would pass. Besides, she was leaving on Friday, and she knew as if by a light flooding some deep part of her mind that all this would be over by then. She lay in the cool shadows of the porch and watched a blue dragonfly float and zip across the high grass.

Theresa closed her eyes in the green shadows of late afternoon. Her body ached as though she'd been riding in a car for a very long time and she tried to relax, still the sensation of someone watching, waiting. She hadn't wanted to tell Camille that Jardine's men had followed her here and sat waiting out front in their blue car. Would they watch the back of the house, too, peer through the slats at her lying there? Or would *he*? She glanced past the old wooden fence by the back alley where purple blossoms climbed in the late day. Nothing there. Not even a dog or a kid on a bike.

I meant no harm, she thought, and the phrase kept repeating itself in her mind: *It was not my fault.* But she could not think what it was that was not her fault or what harm she had been accused of.

Warnings, past lives: Elizabeth's admonition had seemed cloaked in secrecy. Some mysterious code. "We've spoken of this before, haven't we?" The final session—why hadn't she questioned Elizabeth further about that? *Tell me, tell me exactly, Elizabeth, what is going on here? How does Michael fit into this?*

Theresa had never been drawn to the notion of past lives, old karma hanging around for centuries while you changed bodies. That aspect of psychic work had seemed pretentious and phony. People were always claiming to have been Joan of Arc and Mary Magdalene. They had almost certainly been Egyptian princesses, demigods from other galaxies. No one ever had a past life as someone ordinary, a shepherd or a mother of twelve living in a hut. Besides, past lives were too remote to do anything about and there was enough to unravel right now in the mess of the present.

It was Elizabeth who had favored past-life readings. Regressions, she called them. She'd taught that circumstances in one's present life had roots in unresolved conflicts from the past and if understood and clarified, the held energy of the conflict would be released. Healing and resolution could take place. Psychiatrists worked with the same idea, but Theresa had as hard a time remembering any past life as she could remembering her early childhood. Dr. White called it repression. So her father had been a tyrant, yes, he drank too much, he slapped her around sometimes. It was commonplace in her neighborhood. So what else was new?

But what was the warning Elizabeth had given in that final past-life regression? Theresa lay down on the couch on Camille's tilting back porch. A small knot of fear hardened in her chest, as she tried to recall Elizabeth's words.

The first time Elizabeth had ever given a psychic reading for Theresa, she'd seen a large, chaotic family constellation. The light-globes representing the DeVitos were a swarm of flickering dots with an amoebic haze at the left, smothering the smaller dots: Mother. Her father was a pulsating red-tinged point and the child-dots all seemed to cower away from him. Elizabeth referred back to that initial reading when Theresa asked once why some people were psychic and others were not.

"In order to be psychic, you must be able to get outside the confines of your personal boundaries. Some people are more gifted at this than others, they have great empathy or imagination to see into other lives. But some people simply have no boundaries to begin with. You are one of those. You spent your childhood in fear of your father, trying to make it all better for your mother, putting your needs last, forming yourself around the frightening and unpredictable emotions of your family. It's easy for you to hear voices because you spent your whole life listening to the emotional tone of your family to see how you should react—cringe, protect the other children, run away? That's one of the reasons your powers are so strong, Theresa. It's also why they can be so out of control."

During her first year of training with Elizabeth, Theresa learned how to ground herself, strengthen her boundaries, by visualizing a protective white light around her or by meditating on images of solidity—mountains, tree roots, rocks. She also practiced seeing herself within her family constellation, focusing her light-point, pulling it away from the quivering mass of the family until, after several months, she could see the image of her light alone in a dark field, shining, whole and singular.

With her boundaries more secure Theresa learned to

bring in one voice at a time by separating them on a color spectrum—red for angry, fearful voices, yellow for intellectual voices with knowledge to impart, violet for celestial ones.

Elizabeth observed her for some time and then advised Theresa not to read by going out-of-body. "Your boundaries are much more defined now, but you're still—well—absorbent. You lose your body too easily," she'd said, laughing.

It was always the notion of the personal boundary that gave Theresa trouble. Where did she stop and another's influence begin? Therein lay her flaw, her inability to clarify psychic information for herself. Elizabeth told her, "You're better off reading for others, not in trying to decipher your own future. Just realize that every reading you give for someone is also a reading for yourself and you'll be all right."

Everything changed in those months with Elizabeth. Gone was the sense of isolation she'd aways experienced, the feeling of being odd, a misfit. Camille was undergoing a similar transformation as she came into her powers, alternately growing stronger and doubting everything. Both of them had moments when they even doubted Elizabeth and wondered if the whole apprenticeship wasn't some sort of scam—Elizabeth's way of getting cheap labor to help with her sessions, type her manuscripts, cook for her patients. Once Elizabeth read Theresa's doubt and confronted her. "You think I'm just using you? You're free to leave at any time. This is an opportunity for you, not an obligation." She'd been imperious, almost insulted. Then she'd turned to Theresa, her face changed, and said sadly, "Did it ever occur to you that I might need you? That without you and Camille and the others, I would be a very lonely old woman?"

All that year she and Camille worked not only on their own personal powers but on studying various aspects of occult tradition. They spent hours calculating and interpreting numerology equations, paging through ancient texts

197

on the Tarot, throwing the *I Ching*, memorizing *The Book of Changes*. Elizabeth assigned them each to work with her gardener so they could learn about the healing properties of herbs, both physical and psychic. Angelica could purify a troubled house, ferns absorbed emotional chaos—good for bedrooms and nurseries. Blue vervain drunk as a tea or hung in a room would calm the nerves.

When Elizabeth gave lectures, they traveled with her and were privileged to study with friends of hers who were also psychics and healers. Elizabeth called them the "Medicine People of Turtle Island." Aquilla, a feminist witch who led a coven in Pennsylvania, invited them to a new-moon ritual in which blessings were asked for the injured planet. They all lived within an hour of Three Mile Island and felt their vibrations were being destroyed by the collective images of doom that were bound to the area. In Minnesota they were invited to a sweat lodge to fast and share tobacco with a whole school of Native American children. The Red School House was directed by a fourth-degree Midewiwin medicine man, an Ojibwa visionary, one of the last great Native teachers. In Florida they had stayed for several weeks with a shaman from Peru who taught them how to go deeply into trance state, to heal by taking on animal forms. Sometimes, while flying back from a visit or lecture tour with Elizabeth, sitting in the plane drinking 7-Up and listening to the smiling directions of the stewardess, Theresa felt utterly dislocated. It was as if there were two worlds, one the wild spirit world of the ancients and the other modern, urbane, and secular, denying the existence of all magic except money.

At the end of the two-year training period Elizabeth had announced that the apprenticeship would soon enter its final stage. Theresa and Camille would move out in order to set up their own practices without Elizabeth's constant supervision. A two-year separation was demanded. After that they would meet as equals.

The week before she left the cliff house, Theresa had been melancholy and upset. Elizabeth's was the first place she had ever felt safe in her mind. She belonged there, she was almost afraid to return to the world, just as she'd been when she'd gone home from the clinic. Elizabeth's had been her first real home as a psychic.

As a sort of graduation present, to send them out into the world as they started their new lives, Elizabeth had promised both Camille and Theresa a culminating psychic reading. The night of Theresa's final session the ocean sky above Malibu had been clear, brilliant with stars. Elizabeth had taken Theresa into one of the consultation rooms where there was a large table and instructed Theresa to lie down. Placing a crystal in each of Theresa's hands, she had spoken quietly and firmly with the assurance of a master hypnotist. "Tonight you will not resist opening to images from your other lives. Tonight the gates of vision will open and you will see." Elizabeth stood at her head, hands on Theresa's shoulders, breathing quietly. Theresa didn't know if she slept or how much time passed, but the crystals seemed to grow immensely heavy and her arms ached as if she were supporting cement blocks. After a while she not only heard but seemed to feel inside her skin Elizabeth's soft voice chanting, "I am only a channel, only a vehicle. The power belongs not to me, not to you. It only is. Open yourself to the mystery. Allow yourself to carry this power to all the world around you."

Theresa remembered that her whole body began to shudder then. Ripples of energy pulsed through her spine like an electric current and she felt herself grow smaller and smaller, shrinking until she had disappeared. Perhaps she was floating disembodied high over the cliff house, not held by space and time. Elizabeth's voice came from far away. No, it was close, it was inside her, it was her own voice, sweet and melodic, the voice of her mother or a daughter not yet born. "Open to the image of your life before." The image appeared in Theresa's mind, medieval and stone. Gray. Cold dampness pervading.

She saw it like a dream, the fire blazing in a huge hearth, she could even feel the heat from the flames.

Without knowing why, she understood she was in charge of guarding the room so that no one could get at the fire. In her hands she carried a wooden staff which she held in the flames until it caught fire the way a kid sticks a branch in a campfire while his parents have turned the other way.

The door was open, and beyond it, that tunneled hallway. How easy it was to leave the room with the fiery torch lighting her way down that black passage of the mind. There—light the small flares on the rock walls, flame light leaping upward, throwing back shadows like giant arms against the ceiling.

She sensed his presence at the end of the tunnel before she actually saw him, felt him standing there waiting for her in the dark. "Who's there? Who's there?" His breathing heavy, slow. Afraid, she went forward, drawn toward him as the torchlight lit his huge figure, cloaked, hooded, the covered face. Without warning he struck out at her, his fist cracked at her temple and she tumbled to the stone floor, the staff flying out of her hand. Above her he towered. She cringed, covered her face. Sharply, he yanked her up by the hair, bending her neck back so her face was right at his. Voice from far away: "Look at him, look at his—" *"No!"* she cried out. Wrenching from his grasp, she ran, stumbling, toward the open door where wind raged in from a coming storm. Behind her, running. She could not cry out. She stumbled, skull on stone, his hand over her mouth, *can't breathe, can't speak, can't.* Gripping her throat, he dragged her out into a courtyard, spinning buildings whirled around her, dark windows. A bare tree at the center. It was night and cold and suddenly the square was filled with faces watching, mindless crowd chatter like a flock of geese. He bound her, rope squeezing her chest and ankles. He left her hands free.

"Look at his face! Open your eyes!" She forced herself to turn toward him, masked, hooded. Grown over with hair, a terrible animal, hidden boar-face, fanged. Howling he poured cold liquid down her arms. She reached out begging, "Please, please," as he touched the torch to her hands. Flames exploded furiously up her arms, into her hair. Only then did she see that she stood on a huge bonfire of branches and hay. Her long skirts leapt in the fiery wind. She screamed for air as the faces around her lit up yellow-orange, wide-eyed, pointing. "I only told the truth!" she screamed. "I meant no harm!" The fire clawed down her throat and she swallowed it and because she could no longer speak, she sang to herself in her mind as the light consumed her.

Theresa steadied herself on Camille's couch. She was cold, shivering. The pastel California dusk seemed ridiculously beautiful. She remembered she'd felt cold like this after she'd come out of the trance that night at Elizabeth's too. Elizabeth had wrapped her in a wool blanket. The old woman's neat braid had come undone, her white hair hung scraggly and wild, and she'd sighed deeply. "Thank God. Welcome back. I had a hard time bringing you out of that one."

"What time is it?" Theresa had asked.

Elizabeth merely motioned to the open window, where the dawn light was lifting lavender and pink over the calm water. She'd been under, then, for hours, maybe ten, twelve. Elizabeth helped her to her feet and handed her a cup of water.

"I don't like to admit this," Elizabeth had said, "but I didn't know if I was going to be able to get you back here."

"Where was I?"

"You tell me. All I know is your body almost went with you."

"What do you mean? I almost died or something?"

Elizabeth looked long into her cup. She seemed about to cry, her face pained for an instant, then she composed herself. "It's never happened before. The energy release, it was just too much at one time. It was everything I could do to . . ." She didn't finish the sentence. "Do you want to tell me about it? About the images you saw?"

"It was more than seeing. I'm glad it's over."

"Theresa," Elizabeth had said, "whenever you go back to a past life, it's not something over and done with. Time is another illusion we depend on. All lives are simultaneous. The past life you just experienced is also in some way your present life."

Theresa tried to tell Elizabeth what had happened, straining to catch the image fragments before they dissipated like a lost dream. After she'd finished, Elizabeth asked her how she interpreted what she'd been through. Dr. White had always made her do that too. *What do you think the dream means?*

Theresa just shook her head. "Just that someone was after me," she said.

"Here's how I see it," said Elizabeth. "You were guarding a source of light. Knowledge. You used that flame to light your own way and you allowed someone to take it from you."

"How could I help it!"

Elizabeth raised her hand to silence Theresa's protest. "And they killed you for it. I've always suspected you had a past life as a witch, Theresa. You know too much for your own good."

"Are you saying I let someone steal my knowledge and they burned me for it?"

"You were burned by your own light, don't you see?"

"No."

"What is it that Camille's always saying? 'What goes around, comes around.' You misused the light and you were destroyed by it. Do you understand?"

Theresa said nothing. She understood the moral of the story, but she didn't know how it applied to her present life. She was strangely pleased to have had an incarnation as a martyred witch, but she'd never misuse her knowledge like that.

They sat for a while in the room at the cliff house as the sunlight brightened over the ocean. Finally, Elizabeth spoke. "In a few days you're leaving here to go out to make a life

202

for yourself with the gift you have. It's a vast power, Theresa. I don't think you really know what to do with your power. Yet. Maybe ever. But this is the case with our entire race. We have to choose at this point in our destiny to come to terms with our power or we destroy ourselves with it. I think this is the test for you to live out, Theresa. And there is no way I can make you understand it until you actually experience it.

"Use your gift wisely. Don't ever use it for negative means. Use it as a healing force, Theresa. Be a healer, a witch in the ancient sense of that word, a midwife of true knowledge. Be a strong woman-force on the planet, help bring that healing force back into being.

"I keep thinking there's one last thing I have to warn you about. You can't stop this power you have. Especially not now that you've opened to it so fully. I see in the future a time when you will be severely challenged, and if you live up to the responsibility of your power, you will be ready for some very great work. If you are wise, Theresa, if you live through the test, your powers will be ready."

"Live through it?"

"Yes."

"But what are you saying?"

"As the Navajo say, 'I have spoken. It is finished.' "

Elizabeth had then handed Theresa a small package. Inside was a gold chain and pendant, a small golden disc. Engraved on it was a crescent moon and a cross. "Theresa," said Elizabeth, "you are the moon, the woman in the moon. Holder of great hidden knowledge from the ancient ones. But you're also the cross, at odds with yourself, opposing yourself, you're hung upside down in the world like the Hanged Man. You have great power but it can be misused. You have to learn to use it. I wish you well. Blessed be."

Elizabeth rose and walked out of the room. Theresa had the urge to laugh, but only because she was afraid. Who did Elizabeth think she was, some Hollywood guru in her imitation Frank Lloyd Wright house, living off her husband's money while she took in young women and told them tales of their destinies? No way. Live through my test, indeed. Theresa shivered. She looked out the window at the waves rolling in at the beach below. She believed everything Elizabeth had said.

"Resa?" Camille's hand rested lightly on Theresa's shoulder. "What are you doing back here? Here I thought you left while I was on the phone. Sarene comes and finds you out snoozing on the couch. You okay?"

Theresa sat up. She must have dozed off. The afternoon had given way to evening and a single cricket creaked in the high grass along the fence.

"I got to thinking about Elizabeth and her sessions," said Theresa.

"We had some good old times together," Camille whispered.

"Yeah."

"But they gone now, baby. We on our own now."

Theresa stared past the old wooden fence with its missing slats, past the streetlight in the alley and the tall eucalyptus that towered over the stucco houses, into the darkness that surrounded her.

Chapter 16

Oliver Jardine reclined in his squeaky office chair, feet on his desk, and tilted his neck back against the vinyl seat. The room was gray in the dusk. He'd flipped off the overhead lights so he could rest his eyes. The door was slightly ajar and as he waited for Cooper, he listened to the mumbling male chatter in the large room outside. At the mention of his name he eased upright, put his feet down on the worn carpet. He recognized the voices of several young detectives and a senior detective whose office was two doors down from his.

"Yeah, now I hear he's got a position open for a witch. Gonna cast spells on suspects, make them tell the truth." Laughter.

"Really, though"—another voice—"what exactly does she do, wave a magic wand for him? Fortunato—what a name!"

One of them addressed the senior detective: "Is it true she told him where the body would be found before the murder even happened?"

"Can't discuss it," the older detective grumbled. "But I can tell you I don't go for it myself. Whole damn town's full of fairies and gurus and bibbity-bobbity-boo. Next we're going to be required to take seminars in how to astral-project to the scene of the crime."

"That's great! We can save the taxpayers money— eliminate all the dispatchers! Call in using ESP!" Laughter again, caws like a flock of starlings.

"I heard she was okay. Cooper said she looked fine too," offered another. "A friend of mine on the New Orleans force told me they used a psychic once, a Cajun.

Gave them a lot of numbers and letters to go on. Even longitudes and latitudes. Eventually, they followed her directions to some pond. Dredged it. There were bones all over down there, a regular human tar pit. They never did find the murderer, though."

"Is psychic evidence admissible in court?" someone asked.

"Shit," another answered. "If it was my case, I'd take her in for questioning. The fortune teller. Anybody knows so much about a murder, read them the Miranda and let them get a lawyer."

Jardine rose, snapped his office light on, and stepped out into the open room.

"Anyone seen Cooper?" he asked loudly.

The group stood in unison, shifted uneasily, shrugged. "Ah, no, sir." "Uh-uh, haven't seen him," they sputtered nervously.

"Over here, sir." Cooper stepped from behind a wall of file cabinets, holding a stack of papers. The men stuffed their hands in their pockets and one kept passing his hand over his unshaven face, trying to stifle a laugh.

It was dark as Jardine and Cooper left downtown Los Angeles, the night blue, an endless summer twilight. They drove the coastal highway up to Malibu, and a wedge of moon hung out over the water. Jardine was silent and glum, chain-smoking, drawing deep into his lungs, enjoying the raw bite of smoke in his throat.

"You're depressed," said Cooper after a while. "You let them get to you."

Jardine said nothing, just kept driving toward Elizabeth Brandon's house. The woman was impossible to reach by phone. He'd left message after message on her answering machine but she hadn't returned the calls. He had to meet her—anyone close to Theresa. There were missing pieces, holes all over this case, and he felt anxious. He kept thinking of those wildflower jigsaw puzzles he used to get talked into doing at his cousin's farm in Wisconsin when he was a kid. The way he'd get sucked into the stupid edges of leaves and ribs of petals until his mind just went spongy, agonizing over the tiny curves and humps that wouldn't fit together. Sometimes if he just got up suddenly from the table and walked away for a minute, then came back, he could see where the pieces belonged. Bang bang—how could he have missed it?

"Want to talk about it?" asked Cooper.

"What are you, my goddamn therapist?" Jardine snapped.

"What do they know, anyway? They don't know anything about this case. Don't let them get to you."

"I'm getting to myself," he said. "I'm getting to my goddamn self." He stuck another cigarette in his mouth and pushed the lighter in. "They didn't say a damn thing about her I haven't already thought." A fishing boat puttered on the water below and Jardine wished he were on it, dropping a line in. "Let me ask you something, Cooper," he said. "You ever had a psychic experience?"

"Nothing like her," he said.

"I'm serious. You ever had ESP, flashed that something would happen? Déjà vu or anything?"

"Nothing that didn't come from common sense. Only thing out of the ordinary I ever experienced was a faith healer once in Mississippi. Big old brother, must have been six and a half feet tall. He wore a red suit, red shoes, the whole outfit blood red. He spoke in tongues, did laying on of hands. Tent revival meetings, you know? I used to go with my Aunt Lily when I was a kid. I don't know what his story was, but, man, he really did heal those old folks. People be jumping out of wheelchairs, swinging arthritic arms all over the place, casting out the devil every which way. Never got the feeling he was ripping anybody off either. Just had some kind of power."

"What about Theresa—you ever feel she's ripping anybody off?"

Cooper thought for a moment. "No. No, sir, I don't. But I don't get the feeling she's totally straight either. It's like maybe she knows something she don't know she knows.''

"Yeah," said Jardine. "I just can't put my finger on it, what she's not talking about."

Cooper added, "I don't think she sees the forest for the trees. Too close to what's happening. Jumpy. She gets weepy, flies off the handle. That's what I'm looking at." He paused for a moment. "Do you buy it? Her being psychic?"

Jardine sped through traffic. After a while he said quietly, "I'm impressed. I really am impressed with what she comes up with. Yeah, I guess I do buy that she's psychic, but I don't want to. I don't like the idea that this 'information' comes to her in some totally random way out of the blue beyond. I can't let go of the idea that she picks up on the murders with such detail because she's close to them in some way. Like I said, I get the feeling she's holding something back, something just"—he struggled for the right word—"omitted.

"Say she's being set up by somebody, used in some way to make it seem random. Maybe she's even being controlled by someone. She's very impressionable, reactive. That prediction—how could she know that much without being involved? Maybe it's completely unconscious. Maybe someone close to her is involved and she's picking up psychic signals from them.

"That's why I'm trying to get a take on the Brandons. I want to get at Elizabeth Brandon's feelings for Theresa. I may even fly up to Berkeley, talk to Frank Brandon in person. After all, they're the ones who got Theresa into this."

He veered the car sharply out to the left to pass a slow pickup on the incline. "The only thing I feel sure of is that the murderer will eventually go for Theresa. That's why I'm pushing this media hype even though she doesn't like it. The papers, tube, radio, all of them. Let everybody have their laugh. Fuck them. When the murderer knows she's on to him, he's going to go for her."

Cooper whistled. "Bait, then, huh?"

"She's bait."

Jardine lit a cigarette at the stop light. Elizabeth Brandon's should be just up from here. It bothered him when he started liking somebody on a case too much. It wasn't a sexual thing with Theresa. Well, maybe a little. Hell, she was a good-looking woman even if she was flaky, they all were. But he just liked her, that was all. Maybe his attraction to her was getting in the way. Maybe he couldn't see her clearly. But there was just something about her that wasn't right.

"Left up here," said Cooper, "where those stone pillars are."

Jardine slowed and pulled into the long shaded driveway of Elizabeth Brandon's house. Estate, he thought. God, there weren't many pieces of property left in Malibu that were this large. It was a small ranch. He stopped the car off to the side of the circular drive.

A tall woman with an easy smile opened the door and asked them to remain in the foyer while she saw if Elizabeth could meet with them. Jardine slipped his badge case back into his coat pocket and looked around at Elizabeth Brandon's spacious living room. It was not what he'd expected. He'd guessed there would be the similar trappings of new-age mysticism he'd seen at Theresa's and at the bookstores and meditation centers he'd visited. Mandalas, pictures of gurus, altars of Buddhas with votive candles burning and the ever-present perfume of incense clouding the air. Elizabeth Brandon's house was modern, well-kept, expensive, and clean.

"She'll be happy to see you for a few minutes. She's got a dinner engagement at eight," the woman told them when she returned, and with that she led them down a carpeted hall to a small study.

Elizabeth Brandon was older than Jardine had pictured. She was bent over her desk writing, white bun coiled at her neck, prim in a blue cotton dress. But when she stood up from her chair with the elegant grace very tall women

209

learn and extended her hand, she did not seem so elderly or frail. She was tan and her pale eyes glowed with intelligence. Her wrist was ringed with heavy turquoise jewelry and she stood barefoot. Jardine introduced Detective Cooper and himself. She motioned them toward a small couch but Jardine remained standing.

"I've been expecting you," said the old woman without smiling.

"I've left a number of messages on your answering machine," said Jardine. "You're very hard to reach."

"Yes, I'm something of a recluse. I like it that way. Now, I really only have a short time, gentlemen." Elizabeth Brandon checked her watch, then raised her gray eyes, looking directly at Jardine. He patted his suit coat pocket, searching for his pen, set down his notebook on the corner of her desk.

"In your notebook," she said, not taking her eyes off him.

Flipping the pages open, he found the pen clipped to a folded scrap of paper, and he paused. "Thanks," he said. Maybe she'd only just seen him stick it in there.

"Of course, you've come about Theresa. It's all very unfortunate."

"There was a third homicide discovered yesterday," said Jardine.

"Yes, I read about it. Awful. I knew her slightly—Grace. I bought books from her at the store in Topanga Canyon. But when I said 'unfortunate,' I was talking about Theresa's involvement. I hope I don't sound cold. These things happen in the world. We're a brutal, unevolved species in many respects. But I hoped Theresa would not have gotten involved in your investigation, Lieutenant. In fact, I tried to talk her into leaving."

"So that was your idea. She says she's leaving in a few days, Labor Day weekend."

"No," said Elizabeth. "She'll be here over the weekend."

"She told me she was going to Colorado."

"I believe she'll be here," Elizabeth Brandon insisted.

"In L.A.?"

"Here," said the woman. "At my house." She cleared her throat.

Jardine glanced over at Cooper, who coughed into his fist.

"At least," she went on, "that is my intuition."

"It seems you know something about her plans that she hasn't told me."

"I don't have much time, Lieutenant, so let's get right to the center of it. I'm feeling that you—" She paused, eyelids fluttering shut for an instant. Then she held her hand up to silence him. "You would like to trust totally in Theresa but you don't. You don't believe in psychics. Am I right." Statement. Not a question. "So you want to know more. Who is this girl who finds the dead? How can this be in your world of facts and figures, law and order? The issue is doubt, Lieutenant. Not just for you but for her as well. You doubt her. Is she not telling you all she knows? Keeping something hidden, deep in her thinking?

"And you also"—the woman spoke quickly, blinking, fingers held to her temples as if the words she spoke were being whispered in her ear—"there is something you are not telling her either. How she functions for you, for your . . . your procedure. You're not telling her that she is useful to you in ways she is not at all aware of. She is, in fact, essential to you. She is all you have. You like fishing, yes?"

Jardine nodded, smiling slightly. He'd felt like this years and years ago when a mean teacher had known he was lying about the broken window in the boys' bathroom in the fifth grade.

"So she is your bait. This is the word I pick up from you. And I see that this is not good for her, not at all. I tried to warn her about this."

Jardine wished that he'd been able to stop the short, nervous laugh that he blurted out. Quickly, he consulted his notes, composing himself. He was angry for feeling tense around Elizabeth Brandon, but he didn't like the sudden sensation that she knew things about him, just as Theresa had known about his family back in Wisconsin.

"You don't approve of her working with us on this?" he asked.

"Absolutely not."

"Why?"

"Just as I've said. You are pulled into a negative spiral of energy, you are sucked in, you must deal with very unevolved elements of society when your time could better be spent serving people's higher needs. Police work, predictions of movie stars' divorces, the end of the world—all this is a distraction for a psychic. Flashy, yes. A lot of attention. Suddenly, Theresa Fortunato is a great celebrity, the evening news, all of that. Suddenly terribly important. This is bad for the psychic mind. Better to work quietly, healing, focusing on positive energy." Elizabeth Brandon walked over to the window that looked out over the sea.

"Well, your intuitions are very powerful, Ms. Brandon. Theresa has questioned her role with the department, but she's decided to continue working with us and she's been extremely helpful."

"I'm sure she has, Lieutenant."

He wondered for a moment if Elizabeth Brandon were jealous of Theresa's sudden fame. She glanced again at her watch. "May I ask you a question about the significance of the sword cards in the Tarot?" he asked. "This hasn't been made public, but the murderer has used some of the pictures from the sword cards as a basis for the murders."

"Then he will die by his own hand."

He hesitated. "You know this psychically?"

"No. But I do know the first law of black magic—that when one uses the ancient forces of magic for an evil purpose, the evil will always return to one. There is nothing inherently evil about the Tarot or the suit of swords. They simply exist. Like a universal law, like two plus two equals four. Individuals distort the laws, they always have. That is why dealing with them is a waste of time. Better to strengthen the healing forces on the planet. You see, there is so little time. There is so much confusion."

Jardine wanted Cooper to shout amen, break the force her chanting voice created in the room. He could see why she was in demand as a speaker. There was something mesmerizing about her, but he wasn't sure at all that he liked her.

"Love is not good for Theresa." Elizabeth turned suddenly to face him. "One of her difficulties in this lifetime."

"Why do you say that?" asked Jardine.

"Because I sense your attraction to her."

He smiled again. "I didn't know I was coming here for a reading," he said.

"I'm always reading, Lieutenant. Look, I can only tell you that Theresa is very good but she is still in an early stage in her work and she becomes easily, shall I say, attached. I was angry Frank asked her to find this Humphrey girl after I'd refused to do it."

"Should he have asked Camille Taylor?"

"Not Camille, no. Camille only does past-life regressions. No—one of my more accomplished students. Someone who could detach, not get so worked up over it. But it may be Theresa is the only one of my students who would work with you. She's very headstrong. Very emotional. Heart chakra very open. *She wants to help*," she said dramatically, one hand to her forehead.

Jardine put his pen to his lips. He didn't like her haughty, confrontive manner but it was interesting, this view of Theresa as a little incompetent. Everyone he'd talked to had spoken quite highly of her. He decided to push at Elizabeth a little and see what cracked open.

"Would you mind answering just a couple more questions, Elizabeth?"

"Ms. Brandon," she corrected him. "I mind, but go ahead."

"You said you knew one of the victims, Grace Girard. Did you or your brother know the others, Bonnie Humphrey or Carolyn Svedrup?"

213

Elizabeth hesitated, her mouth tightened. "Dr. Humphrey, of course, is a good friend of Frank's. They're both psychiatrists and have taught together for years. That's why Frank suggested that the Humphreys contact me in the first place. But I never met their daughter, no."

"But Frank did."

"I assume he did. I think she might even have worked for him one summer as a research assistant or something."

"And parapsychology is his specialty?"

She nodded.

"What is his focus? Hasn't he studied mind control, the ability of one person to control the thoughts of another? I read that he worked briefly for the government studying the techniques of brainwashing on prisoners of war."

"Well, yes—that study was years ago, after the Korean War. The kind of mind control Frank is most interested in, though, is an individual's ability to control his *own* mind. Frank was one of the pioneers in biofeedback research, alpha waves, that sort of thing."

"What was Theresa's involvement in Frank's research?"

"I think you certainly should consult Frank regarding all of this, Lieutenant Jardine." Elizabeth said, slightly defensively. "I have only the vaguest notion of his experimental procedures. I believe he was testing for psychic abilities in different groups of people. Theresa was in a group of those who considered themselves psychic, and he tested other groups, the terminally ill, those who'd been in comas—I'm not really sure."

"Did you participate?"

She sighed, pressing her hands down flat on her desk and looking at him impatiently. "No. Frank and I keep our professional lives quite separate."

"Just one more question, Ms. Brandon. In your opinion would it be possible for a group or an individual to control someone by planting information psychically in that person's mind?"

"In most of the population, yes." She smiled. "Madison Avenue depends on it."

"I guess what I'm trying to ask is whether someone could be psychically sending information about these murders to Theresa for some reason?"

"What could the reason possibly be?" Elizabeth Brandon stopped here, fingering the turquoise in her ring, looking quizzically at Jardine. "Theresa is very open, a channel. It's her great genius as well as her downfall. But you are talking about hypnosis. Brainwashing, right? Is that your theory, that someone is controlling Theresa's mind? This is why you ask me about my brother's work? Are you suggesting some connection, Lieutenant, because if you are, you're not only terribly mistaken but practically libelous. You are only thinking in this way because your mind is too small to accept the truth of psychic phenomena. No one is sending psychic message to Theresa about these murders. She is tapping into them, not them into her. Now I really must go," she announced abruptly.

Jardine closed his notebook, extended his hand to her. "Well, thank you. This has been illuminating. I may be getting back to you."

"I hope not," Elizabeth Brandon answered, refusing his handshake. "I do not want to be involved in this. If Theresa wants to do it, she can go ahead. Leave me out of it."

As they sped back toward the orange haze of the city, Jardine wondered about the possibility that Theresa might even have met Bonnie Humphrey at some point in her work with Dr. Brandon. But what would that mean? His brain hurt from thinking. He'd better fly up to San Francisco tomorrow night.

"What did you think of Elizabeth Brandon?" he asked Cooper.

"Spooky as hell. She's obviously not your everyday grandmother." Cooper hesitated, then asked, "Sir? *Are* you interested in Theresa Fortunato?"

Jardine snorted. "Are you?"

Cooper turned back to the red line of taillights on the

215

dark road before them. "I think you should have warned her."

"Theresa?"

"No. Elizabeth Brandon. I mean, basically she does the same thing Grace Girard did. You should have mentioned that our boy is after psychics, know what I mean?"

Chapter 17

When Theresa heard the knock, she turned down the sound of the TV news and walked haltingly to the front door, praying it was someone she knew. What if it was the nightmare man, his face hidden, hair-masked or blank? Would she even know him if she saw him? She peeked out the side window and let out a sigh. It was a relief to see Arthur standing there, his light hair messed as if he'd been sleeping. He tugged at the tip of his mustache and grinned widely at her over the sign of the moon and the cross.

"Hi," she said, opening the door. Late afternoon sunlight streamed into the shadows. She toyed with the gold pendant that dangled from a thin chain around her neck.

"I was just wondering," he said, and then he paused.

"Am I supposed to guess? You want to borrow some honey, right?"

"Nope. I want to borrow you. I mean, if you're not busy or anything, maybe you'd like to go for a walk." He palmed his spiky hair. He was sunburned, his mustache sunbleached yellow against his red cheeks. He wore a faded Hawaiian print shirt and army fatigues. "So this is your place?" He leaned in looking past her. "Kind of dark. You always keep the shades pulled?"

"It's cooler that way," she answered. She moved to the side as he eased through the door. He went directly to the wall where her collection of Tarot cards was framed.

"Nice place." He glanced around, his eyes pausing at the camping gear piled in the corner. "These are neat. I like this one, it looks like you." Arthur pointed to a card in a brass frame and Theresa moved closer to see which one it was. "The High Priestess," he read.

As she stood next to him, she brushed his arm and he bent quickly to kiss her. She pulled away but he guided her face back, hand on her cheek, kissing her mouth.

"Was that so bad?" he asked.

Theresa looked down. "No. I guess you startled me."

"Good," he said. "I like surprises. What do you say, still feel like a stroll?"

"Sure," she said. "Why not? I've been in the house all day. I'm getting claustrophobic." In her bedroom she slipped on sandals, let her hair out of the ponytail, brushed it out into a soft, curly mane. If it weren't for the horror of this past week, she'd have opened to him, welcomed his kiss. But why get anything going when she was leaving? As she changed into a cotton shirt, buttoning it over the pendant, she wished again she were on the other side of this whole nightmare, the ritual courtship behind them, wished that she could just take him by the hand into this curtained room, undo the buttons on his shirt, kiss his sunburned chest . . .

She heard Arthur turn the sound up on the TV. "Theresa!" he called from the living room. "You're on the news!"

"A spokesperson for the Los Angeles Police Department," said the newscaster, "has confirmed reports that a psychic has been retained in an attempt to solve several recent murders. Theresa Fortunato of Venice, who has worked with professors at both UCLA and Stanford University in parapsychology research, has so far located the bodies of three victims in the Los Angeles area. All three murders are thought to have been committed by the same person. This is the first time a psychic has been employed by the police and—"

Theresa crossed the room, snapped off the TV. "God, I can't believe this. This lieutenant promised me there wouldn't be anything else on the news. Anybody could see it, anybody. The murderer is probably sitting at his table this very minute watching as he eats his frozen dinner."

"You wanted it to be confidential?"

"Of course!" she said loudly. "Sometimes I just feel like I'm being used by them for their own purposes. Like I have no say in this at all!" Theresa raised her hands over her head, fingers spread as if to grab at something. "Let's get out of here," she huffed, pulling the front door open.

They crossed the courtyard and walked down the several blocks toward the ocean, scuffling through dried eucalyptus leaves on the sidewalk. Arthur took her hand and held it casually as if they'd long been intimate. She was glad for his company, but felt uneasy knowing they were being followed. Turning back for an instant, she saw the unmarked car pause at the corner, then roll slowly toward them. Arthur was gazing into side yards, unaware of their companions.

"So how did you ever come to work for the cops?" he asked.

"I don't work *for* them, I work with them. It's complicated. This family hired me to find their kid and I did. Only she was dead. *Voilà*—cops. Since then I've found two more people, both dead. It's just gotten totally out of hand."

"Did you know they were going to be dead when you found them?"

She nodded. "I don't really *want* to find them. That's what's so crazy. Remember when I told you being psychic was like having a channel open, like on TV? Well, it's like there's this horrible show suddenly playing itself out in my life. Now my privacy is being violated—" She stopped in midsentence, not sure how much she wanted to discuss it.

"Why don't you quit, then, if you don't like it?"

"I am. I'm going away for a while."

"Where?"

"Taos, I guess. I'm not sure." She sighed. "So tell me about you, Arthur. What do you do for excitement?"

"I'm a writer," he said. "At least, I'm trying to be."

Theresa laughed in relief.

"Is that so funny?"

They came out of a small side street onto the boardwalk by the ocean. A woman was practicing t'ai chi exercises in the early dark under a streetlight and a group of people had gathered under the pagoda, banging on conga drums and pop bottles. Someone striking a cowbell was slightly off beat and a drunk lay face down on the grass beside them.

"It's not that it's funny, Arthur. It's just that I had this feeling the other night—remember when I said you were thinking of writing down everything I said?—and I got all paranoid because this cop I work with is always taking notes on everything I say. It never occurred to me you were a writer. God." She feigned hitting herself on the forehead with the palm of her hand. "I even saw the typewriter. So what do you write? Have you published?"

"A few short stories in magazines nobody's heard of," he said. "But right now I'm working on a screenplay. It's about a guy that gets out of the army and is trying to start a new life."

"A post-Vietnam thing?"

"No, a kind of post-post-Vietnam thing. Hey, Theresa," he said, letting go of her hand and sliding his arm gently around her waist, "your life would probably make a pretty good screenplay. Especially now."

"Trying to get new material?"

"We writers never rest." He smiled. "Like this whole thing you're into now. Gruesome as it sounds, it's still fascinating. How did you ever get into this psycho stuff anyway?"

"Psy*chic*, Arthur."

"Yeah."

"You really want to know? A gypsy told me when I was fourteen that I had a star-crossed destiny."

Arthur shook his head. "Nah. We've got to change that. It's too much of a convention. Too predictable. How about: As a child you were kidnapped by a Satanic coven and brought up in the black arts by your wicked uncle who wanted to harness your powers to foresee the future of the OPEC oil market and predict possible assassination at-

220

tempts against corporate officials secretly traveling in South America? We've got to make it more dramatic, more marketable, see?''

"I wouldn't mind reinventing some of my past," she muttered.

"Like what?" he asked.

She stopped and looked in a shopwindow, her arms folded. No, she thought. He probably does want to write this all up. She felt herself close off to him, like a door clicking quietly shut. She wished he would stop questioning her. They all wanted something from her: Frank, Jardine, Michael, now Arthur. Even the undercover detectives down the boardwalk from them pretending to stare at a display of T-shirts. *Where are you going? What are you doing?* She shrugged off Arthur's touch with a shiver and then, without really meaning to, she began to read him. Her mind blurred, refocused, images flashing inside: a suitcase, the name Neal, a blue three-piece suit in a closet, a passport.

"Why don't you tell me about *you,* Arthur? I mean, do you freelance or do you work for somebody? Your pen name is Neal, isn't it?"

Theresa could tell by the way he looked at her that he was surprised, disconcerted, by her knowledge of him.

"Maybe I don't have to," he snapped. "Maybe you can just psych me out, figure it all out by yourself."

"Well, maybe I can." Theresa walked away from him up the boardwalk, the base of her neck aching. She looked at the faces around her and they all seemed masks, hiding something. Falseness, duplicity, all of them. That one there—or even that one—any of them could be a killer. When Arthur touched her arm, she jumped.

"Hey," he said, "I'm just not used to someone reading my mind, okay? You're not pissed off, are you?"

"Let's say I'm distracted," she sighed, looking down. "I'm not myself right now."

Arthur fingered his mustache. "All right. Here's my true confession, real-life autobiography. Ready? I'm thirty-one. A Capricorn. I'm from a little town west of North Platte, Nebraska, my Dad owned a small ranch. After a back injury in seventy-six (I remember the year—it was the Bicentennial), he and my mom bought a bakery. They retired last year and moved down to Tucson. Went to college in Lincoln, dropped out, had a bunch of jobs, some dull, some not. Then, for lack of anything else to do, and some other confused reasons which I won't go into, I joined the army. All my friends thought I was nuts but I guess it worked out. In fact, I just got out about six months ago. Fort Sill.''

"So your screenplay's autobiographical?"

"Well, it's all just notes right now," he admitted. As he spoke, he looked at her with open blue eyes, smiling boyishly with his mouth shut. Then he shrugged, "That's about it, really."

Theresa felt her breathing go all hot, empty and black as a hole inside her, and she knew without question that everything he had just told her was a lie.

She turned from him, began walking, and he hurried to catch her, falling in step beside her, chattering on about being from the Midwest, coming to Los Angeles, how he'd always wanted to write. Why would he lie to her? Maybe he was testing her. She felt certain he had a brother. That his name really *was* Neal. That he'd worked at a bar called Jack's in the Southwest somewhere. Colorado, maybe. Durango. And his family was from Oregon or Washington because she felt ocean, rain, and darkness in him. Forests, thick, tangled with leaves.

Why did she have to go around reading everybody, anyway? All her relationships had been ruined by her psychic powers: parents, sisters, lovers. Michael Ballard? Certainly. He'd thought she was crazy. All the men she'd ever gotten involved with had eventually left her because she was psychic. Told her she invaded their minds, they had no privacy, didn't own their own thoughts. She was too intense. She was a spook, a witch. She was out of her mind. It was impossible to trust any of them. She couldn't

222

get close to a man without reading him and when she did, she saw their lies, their duplicity, saw through their phony romantic posturing, then felt them back away.

Theresa stopped and faced him. "Look, I don't know how to say this without sounding strange, but don't take me for a fool. I know things, right? I'm psychic. I know, for instance, that you're not who you say you are. Your name really is Neal. You're not a struggling playwright. You work for"—she made little scooping movements with her hand as if flipping through invisible cards—"a magazine, right?" Images of pages, palm trees, Spanish, came into her mind. "And you're here to interview me. You just came back into the country from Mexico, Latin America. El Salvador? Was that your last story? And now I'm your latest, is that it?"

The gray-pink clouds far out over the water were losing their last color. Arthur stepped off the boardwalk out onto the sand, backing away from her.

"Okay," he said. "That's right. I cannot tell a lie."

"Then don't," she spat. "Don't come around like an honestly nice person, asking me to dance, inviting me for evening strolls, and then just bold-faced lying to me."

"I'm sorry. I didn't know when I started this assignment that I'd begin to like you. Okay? Sorry I started to care about you. All right?"

Theresa stomped past him down to the water and she heard him behind her. "I'm a freelance writer," he called out over the rolling surf. "I've done pieces for *Rolling Stone, Mother Jones, Esquire*. Right now I'm working on a piece about the occult in southern California. A friend of mine turned me on to you. It was before any of this murder stuff even started. My name is Neal Holton. I'm from Denver. And I was just in Mexico but it was for a travel piece on Baja, okay? I am sorry. I really am. I started to be sorry about this a couple of days ago but I didn't know how to broach the subject."

"Why couldn't you have just interviewed me honestly,

talked to me like a human being, instead of spying on me like this?''

"I wanted an inside story."

"Well, now you've got one, haven't you?"

Theresa kicked off her sandals, stood barefoot on the white sand. Several stars hung in the still-light sky, looking large and close. Two or three sailboats headed back into Marina Del Rey. As Theresa blinked at the pink hem of the horizon, the palms of her hands tingled, hot needlepoints, heat spreading through her fingers and wrists, sickening sensation in a wave through her chest. She slowly turned back toward the boardwalk.

Arthur, Neal—whoever he was—stood head down, waiting for her, roller-skaters zipping past him in silver jackets. A small fire burned in a trash can behind him, some wino stirring it with a coat hanger. She couldn't get her breath. Shouldn't come down to the water at dusk. Burning sun. That's when it would happen. Sky all hot, flaming sand.

She covered her face with her hands, cheeks flushed, feverish. Tried to picture Arthur with a mangy beard, long hair, like the description she'd given the sketch artist. But, no— that face was from a past life. There she went again, confusing her personal life with the case. Nothing was as it seemed. Arthur had lied to her like all the rest of them.

He came toward her then, and she saw the two undercover detectives step out onto the sand, gazing at the remnants of sunset, watching discreetly to see what he would do. At least they were doing their job.

"Well? Are you going to forgive me?" Arthur asked. "Theresa . . ." He reached his hand toward her, held it out, open palm. "It was fucked to lie to you. I know it."

She felt a heavy sadness in her chest. Under different circumstances they'd have been lovers. No chance now. He stepped close to her, offered a handshake.

Her mind was filled with both longing and distrust. A large, dark *no* pulsed at the periphery of her thoughts.

Something about him was false, something else felt solid and honest and warm.

Her eyes blurred with tears and she blinked them back, but they came anyway, soundlessly. She could taste them salty on her lips. She wiped at her cheek with her sleeve. "Look," he said. "I'm really sorry about all of this, the false identity, everything. I wish it hadn't happened this way."

He put his hands on her cheeks, wiped at the tears with his thumbs, and then he pulled her to him, pressing his mouth to hers, waiting for her to relax, to let go into the gesture of his embrace. But she couldn't trust him now. Stiffly, she stood, his arms around her. After a few minutes she pushed him away and looked out past his shoulder at the open stretch of beach where the surf thrust in over and over again, the rush of the rolling water soothing and continuous, something to be counted on.

Chapter 18

I've got to tell someone before my brain explodes. It's getting so loud in my skull, this churning like awful music. The part of me that does this, see—it's the bad part. I know that much. It's what they let out, what they never should've let out because he was better off somewhere behind a locked door. That's what scares me. I don't know what he's going to do next. I really don't.

Hello? What? No, it wasn't a jail, it just felt like one. And I always thought I wanted out, you know? But I can see what they meant with all that "Now, now" stuff and pills given out at certain hours and the television going on and on in the day room like a clock.

My name? No. No, he doesn't want me to say his name. He wants me to hang up. Right now! But I . . . please . . . if I can just say it to someone! Please!

See, I know you've got her after me now, I saw her on the television. But it isn't really me that's doing it, that's what I'm trying to tell you. It was all his fault to begin with. He got me the devil cards and they're the ones that keep telling me what to do, what to do.

Wait a minute. Are you there? I thought I heard him. Just let me, just let me get this out, if I can just talk to somebody. See, I don't talk very good. What? You think I talk just fine? Hah! Are you kidding?

No, I'm okay. It's just I can't breathe too good. I got asthma. Yeah, and they weren't shot, either, those girls, like you said on TV. You lie. You lie. It's a trick, right? No. They were cut up like lambs at a slaughter.

What I did, I went to church. I went to his church because I feel better there. It was morning. Hardly any-

body was there, see—a Tuesday morning and all—but they keep them open because it's sanctuary. Well I tried to pray, but I couldn't. You know why? Because I saw that Jesus was really dead. He always used to tell me that, God is dead, God is dead. Well, I saw he was right. There was God all limp hanging on that cross, skinny feet and arms all dangling down and ribs poking through. He was dead, man. He couldn't hear my prayers. Maybe he never did.

Just then this old guy in a felt hat a couple of rows up turns around and starts staring at me. He was listening in on everything I thought, I could just tell. He knew. He kept staring and staring so I had to get out. I ran outside to the parking lot and I waited for him because the old man was going to tell on me. Just like he told on me. If he hadn't told, I never would've spent my whole life in a hole. He knows everything I do.

But anyway, no I'm okay, I'm okay, it's just I thought I heard him again. No, I'm at home. Right over here on . . . No, I'm not telling you where! You're trying to trick me too. All of you.

Like, I waited for the old guy. He came out of the church and walked out back to this little cemetery, see. And he went up to this grave and he stood there picking old dried-up flowers off this grave and holding his hat in his hands.

I felt better standing there for a minute. Because except for the old guy, every single one of those people in there was dead just like Jesus. They had all made it through to the other side so they were quiet and they couldn't get into my head. Then it came to me, the only way out is if I kill him. That's the only way he'll shut up in my head and not see my every thought, word, and deed.

And then the old guy spun around and stared at me again and he changed! His whole face changed until he wasn't the old guy anymore. It was like he took off his old-guy mask, and it was him, it was him. He started running away, but I grabbed him and pulled him down and pushed hard on his mouth and his throat till he went all limp like the Lord, no breath in him.

227

I left him there in the high weeds by the fence, and lay down for a while on top of a grave, wishing I was down in it all dark and safe with nothing in my head.

No, he's not still there. See, I knew he belonged in church with the rest of them. Now that he was dead, he was good. Once you're dead, you've made it. You can't sin anymore. You're perfect.

So I found the perfect place for him. The sanctuary.

But I never really meant to harm anyone, see? It's just that they go in my head and start screaming and watching and somebody has got to stop me because I know for all my thinking about it that it's just not right. After all, I'm not God. Am I?

Theresa's legs ached from her run back from the ocean to Jasmine Court. She'd told Arthur she'd rather go back by herself. No, she didn't want to have a drink. She didn't know if she wanted to be friends, be his little research project. No, she had enough on her mind. But now, with sandals clicking on the cement patio stones and the dark rustle of the bougainvillea, smell of fog coming inland from the water, she suddenly felt afraid. She stood for a moment outside her door, key poised in hand. Was that just a shadow swooping across the wall inside? As she eased away from the door, a streak of passing car lights washed across the courtyard, headights reflecting on the mirror inside. So that was all. Still, she did not want to go in there alone.

Where were the undercover detectives? Maybe they would go in for her first, check the place out. She had watched them at the beach return to their car, begin to follow her as she headed back, but where were they now? Theresa looked up and down the street at the entry to the courtyard. No van.

She jumped at a metal clank on the stones behind her. A big tomcat sprang after a pop can it had knocked off her neighbor's fence. And then the van pulled up in front of the courtyard, sliding into a parking space. Theresa backed into the dark leaves and watched as the two men inside opened white sacks of McDonald's hamburgers and stuck straws into plastic milkshake cups. She heard one of them say, "Her lights are out."

"Maybe she went to bed," said the other, craning to see past the first.

Christ, she thought. So this was her great protection, zipping out quick for fast food. *Oh, she'll get home okay—I don't see anyone after her.* Anyway, hadn't Jardine said there would be two cars—one to stay here while the van followed her? Where were they? She wanted to know who they were, license numbers, badge numbers, names. First her name on the news, now this. If this was the way Jardine was going to handle it, she would just call the whole damn thing off.

Stepping out of the bushes, Theresa waved at the men in the van. The one on the passenger side nudged the driver, who was busy dipping French fries into ketchup. The driver then nodded to her, an almost imperceptible move, trying to look so serious and professional. Negligent slobs, she thought.

Lying awake that night, she tried to still her mind. *Breathe deep, white light. Going away soon. Away to the mountains, away from the sea. Take car in for tune-up. Get traveler's checks. Let breath cleanse you. Breathe deeply to the middle of your heart.*

Theresa's dream that night was disconnected, distant, as if seen down the tubes of inverted binoculars. She kneeled before the priest with her tongue out. Instead of placing the wafer on her tongue, he placed a coin. She took it out of her mouth to look at it: the golden disc that Elizabeth had given her. "Forgive me, Father, for I have sinned," she whispered. She was embarrassed to be up in front of the whole church wearing nothing but her white slip. When she looked up at the priest in his black and purple

229

vestments, it was Neal making the sign of the cross over her uplifted face.

She shifted in bed, sat up suddenly, throwing the covers back. Her skin itched. Pressure clamped down in her head. That humming behind her—she realized it came from inside her mind. Fly buzz, then plane roaring toward her, rumble of a high storm wind. "Please," she said to no one, "go away. Go." Dizzy. The room blurred, swung in and out of focus. "No." Staggering to the bathroom, she placed her hands on cool tile walls to steady herself. She didn't want it, the vision flooding into her. Sick, her throat clogged, she couldn't breathe, the air too thick. "Stop it, stop it," she whispered, turning on the shower. Water would clear her. *Take away the sins of the world, you only begotten* . . . Water, wine. Blood, heart. She tore out of her nightgown. Tangling, reeling, she stepped into the spray of the shower, but it came anyway, screaming through her like a diesel engine, the voices like sirens whose language she could not understand, a wild speaking of tongues, flames in her head.

She clapped her hands to her ears and slipped, cracking down hard on her knees, grabbing the plastic shower curtain, pulling at it, ripping it down. Water sprayed out onto the aqua tiles. She breathed hard as if she were running, running away. His hands from behind her, hands on her throat. Fingers clawing her neck. Trees swayed wildly green above her, as she sank to the ground, gravestones rising above her. *"No!"* She screamed, then there was no sound, only a face with no features, no mouth or eyes, no nose, only a smooth-skinned globe, horribly empty. The head spun fully around on his neck revealing what was hidden on the back of his skull—a second face leering at her from under the thick hair. This was her final image as her breath left her body forever.

The vision went cool blue like late-night TV snow, pale and shimmering. She was outside of it, then. Watching. From someplace far away she sensed the water splattering on her but she couldn't wake and the image sputtered on again: shut in a dark place. Moving. Being carried, cradled, to a cold place surrounded by stone. Cave? Cellar? Vault? "Let me out of here," came the familiar voice. "I don't have what you want." Dark grave, earth cold around her.

But no, this was different. There was light here, rising slowly like sun through stained glass. *Oh, Heavenly Father,* light streamed in around her as He promised, *Take away the sins of the world.* Blue light, cobalt, indigo. Crimson, red, heart. Yes, a stained glass window. And there was Mary bent lovingly at His feet. Holy Mary, Mother of God. Clean heart. Immaculate.

Theresa grabbed the edge of the tub, pulled herself to standing, and wrapped a towel around herself. Shivering and still wet, she went to the phone in the kitchen, dialing, whispering to herself, "Jardine, Jardine, please be home."

The phone rang three times before he answered with a groan. Only then did she look at the clock on the stove: quarter to four.

"Lieutenant," she croaked, and tried clearing her throat, but her voice was gone. It hurt to swallow. She could only whisper in a guttural grating tone, "It's Theresa."

"Theresa," he said, sounding instantly alert. "Where are you? Are you all right?"

"I think so. I mean, yes. Sort of. Someone is dead again."

"Okay, I'm awake," he said, "It's three forty-seven." She could clearly *see* him sit up in bed, pick up his digital watch in the dark. "What's wrong with your voice?"

"I don't know, Lieutenant." She ached all over, a feverish heat crept through her. "Look, I don't know anything anymore. If it's already happened or going to happen. But it's a church, there's a room off from the altar, it's cement, there's a wrought-iron door like a gate and it's locked. There's a stained glass window of Mary at the Lord's feet."

"Slow down, Theresa," he said. "A church you say—what church?"

Theresa closed her eyes and could hear only the wind and her own heart pulsing hotly through her chest. The words came to her as if someone else were speaking: "Immaculate Heart. It was a strangulation. That's why I have no voice."

"Right," he said. "Room off from the altar—like a sanctuary?"

"Exactly."

"That's what he said."

"Who said?" she cried.

"I'll explain later."

She pulled the phone book out of the kitchen drawer and tore at the pages until she found the address. "I'll meet you there!"

"Stay there," he commanded. "Stay where you are."

"I have to come." She tried to shout but it only scraped at her throat more. "I have to!"

She huddled in the kitchen, wrapped only in a damp towel, her hair still dripping. Dawn light was gray in the trees out back. Theresa toweled off, dressed quickly in pants and sweatshirt, and ran, stumbling, out across the patio court to her car. As she started up the street she glanced in the rearview mirror to see the van pull out behind her, flick its lights on once. She flicked back, then headed up the dim street.

The parking lot beside the church was empty. Immaculate Heart was a large pale brick building with small buildings surrounding it, a school and a convent. A tiny cemetery extended behind the parking lot enclosed by a chain link fence. Two squad cars stood on the street out in front, the red lights on one of them blinking silently, Jardine's car next to them.

Lights were on inside the church and the colored windows glowed in the early dawn. The sight made Theresa deeply lonely. There was no safe place left at all. She wondered if the body would be there, and found herself

232

hoping that it would not. If it hadn't happened yet, maybe they could still stop the murder from taking place.

A uniformed officer stopped her at the front door. "You can't go in there, miss."

"Lieutenant Jardine," she said in a cracked voice. "Let me talk to Jardine."

Cooper strode up behind the man in the pinkish dark, his footsteps echoing in the cavernous church. "It's all right," he told the officer. "She's the psychic." Cooper motioned toward the front of the church where Jardine slouched against a wall, talking to a woman in blue jeans and a white sweater

High vault lights threw an amber glow into the empty church. Theresa instinctively dipped at the knees as she entered, crossing herself. "Up here," said Cooper. As she followed him past the pews, he turned and spoke over his shoulder, "The body is in there, all right. They can't get the door open."

To the left of the altar at the front of the church was the door as she'd seen it in the vision: black cast-iron scroll-work door locking a small sanctuary. The woman beside Jardine was jangling through an assortment of keys on a large brass ring.

Jardine turned as Theresa came up beside him. In a low voice he said, "I thought I told you to stay put."

"I couldn't. I had to come."

"I'll talk to you about this later." Then he faced the nun. "Sister Mary Bridgit, Theresa Fortunato. Theresa, the Mother Superior."

The nun muttered to herself as she flipped through the keys. "The thing is, we never lock this door. It's always open, so I've no idea which key to use. Maybe this one. The only other one who might know is the custodian and he won't be in until afternoon. I suppose we could call him. Well, here, try this one."

Over Jardine's shoulder Theresa could see the body on the front row of several mahogany pews. Jardine wiggled the key into the lock and the grate creaked open.

An elderly man lay ashen blue, his mouth hung open, head lopped to one side. His hands were on his chest, pressed together in an attitude of prayer. As Theresa looked more closely, she noticed they were wired together to keep them from dangling to the side.

Jardine shook his head, opened his notebook, and began scribbling. Theresa leaned against the doors, her fingers clenching the curves of wrought iron. It had been a long time since she'd been in a church, been to Mass. She'd thought that it was all dead for her, the old patriarchal rituals and demeaning of women, always Mary at His feet, always the women confessing to the Father, the Father over all, over everything. The Mother of God was within her, she'd decided long ago. And the rituals of the earth and the seasons had spoken to her far more eloquently than a man with a white stripe around his neck. Now, inside the cool chamber of the church, she held on to the black bars that felt like the bars on the window of her room at the clinic so long ago. There was no sanctuary left, no Father to take care of it all. She had the impulse to pray, to pray for the voice of God in her instead of the voices of the dead, to pray to Mary, to lay her own head at Mary's feet and be healed.

Jardine turned back to her. "No knives this time," he muttered.

Without thinking about it Theresa glanced under the bench where the body lay and saw it there, the small, red plastic sword on the speckled floor. "Yes, there is," she said, pointing, "—under him. But there must be more, more than just one."

Her arms and hands felt warm, her palms stung. She held them out in front of her, closing her eyes, visualizing the cards: Two of Swords was Bonnie, those knives through the hands. Three was the heart, pierced through. That card had not been used yet. She pictured the sequence of sword cards in her mind. Four of Swords was a mausoleum, a crypt. Yes, that was it, the stained glass window, the body at rest, one sword beneath him and three above. Theresa

234

glanced above the body of the old man at the high window where the morning light leaked through. There on the windowsill under the foot of an angel lay three small plastic swords lined up like little colored jelly beans all in a row.

Theresa backed up, lightheaded, pressing herself against the cool bricks. "Four," she said. "Four of Swords, Lieutenant," and she pointed to the sill. "He's just going right through the deck, not in order, but every one. Every last one."

She became aware of the other voices in the church then and turned to see the photographer she'd seen at the other murder sites. Jardine raised a hand to him. Uniformed officers stood talking quietly. The Mother Superior had sagged onto the first pew, pressing her palms to her cheeks.

Theresa turned to go. She was no longer needed and she was tired as if she'd been wandering lost in the mountains for many days.

Jardine crossed the sanctuary and came to stand beside her. "I'll want you to come downtown in a couple of hours, after we've finished up here. I want to talk to you about the vision, every detail. And I'm thinking we'll do the knives. The plastic swords. I mean, have you try to read them, if that's okay. I'll call you. I think we're going to get lucky with this one. Whoever got in here had to have gotten hold of the key."

"Couldn't they just pick the lock?" Theresa asked.

"People usually pick a lock open, not pick it closed. We'll start with people who had access to keys."

She wanted to scream at his plodding slowness. The horrible double-faced head jammed into her mind, leering and monstrous.

"Another thing, Theresa. I want you to listen to this tape."

"I've listened to it a hundred times," she protested.

"Not your answering-machine tape. Ours. Our boy called in last night. Confessed he just killed someone. Even said the body was in a church. Sounds very disturbed, real

235

sick. We've got a psychiatrist analyzing the tape now. We're going to get this guy now because he came inside. They always leave something behind them inside, some trace. Besides, we've got this voice print and the face you described to the sketch artist. Something's going to break."

"I don't know if that's his real face. I think there's another face."

"Pardon?"

"The guy has two faces, the one I described is on the back of his head."

"You're tired," said Jardine. "You go home and get some sleep. I'll call you when we finish up here."

"Yeah, sure. Sleep."

Jardine had stepped back into the sanctuary and was instructing the photographer on the angle of a shot. Through the wrought iron she called out to him, "And, Lieutenant, I want to talk to you about my so-called protection."

He came back, spoke tersely through the curved bars of the gate. "I will call you, all right? I didn't want you to come down here in the first place. I want you to stay put at your house unless I tell you to leave, understand?" Then he went back to the photographer.

Theresa walked out past the altar, down the side aisle of the church, and out the door into the rose light of the morning.

She sat in her car for a moment, waiting while the van behind her started up. Why was Jardine so adamant about her staying at the house? Stay put, indeed. You would think she was under house arrest or something. In fact, the more she thought about it, it seemed almost stupid. The killer probably knew right where she lived. Could look her up in the phone book after he saw her on TV. Home was just a trap now, violated like the rest of the sanctuaries. Being there, she was nothing but a decoy.

And then she realized that must be exactly what Lieutenant Jardine had in mind.

Chapter 19

Our Father who art in heaven, Theresa thought, her silent prayer drifting toward the ceiling like a helium balloon, *deliver us from evil.* She sat at the kitchen table, unconsciously snapping the rubber band that held a deck of old playing cards together. The sky seemed to press down on the house. A dark wind blew the curtains in. Voices hummed faintly in her like Muzak in a discount store. They were tuning up for something. Her longing for prayer fell flat. She no longer believed in deliverance. The future was moving toward her, slowly surrounding her, and she was locked in by it as surely as that inner voice, captive, pleading, that haunted her with its cry.

Nervously, she shuffled the cards, flattening them onto the table in vertical rows. A little game of solitaire to calm her down as she waited for Jardine's call to go downtown. She had promised him two more days. Read those knives. Look at books of lineup shots: frontal, profile. Study them for that blank-eyed hole. But Jardine would have to come clean with her. She wasn't going to do a damn thing more for him if he was planning on using her as some sort of decoy for this pervert to home in on. Not with the spaced-out protection he'd assigned to her.

No, she would not agree to that at all. Two more days to help him and solid protection—that was their agreement. Then she'd have fulfilled her obligation to him and to herself as well. She could leave for New Mexico with a clear mind, having come through all this strengthened.

Everything was nearly ready to go for the trip. She'd called Josh over at the garage and he'd said she could bring her car in this afternoon. Tomorrow she'd finish packing, load up the tent, the knapsack. Out of this nightmare. The cards lined up in sequence, seven, eight, ten. She needed a nine. She needed a jack. She needed a drink and it wasn't even noon yet. She needed to quiet this tangle of voices, this vortex sucking her down into its black pool.

The air around the house was clammy, the trees hushed. Leaf sounds rustled, blending with the breathy voices that steamed in the back of her skull. Then she felt the sound rise up her throat and she spoke the words aloud in a voice that was not her own, "Let me out of here."

"Who are you?" she cried out. Covering her face with her hands, she put her head down on the table, opened her eyes in the shadows of her hands, and stared into her palms at the green surface of the earth, lawn-covered, flower-covered, wreath-covered. Rose-covered. She read the words *Rose, Rosemount*. Along the fingers of her hands floated images of tombstones, tiny white crosses, gray stones with names carved into them.

"Are you a spirit?" she whispered. No answer. Hissing voices boiled inside her. "Where are you?"

"Inside you," said the voice clearly.

"Then are you a part of me? Are you mine?" Theresa cried.

"I'm in you and I can't get out."

Then she screamed, "Well, then, damn you! No one is keeping you here. Get out of my mind, crazy goddamn dead woman! Leave me alone!" She was shaking. *Mad, I am. I am losing it all over, all over again.* And she thought of the bars on the front door of the sanctuary, bars on the windows of the clinic, the invisible bars of her marriage to Michael that still somehow kept her prisoner, and again she shouted, "Yes, let me out! Yes, it is dark in here. It is! And, yes, I can't get myself out of here, you're right." She sobbed into her hands, chest pushing out strange animal cries of despair.

Then she saw them, out of the ground they rose, pink smoke from the graves, blue and pale green puffs of fog with lights inside them, pulsing. They seemed peaceful, at rest, without bodies. Released.

Were the visions, then, merely a metaphor for her own unhappiness? But if that was true, what about the actual dead, Carolyn and Bonnie, Grace and the man, that poor old man laid out in the church in his black suit?

Theresa shoved the chair back from the table and moved across the floor in her bent-leg floating walk, pulling the flowered sheet aside, knocking open the sunroom door. Where had she locked all the decks of cards? There—the cedar box in the bottom drawer of the dresser. She yanked the drawer open, lifting out the small wooden box. As she hurried back to the kitchen, the image of the card hovered, a hologram, a slide picture projected in air before her. She unlocked the box, unwound the silk cloth from the cards.

Theresa shuffled the deck as if her hands were someone else's and she were only watching. Hands trembling, she cut the deck open to the card marked Judgment. There, an archangel played a giant horn. Out of the waters below rose gray coffins, blue-black bodies standing naked inside of them, hands uplifted to the trumpeting angel above. "Please," cried the voice inside her, and Theresa knew it was more than just a symbol of her own cramped and cringing self. She knew there was a real person, imprisoned in an actual place, down under cold ground, long dead and calling out to her over and over again, *"Please help me. Let me out."*

Theresa waited in the hall outside Jardine's office. She dreaded having to tell him there was another body to be found and she didn't want to tell him where it would be discovered. Her mind hummed, gray static. She was numb and exhausted.

As the lieutenant pushed his office door open, Cooper and several other men hurried past her, lighting up cigarettes as they exited.

"Come in," said Jardine, his hand fluttering toward a metal chair piled with newspapers. "Just put those on the floor. Now, where did I put that . . . here it is." He held up a black cassette tape. "We tape every call that comes in about a case this public. Most of them are phony. The news has been carrying these killings as shootings. This guy knew that was a front. Even mentioned the church, the sanctuary. He's our boy. Listen—I'm sure it's the same voice you got on your machine. We're working on getting a voiceprint now to make sure it matches."

"I've got to tell someone before my brain explodes," the tape began. "It's getting so loud in my skull, this churning like awful music. The part of me that does this, see—it's the bad part—"

Theresa nodded, recognizing the voice's uncanny familiarity, its begging and angry tone. She thought she'd heard it before, not only on her answering machine. She shuddered as she listened to the rest of the tape, the confusion and desperation in the words, the violent energy dammed up in them.

"But I never really meant to harm anyone, see? It's just that they go in my head and start screaming and watching and somebody has got to stop me because I know for all my thinking about it that it's just not right. After all, I'm not God. Am I?"

Where had she heard that voice before? The tape blanked to a hushed buzz of air. Jardine pressed the stop button, flipped back a page on a clipboard, and perched on the corner of his desk. His shirttail had come out of his gray slacks and he looked as if he'd been sleeping in his clothes for days. "The psychiatrist has gone over this a number of times and he feels the guy's extremely paranoid, possibly exhibits signs of schizophrenia. All this business of another person watching him or even inside of him. Might be he's psychotic, maybe some sort of split personality. You can't tell. Is the 'He' a religious 'He,' like God or Christ watching him? Anyway, he thinks he's two people."

Theresa nodded, feeling instinctively that this was true. "Last night I dreamt of a coin. Flip sides of a coin."

"And?"

She hated to bring it up, but she had to. "My neighbor was in the dream. Arthur Holton. I mean Neal."

"We spoke to him this morning."

"You did?"

"We've been trying to check on everybody close to you, Theresa."

"You really think it's someone I know?" she nearly whispered.

"We can't overlook anybody."

Arthur. Neal. She wished that she could hate him for using her like that. *Are you going to forgive me?*

"Did he tell you who he really was?" she asked.

"We checked him out. He's a freelance writer. You know he's on assignment to do a piece on you."

"He told me," Theresa said. "I knew he wasn't for real."

"How do you feel about that? Do you mind?"

"It's the least of my worries right now, Lieutenant."

Theresa stood peering through the Venetian blinds at the endless city below, the choked traffic. In the dust on a slat of the blind she scribbled *Neal,* then rubbed it out with the heel of her hand. Next to the smudge, she drew a circle with a cross inside it and a moon, then pressed a small *X* over the insignia.

"Lieutenant, I've got to ask you this right out—are you trying to draw this man to me? I mean, am I some sort of trap for him?"

Jardine tilted the last of a Diet Coke to his lips, then set the can on his cluttered desk. "He said on the tape, 'I know you've got her after me,' right? 'Seen it on the television.' His victims have all been involved in the occult, except this last one. I can't ignore the possibility that the killer may seek you out, Theresa."

"You mean probability, don't you?" she snapped. "It seems to me that you're making it possible. I told you I didn't want my name and where I live all over the news. It's like you're setting me up for him. What am I, his next target?"

"It's very difficult to control the media once they're onto a story. I did instruct them to withhold your name from their reports but I can't make them do it." Jardine paused. "And I hope to God you are not his next target but I want to make damn sure that if he comes anywhere near you, we know about it."

"Oh, sure!" she said. "While your great undercover agents just dash over to McDonald's for a little snack, he could be knocking on my front door! He could be hiding under my bed for how closely they're watching me!"

Theresa went on to explain how she'd seen the two men follow her at the beach, then seemingly abandon her, returning later to her house.

"It's not a good idea to try to monitor our surveillance techniques," Jardine admonished. "I've got at least two rotating teams watching you and your house, twenty-four hours a day. Believe me! You're covered. If they went and got something to eat, they had probably radioed somebody first to pick up your cover. Were you walking?"

She said yes.

"There you have it. One of them must have gotten out to trail you on foot."

"I do not want to be a trap, Lieutenant," Theresa reiterated, pressing her palms down on the windowsill, her back to him.

The lieutenant came over to where she leaned looking out at the gray skyline. "I'm just trying to make sure you're well taken care of, Theresa. I'm not going to let anything happen to you, all right?"

She glanced over at his face, reddened and tired, stray hairs frizzed over his receding hairline.

"What about the knives?" he asked. "Could you read one of them? Could you give it a try?"

She blew out a long sigh, nodding. Jardine opened a desk drawer behind him, lifting out a plastic bag, tagged and marked. Gingerly, he opened it, took out the common black jackknife, and extended it to her, saying, "It's already been dusted for prints."

Theresa grasped it between her two open palms, rolling it slowly like a stick, closing her eyes, trying to relax. *Open mind: let it come.* Her arms felt very heavy holding it. With her thumbnail she clicked open the blade, hefting its weight like a small stone.

The image leapt into her mind—but it didn't seem to have anything to do with the murders. Not at all. It was the road up to Malibu, car swinging smoothly along the Pacific Coast Highway. Hot inside the car. Stuffy. Hard to breathe. Clouds purple and orange at the edge of the mountains, nearly sunset. Always sunset. *See it,* she told herself. *Go deeper.* Sky gone swirling crimson now, red clouds boiling. Nearing Elizabeth's. She pressed one hand over the knife in her palm and whispered out loud, "I'm riding with you up to Malibu. I see—the lights are on, the red lights on top of your car. They're flashing but there is no siren. I see the red lights whirling over the road. I can't exactly—I think it's you driving—we're following someone very quickly. It's so hot in here. I'm trying to open the window but it's locked, it's—"

Suddenly, the vague vision jolted open, swallowing her. She reeled, dizzily, screaming, "Let me out! Let me out of here!" smashing at the car window with her hand, the glass blasting into shards, her fist clamped around the butt of the gun, the shot exploding. The force of the sound jammed into her ears.

Theresa felt Jardine gripping her arm hard. She was bent over, kneeling on the floor of Jardine's office. He pried her grip loose from the jackknife.

"What was it? Did you see him?" Jardine asked.

Theresa shook her head, whispering, "All I could see was the car."

"What make? What color?"

"I don't know. I was in it. Brown, I think. At least on the inside. Lieutenant, it didn't make any sense. There was a gun."

"Where? Who had it? Concentrate!"

243

"I don't know!" she cried. "I had it. I was using it to smash the window. I couldn't get out."

She rose up on her knees and Jardine helped her to her feet, guided her to the chair.

"It's no use," she said. "I can't see him. I think I'm afraid to see him. I won't open to it." She shook her head again. "It's always where I go in my dreams, up the highway, up the coast."

Jardine sat down at his desk and scribbled hurriedly in his notebook while she tried to think it through. There was nothing concrete, no face. Only fear. The sensation of being trapped: that was all. Of trying to escape and feeling closed in. Not a true vision at all, just exactly how she felt.

Finally Jardine looked up at Theresa from his notebook.

"I'm sorry," she said solemnly. "Sometimes it's not clear."

"When it has to do with you," he added.

"Yes," she said, and involuntarily shuddered once, a sudden spasm through her back and neck.

"Now, what about this other card?" Jardine demanded. "The message Cooper gave me said you were bringing another card down."

Theresa dug in her purse, pulled the card of Judgment out, and tossed it onto Jardine's cluttered desk. The Lieutenant picked it up, lit a cigarette.

"Okay," he sighed. "Fill me in."

He held the card out, studying it at arm's length. "It's Judgment, right? Biblical symbolism, Judgment Day. Is our boy a Jesus freak? Fallen priest? Maniac disguised as a nun?"

"We've got to drive," she said. "I've got to take you somewhere."

Jardine tucked his shirt in, tossed the pop can across the room into the wastebasket, where it clanked against the metal rim. "Basket," he said under his breath. "Let's hit it."

*   *   *

The cemetery wasn't far from downtown and Theresa gave the Lieutenant directions. They exited off the freeway and paused at an intersection where an old Hispanic woman stood selling apples and grapes out of a shopping cart.

"How's everything going for your trip?" Jardine asked. "Colorado, wasn't it?"

Theresa nodded. "Everything's just about ready. I'm taking my car in to get fixed this afternoon." As they neared the cemetery, she said, "I've got a distinct feeling of two bodies. I know there is more than one. It's like a double exposure on a camera."

A high brick wall surrounded Rosemount Cemetery and old palms stood at either side of the front gate. At the top of a flagpole a tattered American flat hung limp.

"Here," she said, feeling the presence near to her as if only the thinnest of walls separated her from the world inhabited by the foggy spirits whose physical bodies were entombed in this place. Jardine pulled the car into the driveway and stopped.

Sprinklers spurted across the dry grass. A black family stood in a semicircle near the brick wall, hands clasped behind their backs. Many of the small graves were marked with Oriental figures.

Jardine turned to Theresa. "You're really bringing me to a cemetery to find a dead body?"

"But it's here," she insisted. "The voice is here."

"There have got to be hundreds of bodies here," he said quietly. "What do you want me to do, go around digging up graves?"

Theresa's head ached as if the inward pressure of a vacuum were pushing against her skull, the silence so intense she wanted to scream. She knew she was close to the source of the voice that called to her. She wanted to leap from the car, run wildly over the graves to find just where, just where she lay, but Jardine was right. It was stupid to have brought him here. It was ridiculous. Her mind was spinning out wild images, pink fog rising from graves, shattered glass, water burning. She didn't know anymore what to trust.

Opening the car door, Theresa slid out and walked past a woman in a lilac hat who stood beside a grave. She wound through the maze of headstones and black iron markers set into the grass. It was quiet here among the dead. Several rows farther on she halted and backed up, two steps, three. No voice called out, no vision burned through her mind. There was only silence so still and so empty that she didn't want to leave. The headstone before her was a small concrete angel, the tip of one wing had been chipped off. Inscribed in the stone were the words LEWIS LAUBER, LOVING HUSBAND, DEVOTED FATHER. "Hello?" she whispered. "Is anybody there?"

Damp wind lifted the leathery fronds of the palms above her. Michael had been here, she was sure of it. He'd probably been here a lot. "Are you here?" she said aloud.

"Over here." She was startled by Jardine's voice behind her. "What?" he asked. "What's up?"

"I'm not sure." Theresa stared down the road at a group of workers spread out on the lawn surrounded by rakes and shovels, leaning back on headstones. One man rested his feet on a rusty lawnmower.

"Have you talked to my ex-husband, Michael Ballard?"

"No. Should I have?"

"I thought, you were looking into everyone I know. Besides," she added, "I had dinner with him last Thursday. Didn't your undercover detectives report that back to you?"

Jardine pulled out his notebook and spat on the grass beside him. "The detectives were not instructed to check into the background of every person you had contact with. I'm sure a dinner date didn't appear suspicious to them. I wish you had mentioned this before."

"I didn't mention it before because—I guess I didn't know what to mention. What was significant and what was just my own"—she hesitated, then added, "my own craziness. But I've been having bad dreams about Michael ever since all this began, ever since my very first contact with the Humphreys. Anytime there's a death, I dream of him.''

"He's a mortician. Could it be he's on your mind now simply because of all these deaths?'' He waved his arm over the rows of graves.

The woman in the lilac hat slowly turned from the grave where she'd been standing and proceeded to a gray limousine.

"That's what I kept thinking, too, but it's more than just that. He came around a couple of days ago hyped up asking questions about Bonnie.''

"What questions?''

"Where she was from. Was she from San Diego? Did he know her? Stuff like that.''

"And when was this?''

"Sunday.''

Jardine sighed loudly, shook his head.

"I'm sorry,'' Theresa said. "I wasn't sure what to tell you—what was pertinent to the case and what was just my personal life. At the time it just seemed like another weird conversation with Michael. He seemed really upset. Angry. I wouldn't listen to him, I threw him out.''

"Come on,'' Jardine said, turning back toward the car. But Theresa found it nearly impossible to walk away from where she stood over Lewis Lauber, Loving Husband. She touched the broken wing of the angel and caressed the carved hair. Dipping her finger into a small pool of water that had gathered in the folds of the angel's sleeve, she touched her forehead and crossed herself.

Chapter 20

Michael Ballard stood at the back of chapel number three, checking to make sure things were in order for the funeral service that was about to begin. The coffin had been closed, a blanket of carnations covered the polished mahogany and gleaming brass fixtures. Huge floral sculptures of gladiolas and mums stood at either end of the coffin in the shape of hearts and crosses. A man helped a bent elderly woman with blue hair to her seat in the front row, patting her mink stole securely into place on her shoulder. As Ballard nodded to the organist, vague hymnal chords eased from speakers hidden in the brocade walls.

His secretary tapped him on the arm. "Mr. Ballard? A Lieutenant Jardine is here to see you from the police department." She handed him a white calling card that read, in capital letters at the bottom, HOMICIDE BUREAU.

His heart lurched in his chest and he coughed. "Tell him I'll be right there." Calm down, he told himself. It could be nothing, it could be about motorcades to the cemetery, it could be about the annual benefit baseball game. Maybe it was about the man he'd buried last week who'd drowned in his backyard pool, but he knew it was not. There was no question—it was about Terry.

The detective was balding but not old. Wearing a rumpled blue suit, he slouched on a chair in the reception room paging through a folder on the advantages of prepaid funerals. He stubbed out a cigarette in a standing ashtray. "Michael Ballard?" Lieutenant Jardine extended one hand, with the other, he flipped open a wallet displaying his badge, a long-practiced gesture. "Detective, LAPD, Homicide," he said. "May I have a few minutes of your time?"

"Come on in my office." Ballard shoved the heavy door open across the thick beige carpet. "Hold my calls," he told the secretary.

Lowering himself into a leather chair, Ballard motioned for the lieutenant to sit in the chair next to the desk.

"What can I do for you, Lieutenant?"

"I'll get right to the point, Mr. Ballard. You're aware that your ex-wife, Theresa Fortunato, is working with us as a psychic. We're investigating a series of homicides, seemingly committed by the same person. All the murders have strange cultlike overtones, involving occult symbolism in one way or another."

"I am aware of it, yes. We had dinner last week and she was talking about working with the police. She didn't mention any occult overtones, though."

"You also spoke with her last Sunday, I believe."

"Yes, I did. I went over to take her out for breakfast. We get together a few times a year." Just what had Terry told this cop? He lit a cigarette, hoping the nicotine would calm the hot thumping in his chest.

"You've been divorced five years, is that correct?" Jardine looked up from a small notebook.

Ballard knew this kind of fucker. Wanted to get you talking just to see what you'd screw up on. A red light went on in his mind: *Slow down, slow and easy. Say as little as possible until you knew what this cop wanted.* He nodded. "That's correct. Five years."

"And how would you describe your relationship with Theresa at this time?"

Ballard grinned. "Adequate. You married or divorced, Lieutenant?"

"Neither," Jardine answered.

"Terry and I get along pretty good considering. I mean we see each other now and then, we talk about things. We're friendly. We don't hassle over money or anything, we don't have kids to fight over."

"She told me, though, that you'd had a disagreement on Sunday." The lieutenant looked at his notebook again. "That you were upset and angry with her. Why was that?"

"Sunday," Ballard said. "Yeah." He grinned again, then stood, flicking ashes into the empty wastebasket. *Don't ingratiate yourself, don't smile. Straight arrow. Play the game.* Then he thought, *What is the game?*

"Well, we've got our old patterns like everybody else. If we got along that great, I guess we wouldn't be divorced, you know? I went over there Sunday because I wanted to spend some time with her, and basically, she didn't want to see me. I guess I got a little pissed off."

"She said you questioned her about one of the murders, Mr. Ballard. The victim's name was Bonnie Humphrey. Theresa said you thought you knew her."

"But I was wrong!" *Too quick, buddy, too loud. Ease up.* "Yeah," he continued. "See, when Terry and I had dinner last week she got to talking about that girl and I thought I knew her. I thought maybe it was a girl I dated years ago. She just sounded familiar. But it wasn't her."

"What about her sounded familiar?"

"Her name, that's all. Her name was Bonnie."

"There have got to be a lot of Bonnies in the world, Mr. Ballard. What made you think this girl was someone you'd known?"

How much to say? "I don't know. It was the way Terry described her or something." Okay, yeah, thought Ballard, you know I'm lying, goddamn it. He wanted to throw the cop out. There was only one way out and he was good at it: fake authenticity. In other words, lie. "Look," he said, sitting back down, "here's what happened. Terry and I don't always communicate so well, okay? I dated this broad Bonnie back when Terry and I were separated, see? I hadn't heard from her in years. When I tried looking her up, it was like she'd disappeared. None of her old friends knew where she was. Suddenly Terry finds some dead girl named Bonnie and she has a dream I knew her or something. So I wanted to see if it was this girl I'd gone out with, okay? But it wasn't. The Bonnie I knew wasn't from Berkeley, she was from San Diego and she'd have been in her thirties.''

''What was her last name?''

''Reslow,'' Ballard lied. ''Bonnie Reslow.''

''Anything else?'' Jardine asked.

''No,'' said Ballard. ''Look, I don't really know anything about these cases Terry's working on. She wasn't a real psychic when we were married. I never liked all that messing with the occult and, frankly, we still end up arguing about it. In my opinion it's a crock of shit, no offense.''

''You don't consider Theresa a legitimate psychic, Mr. Ballard?''

Ballard hesitated, swallowing. What was he getting at? ''Well, she's definitely intuitive. She's a sensitive person. She always used these cards, told people's fortunes at parties. It was a party trick, you know? We were all into *I Ching* coins and the stars in those days. Age of Aquarius, remember? I don't know, Lieutenant. What can I say? It's not my religion. Terry's very perceptive around people, but psychic? I mean, you just can't prove it.''

''So she was not a practicing psychic when you were with her.''

''No. It was like a hobby. But she got carried away, you know? I guess that's why it didn't work out between us. You know those people who go follow some guru or go berserk over Jesus—not that I'm anti-Christian or anything— well, that was Terry. It wasn't good for the marriage. She just went nuts.''

''Nuts,'' said the lieutenant.

''Out of control. *Crazy*,'' emphasized Ballard. The conversation was back on track now. Off him, onto Terry. Ballard relaxed, leaned back into the chair. If he gave a lot of information about Terry, he'd appear open and honest. ''To tell you the truth, Lieutenant, she got so carried away, I had her committed to a psychiatric clinic.''

Jardine straightened himself in his chair. Ah, thought Ballard. So he hadn't dug up that juicy little tidbit yet, had he? "When was this?" asked Jardine.

"Let's see, it would have been about six years ago. She'd been acting really odd. Hallucinating voices. Seeing things. Couldn't sleep. She was like a tight wire. Finally she snapped, she got really violent. I decided she needed help so I got her the best care I could. I put her in a private clinic. Hillview."

Jardine was jotting it all down in his notebook. Ballard went on. "She was under the care of a Dr. White over there. Dr. Barbara White. They sedated her, that stopped the hallucinations. After she got out she continued in therapy on an outpatient basis but we never did get the marriage back together."

"This is very interesting, Mr. Ballard. Was there a diagnosis made at that time? What was it, depression or something?"

Ballard picked up a fountain pen, snapping the cover on and off. He cleared his throat. "I don't know if she was clinically diagnosed as schizophrenic, but I tell you it was just like living with two people. Psychotic, manic, something like that. She'd flip in and out. She'd be a normal, everyday person, then without warning, she'd be into this psychic crap, all distraught, sick with migraines, fainting. I couldn't take it. She couldn't take it."

The lieutenant seemed excited as if he'd come on some great new clue in his investigation and something was fitting into place for him. Ballard could tell what he was saying was discrediting Terry. If this cop had any doubts about her, Ballard was confirming them now. Good. The main thing was to keep the focus off him, onto her.

He continued. "So she never mentioned anything to you about her mental illness? I guess she always did want to hide that part of her life. See, sometimes she'd have these intuitions about things or people that were right on. It would blow you away. And then she'd be off on a tangent, start acting hysterical, come up with totally off-the-wall stuff. She'd be like a different person."

Lieutenant Jardine pocketed his notebook and stood. "Just a few more questions," he said. "You ever conduct services out at Immaculate Heart of Mary?"

"Once in a while. Pierson Brothers does a lot of the Catholic funerals over there."

"How about Rosemount Cemetery? Have many burials out there?"

Ballard was glad he was still sitting when the lieutenant spoke so that he didn't fall down. He swiveled the chair to the right and stood slowly, sliding some papers around on his desk and looking at his watch in an obvious way. "Rosemount? We do work out there from time to time, yes. Why do you ask?"

"It came up in the investigation, that's all. Nothing important yet. Well, I thank you for your time, Mr. Ballard. You've been most helpful."

"Anytime."

"I'm sure we'll be talking again."

Ballard pushed the door shut with a quiet click. He didn't like the sound of Jardine's closing statement. Christ— *Rosemount*. What in God's name had she told him? A wave of nausea passed through him. Now she really had to be stopped. He couldn't just stand back while she led Jardine to a grave in Rosemount Cemetery where a dead woman lay next to a dead man under the perfectly green lawn and the innocent sky.

He stood at the window surveying the line of limousines behind the gray hearse shining in the brilliant sunlight. Too nice a day for a funeral. How could anyone die in southern California? He watched the line of cars ready to pull out onto the street with their headlights on, then took a bottle of Scotch in a paper bag from his bottom drawer and a briefcase he kept hidden in his closet, quickly checking its contents. Notifying his secretary that he'd be taking the rest of the afternoon off, he drove one of the funeral-home cars from the garage, joining the caravan to the cemetery, in a black Fleetwood, leaving his own car sitting in the front on the street. *Fuck you, Lieutenant,* he thought, sure now that the cop would have him watched. After a few miles in the slow procession he pulled out and drove around for a while, going nowhere in particular. When he was certain he was not being followed, he pulled in beside a drive-up telephone outside a shopping center and dialed Lowell's number.

"Just a minute, Mr. Ballard," answered a woman's voice. "He's out back by the pool." Ballard jerked down the sun visor. With the window rolled down the near one-hundred-degree heat seemed almost to roll into the air-conditioned car.

"Qué pasa?" Lowell's voice snapped on from what Ballard assumed was a cordless poolside phone.

"She knows. Terry knows where it is. Cops came around asking all kinds of questions. She told them I was asking about the murders. I knew talking to her about this was a mistake, Lowell. She told them something about Rosemount Cemetery, I don't know exactly what."

"First of all, please confine your comments to a more general terminology. Second, if what you say is true, she's going to have to be silenced. *Silenciada.*"

"Cut with the fucking Spanish, Lowell."

"Ella no hablará más," said Lowell. *"Ella desaparecerá. Comprende?* She will disappear. Just like the other one disappeared. Is that clear?"

"No. I'm not doing it again. It was a mistake the first time."

"If you won't take care of it, I'll get somebody else to do it."

"There's got to be some other way!" Ballard lit the cigarette he'd jammed into the corner of his dry mouth. "Look, I'm going to talk to her one more time! I'll see what I can do. I'm not covering up any more of your goddamn murders, man."

"Don't ever speak like this with me on the phone again, Ballard, or your file is terminated." Lowell hung up.

Ballard slammed the phone down in its metal cradle and it bounced out, dangling, swinging on its silver cord.

It was all converging—clues, leads, information, past, present and future all funneling together into a tight spiral of lies with himself at the center. He hadn't killed her! He hadn't! He'd tell them the truth, that was what he'd do. Lowell had blackmailed him, threatened to have him killed if he told the truth. He'd see if he could plea-bargain for immunity. They could catch Lowell and probably the whole southern California syndicate if they'd just listen to him. He'd set Lowell up, that's what he'd do. Ballard could hardly hold the cigarette and he smashed it out in the clean ashtray.

Your file is terminated. . . . Lowell would do it too. There was very little time. Lowell would not wait. He hadn't waited to kill Bonnie. It must have been Lowell who'd killed her. And it was totally stupid to think he could set Lowell up. All of it, funeral-home files, bank accounts, it all pointed only back to himself. And even if somehow Lowell could be set up, even if Lowell stood trial, went to prison, he'd have Ballard killed. And it would be clean, so clean. Car off a road on a wet night. Fall from a boat and drown—he knew Lowell's people would make him pay.

And they'd make Terry pay, too, because she was the one who was going to spill it all. He had to do something, had to stop her from telling Jardine any more.

Ballard dropped a coin into the pay phone and was relieved that she answered in person.

"It's Michael, Terry. I've got to talk to you."

"Michael, please," she pleaded. "Stay away from me. *I cannot see you*." She pronounced every word as if she were spelling it out.

"Terry, you've got to. I'm serious. It's life or death."

"I know, Michael. That's exactly why I can't see you."

"It's about the police!" he shouted into the phone, but she had already hung up.

*   *   *

Afternoon traffic was already heavy and he cursed the standstill maze of cars on the freeway. Snapping the radio on, he jammed the buttons down searching for quiet music to calm him. It was necessary that he make some kind of sense when he saw her, not babble, not shout. How could he get her to stop thinking about Rosemount Cemetery, keep her imagination from veering toward the truth? She just had to be stopped, or he'd be found out. Cars snaked forward and he pushed down the accelerator, roaring down the exit ramp toward Venice. The air always felt cooler over by the ocean. A clean wind off the water blew through the midday dust and smog.

He parked half a block down from Jasmine Court and sat in the car smoking a cigarette. Looking up, he saw a car stop in the street beside a van that was parked outside the entrance to her courtyard. The driver slid across the front seat, rolled down the window, and handed a white sack toward the van window. A hand poked out, grabbing the sack, and the car pulled quickly away.

Of course, he thought, sinking down into the plush gray seat. They were watching her house. Fucking undercover cops were always so obvious on a stakeout in their Fair-monts and their tinted-window vans. He'd never be able to get to her front door without being seen, and even if he could, she'd never let him in anyway, he knew that. He'd have to go around to the street in back of her house, cut through to Jasmine Court, and get in somehow. She'd have to listen. He'd make her.

He backed the Fleetwood out of the parking space and drove past the brown van. Glancing in the rearview mirror, he saw that the van appeared empty, which confirmed his feeling that the car's inhabitants were trying to conceal themselves. Stupid pigs! He took a right, then another, parking on the street behind Theresa's. After waiting several minutes to make sure the van had not followed him around the corner, he got out and made his way through the yards.

The alley behind her house stopped in a dead end of

tangled vines before it got to Jasmine Court. He jumped the neighbor's fence, crouching under a huge flowering bougainvillea. If he sneaked low along the bushes, he could scale that eucalyptus, drop down over the high fence in back of her house. He was glad she didn't own a dog.

He peered quickly out from under the leaves, bolted to the tree, shinnied up, and flung himself down into her yard. Squatting low, he glanced around. No one. Midafternoon. Everyone at work or at the beach. Good thing he was still wearing his suit; at least he didn't look like some junkie daylight burglar. Brushing off his pants, he hurried across the small yard, up the steps to her back door, quietly pulled open the screen, and tried the knob on the inside door. Locked. Damn—no time, no time. He slipped off his suit coat, pressed it against a small square of glass in the door, and beat it once hard with his fist. Glass shattered to the kitchen floor.

Ballard reached in, twisted the inside knob, and nearly fell in the door as it swung open. When he pulled his hand out, his wrist dragged over the broken glass. It sliced into his skin.

Theresa ran into the kitchen, her face gray-white. When she saw him, she let out a short startled scream and he threw himself across the room, diving on top of her, knocking her hard against the wall. Pushing her down to the floor, he jammed his suit coat against her mouth and held her there, his whole body pressing down on her until she lay still, eyes wide with animal fear. His wrist was bleeding badly, it was staining his suit coat, smearing the side of her face as she lay, not moving, beneath him.

Chapter 21

"Don't scream." Michael's mouth was very close to hers, cigarette smell of his breath in her face, men's cologne and alcohol, his eyes blue slits, metallic and cold. "It's not what you think. I'm going to take my hand off your mouth but if you scream, I swear I'll—I'll have to stop you. Okay? Okay? Say Okay."

Theresa tried to nod. Tentatively, he lifted his hand from her mouth. She gasped for air. How in the hell had he gotten around back? If she screamed loudly enough, would the men in the van hear? Michael: she'd known he was in on all this. The room almost smelled of fear, acrid smoke scent, smoldering. Everything moved slowly, dream-speed. "Please don't hurt me," she begged.

"I'm not going to hurt you."

"You are hurting me."

"I've got to talk to you. Will you just listen to me for once?" He continued to sprawl on top of her, pinning her down with his weight, hand poised over her face.

She saw that he'd cut his arm on the broken glass, his wrist an open wound. There was blood on his cuff, his white shirt, just like years ago in the funeral home basement when he'd come at her, kicked her back against the wall. It always came to this, always would—the vision Elizabeth had told her to ignore, mistrust.

"Terry, the police came to me, this Lieutenant Jardine. What did you tell him about me?"

"That you've been harassing me."

"I haven't been harassing you!"

"What do you call this? Let me up!"

"Shut up!" he hissed.

If she could get to the door, out to the courtyard. "This is breaking and entering, Michael. Assault. I swear I'm going to have you arrested for this, I'm going to call the cops, I'm going to—"

As he pressed his hand down, her teeth cut into the sides of her mouth. The sour blood taste leaked over her tongue. "You're not calling anybody, understand? You think the fucking police can help you? They're sitting out in front of your street like a sore thumb, most obvious fucking surveillance I've ever seen in my entire life. An idiot could get around those cops, so don't expect any help from them. Look. All I want to do is talk to you. You never listen to me, never fucking once have you listened to me!"

Slowly he rose off her and she sat up, rubbing the back of her head, wiping her mouth with her hand. "I think I bit my lip." She winced. Pointing across the room, she said, "Give me that towel by the sink."

He turned to reach for the towel, then spun quickly back around. "Stay there!" he said, holding the towel to his own bleeding wrist. "Just stay put. What did you tell this cop?"

"That you've been in my dreams, my visions. That you came around asking me about that dead girl."

"You think I have something to do with these murders? You're crazy!"

"No, I'm not, Michael. Four people have been killed and I know you're connected, I just don't know how."

"What did you tell him about Rosemount?"

"You really want to know, Michael? I took him there. I had a psychic feeling there was a body there. I stood right over an old grave of someone named Lewis Lauber and I knew there was someone else down there, someone who'd been murdered. There were two bodies. Of course Jardine thought I was stupid taking him to a cemetery to find a dead body. But I could hear this voice. It's locked in down there and I've heard it for years. When I was at the cemetery, I knew that's where the voice was coming from and I knew it had something to do with you. Jardine said

259

of course it has to do with you. You're a mortician. You hang around dead bodies all day. I haven't figured it out yet, Michael, but I will. You can goddamn bet I will.''

A small line of blood ran from her lip to her chin.

"Terry, listen to me. You're in danger. I can't explain, but you've got to get out of L.A."

"Tell me about it." She licked her lip. "The least you could do is give me a Kleenex," she sniffed. "On top of the fridge."

As he turned to reach for the Kleenex, she sprang forward, wheeling around the corner into the front room and yanking at the chain lock on the door. Her fingers fumbled with the chain. Helplessly, she pulled at the locked doorknob and it bled into her mind like spilled liquid, the vision: inside a car, reaching to open the door, fists slamming at the window, because—why? No handle, no knob. Look up. Orange sea to the west, burning sky of sunset, Michael coming toward her, gun raised—

She spun around as Michael came up behind her. "Don't touch me!" she cried, pressing back against the locked front door. Her eyes widened and she gasped. Covering her mouth, she looked past him, horrified, toward the kitchen door. "Oh, my God!" she shouted, pointing.

As he glanced back over his shoulder at the empty doorway, she raced past him back to the kitchen. He rushed after her. She had the phone in her hand, she was dialing. He grabbed it from her, ripped the cord and jack out of the wall. She cowered back from him, slid down to a crouch against the wall. "Trust me," he rasped hoarsely. "For God's sake, I'm trying to help you."

Help me, Jesus—he was mad. Out of his mind. Her eyes moved about the room looking for a way to escape. He pushed her down to a sitting position and shoved her feet together, binding the phone cord around and around her ankles.

When she started to scream again, he slapped her backhand across the face.

"Shut up! If you scream, so help me, I'll, I'll . . ." He

260

bent over her, hand raised to hit her again. She cringed back against the wall. Double vision: the present—this slow black moment of him threatening above her. The second scene superimposed—through a broken car window, gun in his hand, held up, shot blasting.

Theresa fell back, waiting for the blow the way she had as a kid. *Her father. Get it over with. Belt, strap, ironing cord. Close eyes and endure.* Michael slowly lowered his hand, covered with blood, his face stunned and pale. Stood there staring down at her.

Easing down on to the floor next to her, he wiped at his wrist with the palm of his other hand, then reached into his shirt pocket, pulled out a bent cigarette, lit it. Inhaling deeply, and without looking at her, he began to speak.

"Rosemount Cemetery. There's a girl buried there. Her name is Bonnie. She was killed six years ago in a drug deal. Terry, I didn't kill her, I swear. But I buried her for the person who did." He couldn't bring himself to look at her. "Yeah, it was one of those Miami deals. You picked up on it way back then. All of it—the voices you heard, somebody crying, 'Let me out, I don't have what you want.' And that card, the thief. I hated that occult crap, I hated you being psychic. It scared the shit out of me, and then that girl was murdered and you knew about it. I just couldn't have that, so I put you in the clinic. I wanted you to be the girl I married, the girl I loved. Not some crazy psychic."

He stopped, lit one cigarette off another, continued. "But I'm telling you, I didn't kill that girl. I just got rid of her. I know it was wrong. Okay. That was a mistake. Right there. So now, after all this time, you start finding bodies for the cops and the girl's name is Bonnie and somehow it brings it all back up, your psychic memory of what I did. But I swear on every Bible in the world these deaths are not connected except in your mind. I don't have anything to do with these murders, you hear me?"

Holding the cigarette in his lips, he reached over, unwinding the cord from her ankles, rubbing her legs where the cord had dug deep red lines. She said nothing, just pulled away from his touch, raising her knees up to her chest, taking in the words that confirmed all she'd ever thought was true.

He went on. "I've always been afraid you'd eventually figure it out, and you did. You went to Rosemount. Jesus, you stood right on top of her grave. Terry, she's buried in that guy's coffin, Lauber. I buried them in there together." He spoke with the relief of a man confessing. "I just can't handle it anymore. I've hidden it too long and I can't hold it in. I'm putting myself at your mercy. I'm begging you not to tell the cops about that body, Terry. You've got to realize that they're two completely separate things. It's over, it's all past. You've got to believe me. *I'm not this killer.*"

His voice broke and he nearly sobbed. He put his head in his hands.

"You mean I was right all that time?" she whispered. "You've been lying all these years, you convinced me I was mentally ill, you had me committed, you ruined our marriage, because of a drug deal?"

Ballard couldn't speak. He was trembling.

"What am I supposed to do with this, Michael? Why should I even believe you?"

"You know I'm telling the truth. Why would I make this up? All I can do is beg you not to tell anyone. Just let it be past. I know it was a terrible mistake. I couldn't go to the police because of the dealing. I'd have been arrested in a minute. I was in too deep. I was an accomplice to murder. I was afraid, Terry, and I'm still afraid. Lowell knows about everything, he knows that you know the girl's body is in Rosemount."

"Lowell?" she interrupted. "You don't mean Lowell from Topanga Canyon, that dealer who used to throw those big parties?"

Michael nodded.

"You're still dealing for him?"

"Not dealing, but I still work for him. He was the one

who set up all those deals for me and Travis. He was the one who killed Bonnie or had her killed. He blackmailed me into getting rid of the body. Ter, he's part of a huge drug-traffic network now—cocaine, heroin, you name it. He threatened to have me killed back then, so I just shut up and went along with it."

"Bonnie," she whispered. "Wasn't that Travis's girl-friend?"

He nodded. "Lowell told me I was being watched, so Bonnie made the delivery instead of me. But Lowell must have freaked, thought she was trying to rip him off. Maybe she was, for all I know. I never knew what went down, but when I got there she was dead. I got scared, Terry. I didn't know what to do so I went along with it."

"Why didn't you just tell me back then? Why couldn't you admit to it, Michael?" She kept shaking her head back and forth in disbelief.

"I didn't want you involved."

"*Involved?* Michael, how could I not be involved? And how can you expect me to keep this a secret? What am I supposed to do, walk around for the rest of my life helping you carry your bad karma? Why should I do that after all that you've done to me? Why?"

He leaned forward, holding his stomach. She thought he might be sick. "I don't know," he groaned. "Because you loved me once."

"You fucked me, Michael. You fucked up my whole life and you're still fucking it up."

"I'm begging you to forgive me."

"I'm not a goddamn priest."

"Please, I don't know what else to do. I *don't want you to be killed.*"

The details of Michael's revelation swam, blurred, in her mind. She'd met Bonnie at one of those parties at Lowell's. Bonnie had spoken in a musical, lilting voice, had a deep Miami tan. Theresa had even read cards for her, hadn't she? Sitting on somebody's waterbed, candela-bra lit on a crate beside the bed. The high moan whined in

263

her head, old sad, dead voice trapped in a locked grave: *Let me out, please let me out.*

So she'd been right all along, about Michael, the girl's voice. Elizabeth said don't trust them—the visions about your own life—but they were true. Every last one of them.

Michael continued. "I didn't have a choice but to tell you, Terry, because Lowell knows all about you. Don't you see? You've got to get out of L.A."

"Get out of here, Michael," she stammered, standing.

"What are you going to do?" he asked.

"I don't know," she whispered. Then she turned to face him, looking at him as if she were seeing him for the first time in her life. "I really don't know what I'm going to do."

Michael stood, weaving slightly as if he were dizzy or drunk. He moved like a sleepwalker through the living room to the front door, clacked the chain-lock over, swung open the door, and then he was gone.

Chapter 22

He knew everything, his mind leaked into mine, injected like a poison into my thinking, taking me over. I'm a prisoner in my own skull. That's why when it came on the midday news while we were eating lunch, I tried to turn it off. There, on the screen: the church, his church, his holy cleanliness. The body under white cloth, pure and dead. That's when he started screaming into me, his face shaking, splitting apart like a cracked mirror. I could feel him clawing into me the way he does, picking my bones apart. That's when he finally knew. There could be no more secrets.

He made me tell. I bent down holding on to my head as he told me I was bad, bad, like our mother always used to do. I was never good enough for her, for him, for anyone. Yes, I killed the man, I cried. I killed all of them and I told him everything—the knives, the cards, and how when evil gets near me I get scared. I have to get rid of it before it enters me. The way his cards did, took my brain by force, instructions from darkness to darkness.

That's when I saw her again. I looked up at the screen and there was her face and I knew we were all connected just like we had wires going from head to head: his, mine, Theresa Fortunato. Skin holds nothing in but blood and bone. Our minds are the same.

He said he was calling the police and I half wanted him to. I half want to die and rise up like light straight into God's mouth. But I just started laughing, "I already called them! They know all about us!"

"What do you mean us?" he said, and picked up the phone then, so I had to stop him. He who has always been

265

locked in me, jail cell, no key, forever and ever amen. I grabbed the kitchen knife, tore my shirt open, and cut myself, "See," I shouted, "blood brother, how you make me bleed?" When I cut the second time, he came out, ripped right out of the world and out of my screaming mind.

It was God's mistake. No one should have two faces and be exactly the same.

Now all that's left is her. One two three. Him her me. Three of Swords. Pure heart, broken heart, heart of the matter. I am walking to her house. I put my glasses on so I'm invisible. I'm taking her an offering. I'm going there because now that he's gone, she is the only one left who can touch me.

Theresa leaned her forehead against the closed door, listening to Michael's hurried steps exit the courtyard. His blood had dried on her hands, her shirt. She felt silent inside, the emptiness of shock. Truth had a vibration, an energy so sharp and clean, it cut through everything, and when she'd heard Michael's long blurting confession, her whole body knew it was true.

In the bathroom she rinsed the blood off her hands, splashed water on her face. She changed into a magenta blouse, black jeans. Enough of white purity, angelic cleanliness. The world was too dirty, too full of lies.

As Theresa returned to the kitchen to call Jardine, she remembered with disgust that Michael had ripped the cord out of the wall. It lay coiled on the floor by the sink. Glass shards were splintered across the floor, the back door now impossible to keep locked. No phone, no door. She didn't even have her car—she'd dropped it at the garage on her way back from downtown. She could not stay here in this house.

Get to Jardine. Just get him to come, take her away to a safe place. Theresa threw open the front door and ran, stumbling, across the patio to Neal's, banged on his door. "Neal!" she called. "Are you there? Neal?" Her voice broke into a sob. The house was quiet, no music. Late afternoon, no one home. Next door was Number Five—no answer. At Number Six the shades were drawn, the house empty. It was nearly dinnertime. Where was everyone? She knocked on doors, running wildly from house to house, crying out, "Where is everybody?"

The van—they could drive her to a goddamn phone. Theresa raced to the front of the courtyard and out the front gate, but the van was not there. There was only an empty space where it had been parked all day. They must have followed Michael when he left. It was the only explanation. Why would they have left her? Jardine had promised, promised.

She stood outside Jasmine Court, clenching and loosening her fists, trying to keep from screaming. "Just go," she said out loud. Go up to The NightTime, use Spider's phone there.

Her sandals scuffed on the crumbled sidewalk. She fell forward into her steps with thick movements as if she'd been drugged. Everything blurred, the green dusk light spun dizzily around her, and she heard the woman whining in her mind, that old singsong, *It's so dark in here, so very dark.* Theresa staggered against a car, tried to steady herself.

"I know," she whispered. "Bonnie?"

Get me out of here, came the high voice.

"I will," she moaned. "I will get you out—only I need to get out too. He's after me now too." And she tried to recall what Lowell had looked like, small man, long brown hair in a scraggly ponytail. But that had been years ago, early seventies. Beard? Did he have a beard like the dog-faced picture the artist had drawn? A mustache, surely he'd had a mustache. She couldn't picture him, didn't think she'd recognize him if she saw him.

With Michael's confession so much of the past made sense. The buried voice, its insistent plea for release, Michael's lies, his fear of her and violence toward her.

267

The death vision now was more enigmatic than ever, but she no longer wanted to question it.

Please, whined the voice within. *Don't go away. Don't leave me here.*

Theresa put her hands over her face, cried out, "Bonnie!" Then she muttered, "Stop it, stop it. Don't go crazy. Just go back to the house. Go back to the house, get your purse. Traveler's checks, money. Leave the rest. Jardine or Cooper can come back for your stuff. Then walk over to The NightTime, call Jardine."

Theresa hurried back up the quiet street to Jasmine Court, in through the gate, past the thick bougainvillea now shadowy in the twilight, through the white picket fence. On her front step she saw the package, small and flat, wrapped in wrinkled white tissue paper. Had she dropped something as she'd run out? As she bent to pick it up tremors ran through her slender fingers. She dropped it. It was hot, there was fire inside it. Could it be a letter bomb? No, a letter bomb had to be sealed. This was a loose square of tissue folded over what appeared to be a small rectangle of paper. Willing her hands to be still, she bent over the package, picked at the tissue paper, opening it. Inside was a single Tarot card, face down. And three small plastic swords.

Her mind went black and quiet. She tried to turn the card over, already knowing what it was, but her hands blinked into flames, then off again. *Only in my mind,* she thought, *only in my mind.* Fire laced over her fingers. She flipped the card to see the Three of Swords piercing the red heart. Lettered across the card, scribbled in red felt-tip pen, were the words *I saved this one for you.*

Red pen, just like on that strange letter, what had it said? *Witches get burned.*

Her hands were glowing red embers of skin, a crimson light inside them. She felt nothing in the rest of her body, only a numbness spreading through her. When had she felt this before? This burning in her hands, this image of fire in her mind. It was all connected, not just some symptom of imbalance. All last week the cards had shown swords, but in one of the readings this heat had burned her hands red. And they'd burned again when she saw Michael, but what was the connection?

Listen to yourself, Theresa, believe in your visions, all of them, no matter what Elizabeth says.

Pure fear opened at the center of her heart, blossoming through her body like a black poisonous flower as Theresa realized he had just been there. He could be inside even now.

Chapter 23

Lieutenant Oliver Jardine leaned into the rounded edge of the bar, curved both hands around the cool glass, and stared down at the amber swirl of the Manhattan. He liked bars during the day, they were quiet and dark, out of the pretty sunshine. People left you alone and you could sit hunched over, depressed, glaring at a matchbook, and no one would bother you. He couldn't think in the sunlight unless he had a fishing hat on and was gazing out over empty blue water. Tipping the glass to his mouth, he swallowed the last of the drink down, raised a finger to the bartender, who said, "yes, sir," and brought him another.

That Ballard was a snake in a well-cut suit. A good-looking snake with handsome stripes but he didn't blend in well with his surroundings like a good reptile should. He was nervous as hell, fast talk, flicking cigarette ashes around.

Bonnie Reslow, Jardine penned in his notebook. Check San Diego directory, and Missing Persons. That was a phony tale, they had the same name. Give me a break, he thought. Why would Ballard be questioning his ex-wife about an old girlfriend he'd lost touch with years ago? And · why was she so upset about it?

Jardine lit a cigarette, watching the coil of smoke spread in a square of sunlight that came through the hanging plants in the front window. Theresa, Theresa. His head ached and the drinks weren't helping. A vein on the top of his head throbbed. He'd been up since four-thirty A.M. scouring that sanctuary for prints, overseeing the photographer's laborious snapping of the room, the old man on the bench, those hands wired together, little plastic swords lined up on the windowsill like a kid's game, and he'd be up late tonight. He had a reservation on a flight to San Francisco in about four hours and an appointment to see Dr. Frank Brandon first thing in the morning. "Goddamn it," he said aloud.

The bartender looked up. "Sir?"

"Bring me another. Forget the cherry." At least, he'd discovered what Theresa had been holding back from him. He wondered if Brandon knew about this. Why hadn't she mentioned a history of mental illness when she signed the release form? "Anything else I should know about you, Theresa?" Mental imbalance. Religious fanaticism, martyrdom, Saint Theresa, bleeding hands . . . he couldn't put it together. And Ballard was no Mr. Clean either. There was some way Theresa and her old man were still connected.

The bartender set the drink before him and Jardine rubbed his forehead. He didn't need that one, he knew. It was getting to him, that's what. All the gears were turning properly but nothing was moving. Logic was not serving him well. The answer would come at an odd angle, off to one side, crazy tilt of the truth. Theresa had once been psychotic, manic, maybe schizy. So was this killer whose voice he had on tape. He'd taped conversations with all of them—Theresa, the esteemed Ms. Brandon, and Ballard, too, just this morning. He'd get the tapes into the lab tonight while he was up in Berkeley to see if there were any similarities.

A crack in Theresa, a hole. What about those experiments Elizabeth had spoken of? Just what had been Brandon's purpose and exactly what part had Theresa played? Check back further on him—criminal record, malpractice. Maybe that was too far off. Not a ninety-degree angle, but closer. Closer was Ballard, his questions about girls named Bonnie, his well-dressed lies, his enthusiasm over dumping on Theresa, turning the questions away from himself.

Jardine paid the tab, stood at a pay phone at the back of the bar, loosened his tie. He felt lightheaded.

"Cooper's out, sir," said the clerk downtown. "Left a

message for you though. It says, 'Three keys to church sanctuary—Mother Superior, janitor, and one hanging on a board in the church office anybody could have gotten to.' "

"If Cooper calls in, tell him to meet me at Hillview Clinic as soon as possible."

"Yes, sir."

The afternoon's white sun made him squint as he walked out of the cool bar. Before driving to the clinic Jardine radioed the car he'd stationed outside Ballard Mortuary. The static crackled through the radio receiver. "Red Monte Carlo, California license number MB Four seventy-seven, still in the side parking lot. Over," reported the detective on duty.

"Right," Jardine growled into the mike. "Keep on it. Let me know when it moves. Over."

Next he radioed the van parked at the entrance to Jasmine Court. The detective called in his response in an excited monotone. "White male seen leaving premises of Number Three, sir. Had not been observed entering. When he saw our vehicle, he ran. We pursued, picked up his tail several blocks over just a few minutes ago. Black Fleetwood, California license number BAL Three-fifty, registered to a Ballard Mortuary. We're on him now, sir. Please instruct. Over."

Damn, thought Jardine. Bastard sneaked out in another car.

"Is she all right?"

"Sir."

"Did you check on her before you followed the Fleetwood?"

"Sir, we did not."

"No one is now watching Number Three?"

"That is correct."

Jardine held the microphone button down, crackling static across the airwaves. "Return immediately. I'll have another car pick up the Fleetwood. Over."

"Fools," he said aloud. Returning to the phone booth in

272

the bar, he dialed Theresa's number. No answer. He'd radio the detectives to check on her house. Glancing at his watch, he realized he'd have to hurry to make the appointment with the psychiatrist. It was only a few blocks away.

It might be just as well if a second car picked up Ballard's tail anyway. That way he'd think he'd lost the van. Jardine wanted him to think he was moving about unobserved so that if he tried anything funny he could be arrested in the process. Jardine had seen so many suspects taken in too early before anything substantial happened, and it always fell apart in court. Reasonable doubt. If Ballard was in this somehow, let him get caught at something.

Jardine's car grumbled to a start and he wheeled out into traffic, welcoming the slight movement of air through the open windows. He reached over, unlocked the glove compartment, and pulled out the medical release form Theresa had signed.

Hillview Clinic stood on a slight rise surrounded by acres of trees, perfectly manicured gardens, and lawns so green they seemed to glow with a light of their own. The grounds, once the estate of a wealthy family, had retained the calm of a well-protected place. Only the bars on the second-floor windows of the main building gave it away as a psychiatric clinic.

Jardine parked his car and paused at the information desk where the receptionist directed him to the psychiatrist's office. DR. BARBARA A. WHITE, M.D. was inscribed on a small brass plate on the door which stood slightly ajar. He pushed the door open, knocking lightly as he entered.

"Lieutenant Jardine?" the doctor said, standing and firmly shaking his hand. "Come in, please. Thanks for calling ahead before you came. It gave me some time to review this file."

She was younger than he'd expected, in her mid-thirties. Her coarse hair was cut short, bangs curled down over thick eyebrows. She smiled as she stepped back behind her desk and adjusted the shade of the window behind her. "Coffee, Lieutenant?"

"Thanks, it's been a long day."

"So. Terry Ballard." Dr. White slid a wooden chair up close to her desk and folded her hands. "Or shall I say Theresa Fortunato? I've been reading about her in the papers, of course."

"Are you surprised at all?"

"By what?"

"Her profession."

"No, I can't say that it surprises me. She was always interested in quasi-spiritual dimensions, ESP, that sort of thing. If there is any surprise on my part, it has to do with the focus of her work, these murders and so on. She was always very afraid of violence."

"How so?"

"Her ex-husband was a mortician. Did you know that? Terry had a very strong fear of death, in fact, she was terrified of blood, any sort of physical pain. It was very difficult for her being around corpses and funerals, so of course, I did think it a bit odd that she'd end up working with the Homicide Bureau. Then again, I've found many people do eventually create situations where they're forced to confront their deepest fears in one way or another. They almost bring it on themselves."

"Could you describe her case to me, Dr. White? Why was she here? What exactly was her diagnosis?"

The woman opened a file on her desk, pushed her glasses up farther on her nose, and read for a moment. Jardine handed her the signed release form and she looked it over. "I must admit, I'm somewhat hesitant to give out information at this point, Lieutenant, even with the form. I'd have preferred to talk to Terry first. In fact, I took the liberty of phoning her to double-check on her permission to discuss her file with you but there's been no answer at her house."

Jardine took out his notebook, scribbled *no answer* on a

blank page. That was strange—Theresa always left her answering machine on if she went out. He did not like it at all that Ballard had gone directly to her house after he'd questioned him and that the van had left her unprotected. Jardine asked the doctor to try Theresa's number again.

"It just rings and rings" she said, holding the phone away from her head.

Okay, he thought, make this quick. Maybe he should have an operator check on that phone and then get over to Venice in a hurry. He realized that he might have to take a later flight than he'd planned. He went on.

"I can assure you, Dr. White, that the form is perfectly legal. Theresa just signed it last week after she had some kind of seizure. Did she have any history of epilepsy or blackouts that you're aware of?"

"Not to my knowledge," said the doctor. Then she paged through the file and handed Jardine a photograph. "This was taken several days after Terry was admitted here." The young woman was hardly recognizable as Theresa. Her dazed eyes were half-shut, thin cheekbones protruding sharply from her drawn face. It looked like a police lineup photo, or worse yet, a shot the coroner's office would get of somebody already cold.

"Terry was legally committed by her husband, Michael Ballard—it would have been six years ago last spring. She was restrained at that time and sedated. She'd been in an extremely agitated, aggressive, and violent state and had, in fact, attacked her husband with a fireplace poker. He suffered lacerations on the forehead which required stitches. We kept her under observation because we feared she might transfer her violent actions from him to herself, and in fact, we considered her suicidal for several weeks. She chose to stay on and continue her treatment here for another two months and I continued seeing her in therapy for another year thereafter.

"Her behavior was described at that time as delusional, leaning toward something we call schizo-typal. She claimed to hear messages, voices, thought that her husband and

275

others were plotting to kill her. She experienced visions, hallucinations. Much of her behavior was compulsive and ritualistic. For instance, she was obsessed with cleanliness, refused to wear clothes that weren't white, refused food saying it was impure. She said she was fasting. She claimed that these activities were of a spiritual nature. She was comfortable only under highly regimented and controlled circumstances and could tolerate very little freedom of choice or decision making.

"We treated her with medication to calm her—Dalmane and Haldol, I've noted here—and she also underwent tests for a possible brain tumor. This is always a fear in cases where there are problems with the vision. We found nothing conclusive on that score." Dr. White looked up over her glasses. "That could be something to look into again if she is experiencing blackouts or seizures. She should see someone about that. Get a special EEG lead to rule out temporal lobe epilepsy."

Jardine was writing quickly in his notebook, having difficulty in concentrating. *Thought he was plotting to kill her*, he wrote. Ballard had not mentioned any violence in the past. All Jardine could picture was Ballard running from her house, the undercover car chasing after him.

The doctor sighed, shut the file. "Terry responded quite well to treatment. Her behavior became appropriate after several weeks here. The aggressive and suicidal tendencies subsided and she became, in fact, quite docile."

"Doctor, could you talk about the violent behavior toward her husband?"

"It appeared to have been an isolated incident."

"And what about Michael Ballard? Was he a violent person? Any abuse, that sort of thing?"

The doctor thought for a moment, then spoke. "Theirs was a troubled marriage, but I don't recall any mention of battering or abuse beyond that one occasion and it was, after all, Theresa who was the aggressor in that instance. That was six years ago, however, and I'm sorry to say our methods back then for uncovering hidden abusive relation-

276

ships in our patients' lives were rather poor. The current literature now suggests it's quite common for a battered wife to conceal marital abuse out of shame and guilt, feeling they're actually somehow responsible for it. Terry may well have been more abused than we were aware of."

"What about her psychic abilities? How did you view that?" asked Jardine.

"I guess it boils down to beliefs at some point, Lieutenant. Does one accept psychic phenomena or not? Terry believed that everything was alive, that all matter was energy, that life force travels in waves, and so on. She felt that her mind was more open to these waves than others'. As for me, I'm a great believer in matter, and in the integrity of the individual self. Call it a good strong ego if you like. Terry said she could pick up on other people's thoughts, even enter their minds or go into their lives. I'd say that these personalities or 'lives' she picked up on were all parts of herself."

"So she was never cured in that respect."

"Well, you don't cure someone of their beliefs, Lieutenant. Our concern was to bring her behavior under control. As I said, she responded well to the medications we used, and after therapy she began to exhibit more conforming behavior. She stopped wearing her spiritual costume, the white clothes, she ceased fasting, and so on."

He decided to throw out a wild shot, his odd-angle question, though he knew it might be too far off. "This is on a slightly different tack, Dr. White, but what is your opinion of split personalities? Is it ever possible that some part of a person is very different from the way they appear on the surface?"

The doctor placed her hands together, pressed her lips to her fingertips. "Clinically speaking, Lieutenant, cases of true multiple personalities are very rare. In the schizo-typal personality, the person processes his imbalances by claiming that some information or message is coming from outside himself. The problem is that such people lack a strong personal boundary. They're spongy. They absorb emotional information from others and claim to be clairvoyant.

"In other cases stressful situations from the past might recur in the patient's mind in such a way that he actually relives them. He blacks out the present and is living out a nightmare vision. This is what happens to many Vietnam veterans, for instance. Let me ask you a question, if I may, Lieutenant."

"Go ahead."

"Is Terry a suspect in this case?"

Jardine sighed and waited a moment before speaking. "Doctor, I'll level with you. In Theresa I have a person who has extremely specific knowledge of four recent murders, information that no one who had not actually viewed the bodies could possibly have. She claims to be psychic. I'll admit that before I met Theresa, my beliefs coincided pretty closely with yours on the subject of psychic phenomena. So I have a dilemma. I can't let go of the feeling that there is some connection between her and the murders. What she knows—it is too uncanny."

The doctor was silent then. Jardine closed his notebook, looked again at his watch.

Finally, Dr. White said, "I'm very troubled by the thought that Terry could be connected with these murders in some way."

"Maybe it is someone she knows," he offered. "Someone close to her."

The doctor stood and walked to a bookshelf, poured a cup of coffee from the glass pot on a hot plate.

"She was always drawn toward spiritual groups. She isn't in any sort of coven or anything like that, is she? Perhaps she has unconscious knowledge of the murders but is unwilling to bring it up into consciousness. If she were aware of these killings in a subliminal way, she might repress the knowledge for some reason and the information might surface 'psychically'; that is, she'd only let herself be aware of it through so-called psychic channels."

"That's interesting. Can you go on?" Jardine asked.

"Is a schizo-typal personality more likely to be psychically open than a healthy person?"

"You know, the person to talk to about all this is a Dr. Frank Brandon up at Berkeley."

Jardine swallowed too large a gulp of coffee and his tongue burned.

The doctor continued. "He's even an acquaintance of Terry's. I believe she worked with him on some parapsychology experiments; I remember reading about it in a medical journal. Lieutenant, you seem surprised that I know of him."

"It's a coincidence. His name came up in another conversation just yesterday."

"Well, the reason I suggest you talk to him is that he's done some very interesting work recently in the area of clairvoyance and psychosis. He studied patients who were hospitalized for various mental illnesses to see if they were any more likely than a healthy person to be psychic, or, as I see it, to absorb information from outside of themselves."

"What about programming, brainwashing, that sort of thing?"

She shook her head. "I don't believe the study touched on that at all," she answered.

"Pandora's box," he muttered.

"What, Lieutenant?"

Jardine tapped the pen on the cover of his notebook. "Thank you, Doctor. Thank you very much. You've been a great help."

"I will be letting Terry know what I've told you, Lieutenant. If there's anything else I can do," she said, taking off her glasses and putting them in the pocket of her white coat, "please call me."

"Do you mind dialing Theresa's number again?"

"Not at all." The doctor picked up the phone, dialed, then shook her head. "Still no answer."

Jardine took the phone and dialed the operator, asked him to check on the line.

"I'm sorry, sir, there does appear to be some sort of

trouble with that line," the operator reported. "We'll have one of our repairmen check on it."

He had to see Theresa, get over to Venice right away. The case was falling open but he had to move quickly before something fell out. He hoped to God Cooper would be waiting for him in the lobby.

The corridor of the clinic was hushed. His shoes even sounded quiet on the shiny tile floor. When he reached the lobby, he looked about for Cooper but he was not there. He tried, for a moment, to imagine Theresa Fortunato in a straitjacket in a padded cell on the second floor, slumped in a corner, in a stupor, a vapid expression on her face. As he walked out into the pleasant light of the afternoon, he did not look back at the barred windows above him.

Cooper's car was pulled up next to Jardine's in the lot outside Hillview and he raised a hand as Jardine stalked hurriedly toward him.

"It's blowing wide open but I still don't know what we've got," he called out. "I don't know where to begin. Theresa did a little time here. Turns out she's got a history of mental illness and violent behavior. Get this—she was locked up because she attacked her ex-husband with a fireplace poker. I talked to her ex-husband this morning and he's jumpy as hell. He'd been questioning her about the killings. Then when I radioed the van at her house, he had just left there and they were on his tail."

Cooper just whistled.

"And the doc didn't buy the psychic bit either. Thought it was compulsive, quasi-spiritual, how did she put it?" He flipped through his notebook. "Anyway, Cooper, I knew this random-killer thing just didn't make it. On top of all this, Dr. Brandon's latest specialty is psychic phenomena and aberrant behavior. Clairvoyance and psychosis. Now, what I want you to do is—"

"Sir, I've come up with something too," Cooper interrupted. "I tried getting hold of the janitor over at Immaculate Heart. He never showed up for work. He was due in at one o'clock and he doesn't answer the phone at home. Operator says it's out of order."

"Shit. So is hers." Jardine scowled, angry that his line of thinking was being muddled by this new information. "Maybe he's just home sick or something. Pulled the plug."

"The sister told me he's never taken one sick day in the three years he's been there, never once come in late. Then I got to thinking—remember on Svedrup's body, the traces of industrial cleaning fluid and the possibility of the murderer wearing rubber cleaning gloves?"

"Goddamn, Let's go check him out. Where does he live?"

Jardine's headache eased up in the excitement.

Cooper reached into his car, picked up a clipboard from the front seat, and read the address out loud. "Forty-eight seventy-two Breezeway. Venice Beach."

"What did you say this guy's name was again?" asked Jardine.

Over Jardine's car radio came the call for Lieutenant Jardine, and he responded.

"Mead," read Cooper from the clipboard.

The detective's voice came on. "This is Crain. We checked out Number Three and we've got Theresa right here. She wants to talk to you."

"Raymond Mead," said Cooper under his breath.

Jardine was relieved that Theresa was with the detectives.

"Should this be a secure line?" he asked.

The radio crackled for a moment, then the detective's voice again: "Better talk to her now, sir. Over."

"Go ahead," he responded.

Where had he heard that name before—on the list of people who took classes in astrology or the meditation temple? No, he thought. Theresa's list of clients, he was sure of it. Reed? Mead?

"What was that name again?" he asked Cooper.

Chapter 24

"Raymond Mead." Theresa pronounced the name slowly into the radio microphone. She sat on the passenger side of the brown undercover van. Running out of Jasmine Court with the Tarot card in her hand, she'd flagged the van as it returned to her house. Now they were parked behind a dry cleaner's several blocks away. "I'm certain it's him." Letting go of the button on the side of the radio, then quickly pressing it again, she added, "I've even got his address, Lieutenant."

Jardine's voice barked onto the radio, flat and loud. "Check. I've already got it. This is not a secure line, do you understand? Keep it simple. Are you all right?"

Pressing the red button: "No. Yes. Michael—he broke into my house, then—look there's too much. I have to see you. My phone is pulled out. I need to see you right away!"

"There's no time right now. As long as you're okay. Do exactly what I tell you. I want you to go back to your house and stay there. Do not leave under any circumstances, do you understand? I'll come over as soon as I check out this address."

"Are you going to Raymond's house now?"

"Let me talk to Crain."

The detective who'd been holding the van door open for her took the radio and she heard Jardine's orders: "Keep her at Number Three, is that clear? Secure the residence and wait. Do not leave and do not let her leave." His voice blared out in the hot van. "Continue as directed. Proceeding to residence. Over."

The detective named Crain hooked the microphone onto

a metal groove on the dashboard and looked at Theresa, his face close to hers. "Guess I'm taking you back home."

"No," she protested. "I can't go back there. You saw the place. It's not safe!"

"The man says—"

"I don't give a shit what he says. Take me to Breezeway or let me just go on my own." She tried to squeeze past him and he blocked her, gripping her forearm.

"Miss Fortunato, I'm sorry. Orders."

"You can't detain me like this. I'm not under arrest."

"He wants you protected, that's all. He doesn't want to lose you."

"The hell he doesn't!" She pulled her arm away and he slammed the van door, went around to the other side, and slid in.

Late-summer dusk glowed outside as she swept up the broken window from the kitchen floor, slivers of glass clattering into the wastebasket. She found a piece of cardboard leaning behind the refrigerator and taped it across the hole in the door. A lot of good that was going to do. The one place that should be safe was the one place she was sure she should not be. Jardine had to know that, damn him. He must be using her as bait. He must! But if that's what he was doing, at least he could give her a bodyguard inside the house! A radio, a remote control microphone, something. If Michael had gotten in here, anyone could.

All the shades were drawn, the house dark except for one light, a yellow circle in the bedroom where she tried to sit still, but she kept getting up from the wicker chair beside the bed, peeking out into the living room. Noises, street sounds, dusk traffic. Music from an open window.

Her ankles were sore where Michael had wound the phone cord, the blood salt taste of a cut still inside her mouth. *Oh, Michael, why did you lie to me all that time? You were always sucked in by money, that sad hipness of*

283

your dealing friends. Old canyon days. We had something then, we really did. Something young and pure before all the bad dreams started.

No, she told herself. *Don't even think that way. Don't even remember the good times, it only burns in you.*

Burns, body hot, searing skin from the inside. The Three of Swords lay face up on the bedside table. Next card, next death. *Jesus Mary Joseph, Sweet Mother of God.* Theresa moved her hand over the card on the table, testing to see if fire would ripple through her. Nothing. She picked the card up, put it in her pocket. She'd give it to Jardine.

How stupid she'd been. Partial truths, that's all she'd ever seen with her almighty psychic gift. No wonder she doubted herself. One third of Michael—the rest was a wash of lies. One half of Raymond—my God, she'd read for him. Almost the whole reading had been swords. How could she have misread it so completely? The way his face had blinked, one face to another, the two men crossing each other, opposition. That must have been the split personality Jardine had talked about, the light-points merging, one swallowing the other. Raymond must have invented the brother completely. He'd meant himself, his dark side rising up inside him, part of him still sane enough to want to stop it all. Raymond's pathetic face hidden beneath the beard, the scraggly hair. The hidden face. Of course, that animal image she'd given the artist, straight out of a past-life dream. But there was no way she could have known. It was all too close in, subjective, confusing. All the readings that week had been cluttered with swords, Josh's, Evelyn's. Just having swords in a reading didn't mean you were a killer. But Raymond was. And within a few hours he'd be in jail, this nightmare over at last.

Theresa went into the bathroom to splash cold water on her face. Her car would be ready tomorrow. She'd leave a day early, fly down that hot road through the desert, all this behind her for good.

As she stood before the mirror, a terrible silence pressed in on her ears, that vacuum that preceded the choir of voices she'd come to dread. She steadied herself against the sink as the stammering swelled, frantic, high-pitched like a thousand people all humming at once. Clapping her hands to her ears, she moaned in a childlike voice, then looked up at the mirror, her hair like a crimson Medusa's leaping with fire, long strands of smoke snaking upward. She pulled at her hair, running her hands through the red flames she knew existed only in her mind, and her face blinked once, twice, to the open-mouthed image of him. "Raymond!" she screamed out as hair grew over her cheeks, and she clawed at the face that was not her face, but his. All his tormented sickness twisted into an open-mouthed howl, a tragic death-mask.

Raymond reached out toward her, pounding on the glass as if he were locked behind the mirror, screaming at her words she could not hear. She felt the stinging in her back over and over, sharp jabs of the knife, his voice roaring, counting as he stabbed. "Not me, not me!" she cried. "Not my death. Only a dream, only a bad, bad dream," as the stabbing continued, the voice raging, "One, two, three, four—"

Theresa fell forward against the sink as the vision snapped off and the mirror reflected again her own terrified face. She couldn't stay here waiting like the good girl everyone wanted her to be. She had to see him, handcuffed, gun at his back, led to a squad car with grilled windows. Had to know they had him in locks and chains. Otherwise, she'd never feel safe. She could not stay here a minute longer in this broken house, with its smashed window, shattered moon.

Theresa staggered to the front door. Neal's house was dark or she would have run to him, in spite of everything. She could see the back of the van at the entrance to the courtyard. She'd have to go out the back way into the shadows of bougainvillea and eucalyptus. After standing at the open back door for several minutes while her eyes

285

adjusted to the dark, she crept out, moving slowly over the grass to the fence.

Light-headed, she steadied herself again. A few stars dotted the dark sky. She stumbled, her legs rubbery, weak. Shadows rustled in the leaves and the soft summer evening swam before her. Waiting until she felt stronger, she looked first one way, then another before scrambling up and over the high fence. She avoided the street for several blocks, sneaking quietly from yard to yard until she came out at the corner. Street dark. No van. Windows lit yellow in the night, blue fleck of TV. Everything quiet.

She hurried north past tiny bungalows covered in vines, shabby wood cottages buried in flowers. The voices' buzz grew still as she neared Breezeway and she recognized that this scene had been played out before, a déjà vu of the most trivial details, that tree bent just so, that line of dried flowers along the sidewalk, a cat crying out by a mailbox, as she was drawn slowly forward.

Peering around the corner of a house onto Breezeway, she saw what must be Raymond's house at the center of the block. Three squad cars were parked on the street, cherry lights blinking silently, red flashes. She didn't see Jardine's car. He must not be there yet. Pulled forward, a sleepwalker obeying some inner voice, she walked down the sidewalk toward the house, entering the whirling circle of lights. Two policemen stood near the front door. Several others hovered around the squad cars. They almost didn't notice her approaching the small yellow house set back behind ragged overgrown bushes. Finally, one called out, "Hey! Get her out of there!" And a man in uniform pulled her off the grass onto the sidewalk, then looked at her face and recognized her.

"It's the psychic," he said to the others. "Miss Fortunato?"

"Yes," she answered. "Is Jardine here?"

"He should be any minute."

"Is *he* in there? Have you got him yet?" she asked, voice quiet, strange distance of a dream. She heard several cars pull up on the street, clack of car doors ease shut behind her. *Please,* she thought, *let this be the end of it.* As she tried to push past the officer toward the house, she felt someone grasp her shoulder roughly, spin her around. It was Jardine, red-faced, his pale eyes shooting anger.

"I thought I told you to stay put, goddamn it."

"I can't stay there. I'm telling you it's not safe."

"It's not safe for you to be anyplace where you can't be protected."

"What fucking protection! Michael Ballard breaks in my back door this afternoon, beats me, ties me up, pulls my phone right out of the wall, while your macho detectives are taking a goddamn nap or something!"

"We're tailing him now."

"*Tailing* him? Why don't you arrest him for breaking and entering! For assault! I'm trying to tell you—" Frustrated, she pulled the Three of Swords from her pocket, the red message inked across it. "Look! I'm next!"

"Theresa." Jardine said loudly, then quieted to a gravelly whisper. "Get in that goddamn squad car till we can talk this through. I've got to deal with this situation first."

"I have to talk to you now!"

Jardine pulled her by the arm across the sidewalk and shoved her down into the squad car.

The officer who had recognized her exchanged a few rapid words with the lieutenant. "Yeah, he's inside," was all she heard. Jardine ran quickly up to the door of the yellow house on Breezeway, and went in. The windows were dark except for the shimmering light of a television. Inside the house one light blinked on. The front door opened a crack and Jardine let a plainclothesman in, signaling for another to follow.

Theresa waited for several minutes, then slid out of the car and walked up the sidewalk into the house.

Inside, a black-and-white television flickered silently on the kitchen table. The living room was neat, stacks of newspapers piled next to the door, a dried plant hung in front of the window. There was secondhand furniture arranged around the room in a square. Theresa rubbed her eyes, tilting her head to the side. The whole house was permeated by a gray fog. She watched it swirl around her feet, drift like fake dry-ice smoke over the furniture, up the drapes. She knew no one could see it but her.

The two plainclothesmen stood outside a door midway down a hall. A light was on in the room, beaming out blue-white fluorescence into the dark. Jardine stood writing in his notebook. "Go ahead and call it in," he muttered. "Use the phone here."

"It's dead, sir."

"Go next door," he ordered.

Brushing past Theresa, the officer said, "Don't go in there. Get back out to the car."

As the officer left the house, she waded slowly through the dream fog down the short distance of the hall and peered past the detective's shoulder. Jardine was bending over a body that was slumped forward on the bathroom sink. The man's white T-shirt was shredded, smeared red-brown, and there was a single knife in his back. The tiled floor was also wet with blood. Just as Jardine touched the body, it tumbled over, falling face up on a worn green rug.

Faint, nauseous, Theresa fell back against the wall as Jardine knelt down over the mutilated body of Raymond Mead on the floor, his face petrified in the exact howl of fear that had leapt out at her from her own mirror not half an hour before.

"He's been dead awhile," Jardine said in a low voice. "I'd say not more than five or six hours." Glancing up, he saw Theresa in the shadows.

"Get her out of here," he barked to the officer. "Get her back to her house!"

"But why?" She forced out a cracked whisper. "Are you using me as bait? Please tell me if you are."

Jardine stood, wiped his fingers on a handkerchief. "Yes," he said quietly.

The officer took her firmly by the arm and Theresa

didn't resist. He led her back out into the night, opened the door of a squad car, and told her to get in. She sat in the back of the car, her arms trembling. She was unable to still the shaking in her hands.

As the car moved up the street taking Theresa home, she turned back to see, through the rearview window, the lights of the remaining squad cars, quick rotating flickers across the houses, round and round, the red whirling.

It was clear to her that the police could not adequately protect her. The protection had been a sham all along anyway. They'd set her up to be killed and lied to her about it after she'd tried to give so much. She recalled Elizabeth's final session with a sickening feeling. *"You let someone steal your knowledge and they burned you for it. You were burned by your own light, don't you see?"*

It was obvious what she had to do. No one, no one, must know where she was. Not Michael or Lowell, not Jardine, not whoever had really killed Raymond Mead. She had to perform some ultimate magic and disappear.

The officer pulled up in front of Jasmine Court and escorted Theresa to her front door. "You heard the man" was all he said.

Pushing the door shut with a click, she stood for a moment in the dark living room, peering out the window at the cop, who signaled with a raised thumb to the invisible Crain and his companion in the brown van.

As she turned around, she saw the large shadow move at the edge of the room.

Chapter 25

Theresa flattened herself against the living room wall, shuddering in small repeating waves as if tiny electrical shocks were shooting through her. This was not a dream, not vision or illusion. Once, the present had felt like a tunnel into the future. Now there was no tunnel, only a locked door behind her. The future had arrived and that meant one thing. The few seconds of silence seemed dizzyingly long as she cowered in the darkness, unable to move. All possibilities had converged into this blackness where a figure stood just out of sight in the shadow by the sunroom door.

The voice repeated, "Theresa?" He moved toward her, stepping into the pale illumination from the streetlight outside her window.

She screamed, "Let me go!"

"I'm not touching you." Stepping from the darkness, Neal Holton held up his open hands as if to prove some innocence. *See? No weapons.* And he spoke rapidly, excuses tumbling out. "I was sitting outside my house drinking a beer—you know, where you sat with me the other night? And I saw you at the window. I waved but you didn't see me. You looked dazed, like you were high or something. I got scared you'd been hurt. Pretty soon this guy came running up knocking at your door and you didn't answer. I watched him go back out to the street, get in that brown van that's been parked out front off and on for the last day or so. At first I thought they were cops. Then I got real worried, why didn't you answer the door? After a while there were still no lights or movements in your house so I got nervous. I came over and knocked and when you didn't answer I went around back and your door was wide open so I came in to look around. Theresa, I was afraid you'd been hurt or something and now here you come walking in, honest to God, Theresa—"

He stepped toward her and she grabbed a letter opener from the top of her desk. "Don't come near me!"

"Look, I know you're scared but believe me—"

"I can't afford to believe you. Or anybody." She opened the door behind her and stepped to the side. "Get out of here."

Neal sat down on the couch and rubbed his face. "I'm not going to harm you," he whispered. "Please trust me."

When he looked up at her, his eyes were pleading and her whole body shook once, violently, as if in shock, and she broke into a silent weeping. She stood in the dark house, sobbing. "I don't know what to do. I don't know what to do."

Neal came over to her slowly as if approaching an injured animal. He eased the door shut, then put his arm around her shoulder, stroking her back. She nearly fell into his embrace and could not seem to stop the wild shaking of tears that jolted through her.

Finally, when she was able to catch her breath, she sucked in air like a drowning woman who'd been pulled from a pool. He led her to the couch, where she sat, and he went into the kitchen to get a glass of water.

"What in the hell is going on with you, Theresa?" he asked, sitting down next to her.

"Do you remember that guy you saw leaving here the day you moved in? You know, the guy in the bar." Neal nodded. "Well, he's dead. They just found him, Neal, not six blocks from here. I thought he was the murderer, I was sure it was him, but he's dead so that means it is someone else, it's someone else, and I'm so afraid. It could be anyone," she continued hysterically. "He could be right outside this house! It could be you! I have to get out of here, I can't trust—"

"It's not me, Theresa," Neal said emphatically. He

took her face in his hands. "Look, I lied to you once but I came clean, right? You had that cop check me out, right? That Jardine. He ran me down and I'm straight, my whole history, it's all on record. He must have talked to you. There are still a lot of things we don't know about each other, Theresa, but I'm not a killer, I'm here to help you. I care about you far beyond all this bizarre bullshit. Use your powers, if you have them. Look at me. You know I'm telling the truth."

His hands were warm on her cheeks. He was right. She did believe him, or she wanted to. "Okay," she whispered. "Neal, I'm so scared. Nothing makes sense anymore. This killer is wandering around loose, he was here earlier, he left this card." She reached into her pocket, realized she'd given the card to Jardine. "Well, a Tarot card, it's like his sign, a sword. The cops are using me as a decoy to pull this guy in. That's why the van is out in front—to protect me—but they're so stupid. All I know is that I've got to get out of here, not just my house, but out of L.A., and I can't have them find out where I am. Any of them! Neal, you can write this all up in your article someday, but it's no joke. It's not a story, it's my life or it's the end of my life. I don't want to die! But as long as I keep playing cops and robbers, as long as I stay in this story, that's all that can happen. It's inevitable."

"What are you going to do?"

"I don't know, I don't know." But she knew exactly: Wait until morning. Pick up her car. Drive east through the desert into the mountains just as Elizabeth had told her to do.

"I don't think you should stay here tonight," Neal whispered. "Why don't you stay at my place? You can sleep on the couch."

Neal took both her hands in his and bent toward her, kissing her on the mouth, hand curved on the back of her neck. His touch was comforting, protective. She moved over into his arms and he held her, rocking her slightly as if she were a child. "This is so weird," he said, "because

292

it's no time for romantic declarations. But I just want you to know when all this is over and it's all been sorted out, that I—" he stopped, kissed her again—"that maybe it is inappropriate, but I'm a little in love with you. Just a little. Okay? Will you try to remember that on the other side of this chaos?"

In the dark his face looked very young. Theresa didn't know what to say.

She rose from the couch and went into the bedroom, where she filled a small, nylon athletic bag with a change of clothes. In the bathroom she reached for her toothbrush and comb without turning the light on, averting her face from the silvery mirror, still afraid that, if she looked into it, the reflection would be the image of Raymond's twisted face.

Returning to the living room, Theresa whispered, "I'm ready. But how am I going to get across to your place without the cops in the van seeing me?"

Neal rose, peered out the front window. "Tell you what. They're not only watching you, they're watching everybody who goes in and out of this whole courtyard. I'm going to run out and yell like I'm calling my dog or something. They'll be watching me for a second, instead of your house. But only for a second. You go out the back and over the fence. Stay there for a minute until you hear me at my back door. Then come around. I'll be holding the back door open. Got it?"

"What if he's out there in the back—the killer—hiding or something?"

"Scream. I'm right here and so are the cops. Okay?" He kissed her again. She stayed at the back door watching as he exited, dashed around to the front of her house, hopped the small side fence, and shouted, "Here, Duchess! Here, girl!" followed by a loud whistle. As Theresa clicked the back door shut behind her and stepped out into her small yard, it was with the certainty that she would never enter that house again alive.

She threw herself into the darkness across the grass,

over the high fence, and crouched there panting. "Duchess! Here, girl!" She could hear Neal talking in an excited voice, word fragments came through the leaves. "Black Lab—leash broke—" God, he was even talking to them. She recognized Crain's voice. Slam of the van door.

After several minutes she heard Neal's front door creak open, ease shut. A second creak: back door. The alley shuddered with shadows, every leaf movement seemed a hand, an ear, the darkness alive and watching as she moved slowly around the side of Neal's house. Quick— flatten against the stucco wall. Press into the blackness. Only a sheet of newspaper flapping, caught at the base of a telephone pole.

"Duchess?" she heard a soft whistle. "Are you out there?"

She scrambled around the back and into Neal's open door.

"Do you want me to keep the lights off?" he whispered as she entered his house.

"Please," she said.

"How about a candle?" The match struck a flecked light into the room and Theresa lowered herself on to the Navajo rug, sitting cross-legged in the center of the floor. "I wish we were somewhere out in the woods," she whispered. "I'd feel safer in the middle of nowhere."

"You're safe here," he said. "I promise you."

He brought a bottle of wine and poured two glasses. Theresa drank a glass quickly, then sipped another. There was so much she wanted to tell him, but it was too complicated. She didn't want to mention Michael, not now. Besides, though she believed she could trust Neal, she wasn't sure if he was still doing research for his article.

"There's a lot you don't know about all this, Neal," she whispered.

"I can imagine."

"It's not just these killings. It's all tied in with some things that happened a long time ago. Things I can't talk about right now. I never knew secrets could kill you, but they can.''

"How do you mean?"

"I promise I'll tell you sometime."

"So there might be a sometime?" he asked. "I mean for you and me."

"I hope so," she said. "I really mean that."

Neal took a piece of paper from a low table constructed of concrete blocks and a sheet of plywood and he jotted down a telephone number. "When you're out the other side of all this, call me, would you? This is my number. In my real life."

"You've got a whole life I know nothing about. This has all been false, hasn't it?"

"The core of me is real. I swear to you, Theresa."

"I can feel it," she whispered. She reached toward him, pulling him down to her, kissing his face and mouth. Her confusion funneled into an aching desire for something loving and human at the black center. She pressed herself against him with a passion born of fear, her subtle movements a release. She wanted to obliterate the reality of this night, escape totally into his warm embrace. His shoulder was naked against her mouth. His lips pressed down hard against hers.

"Make love to me, Neal. Make me forget all this craziness."

In the stillness she laid her cheek against his chest, listening to him breathe. He was not asleep in the ease that usually followed lovemaking. She could tell he was thinking, his mind stirring as if he were listening to every sound in the house. She could almost feel his thoughts scraping around inside him.

"You didn't really want to do that, did you?" she asked. "I mean underneath it all, there was some doubt, wasn't there? Why?"

He kissed her hair. "I just wasn't sure," he whispered, "if it was the best time."

"It was," she protested. Then without knowing why, she added, "Maybe it was the only time we had."

She couldn't sleep but lay awake listening to his breathing shift, deepen into a slow rhythm. The room swam in shadows. How long before they knew she wasn't at her house? Jardine would surely come over after Raymond's body had been covered, strapped to a metal stretcher, after the photographer captured his still shots, angle of the body on the green rug. And what if Michael were right and Lowell was also after her? Then there was the murderer, whoever he was, watching, waiting. She couldn't stay here, even in the safety of Neal's arms. It was too close to home.

She wondered if she should get up and leave, but she was afraid he might wake. No, she thought, wait another half hour. Unable to fall asleep, she tried to replace, in her mind, the blurred image of Raymond's face, his stocky back soaking red, that knife imbedded in his skin. Instead she pictured the road into Taos where she'd be in a day or two. She tried to imagine a new life there. Fantasy soothed her. She'd take her savings, buy some land on the mesa, build a dome house like she'd always wanted, chop wood, go for long walks until this crazed stain of death was cleansed from her life. When she felt sane again, and rested and beautiful, she'd call the number Neal had given her and he'd join her. She could picture it so clearly, the life they would have. She saw it as plain as a photograph—her sitting on the wooden steps of a cabin with a small dark-haired daughter playing before her in the dirt, drawing designs with a stick. Neal chopping wood out back. She would step into the cabin to stir a pot of soup. Blessed domesticity and peace.

Then in the picture she saw herself pick up a small green knapsack that lay beside her on the step, rise, and begin walking down the road. The knapsack grew heavier and heavier as if something of great weight and importance were contained in it.

She was aware that this was no longer a fantasy or a

daydream, yet she was not asleep. It was a vision, a mind-leak. *Open it,* sang a voice inside her.

She put the knapsack down on the ground and could feel heat emanating from it. *Open it, Theresa.*

Carefully, she unlaced the ties, reached inside, and pulled out the gun. The metal was cool in her hand, though the bag felt hot. She held it for a moment and then, as if controlled by something outside herself, she pointed it across the road to a small shack. Michael stepped from the doorway, shouting at her in another language. She raised the gun and pointed it at him.

Theresa sat up in the bed, heart slamming in her chest. Her right hand ached as if she'd shut it in a car door. Neal was still sleeping. She touched his back softly, then stumbled into the kitchen, ran cold water over her hand. She flipped on the small light over the stove; as she turned around she saw it in the small spot of light and her heart leapt into her swollen throat.

The green knapsack hung right there on a peg by Neal's back door. She went to it, lifting it down. It was heavy, just as it had been in the dream. She placed it on the table, watching the double-dream image appear, future and present moving closer and closer until they were one. She reached inside, wrapping her fingers around the cold metal of the gun.

Quickly she let go. Don't hold it, don't even touch it, she told herself. She opened the bag and peered inside. Lie. He was lying, they all were. I *care about you far beyond . . . Will there be a sometime . . .* Oh, God, she thought, her mind clear and empty as the night sky. "Neal," she whispered. "Not Neal."

Reaching farther into the knapsack, her hands fumbled, searching for something she knew was there, and her fingers closed around the bag, lifting it out, crumple of plastic, bits of bright color inside. She didn't have to open the bag to see but she did, slowly, with the cold spreading through her in utter certainty as she stared down at the jumble of brightly colored plastic swords.

297

Chapter 26

This time it was not a dream voice but her own that whispered, "Get out, Theresa. Get out of here." She reached up, clicked off the stove light, waited while her eyes adjusted to the dark. In the bedroom she heard him turn restlessly in the covers. She stood naked, rigid, staring down into the knapsack at the silver gun and the bag of plastic swords. *I'm saving this one for you,* the card on her doorstep had read. Lucky, lucky three. Not me, baby, she thought.

Her heart jackhammered in her chest, but her mind felt bell-clear, an impersonal witness, as if this moment were itself a dream belonging to someone else.

Tiptoeing back into the living room, she found her jeans and shirt, slipped them on, fingering the buttons Neal's hands had opened one by one, hands lovingly stroking her neck and breasts, the chest he'd planned to stab, neck he'd planned to choke. He was sick, sick. Never open, she thought, never love anyone again. Only betrayal, all they want to do is eat you alive, then cut your throat, all of them, even Jardine slipping her life onto his hook and publicly dangling her until he found his killer. Neal. For a moment she wanted to break down sobbing again, but no, she thought, stay far from it all, distant as a star.

She started for the front door, hesitated, turned for the back of the house, passing Neal's bedroom. The door was open a crack and he lay naked, face up on top of the sheets, looking childlike and vulnerable. So Jardine had been right after all. He had to be a split personality. No one could touch her as he had knowing he was going to kill her. She had to believe that the man who'd just made love to her and the murderer were separate selves.

They must not see her, not Neal, not the men in the van. They must not know where she was, not Ballard, Lowell, or Jardine, or the ghosts she could hear whining just below the surface of her thoughts. None of them would know. She would disappear. Evaporate. Die to this life. Cut the rope of circumstance that was being pulled tighter and tighter around her.

In the kitchen she laced closed the knapsack, shutting the gun and swords inside, then hoisted it to the peg beside the door and it came to her, a fact as irrevocable as night following day: the gun in the sack was the gun that killed Michael.

"No," she whispered. "Will kill. Not yet, it hasn't happened yet." Or had it? Suddenly she was not sure. Past and future ran together like watercolors washing through her in black and red until the color was that of blood and night. Time made no difference. Dream and waking, there was no boundary. Just then, she heard Neal turn again in the bed, the changed breathing of sleep broken. Silence, as if he was awake. Knew she was gone.

Quickly she slid the door open and glancing around his small yard, she stepped into the cool air. A hunted animal feeling the night with her entire skin, Theresa stole out of Neal's yard into the alley and broke into a run.

There was only one place she could go, to Camille's. Five blocks to freedom. She thought of Camille's house as her door to safety, a hole that was growing smaller and smaller, and if she could just get to it and go through that hole, she would be saved. If not, she would remain here, death closing in around her.

The residential streets of Venice were dark, cars prowled slowly down the thin streets. She stuck to alleys where she'd be hidden. Once when a car wheeled slowly past she crouched down behind a parked car. A group of teenagers walked by smoking a joint. They passed without seeing her.

But every cat howl or door slam made her draw in her breath, heart thudding wildly. Near Camille's she stopped dead-still in an alley, twisted back, listening to the neighborhood night, car horn, passing boom-box a block away. Rap voice and zag of percussion. What was that? Presence in a side yard? Looking closer, she saw it was just an old man in a sleeveless ribbed undershirt and baggy pants, wrapping a hose around and around his spindly arm, staring at the moon.

A streetlight brightened the front of Camille's building, a safe globe of light guarding the entrance, but what if they were watching her house too? She went a block out of her way, circled back to the rear of the building, eased sideways between the break in the boards used all the time by kids and dogs, up onto Camille's back porch.

She rapped on the wooden door, twice, sharply, on the glass. No answer. She knocked again, short staccato alarm. *Please be home,* she prayed. Suddenly a light flashed on in the hallway, the shade over the door window flapped up, and Camille's face appeared, scowling. After a clatter and click of locks the door creaked open.

"Were you sleeping?" Theresa could barely speak. She realized how out of breath she was, her throat aching.

"What in God's name"—Camille grabbed Theresa's hand, jerked her into the house and slammed the door—"is going on? Get in here. Why you sneaking round backs of people's houses like some common thief, girl?" Her voice was both agitated and imperious.

Theresa walked down the hall into the kitchen and paced the room in a tight path.

"Camille, you've got to let me hide here."

"I ain't got to nothing. Now what in the hell is going down?"

"I know who it is. The killer."

"Why don't you go to the police with this grand revelation like you been doing all along? Why you coming to me? You know I don't have time for this nonsense!"

"They promised me protection but it's full of holes.

They're not watching the back of my house. Jardine wants to use me for bait, bring the killer to me, but he wasn't even straight with me about it. He lied. They'll just suck him in and then they won't be there. Besides, I've just got this feeling"— Theresa pictured that repeating fragment, red whirling spin of the squad car lights—"I can't have anything to do with the police anymore."

"First smart thing you've said in three weeks."

"You were right about the cops, Camille. It's only gotten me in deeper."

"You were digging your own grave, girl."

"God, don't say that! I've got to get out of here. I'm leaving tomorrow for New Mexico, my car's in the garage, and as soon as it's ready I'll be gone. It's all a pattern, Camille," she went on, "and the only way out is to leave all the components of the pattern—the cards, police, Jardine, Michael, the gun—"

"What gun? You don't mean it's Ballard?"

"No. It's this man who moved in across from me. Camille, I've always known there was something false about him, but not this. I still can't believe it. I found a gun in his house and a whole bag of those plastic swords, the ones he leaves at every murder."

"Slow down, girl. You talking completely crazy but I trust you're making sense to yourself. I don't understand all this about components and patterns and Ballard and a man next door but I'll help you if I can because you're my sister. Now, what is it you want me to do?"

"Just let me stay here until tomorrow, Camille. When my car is ready, I'll go get my stuff and leave."

Camille sat down on a wooden chair by the table, and nervously spun the bead on the end of one of her braids, thinking hard, her brow wrinkled into a frown.

"Camille, I'll—"

"Hush," she said. "My spirit guide is talking." Camille closed her eyes, breathed deeply. "I got to take this to my spirit, Theresa, because you're talking life and death. Now, this ain't no game!" She was almost shouting, then low-

301

ered her voice to a whisper. "You can't stay here, Resa, because the pattern you speak of is the pattern of death and I can't have it here. For one thing I got Sarene to think of. For another, these cops know we're friends and you know they going to come by here looking for you."

Theresa was about to speak, but Camille held out her hand, long plum fingernails cut through the air. "Let me think now. Let me think. What we need is a proper course of action. That's what you needed all along. Thought. You just been racing blindly along not seeing consequences. Okay—you leave tomorrow as soon as you get your ride together."

"And I can call Jardine when I get out to New Mexico— tell him who this guy is from there, where I'm safe."

"That's good. But you do got to hide and I'm thinking you got to be somewhere so out of the way, no one think to look for you. And it also got to be a place that's righteous and holy and upright so the vibration of the place helps you be invisible."

"Elizabeth's?" whispered Theresa.

"No way, honey. I'm talking about my mama's house in Watts. No white boy killer going to find you at Hattie Taylor's and she got a whole choir of angels going to be watching over you there."

Camille went into her bedroom, changed out of her robe into clothes, then emerged in the hallway, cradling the sleeping Sarene in her arms. "I'm going to bring her cross the hall to Mrs. Steele's. That's where she always goes when I'm at work."

Theresa heard a knock, quick flurry of whispers, and Camille appeared again in the kitchen, snapping the light off.

"Okay, now, here's the plan. You go out back and down the end of the alley to that big old corner house with the driveway and wait for me there. I'm going to drive around a block or two, make sure nobody is following. Then I'll swing by and you hop in."

Theresa nodded and Camille followed her to the back

door, standing watch as Theresa sneaked through the high grass out into the darkness behind the houses. Crouching under a bush beside the driveway as Camille had instructed, she waited for several minutes until she heard Camille's VW sputter up the street. It turned in the driveway, Camille threw the door open for Theresa, and she quickly backed out, heading inland toward the freeway.

"Stay down," Camille commanded. "Hunch down in the back so no one spots you."

They drove in silence and Camille flipped the radio on, spinning the dial until she settled on a Bob Marley song. Theresa watched streetlights zip by overhead. She felt a tremendous sense of relief, almost embarrassment, as if she were a small child caught in a lie that was too big for her, one that had drawn in all the adults around her.

Finally Camille spoke. "Elizabeth warned you about all this, didn't she?"

"Yes," Theresa said. She thought if she said more, the tight knot of tears in her throat would begin to unravel and she'd lose control.

"This test of yours is some heavy karma. I wonder what past life you messed up to make this one so bad."

"It's not just bad karma, Camille. Elizabeth said it's an initiation. I had to sort some things out and I am. The way I look at it is if I pass, my slate should be really clean."

"Well, I hope so. I don't know if running away will solve anything, but for now I think you're doing the right thing by leaving."

"Do you think so?" Theresa asked.

"If you don't, you gon' be dead."

Chapter 27

Now I'm completely alone in the world. I lie awake in the dark, imagining her sleeping so perfectly. So pure. Only in sleep is she that beautiful. Awake, she could kill me. I know it. She knows it. It's all been decided already one way or another. If I just obey the rules, then whatever happens will be God's will.

Last night, was it? I stood in the hedge beside her house and looked in her window. She lay face down, her hair all stretched out across the pillow. Rock-a-bye.

I should never have revealed myself to her that night in the bar. Just should have stayed in the background, in disguise. Maybe I should have stopped it all right then, gone home with her that very night, made her die for me.

Oh, Jesus, Jesus, I get so confused. I know I'm not all bad like you say. Was I really born evil in the world, a dirty human animal? Some part of me must be good. It's just that Raymond was too close to her. I could see it. He counted on her every word like she was some goddess he was afraid of. When I told him she had to die, he cried. His face got so puffed up, red, I thought he'd explode. He said, "You poor, sick bastard." I said, "If I'm a bastard, so are you."

He told me he felt sorry for me because I knew not what I did. But, God, so help me, I knew! He said he was going to go to her and tell. Tell on me. Bad, bad boy. That's when I knocked him down. He hit his head on the bathtub. I made him hit it again and again, smashing his doll head down and down. I got out the cards and looked for one that would be right for him but there was no card for a smashed head. So I chose the ten, most swords of all. I

*was going to stick all ten of them in his back, but when I
looked I only had two knives left, so I just used one, stuck
it in ten times, counting out loud to make sure I was doing
it by the rules. Now there's only one knife left, Theresa. . . .*

*No one can help you now. I know they're all watching
you, I see them behind you, outside your house. I'm not
that dumb. And you have no idea how often I am watching, following as you go to the bookstore, the café, the bar
where the dancer dances, the long walk down to the pier
and back. I know all the places you are likely to be. Once
you turned and saw me, stared right in full daylight right
into my eyes. You got off your beach towel just like you
were going to wave at me. Hello, my love, my deadly one.
But I was invisible. You couldn't see me.*

*I know where you are, Theresa, and I'm waiting for the
sign, the time, the message in the stars, for the one thing
left for me to do. I'm sorry, but it's the only way I can
survive.*

"Mama? It's me, Camille." Camille knocked again and
a porch light flicked on above them. Eyes squinted out
from under a shade, then the door opened. A small black
woman pushed at the screen door while holding a pair of
glasses to her eyes. She was wearing a fuzzy yellow
bathrobe, her hair up in pink foam rollers. She stood with
one hand on her hip, the other hand jabbing a pointed
finger as she spoke.

"Girl, what fool business you up to in the middle of the
night? Don't you know decent folks sleep at this hour?"

Camille bent down to stroke the back of a mangy cat
that rubbed against her ankles. "Aw, big guy, what happened to you?"

"Come on," Hattie Taylor scolded, "before you let that
flea-bitten cat in with you."

Inside, Camille set her purse on an ironing board and
flopped into a large chair. "Mama, I can't explain the
whole thing, you got to trust me. Theresa's got to stay
here for the night."

Hattie eyed Theresa over her glasses. "You got thin, girl. You sick?"

"Kind of, Mrs. Taylor."

Hattie Taylor clucked her tongue and shook her head. "I suppose you got man trouble."

"That's it, Mama," cried Camille. "And Resa's got to hide from him."

"Some fool nigger with a gun?"

"Mama, I swear you got ESP. He's got a gun but he's a white boy."

"In my mind, no man need to be holding a gun to a woman to show his strength. Let me make up this couch. You can sleep right here, Theresa."

Hattie Taylor muttered as she hoisted the day bed open and flapped out sheets and blankets, shooing Theresa and Camille away when they tried to help. Camille perched on the arm of the chair where Theresa had slumped, her hand patting her friend's shoulder. "You got bread, Resa?" She held out a clump of bills folded in half.

"I've got traveler's checks. I got them for the trip."

"Well, take this. You might need some more. I'll come back here in the morning to get you. Call first and make sure your car is ready, Okay?" Camille put her arms around Theresa and held her; then she left the house. Theresa could hear her car drive off down the dark street.

Theresa lay awake watching the gray room grow pink with dawn. She huddled in the blankets, waking and drifting in short meaningless dreams. Her father cutting cheese in the grocery store in Boston. Sarene picking goldenrod in an open field and then heaping it in a pile on the ground. Michael kissing her on the throat. Theresa running after the mailman, shouting and holding a miniature baby in her pocket. She had no idea that she'd given birth.

First she covered her head with the pillow so she wouldn't have to hear the news droning about trouble in the Middle East and then she jerked up in the day bed. The morning news blared in the kitchen and the smell of bacon frying filled the small neat house. Theresa rubbed her eyes and remembered: Today was the day she was leaving. If she could only make it through this day, she'd be done with it. By midafternoon she'd be speeding along an empty highway in the desert, far from the ocean. By sunset she'd be sitting in some bar watching a few men in cowboy hats shoot pool.

"Well, you finally up. I thought you was going to sleep till noon," Hattie Taylor called from the kitchen door. "I got you some breakfast because you thin as a scarecrow and you look awful too. I swear you girls never learned how to cook or take care of yourself in a proper fashion. What you really need is liver. Anybody can see that. And leafy greens. Liver and leafy greens. Collard, turnip, and some chard. Iron and folic acid. Don't say I don't know my nutrition. I heard it on Gary Collins's show. You think it's just soul food—no, ma'am. You been eating that funny brown rice again, haven't you? Now I say any American who can't eat Uncle Ben's is something wrong with 'em. Here's a cup of coffee. Now, you go wash up and get back in here in five minutes and sit down at this table and I don't want to hear another word about it."

On her way to the bathroom Theresa passed a hallway hung entirely with pictures of Camille and Sarene. There was Camille with a huge Afro, red graduation cap perched high atop her poofed-out hair. Sarene, a squawling newborn swaddled in a lavender blanket. She wondered briefly if her mother kept a picture of her in the second-floor apartment in Boston's North End. It had been ten years since she'd been back East. Maybe that was part of the karma Camille had spoken of. None of her past relationships had ever been resolved, not her family, not her marriage. Maybe after she'd gotten safely settled in Taos, she would go home for a visit and try to make amends.

Before she sat down to breakfast, she telephoned the garage where she'd left her car yesterday afternoon after going to the graveyard with Jardine. How could it have been only yesterday? It seemed like a month.

307

"The Opel? Just a minute," said the loud voice, and she was put on hold, forced to listen to a Muzak violin version of "Strawberry Fields Forever."

"Yah, lady? Yah, we're just getting to it today. Yah, we run into a little trouble yesterday, got backed up."

"Well, when can I get it? When will it be ready?"

"Can't really say. Might not be till tomorrow morning."

"Tomorrow!" she moaned. "Look, this is a life-and-death situation!"

"Yah, it's always a matter of life and death. You let 'em run down for years and then you got to have it yesterday at noon. It's the big weekend, lady. Everybody is in a big hurry. If it's done any sooner, we'll give you a call, Okay?"

Theresa gave the man Mrs. Taylor's number and as she hung up, she realized what a fool she'd been. She couldn't leave the city driving her own car anyway. Jardine would be looking all over for her now, not to mention Lowell and Michael and Neal. She was going to have to fly out, get a plane into Albuquerque and rent a car or something. She wondered how much credit she had left on her MasterCard, or maybe Camille could lend her the money. A bus would be cheaper. But that was stupid too. If the police were looking for her, they'd be checking all the depots and the airport. Camille's car! She'd borrow her ride—but that wasn't safe, either, they knew her license number too. Desperately, she reached for a way out and could think of none. The only possibility was Josh. Once when he'd been working on her car, he'd said he had a couple of old beaters out back that she could use instead of renting one.

Picking up the phone, she dialed the garage again and asked to speak to Josh. She held the phone out from her ear so she didn't have to listen to the Muzak. Finally, he came on the line.

"Josh, here."

"It's Theresa Fortunato, Josh. I'm in trouble, really bad, and I need your help."

"Sure, man, anything I can do."

308

"Once you told me you'd lend me a car if mine wasn't ready on time. Well, I need one now. But not just for a couple of days—a couple of weeks. I need to get out of town in a car that's not mine. I can't explain—it's just, I know I can trust you and—" She stumbled over the words, not sure how much to tell him.

"Don't say another word, Theresa. I got this old pickup out back I been working on. It's just about ready. I got a car to finish up this morning and then I'll get to work on the truck. I think I could have it for you by about five. Can you come and get it then?"

"Oh, thank you, Josh, thank you. Five, then. And it's okay to keep it a couple of weeks?"

"Long as I get it back eventually!"

As Theresa hung up, a wave of despair passed through her at the thought of the long day before her. She dialed Camille to tell her not to come out and pick her up.

"They'll be watching your car, too, Camille. I'm sure of it. It would be better for me to take a cab back to the garage."

"I guess this is the way it's going to have to be," said Camille. "I was hoping to say goodbye to you before you left."

"I'm not leaving for good."

Camille was silent. "I hope not," she said. "Now just lie back today at Mama's and get some rest for the drive. You leavin' tonight, then? I'll be at The NightTime tonight if you need me for anything. Take care of yourself."

The morning stretched endlessly before Theresa and though she felt safe in Hattie Taylor's prim house, she also felt caged. Hattie chattered cheerfully through breakfast, flipping the television to an exercise show—"You ever watch this? It's good"—then to a game show. The TV and the sound of Hattie's voice kept her mind empty. Theresa took a second cup of coffee out to the side porch, a small wood platform with steps leading down to a neat rectangle of lawn.

Watching some lost seagulls circle over the telephone

wires, Theresa felt a great stillness in herself, a sadness. Her life in L.A. was at an end. She knew she could never return. Even if they did catch Neal, and she was sure they would, she couldn't live here anymore. She had another task to complete, another life to live out. Ten years ago she'd come to southern California because it was as far away from her family as she could get. Maybe that was the trouble. She was always leaving, always trying to escape something, only to find it existed inside her and she would never be able to get away.

In the early afternoon Theresa lay down on the couch, paging through back issues of *Ebony* and *Jet*. There was an article about an elderly woman who had taken in seventeen foster children in Houston. The picture showed a tall, gangly woman in a white suit and a black church hat, surrounded by nine tall boys in suits and eight grown girls in elegant dresses. It made her think of Elizabeth taking in her "daughters," and she wished she had a picture of her in her old brown pants and worn sweater. Suddenly she had the urge to talk to her, to tell her that she was all right, that she wasn't going to give her power away after all. She was going to pass her initiation. She would survive.

She was surprised when the familiar voice answered. She'd expected the answering machine or one of her assistants. "Elizabeth, this is Theresa." She wondered if the old woman would just hang up, but she was silent, waiting. Theresa cleared her throat, continued. "I'm leaving California today and I guess I'm calling up to say goodbye."

"You'll be back," said the stern voice.

"I'm in the middle of it all, just like you predicted."

"I didn't predict it. You did."

"I don't know if I'm doing the right thing. I just have to get out of here." Theresa paused, waiting for Elizabeth's approval, advice, some word she could take with her. "I take that back. I am doing the right thing. I know I am."

Well," Elizabeth finally said, "it's your test. If you sort it all out, you'll have some very great work to do, Theresa."

"Am I going to live through it?" Theresa asked.

She heard, on the other end of the line, the sound of a match, Elizabeth lighting a Camel. Theresa could picture her in her office, the old cat in her lap. Elizabeth did not answer Theresa's question but said, "Your friends were out to see me yesterday. Your police lieutenant."

Theresa cringed.

"When did you say you were leaving?" asked Elizabeth.

"This afternoon. I'm going to the mountains like you told me."

There was a long pause, exhalation of smoke into air. "Don't come by the water, Theresa. Stay away from the ocean." Then she hung up.

Suddenly it flashed through Theresa's mind that Elizabeth had set this whole thing up, the test, right down to the murders. They'd all been faked, right? Hollywood blood and plastic swords as props. She and Frank Brandon probably arranged it all, the Humphreys, all of it. They'd even hired an actor to play Neal, the madman killer in disguise, to see if she could tell real from unreal. That was why he'd always felt so duplicitous even after he told her who he was.

But that was silly. That was paranoid. Delusional, as Dr. White had once described her to Michael.

She got up and walked back into the kitchen, where Hattie Taylor set a plate down on the table and ordered Theresa to eat. She wasn't hungry and she had to force herself to swallow the liverwurst sandwich, baked beans, and potato chips. Hattie Taylor watched her chew every bite, sitting on a kitchen chair in her striped dress and spotless apron.

"Theresa," she began, "I got this strange feeling about you. You smart but sometimes you dumb. Camille is the same way but you're worse. The two of you got such a roundabout way of getting in touch with the spirit, it gets you in trouble. Now, I don't know where this man fits in and I ain't got no second sight and if I did I'd pray it go away. But I do know this—you can't solve it yourself. Whatever mess you in it's bigger than you and it's going to take something bigger than you to get you out. You got to lay it down, girl. I'm talking 'bout your burden. Your heavy load. It's making you old before your time. You just put it down right into Jesus' hands. He carry it for you. You take it to the Lord, girl, He make it right. You get down on your knees and give it up to the Father. You think you know so much about the spirit world, both of you girls, you ain't nothing but a pinhead to the sun. Just you go get deep down in your heart. And once you give up your life, He'll tell you what to do. And that's the gospel truth.''

Theresa stared down at her plate. ''I guess that is what I'm trying to do, Mrs. Taylor. In my own way.''

Hattie Taylor crossed her arms and leaned back in her chair, shaking her head.

Theresa couldn't stand it anymore. She called a cab and sat watching for it on Hattie Taylor's front porch. Just as the cab pulled up, Mrs. Taylor opened the screen door and handed her a brown paper bag. ''Oatmeal cookies,'' she said. ''And some vitamin C. Now you come back here when you ain't in such a state of mind, you hear me? And tell that daughter of mine to call.''

Theresa hunched down in the cab as it streamed through late-afternoon traffic, holding the athletic bag and the brown bag on her lap. The sky was dull with fumes and a hot wind sailed in the open window of the car.

The streets of Venice looked, to Theresa, like a scene in a play that had finished its run and was about to be torn down. She was seeing it all for the last time, the small stucco houses, pink and pale blue, the scrubby trees and dusty cars, that particular group of Hispanic children drawing chalk squares on the sidewalk, this exact red-striped awning torn in the middle. Here she'd lived out the script of her life. How had it become, in these three interminable weeks, so hopelessly confused?

The cabbie let her out at the gas station at the corner on Venice, half a block down from the bookstore. The smell of gasoline and hot tar was overwhelming. She glanced around at the cars parked in the crowded lot and the rush-hour traffic speeding down Venice Avenue, looking for the brown van or Michael's red car. When Josh came up behind her, she spun around, nearly losing her balance.

He was wiping his hands on a blue paper towel, wearing greasy coveralls. A red bandana headband was wrapped around his forehead over his long hair.

"It's ready," he said. "Do I get a free reading for this?" He winked and she wanted to throw her arms around him.

"Josh, you'll get a year's supply, I swear to God."

"I hope everything is all right. It isn't all this murder shit I been hearing about, is it?"

"Josh, I can't talk about it."

"Yeah," he said. "That's cool. Listen, let me go on back and get the keys. I even got you a full tank of gas."

Josh strode into the dark garage and Theresa leaned back against the plate glass window staring out into the passing traffic. She looked across toward Washington, the bookstore only half a block up, The NightTime a bit farther down. Her own house, to which she could not return, was just a few blocks closer in toward the ocean. Maybe, if she was lucky, Jardine would think she'd just left early for her trip and wouldn't be actively looking for her, but she doubted it.

Stepping out into the sunshine, she dug in her bag for some change to get a can of 7-Up from the machine in front of the garage. When she heard her name called out, she looked up. Turning toward the traffic, she saw him waving at her.

"Theresa!" he shouted. "Wait!"

But she could not wait. Where was Josh? She ran into the garage, shouting, "Josh! Where's Josh!" But the old man inside merely raised his hands and shrugged. Outside the plate glass window she could see that Michael was crossing the busy Venice traffic, standing on the dry dirt median under the telephone poles, searching frantically for a place to cross.

Again she called out for Josh, but Michael had broken out across the busy road in a long-legged run. She couldn't wait. Pushing out the side door of the garage, she ducked behind a white van and burst across the street into the courtyard of a motel, around the edge of a small pool, and into the alley behind a row of rooms. Then she took off running down the back streets toward the pier.

Chapter 28

Michael Ballard charged into the garage, shouting her name. "Wasn't there just a woman in here with dark hair? Short? Terry!" he shouted again. An overweight biker came out of the back office, glanced out the side door, crossed his thick arms over his chest, and glared at him.

"Who wants to know?"

"I just saw her. Where the fuck is she!"

"Maybe she ain't here. Why you looking for her?"

"Who in the hell are you?" Ballard demanded.

She must have dodged out that side door. He pushed past the biker and caught sight of Terry racing into the courtyard of a motel across the street, the flash of her pink shirt against dull brick. Ballard followed her into the motel parking lot where some scrawny kids were splashing and screaming in a dirty pool, and a tired-looking woman sat drinking a Coors in a lawn chair beside a car.

"Terry!" he called out again. He ran between the units into the back alley. Stopping to catch his breath, he stood and listened. Rush-hour traffic din, impatient honking. Quickly, he crossed between two houses over to the next block and there she was, heading west down the back streets toward the pier.

She looked back then over her shoulder and saw him, serpentined around some parked cars, and cut through the houses, disappearing into the thick shrubbery. He chased after her, out of breath now. Had to catch her, stop her, get to her before Lowell did. She had to understand.

On the next block he saw her cut back toward Venice Avenue. Coming around the corner, he almost missed her ducking into an Oriental restaurant. As he pushed through the door of the restaurant just after her, she turned and screamed. The proprietors behind the cash register looked up in alarm. She dodged around small tables, and through the reddish shadows, he could barely make out her figure knocking against a table at the back of the room before fleeing down a hallway.

His eyes weren't adjusted to the dark inside and a waiter tried to stop him as he threw himself after her. As he passed the kitchen door, a cook ran out yelling in Chinese. Ballard shoved him against the velvet wallpaper. His white hat fell off. Pushing out the fire door into the back parking lot, Ballard heard them calling behind him in broken English, "Hey, you! What doing—you no run! Hey, you!"

Down the alley, he thought he saw her, a shadow in his peripheral vision, or was it a cat, a dog, the wind in the flowers? He pressed himself back against the building, crouched behind a dumpster. Then he was sure of it, the shadow in the bushes moved slightly. When he heard footsteps on gravel, he stayed hidden and the figure moved by him, but as he emerged from his hiding place, he saw it was a fat woman being yanked forward by a dog on a leash.

Damn, Ballard thought, kicking at the small stones.

He hurried back out to Venice Avenue and glanced up and down the busy street but did not see her. Crossing against the traffic, he walked the several blocks back to his car. The pier, the boardwalk. That's where she must be heading. Even though it was close, he'd drive his car up there and park so he could be ready in case he spotted her again.

He drove the eight blocks down toward the ocean and pulled up behind a small sushi restaurant. Out back, boxes of trash were stacked next to a large blue mural of a tidal wave. Opening the hatchback, he lifted out the brown bag and the briefcase, slid them onto the front seat, looking over his shoulder to make sure that no one was watching him. The briefcase clicked open and he fingered the barrel of the gun inside. He wasn't sure he wanted to carry it on him. It would be hot and uncomfortable against his skin, tucked in under his belt. He'd had the gun for years and had never once used it except for target practice, long afternoons smoking dope and shooting pop cans thrown into the air in the hills up from Topanga Canyon.

He gripped the gun, then opened the chamber to check—six bullets—and placed it back in the open briefcase. Taking the roach from the ashtray, he lit it and smoked it down until it burned his fingers. In the rearview mirror the late sun gleamed across the boardwalk.

After he'd left her house yesterday in the stupor following his confession, he'd spotted the brown van tailing him. Heading for the San Diego freeway, he'd laced through afternoon traffic, taking the Santa Monica toward downtown, and then the Hollywood, swerving across lanes at seventy miles an hour until he was sure he'd lost them. But he'd known he couldn't stay in the Fleetwood once they'd seen it.

In melon-colored darkness he'd driven out to the airport, parked in the lot, and changed from his blood-smeared shirt into a T-shirt he'd stuffed into the briefcase at the last minute. Inside, he'd rented a car, taken the shuttle bus to the rental car lot, and driven out in a white Mustang. By that time it was almost nine and he'd checked into a nearby motel. Unable to sleep, he'd stayed up late watching the cable channel, drinking warm Scotch straight out of the sanitary plastic cup, and trying to think it all through.

Now as he sat in the hot car watching the boardwalk crowded with late-afternoon joggers, the vendors beginning to close up their booths, folding up walls of sunglasses as sunset approached, he knew it was all over, the game, the lie that was his life. He could never go back now to that deception. It wasn't just the hidden body, his betrayal of Terry, not to mention Travis and Bonnie, his fear of Lowell. It was everything—the funeral home, his uncles, hearses, three-piece suits, gladiolas, coffins with satin interiors. He didn't want it, any of it. That apartment above the funeral home had locked him in just as surely as

317

any prison he could be slammed into, and he no longer wanted his father's legacy. He should have sold out to his uncles long ago and left California for good. Gone to Hawaii as he'd planned and bought a sailboat, gotten a job as a bartender. Why, why, had he ever stayed?

She had been right all along—he was nothing but a fraud. There was not an authentic word in his mouth or thought in his aching mind. He'd worn the mask of lying so long, he no longer knew what was true in himself or in anyone else. He'd not so much fallen from grace as he had always been excluded from it, and Terry, Terry had been his salvation and he'd blown it. Now he'd confessed to her and it hadn't even mattered. Terry might have already called the cops on him by now. They might have already dug up that grave in Rosemount for all he knew.

His eyes hurt, his pulse was a dull throb in his temples. There was only one possible way that he might redeem himself, and that was to save Terry from Lowell. If he could do that, he could save himself. Exactly how, he was not sure, but he had to find her. She'd never come with him of her own will, he knew that. He'd have to force her. She'd come to realize it was best. They'd drive south toward Mexico, be there in a matter of hours, safe at some cantino, drinking tequila, and she'd understand at last that she needed him. She really needed him now. He'd stay by her, he'd be her dark guardian, her secret angel protector. If he could just save her, be there at just the right moment, she might forgive him everything, he thought, placing his palm over the warm metal of the gun at his side. Lowell would never find them in Mexico.

Before getting out to search the boardwalk, Ballard fumbled in the glove compartment for a small box. Bending over the passenger seat, he scooped a tiny spoonful of cocaine, held it to his nose, and sniffed. He straightened up, inserted the gun into his belt, and tucked his shirt in over it. His mind rushing with heightened resolve, he stepped out of the hot car into the breeze that was coming up off the ocean, rustling the palm trees on the boardwalk.

Terry had always talked about omens, and he watched for one now. It was more than just the rush of the drug, he could feel something moving, breaking open. She was coming, coming.

Theresa raced up the street, sandals flapping on the pavement, and nearly collided with a man whose Rastafarian dreadlocks were stuffed under a brightly colored cap. He shouted after her and she had to swerve to avoid a Japanese family posing for a photograph in front of a drugstore. After she'd run for several blocks, she stopped in a doorway, pressing back against a metal door which was hot from the afternoon heat. For several minutes she watched the pushy traffic, the slow passersby. From her vantage point in the alcove she could see up Venice Avenue: no sign of Michael. He hadn't seen her.

Trying to catch her breath, she clutched the small athletic bag to her chest as if to hide behind it. Fear spread through her, spilling outward like a slow stain. It was always black, an absolute emptiness. That's what death would be. Black and nothing. The dark under the bed, blank and gone, gone beyond . . . She couldn't think. Seeing Michael had made Theresa's thoughts frenzied.

When she was sure that Michael was not waiting for her in some hiding place up the street or cruising past in his red car, she cut back to a side street and down toward the ocean. Just blend in with the crowd, she thought. The boardwalk was busy with skaters and strollers catching the last hot rays of afternoon. It was a weekday, but on Venice Beach, Labor Day weekend began several days early. A large striped tent was being erected on the grass and vendors were staking out territory, hawking T-shirts, tiger-striped swimsuits, sunglasses, and metallic socks in small booths that lined the sidewalk.

She hurried out onto the cement pier and stood, leaning out over the water, remembering Hattie Taylor's advice and the words of an old gospel tune Camille used to hum:

"I shall walk down to the water / And lay my burden down / And for one moment in my life / I shall be free."

"God?" Theresa whispered, but it was no use. Her burden was her mind. To lay down her heavy load, to stop the wheel of fortune, she would have to stop thinking. Her brain would have to be blanked out, erased. She'd have to die.

"Oh, God," she whispered to the ocean, gorgeous, rolling below her in peachy western light, "please, someone—angels, guides, devas, Buddha, Mother Mary" —and then she broke off into silence, feeling that she had brought all this on herself and that she was absolutely alone.

She stepped off the pier, followed the shore north, walking up along the hard-packed sand at the water's edge, back far enough from the boardwalk that she could see quite a distance in either direction. The surf foamed rhythmically at her feet. She stared over the crowded sand and the boardwalk but did not see Michael. But she couldn't stay here on the beach, she was sure of that. She couldn't return to her house. If she could just get to a phone and call Josh, maybe he could bring the truck down here. She'd been so close to getting away.

Up the beach she saw an old brick building where one of her clients lived, a beachfront hotel that had been converted to shabby apartments. Wasn't there a pay phone in the lobby there? She stayed down near the water, making her way up past the jetty, the sidewalk café. The hills above Malibu loomed before her in a dusty haze. Crossing the boardwalk through the late-afternoon joggers, she cut down a short side street to the apartment-building entrance and pushed open the wooden door with the small window that had been broken out. The lobby always reminded her of New York, its stench of urine from winos who slept there on cold nights.

Fumbling with the zipper of her bag, she reached in to find a quarter, inserted it, and began dialing the number of the garage: six-four-seven, pause . . . Across the dark lobby a wooden chair leaned sideways against the wall and she regarded it as if it were something seen in a dream, a Magritte painting, some perfectly ordinary object carrying tremendous meaning. As in a dream the elements slowed and separated—the sea breeze seemed disconnected from the sound of the door opening behind her. Just at that moment she noticed, with microscopic detail, the heart-shaped hole someone had dug in the plaster next to the phone, as the gloved hand reached past her and clicked down the metal hook of the telephone.

Unable to move she could only stare at the scribbled initials on the wall before her. Then she pivoted slowly, air still and hot, pressure of a vacuum, and saw the ghost of his bearded face, the amber eyes, nearly human. "But you're dead," she whispered.

Without knowing why she cringed, expecting a blow. It was not until then that she screamed, clawed out at him to push him away, and he lunged at her, knocking her back against the rough wall, pressing his small body against hers, his hand over her open mouth.

She closed her eyes, tried to scream again, short gasping sounds that would not come out of her throat. Raymond Mead whispered, his mouth against her ear, "Please, Theresa. I didn't mean to hurt you. You're the only one who can help me. Please don't scream. Please don't."

Theresa froze in his arms. She could not see his face. "Promise," he begged, and she nodded stiffly at he lifted his hand from her mouth and took one step back from her. She couldn't believe she was seeing his face, delicate and boyish beneath the mange of beard, the same face that had lolled back, open-mouthed, slack, on the green floor, Jardine bent over him. Had she mistaken that body for Raymond in her fear and haste, simply because it had been Raymond's house? Jardine had rushed at her, yelling at her to get out, they had pulled her out to the car. The whole scene had been hallucinogenic, the pale fog floating at her feet.

"You were dead," she said. "I saw you with my own eyes. It wasn't a dream. It wasn't a vision."

He shook his head and leaned close to her, keeping her flattened against the wall, one of his hands on the chipped plaster, the other on her shoulder. She saw that his eyes were bloodshot, frightened.

"My brother. He killed him. I saw the whole thing. He's dead. He's dead," Raymond stammered. "I don't know how it happened. He brought this dude home for breakfast, he'd been out all night drinking down at the pagoda. That's the kind of shit he'd been up to. Drugs too. Some guy I didn't even know, he was a young dude. I'd seen him a couple of times around Venice, in the Seaside, The NightTime, that kind of place."

Theresa shuddered. Raymond had a sour smell. His brother—but he had looked almost exactly like him.

He went on, "But, like, I had to go to work and he brings home this guy, they're both shit-faced and I start screaming at him 'cause I can't take it anymore. And the TV was on, it was the news and all of a sudden, it's you. You come on the news and my brother—Ron—" He stopped. Theresa thought he might break down. He took a deep breath and spoke again. "So Ron says, 'I hope they get that fucker and cut his nuts off,' and then he says, 'I know that psychic is going to get him,' and then the guy, he just went berserk. Theresa, he picked up a kitchen knife and he started stabbing at my brother, he dragged him into the bathroom, I tried to stop him, I tried, I really did try!"

Here Raymond broke into a convulsive, soundless sobbing, his head sagged against Theresa's shoulder. She tried to cringe away from him.

"I tried to grab the knife out of his hands and he cut me with it, see?" Backing away from her at last, he pulled his shirt open to display a large, clean wound across his chest, blood dried at its edge, the skin around it inflamed. "I tried to get the knife, but I couldn't! He came at me. I ran, I was chicken, my brother was dying and I was chicken-ass scared," he cried. "I just ran. I didn't know what else

322

to do. I guess I was in shock or something, you know? I hid in some bushes. After it was dark for a long time, I just came and sat down here by the water. I must have been in a daze.

"Then I came out of it, I headed back to the house. I figured I'd better call the cops. I didn't know what the hell time it was or anything. There were cops all over the place. They saw me coming and they started shooting at me! I guess they thought I was the one that did it. I took off again and I circled back, went into the back door of this garage down the street where a friend of mine lets me keep my car and I stayed in there all night, hiding in the back seat, sort of sleeping and sort of not, and I stayed in there all today until about half an hour ago. I must have known I'd find you down here. That must be why I came, right? You've just got to help me, Theresa. I don't know what I'm going to do. I guess I should go to the cops and tell them it's not me, right? Will they believe me? Do you believe me?"

Theresa didn't know what to believe. "I saw his body, Raymond. At your house. I thought it was you, I swear. He looked exactly like you."

"He's my twin." Raymond sobbed, lungs heaving for air. "My twin brother."

Theresa put her head back against the plaster wall, remembering the oddly merging pin-lights of her vision, the night he'd seemed not to recognize her in the bar. "Why didn't you tell me he was your twin?" she begged.

"I must have told you. Maybe I didn't. We weren't close. I hadn't seen him in years. I tried to forget about him. I think part of me wanted to block out that I even had a brother until he came back into my life."

"I must have seen him in the bar that night. That was him, then, wasn't it?"

"Maybe it was. I didn't even know he was in there. Theresa! What am I going to do!"

"I don't know. Jesus, how can I help you? I've got problems of my own. I've got to get out of town. I think I know who this killer is, but I can't talk to the police until I'm safe, until I'm out of L.A. It's too dangerous, the whole thing."

He grabbed her shoulders. "What does he look like—the killer?" Raymond demanded, eyes wide, pleading.

"Sandy hair? Mustache? He wears a piece of turquoise on a chain."

"That's him! My god! Kind of skinny! I saw him up at The NightTime. I knew I saw him before! Doesn't he live by you?"

Theresa nodded, her heart hollow.

"I witnessed the whole thing," Raymond rasped. "I know I got to go to the cops and identify the dude, but they got to know it's not me! I think I've got to get out of here too—just for a couple of days till everything cools down and I can think straight. Where are you going to go?" he asked her.

"I'm not sure, but I can't stay here."

"Where's your car?" He backed away from her. "I'll walk you to your car."

"That's the thing. I don't have it. It's in the shop. I was just calling there now."

She turned back, picked up the dangling receiver, put in the quarter again, and dialed the number, but it just kept ringing. She placed her forehead against the cool black metal of the phone. "They're closed," she moaned. "Now what am I going to do?"

"I've got a car," he offered. "I'll drive you. We can go together. Where do you want to go?"

"I don't know," she cried. Maybe she should stop it all right now. Put the quarter back in and call Jardine. She turned and looked at Raymond's face, the sad beauty beneath the pocked skin, the haunted eyes. She couldn't sort it out, but knew she had to be alone. She could not stay with Raymond even if he did need help. She could not be responsible for anyone but herself right now. She hesitated, swallowed. "I've got to get out of here."

"Go with me! My car's right outside!"

"No!" She pushed past him, pulled open the door, and ran out into the street, nearly tripping on the cement curb. At the edge of the boardwalk, not half a block down, Michael stood with his back to her, hands in his pockets, surveying the stretch of beach before him.

"Theresa!" Raymond yelled from the door. "You can't leave me!"

With that Michael flung himself around, looked wildly up and down the boardwalk. Theresa hurled herself toward the car, ducked down beside it. "Raymond—is this your car?" she hissed. "Open it!"

Raymond unlocked the door, swung it open, and she crawled onto the hot vinyl seat. Slamming the door, he ran around and slid in beside her. She crouched low under the dashboard. "Just go," she commanded.

He revved the engine loudly, backed up with a jerk, then the car shot forward onto Pacific Avenue.

"Where should we go?" he asked, glancing up at the rearview mirror.

Theresa put her head down on the seat, held her breath, realizing she'd forgotten the nylon bag at the apartment building, her change of clothes, her keys, her money. Now where could she possibly go? And then she thought of it, the only safe place that remained.

"Just go up the coast highway," she instructed. "Malibu."

After a few minutes Theresa crawled up onto the seat, peering behind them into the snaking traffic. She couldn't tell if Michael was following them but she didn't see his car. "Just get me up to Malibu," she said again.

As they sped along the highway next to the water, Theresa watched as the intense disc of the sun lowered over the Pacific, the late light flashing on the rising waves and glaring down on the hot metal hood of the tan car.

Chapter 29

The Pacific Coast Highway was still busy with early-evening traffic, cars swerving out to pass and spinning off sharply into driveways at odd angles. Quickly, they followed the winding road that cut along brown rock cliffs, the ocean below them on the left in a dazzle of light. They passed the turnoff into Topanga Canyon, where Theresa had waited for Jardine to meet her not a week before. On the hills above them expensive houses stuck out of the dry hills on stilts, glass windows reflecting the rosy sky.

Looking out over the stupidly bright water, Theresa felt her fear turn to a dull aching that spread over her back and legs. With one arm thrown over the top of the seat, she kept glancing behind her at the line of rushing traffic to see if she could spot Michael's car. Had he even seen her? She'd huddled down so fast under the dashboard, she hadn't known if he'd followed or not. Elizabeth's was so close. She'd be safe there—but that was wrong too. She knew it. The blue horizon of the Pacific glittered below her and Elizabeth's words had been clear—*Stay away from the ocean*—but where else could she go? Maybe she should have Raymond just drop her off somewhere on the road, she could hitchhike back to the airport, the bus depot. But she didn't even have any money. If worse came to worst, she could just run up into the mountains, up through the residential areas above Malibu, and hike over into the canyon, hide in the dry bush hills. If worse came to worst, she could always call Jardine. Glancing back again, she looked for Michael's red car, or the blue car she'd seen last week, the man with the mirrored sunglasses. For a moment she even wished she could see Crain at the wheel of the brown van.

Raymond drove stiff-armed, bent forward at the wheel, peering just over the dashboard, concentrating fiercely as if navigating an icy road. He wore a single black driving glove on his left hand. With his right he wiped the hair out of his eyes. His hair was shorter than she'd remembered. He must have gotten it cut. He squinted into the western sun.

Turning back to the road ahead, Theresa closed her eyes, the old light-points of Raymond's family blinking into the black of her inner sight. They shone there, quivering, and then all the lights disappeared except for a single star, just one, not two, not merging and separating. Just one, pulsing in time with the ache in her head. All dead but one, all gone beyond. Had she perceived his brother's death all along?

"Oh, Raymond," she said, almost crying. "I could have foreseen all of this, your brother's death, everything. . . . I've failed everyone so terribly." She talked nervously, afraid that if she were silent, she'd begin to sob and would never be able to stop. It was comforting to see the mountains ahead, dry brown in the haze of sunset. Beach houses now on the left, a long unbroken line of them with Mercedes and vintage Cadillacs pulled precariously into driveways directly off the highway. Elizabeth's was not far.

"What we'll do when we get to my friend's house is—we'll—we'll call the police," she said. "And I'll tell them about you, I'll tell them that you're all right. I mean that I know you and everything. I'll vouch for you and—Jardine," she stammered, "he'll understand, I think he'll understand."

Raymond Mead looked over at her, his eyes wide and childlike, then straight ahead at the road. When he glanced at her again, she moved unconsciously closer to the door. The look was brief, but unmistakable, full of scorn and disgust. But now, facing the traffic, he seemed again just sad and frightened.

"Raymond? Are you all right?" she asked, and when he did not speak, she thought, *Talk. Just get Raymond to talk.*

"What was his name again—your brother?" she asked.

"Ron," he said very slowly. "His name's Ron. I mean, it was."

"What was it between you two?" she asked. "We never did get to that in the reading, did we? Why you didn't get along with him."

"No. We didn't. We never did get along. I didn't want him to go to you for that fortune telling and I told him so. I guess I didn't want you to know how much I hated him, really. Knowing the Bible says that hate is wrong. I figured if you could read minds, you'd know things about me no one should know."

A tremor went through Theresa, and for a moment she thought she might be sick. "You mean *you*, don't you? *You're* the one who came to me for the reading, not your twin brother, right? Raymond?"

He went on speaking, almost as if she weren't there, staring blankly at the road ahead. "See, I found those cards in his drawer, the fortune cards. And they were the same ones she had the day they tested me with those wires in my head and wires in my hands. The very same pictures, the ones they projected into my head for their purposes, with their machines that monitor your thoughts on a TV, reducing all of God's will to a green blip on a screen. Those cards—I knew right then they were evil."

"Raymond, what are you talking about?" Theresa huddled against the door. His face had changed, a dull look in his eyes, not the sad child-eyes, but something cold. He went on and she listened, closing her eyes with a sensation of falling slowly backwards. Just whom was she talking to?

"See, the first time he saw those pictures, he was still in the hospital. All the doctors came in, they were always trying to probe their brains and pick them down to the bones. But he wasn't going to let them in. Not for a second. I knew we were their experiment like a bunch of Nazis. I'm not that stupid. I read some books too. First they started with regular playing cards, holding up the aces and spades and hearts and diamonds, and then they brought out those other ones. What's the first one they hold up? The Devil. The Hanged Man. The Lovers. The Tower. 'Can you tell what is the picture on this card? Can you see it in your mind?' I knew right then they were trying to take me over, do me in.''

Theresa looked straight ahead as the road veered off up toward Pepperdine University. Elizabeth's was not five or six minutes away. At the next stop she could jump out onto the shoulder, flag down a car. She nestled against the door to be ready. She'd not trusted Jardine, but she should have. His instincts had been right all along, he'd had the distance, the objectivity. She should have told him everything right from the beginning—every reading that had gone badly—check these people out, my clients, my friends, my ex-husband, all of them. Was Raymond schizophrenic? He had to be—listen to him babbling about wires and cards. One minute he said "he," then he said "I." Maybe if she didn't let him know she was on to him, he would just let her out.

Ahead, the road was carved into the red cliffs by the sea. When the car halted at the stoplight, Theresa searched with her fingers for the handle, slid her hand over the hot vinyl of the door, touching the holes where the door and window handles had been removed.

Theresa swallowed once, her throat dry. The light changed to green and the car jolted back into traffic.

"Raymond?" she said softly. "My friend's house is right up here around the next curve. You'll see some white pillars at the top of the hill, it's going to be a left turn. I know we're going to be all right once we get there. We're all going to be safe.''

He was sweating, wet lines down the side of his face.

With his gloved hand he was squeezing the steering wheel in a rhythmic movement.

But if Raymond was a split personality, if this twin was just a sick invention of his own mind, who had been dead on that green rug? She was sure that had been Raymond but maybe it had been someone else altogether, a total stranger. She must have been wrong, seen it wrong.

Wild hope flooded through her as they neared the top of the rise and Elizabeth's driveway came into view. "There it is"—she pointed—"right up there!" And as the car whizzed past the turnoff, she rammed at the door with her shoulder, and shouted, "Let me out of here! Stop this car!"

She beat once against the window with her fist and he reached across the seat, grabbed her arm, digging his fingernails into her skin. She lunged at the wheel, and the car swerved wildly toward the cliff. Sliding over toward him, she tried to take the steering wheel in her hands, stabbed her feet at the brake pedal, screaming, "Stop this car, stop it right now! Let me out!"

He tore at her hair and, reaching under the driver's seat with his gloved hand, pulled out a pistol and held it to the side of her head. Theresa cringed helplessly away from him against the locked door.

"Be quiet,!" he hissed. "He doesn't want to have to kill you like this. He really doesn't want to have to shoot you. He wants to do it the right way."

She could flag down a car. Occasional traffic was passing them on the outside lane. Someone would see her struggling, they'd call the state patrol. She tried to sit up in the seat and flail her arms around, and he struck her sharply on the forehead with the metal butt of the gun. She cowered against the door, palm to her head.

The only way was to talk to him. She'd read it in an article about rapists. Talk to them. Make them see you as human. Call him by name.

"Raymond?" she whispered.

"Don't call me that!" he shouted. "Don't mention his

name again!'' He tore his glove off. "Can't you see this?'' He flapped his hand at her, a fleshy leaf of skin, a bony shriveled palm with flipperlike fingers.

No, she thought. This was no schizy Raymond. Raymond really was dead.

His twin pointed the gun at her, talking in a dull monotone. "See this? See this hand? This was Raymond's first act of life. See, he came out before I did. Out of our mother, I mean. They didn't even know I was in there. They never even thought about me. They just let him be born and left me in the dark hole with the cord all wound around my neck until I just rammed out on my own, all blue and screaming. At least that's the way my mother always told it to us.

"Yeah, she'd tell me over and over again, just like that. Raymond was first, he was the perfect one. I was the replica, the one who went wrong, the one that just didn't quite make it. The error. She'd tell me she didn't want me, didn't want me, didn't want me, she already had her perfect little baby Raymond. Raymond Raymond Raymond. Whenever she got good and drunk she'd tell me, boy, would she tell me, so I had it seared into my brain what a fucking mistake I was.

"He was always the perfect one. Angel boy, good and pure and full of light. It was he who made me imperfect. He betrayed me in the womb, right from the beginning. I tried to ruin his hand once so we'd be more alike. So she'd love me better. Poured gas over it, that's right. And then I lit it. We were just kids then. It didn't burn too bad, but at least there were scars.''

Theresa tried to sit up. Maybe she could somehow throw herself into the back seat, grab him from behind, hit him with something, get the gun. Get at the door handle on the driver's side. Very slowly, she eased up to a sitting position. Maybe if he had to hold the gun up higher in the car, someone would see what was going on.

He went on. "At the trial, they said I was numb, I had no sense of morals, I didn't know good from evil, I

331

couldn't tell fantasy from reality, but that wasn't true, see, because I know evil better than anybody and I know the will of God. We went to church every day. Friday nights, all day Saturday, all day Sunday, she made us go down to that wet dark basement where we sat for hours on those benches, watching grown-up people fall down twitching and writhing on the floor screaming wild nonsense they claimed was the tongue of God in their heads. But I knew better. God is totally silent. He has nothing at all in his huge mind. I could hear the perfect nothing of his holy emptiness but I got good, so good, at faking the speaking in tongues. All because I wanted her to love me.

"And don't you think she liked me better since I was best at the God game, best at bended knee and holy talk? No! It never worked. Not for a second. She never loved me. She never wanted me at all. I was a wrong turn. And she never let me forget it.

"Raymond was good, I was bad. My whole life. 'Ronnie did it,' was all he'd have to say and I'd get beat. 'Ronnie broke the cup, spilled the milk, put the cat in the oven.' But I showed her who was smarter, stronger. When she started having that man up after Daddy died and she was sleeping with him, I knew that was sinful wrong. I just listened to God's message to me in the silence. It was so easy! I got the knife from the tool shed, the one she chopped chickens with. Yeah, just like the jackknives. A lot like them.

"I slit his throat first. Right while they were sleeping. Then I held the pillow over her face so there was no more breath, no speaking prayers, tongues, lullabies, lies. Nothing. Because I wanted to show her I did know good from evil.

"I was fourteen years old. After that it was the juvenile hall, jail, and then the hospital, which was also a kind of prison. They kept me in that barred room with those filthy idiots and Raymond was sent down here to live with Aunt Elaine and Uncle Herb. I was in there that whole time. Ten years in that stinking hole."

His eyes were dilated, widened, as he stared at the road ahead. They passed Point Dume and there were hardly any cars on the road now.

"All that time I was waiting for a sign, though," he continued, "and when that doctor came with his tests and his wires and his cards and his assistants in their white jackets, that's when I knew. Bonnie," he said quietly. "That was her name, the one who gave me the pictures." His voice was quiet, calmer. "So when they let me out the next year and I came down here to live with Raymond, 'released to his custody' was how they put it, what happens? The first day I find the very same cards in his dresser drawer! And the next day I see that exact same girl on the beach, the doctor's girl. Bonnie Bonnie Banks of Loch Lomond. So there it was, God's plan, leading me to get rid of the rest of the evil my mother left behind. And that's what I've been doing. But I was going about it all wrong. None of them was as pure darkness as you, Theresa Fortunato."

He straightened his arm, thrusting the gun at her, and she screamed, pushing his arm away. The gun blasted once at the floor and she had her hands over his, biting into his arm. He shoved at her again, then he swung a sudden left turn, crossing in front of the oncoming traffic, on to a dirt road that led down a steep hill. A truck blasted a long honk at them. MATADOR STATE BEACH, read the sign at the entrance to the road where they had turned off. The car rocketed out of control down toward the cliff. Bouncing wildly over the dry brush and through the small parking area which was down from the coast highway, the car flew over a railroad tie partition, past an outhouse, a picnic table, coming to rest a short distance above the sharp cliff that jutted out over the ocean. Through the dust, the sun blazed golden on the water.

Back up to the west Theresa saw houses not far off. Maybe half a mile. If she could run to them. If she could scream. The coast highway was visible above them. Surely someone passing would look down and see them. She let out a loud, high, piercing shriek and clawed at his eyes. He grabbed a rag from the seat between them and stuffed it into her mouth, forcing her back. He took a rope from the back of the car, wound it around her hands in front of her, tied a second rag around her mouth. Theresa struggled, kicking at him, gagging at the stuffed cloth in her throat. He kneed her hard in the belly and pushed the gun to her mouth.

"I'm not going to kill you with this," he said, out of breath, "because I promised I'd save the Three of Hearts for you, Theresa." Then he whispered, "I swear to you, I'm not all bad. I only get confused and he's so loud in my head. All of you in my brain. That's why you have to die, so I can hear again."

He eased off her then and, still pointing the gun, lifted a brown paper bag from the back seat, brought it slowly into the front, and set it on her chest. From the bag he took a small red can of gasoline, reached out of his open window, opened the driver's side door, then wound the window back up and got out.

Theresa squirmed to a sitting position and watched as he opened the can and began pouring gasoline in a wide circle, splashing it on the hillside above the car and into the dry brush at the edge of the cliff. With her hands still bound in front of her she tried to open the driver's side door but the handle on that side had also been removed. She pounded at the glass with both her fists as he threw the can over the steep cliff toward the water. Turning back toward her, his face looked blank, empty, not even angry. As he came toward the car, she threw herself back against the seat, prepared to kick him as he opened the door from the outside.

He yanked the door open and half-sprawled on the seat. "Yea, though I walk through the valley of the shadow of death," he chanted, cocking the gun and lifting it to her face.

Chapter 3o

In front of them the white Mustang careened in and out of the right lane, veering swiftly through traffic up the Pacific Coast Highway. Jardine gripped the wheel tightly, hung several cars back, glanced in the rearview mirror to check the squad car in back of him.

"I think we should pull him over, sir," said Cooper. "He's got to be doing seventy. He's bound to have a piece on him. At least we'd have him on that."

"No," protested the man who sat in the front seat next to Jardine. "Just wait. He wouldn't be driving like that if all he was doing was leaving town. All this time we waited to pick him back up—let him go, I just know he's going to take us to her."

"You're the one who lost her," Jardine said sharply.

"Look, Crain didn't see her leaving either. None of us did, all right? Besides, I wasn't there to follow her. That was Crain's job. I was supposed to get in close, find out what I could."

"Which wasn't much," Jardine added.

"Bullshit."

Jardine pushed the lighter in, stuck a cigarette in his mouth. He was sorry he'd said that. The man was good at surveillance, at acting. He was the best of the young undercover detectives. And it wasn't true he hadn't found much. It was just that Jardine hadn't been able to act on anything he'd discovered. He'd even told Jardine about this Mead visiting her house last week, how upset she'd been, crying. That he'd spotted Mead again at that bar acting suspicious. But how could you pick somebody up for making a woman cry? Now the poor guy was dead.

The Mother Superior had had to make the identification. She'd hesitated for a moment, then said, yes, it was him.

Damn Theresa and her bullheaded ideas. Maybe he should have told her about the undercover detective in the first place. She'd lost her faith in him and after he'd seen the mess Ballard had made of her house, he didn't blame her. He prayed to whatever God might possibly exist that she was still alive.

"If she'd just stayed there, she'd be safe now," muttered the undercover detective.

Jardine dragged on the cigarette, flicking ashes nervously toward the ashtray. "Whoa, baby," he said under his breath. Up ahead the Mustang pulled off the side of the road in a flurry of sand dust and let the traffic stream by him. "Look at this, he's pulling over. Wonder if he spotted us."

Jardine slowed slightly and passed Ballard's car.

"What in the hell is he doing?" asked Cooper, looking back. "Is he pulling a U-turn?"

In the rearview mirror, Jardine saw Ballard wheel his car out on to the highway and head back the other way. "Maybe he's going back to Elizabeth Brandon's," he said. He picked up the radio microphone and called to the squad car behind him. "We're turning around. Prepare to move in."

Braking to a stop on the shoulder, Jardine spun toward the sharp rocks, then turned the car around as the Mustang sailed out of sight on the rise back to Malibu.

Her vision had never been more clear. The siren voices in her head at last were silent, stunned into mute witness. She had seen it all before, the cliff, the glow of the sky, water far below. The crack of a chance opened inside her and she took it. Just as the twin lowered the gun toward her face, she kicked up hard at his arm, tried to roll off the seat to the floor. The gun blast screamed through the car, shattering the windshield into shards that remained frozen in place. She choked out a cry from under the gag as he fell forward onto her, slumping over her, a heavy sack of skin. She pushed him off with her hands still tied together and tried to squirm from beneath him. The driver's door was open, his feet hung out. She could smell gas fumes rising off the grass. Wriggling out from under his body, she tore with both hands at the gag, jerked the rag from her mouth, and stumbled out of the car.

Above her on the hill stood Michael Ballard, a gun dangling loosely from his fingers. When he saw her he rushed down through the brown weeds.

Theresa backed up, glimpsing behind her the long jagged drop to the ocean, giant boulders jutting out from the side of the cliff and pointing up from the sand below. Involuntarily, she crouched down to a squat as Michael ran toward her, though there was nothing to hide behind, nowhere now to escape. She covered her head with her hands.

He knelt down beside where she cowered on the edge of the cliff. "Terry!" he shouted, though he was right beside her. He tried to pull her hands from her face. "Look at me!" he cried. "I've been looking all over for you. Are you okay?" he shouted again. Then looking for a moment up the hill at the tan car. "I think I killed him. I think he's dead."

Finally, she raised her eyes to Michael. His face was huge and close, hair scraggly, uncombed, a day's growth of beard on his cheeks, his dark eyes wild. He spoke in a gravelly slur, she smelled alcohol on his breath. He palmed her cheek, a rough caress, and with the other hand moved her hair from the side of her face. In that hand he held the gun and she felt it scrape against her scalp as he stroked her head.

"Baby, baby. I got to get you out of here," he said in a boozy voice, pulling her to her feet. "I knew Lowell was going to send someone after you. I told you. Oh, baby." He drew her toward him, and finally, she let herself feel the relief, pushed her face against his warm chest, listened to the loud thump of his heart.

"I guess I better be glad you were an asshole enough to follow me," she choked out, pulling back from him, looking over his shoulder at the twin face down on the seat of the car. "Thank you, Michael."

"Now we got to split, Ter. I'm thinking Mexico. At least for a couple months. There's this little place down in Baja," he rattled on. "We could live there real cheap. Until everything blows over. You didn't tell the cops about Rosemount, did you?"

She shook her head.

"Oh, thank you, thank God, baby. I knew you'd end up on my side."

"What do you mean 'your side'? I'm not going to Mexico, Michael."

"You still don't get it, do you?" he yelled.

"You're the one who doesn't get it! That man up there isn't anybody Lowell knew!"

Michael drew a bent cigarette from his pants pocket, cupped a lit match to his lips, and threw the match down into the grass. Instantly, the small rise breathed into flames with a windlike sigh, the dry grass crackling at their feet.

"What the—?" Michael began stamping at the weeds, the cigarette still in his mouth. Then he took her arm, pulled at her. "Come on!" he insisted.

Theresa placed her hand on his arm and slowly pushed it away. The light was golden, the air itself seemed lit. Suddenly, with a clarity that seemed inevitable and pure, she realized that everything was present, detailed as a photograph she'd memorized, stared at for years. The tan car just above her, the fire shooting spindly red points through the tall weeds, gray smoke beginning to waft in the air. The cliff behind her, the orange sun—all of it in perfect order, this seen death of hers. All of it was there. Michael's presence had made the vision complete. No sound of whine-song voices in her head. Everything was slow and eternal, these last moments of light. No matter that if he'd not come, Raymond's twin would have murdered her. There was still the vision, the truth of the dream she could not disbelieve.

Again, Michael grabbed her hand. "Don't just stand there, Ter, let's get out of here!"

He tried to jerk her around the burning grass that was spreading up the hill.

"No! I just can't go with you!"

"I'm not leaving you here. I'm taking you with me."

"You're killing me. You are all killing me!" she screamed.

"I'm saving your goddamn life," he shouted. "If it wasn't for me, you'd be dead. You're not getting away now! I've waited too long! Get over here," he commanded.

As he reached out at her, she charged past him up the incline. He caught her at the ankle, pulled her down to the red-brown dust. Above her the rising air glimmered in the heat from the flames.

"Terry! Terry!" he cried, "Listen to me! You've got to go with me. Lowell's going to kill you. He's going to kill both of us. Don't you see? It's the only way!"

Theresa pushed at the huge weight of his chest, a wave of smoke blurring her eyes, dirt in her mouth.

"I saved you," his voice shaking. "I'm the only one who can save you."

"Michael, get away from me!" She clawed at his back with her fingernails. He reached behind her, yanked her hair down, holding her to the ground. She could feel, lodged between them, the hard gun against her ribs.

"I'm doing this because I loved you"—his voice deep in his throat, an alien growl. "Maybe I still do. Maybe I could never stop loving you even though I hate you half the time." Then he cried out, howling, "Goddamn it, Terry!"

Theresa felt him give for just an instant and she pulled suddenly to the side, trying to push him off, her hands up at his throat, thumbs digging into the muscles. He rose just slightly, hunched half kneeling over her, and as she squirmed up from beneath him, she felt his whole body jolt, the

339

gunfire caving in her ears. Once. Then a second time. Michael's eyes widened, stunned, incredulous. One second of recognition.

"Ter?" he whispered in the final moment before he collapsed on top of her.

Red lights strobed above on the hill as squad cars wheeled into the parking lot. The high whine of sirens hurt her ears. A rhythmic flicker of red spun across the high grass, over the side of Michael's unshaven face, his cheek nearly touching hers.

Suddenly, they were beside her, Jardine and Cooper, pulling Michael off her. The gun that had been pressed between them fell onto her chest from Michael's open hand and Theresa could not stop screaming, "Oh, my God, no. I shot him!"

Several men with guns ran to Michael's slack form; one of them picked up the gun with a rag. Jardine held Theresa in his arms and she sobbed long, breathless wails into his white shirt, clung to him, and did not want to look up.

"Somebody call the fire department." Jardine shouted, "before this thing gets completely out of control!"

Then he held her face in his hands. "You're all right?" he asked. "Are you sure you're all right?" He touched the welt at her temple, bleeding now. "Where in the hell did you go? I told you to stay at the house!" Still angry, still the scolding father, but then he embraced her again. "Jesus Christ, I thought I was going to lose you," he spoke into her hair, helped her to a sitting position, took off his suit coat, draping it over her shoulders.

Above them the flames snapped over the hillside, spreading wildly, smoldering, crackling upward in the wind off the Pacific.

Theresa looked over several feet at the man who was covering Michael's body with a sheet of transparent plastic. He dragged it over Michael's upturned face, then stood, his lips pursed together, and stared down the hill toward her. He lifted his arm, inserting a gun in an underarm holster, and a shock went through Theresa's body. The sandy hair, sunburned face, the handlebar mustache. As he came down toward her through the high weeds, she stiffened.

Staring into the eyes of her lover, she cried to Jardine, "Lieutenant, he's—no! He's—"

"Our undercover detective, Theresa," said Jardine. "Neal Holton. He's been with us since the beginning. I put him in the house across from you so we could have somebody near you all the time. If you'd only stayed put like I told you!"

Neal knelt down beside her, took her hand. "I'm sorry," he said, "it had to be this way." He looked at Jardine, then down. "I couldn't tell you what I was really doing. Orders," he mumbled.

"Oh, Neal," she cried. "I thought you were—" The words were thick in her mouth. Like a drugged sleeper, she stammered, "He's my ex-husband. I can't believe I killed him. The gun just went off, I don't even remember touching it."

"You didn't," he said, shaking his head. "You didn't kill him, Theresa. I did. Didn't you see the wound? It was in his back. I shot him from behind, Theresa. If you'd shot him, it would have been a chest wound."

She put her hands over her face, then looked over again at Michael's body, still now under the plastic. "Is he dead? Is he really dead?"

Standing, she stumbled over to him, his skin already pale through the clear sheet, eyes closed. She pulled the sheet off him and touched his chest. No bloom of blood where she'd imagined it to be. He was still warm, no breath. Just a stillness. She heard the loud sirens approaching from a distance down the highway.

There was another sound to the fire now as the wind picked up—a roar, a rumbling. The red-orange flames reached away from them toward the parking lot, the wind bending the flames, combing the fire upward through the grass.

Covering Michael again, she touched his cheek through the plastic and whispered, "Yes, I did. It doesn't matter who shot you, Michael, it was me that killed you. Just as I'd always seen it. And now you'll never let me go, will you? Your death is bound to me. We'll always be together like this, won't we, my darling, my bastard?"

Lieutenant Jardine stood over her, put his hand on her shoulder. "Come on, Theresa," he said. "This fire's getting wicked. Let's get you up to one of the cars. At least we finally got him. You're safe now," he said, looking down at Michael's body. "I knew the murderer would go for you sooner or later."

As he spoke, Theresa looked up to the hill at the empty door of the twin's car.

"Where is he?" Her voice would almost not come out. "Did they take him away already?" She pointed to the car.

"Who?" asked Jardine.

She took his arm and said slowly, "You didn't think that Michael—Lieutenant, Michael Ballard was not the killer. The killer was in that car with me. Raymond's brother, his twin brother! Right over there. I swear he was right there. It was Michael who shot him! He came just in time!" She was shouting now, the wail of sirens louder.

Jardine looked at her for a long moment, "Twin?" he muttered, then gazed up at the empty car. "What are you saying?" He strode up the hill, pulling a gun out of his shoulder holster.

The fire engines had pulled to a stop in the small parking lot several hundred yards up the hill. Confused voices shouted around them. The sky was a brilliant Day-Glo orange, unreal, as if it all were happening in a vision, not to her but to some dreamed part of herself. Suddenly the wind shifted and a wall of fire seemed to lift diagonally across the hill spreading downward in their direction.

Jardine looked up at it in alarm, then poked the large

gun into the car, peered over into the back seat. Theresa came up beside him.

"But there's no one here, Theresa! Tell me again, what you think happened. You weren't driving this car?"

"No!" she cried, "I'm telling you it was Raymond's twin brother. He tried to kill me. It was just then Michael pulled up and shot him and he was lying right here!"

"I want you to get out of here now," Jardine yelled, "before the fire cuts us off from the cars!"

Theresa nodded, but first she hurried around to the front of the car, squatting to examine underneath. Then she turned and ran down to the rounded edge of the cliff. Looking over, she saw that there was a ledge below her, just before the cliff fell off, a sheer drop to the sea. The twin was crouched there, grinning madly up at her, his shoulder wet with blood, clenching an open jackknife in his fist.

Howling, he sprang straight up at her, knocking her to the ground. Grabbing her by the throat, he scrambled to his feet, hauling her up with him, the knife razored against her neck. He stood with his back to the ocean, holding her in front of him, drawing the blade in a long line across her skin, then again and again.

"Three of Swords," he rasped.

The dry hill above the car was lashing with flames, the fire moving quickly down now, the smoke a black swirl in the light. Jardine, Cooper, and Neal all stood, legs straddled, guns held in two hands, still as hunters taking aim. The fire crackled toward them, flames needling high into the air. Other officers and firemen stood waiting on the rise, a tableau in the waving heat, Theresa thought, exactly like the crowd in the past-life vision Elizabeth had once taken her to. Exactly that circle of witnesses to her burning.

"Let her go!" Jardine shouted. "You don't have a chance of getting away, buddy. Just push her out in front of you and throw down the knife!"

Theresa watched as, behind Jardine, a sudden gust of

wind shoved a river of fire across the grass. In an instant it flowed under the car. The knife blade stung at her throat.

"The car!" she screamed, and then there was the roar of light. She broke from the twin's hold, threw herself down to the ledge below, clutching at the loose rocks, the dried roots of a stunted tree, watching as he was blown back by the shots that broke the air. She clung to the rocks as he sailed out over her into the red light the way a large bird would fall heavily to the water below.

Epilogue

The room was dark, the windows hung with thick, heavy drapes. As Camille dragged them to the side, intense daylight illuminated the room. Theresa moaned, turned over, her face nestled in the pillow.

"Hey. Bum," Camille said softly. "It's eleven o'clock, Pacific Standard Time. Somebody's here to see you." She sat down on the bed beside Theresa and rubbed her friend's back. "It's that Lieutenant Jardine. Right now he's talking to Elizabeth out on the back deck. You best get yourself up and dressed, girl. You look too raggedy to be seen."

Theresa rolled over and sat up, palming her eyes. Her old room at Elizabeth's cliff house looked much the same as when she'd lived there. Camille's braids swayed as she spoke, the multicolored beads clacking softly. Framed in the window beside her the sky was clear, brilliant and white, a thin wash of yellow at the horizon. She fingered the bandage at her throat. It felt wrinkled and damp. The skin underneath it itched.

"How you feeling today?" asked Camille.

"I think I want to take this off," Theresa said, tugging at the dressing.

"Let a doctor take a look at them stitches, honey, before you start messing with them. You might go and tear something open."

"You sound like a mother."

"That's because I am. Now get your ass out of the bed, Miss Mary." She wagged her finger at Theresa, and for the first time since the fire, Theresa smiled.

The fire, that's how she thought of it. Four days ago. The explosion. The end of it all. The death vision. No,

345

that was not right—it was not just a vision. It had all been very real. Michael's death; it had very nearly been her own.

Following the initial tremendous relief at having survived at all, Theresa had experienced a curious sensation as if in some way she really *had* died and her present self were merely a ghost observing the days just after her own death. She felt disjointed, distanced, thinking: Now they would be notifying my parents, now they would be telling the papers, now they would go to my house, now they would ship my body back East. *If I had died.*

Four days. She'd requested that Jardine bring her to Elizabeth's that night. She hadn't wanted to go back to Venice, to her house in Jasmine Court. Not for a while, anyway. All she had wanted to do was sleep Labor Day weekend away, lie in a chaise longue on Elizabeth's deck in the sun and drink mint tea. Now it was Tuesday, the workweek resumed, everything normal again. Tomorrow was Michael's funeral out at his uncle's mortuary in the valley. She'd read about it in the obituary on Sunday and she had asked Camille to go with her. It was still in her mind—she supposed it always would be—the image of Michael's face, almost sad in death, but finally not afraid, the eyes closed under the clear sheet of plastic.

"Elizabeth made you some breakfast, Resa. You're supposed to come out on the deck when you're dressed. The lieutenant says he'll be waiting for you out there."

Jardine had come by Elizabeth's the day after, but Theresa had been extremely distraught, only able to talk to him for a few minutes. She'd told him about Bonnie, the body in the double grave, "Lewis Lauber, Devoted Father," and about Lowell, Michael's feeling that he, too, would be seeking her out. After she'd spoken, she felt dizzy, unable to go on. Elizabeth had been protective and had sent Jardine away, ever mistrustful of the police.

Theresa dressed and joined Elizabeth and Jardine on the long sun deck that ran the length of the house, perched out over the cliff that dropped down to the sea only a few miles from where she'd almost fallen to her death. She shivered as she stood for a moment at the glass doors, wondering if she'd ever be able to look out over the ocean without remembering. Elizabeth had made her stand out here on the deck the next morning. "Face your fears, Theresa, so you can let them go. Wasn't that what all this was about in the first place?" So she'd walked out to the edge of the cliff below Elizabeth's house, sat there for several hours alone, just feeling empty and grateful to be alive. The ocean was just the beautiful surf, the sunset just a postcard view—no demons, no hidden messages, no voices of death.

Jardine looked over at her as she emerged from Elizabeth's living room. She had dressed in white, the way she'd always done before any of this had happened. He stood, extended a hand as if to shake it, then wrapped his arm around her shoulder and hugged her. "Hi, there."

"Hi," she said. "I'm better."

"Good," he said, indicating an empty chair beside Elizabeth. "How's that neck?"

"It itches. I guess that's a sign it's healing, right?"

Elizabeth sat smoking a Camel; her long white hair blew softly back in the warm wind. "Lieutenant Jardine," she said, "tells me he's discovered that Frank actually knew this—this murderer, Theresa."

Theresa lowered herself into a blue deck chair. "What?" she whispered.

Jardine flipped open his notebook, paged toward the back. "When I found out about Dr. Brandon's research in the area of clairvoyance and psychosis, I remembered that Dr. Humphrey once mentioned Bonnie had been a research assistant to Dr. Brandon one summer. What I found out was that Ronald Mead, Raymond's twin, was a patient at a hospital for the criminally insane where some of that research was conducted. Dr. Brandon looked back through his notes and found that Ronald Mead was in a halfway house at the time. He'd served ten years for matricide and was about to be released. The doctors claimed he was 'well' but Dr. Brandon said it was the cutbacks to state

347

facilities—they were letting everybody out who wasn't in a straitjacket.

"The research involved clairvoyant perception of visual archetypes, pictures. In other words, which could a person psychically perceive more easily—a picture, or numbers and letters? In fact, Theresa, Dr. Brandon used pictures from Tarot cards for those experiments."

Theresa shuddered, looking down at her hands. "God, I think I even suggested that to him. So there was some connection. It was just as you thought."

"Not exactly what I'd thought," Jardine said.

Theresa told him about the twin's wild babbling in the car as they'd driven north to Malibu, his talk of evil experiments, wires, pictures in his head.

"Bonnie Humphrey was the research assistant the day Ronald Mead was a participant in the experiment. What we're assuming is that he must have run into her when he came down to Los Angeles to live with Raymond, that he met her somehow, remembered her, and associated her with his past fears and preoccupations."

"I wonder if he ever met me before. I worked with Dr. Brandon at some of those hospitals."

"Dr. Brandon checked on that possibility in his notes," said Lieutenant Jardine, "but he said you hadn't wanted to go that particular day because it was a mental hospital. You'd only wanted to work with the cancer patients and with children. He knew nothing about your history of mental illness. And neither did I, I might add. You might have told me."

"I thought you had me all checked out."

"I did, but somehow that didn't come up until later. In fact, it was Michael Ballard who told me."

Theresa glanced over at Elizabeth. "Some things you put behind you. Or you try to, at least."

Elizabeth rose then, excusing herself. "Theresa?" she said. "Do you still want to take that walk later?"

Theresa hesitated. "I guess so."

Jardine closed his notebook, fumbled in his pocket, and

348

pulled out a match, along with some coins, a crumpled piece of Kleenex, and several plastic swords.

"Must you?" said Theresa. "I don't think I'll ever want a club sandwich again in my life." She thought of Neal, then, the backpack in the kitchen. "Lieutenant, when I left Neal's that night, it was because I found a bunch of those in a plastic bag in his backpack. When I found them, I assumed that Neal was the killer. That's why I ran away."

"You thought it was Neal?" Jardine asked.

"Well, why else would he have a gun and a bunch of plastic swords hidden away?"

"All of us were trying to locate establishments in Venice that used plastic swords. Neal said he'd picked up a handful at the bar where he met you, The NightTime. That was one of the reasons we talked to Camille—because she worked there and was familiar with the clientele and the staff. Which reminds me."

He pulled a sealed envelope out of his notebook and handed it to her. She opened it, unfolded the note inside and read:

Theresa—
I meant what I said about wanting to make contact with you on the other side of all this craziness. If you lost my number, here it is again. You asked me why I seemed to hold back that night—now you know. I remember you once saying there were times you didn't want to be "on duty." I didn't want to be, either, that night. Can we meet in real life as normal people? Not that either of us is.

Your friend, Neal.

She could see where he'd written *Love*, erased it, and scribbled *Your friend*. Not wanting to be embarrassed, to go too far, she supposed, smiling slightly.

Theresa folded the note and continued holding it in her hands. She sighed. "Lieutenant, if you had it to do over

349

again, would you have told me what was really going on? I wish to God you had trusted me."

"But I had to trust *me*, Theresa. Hey—I didn't know you, all right? To me you were just—"

"A crazy witch, right?"

"No," he protested. "A very intriguing and intelligent woman." He looked down. "Well, okay. A little weird, I admit it." He laughed then, stood to leave, hands in his coat pockets. "I won't keep you long. I'll want you downtown in a day or so to answer some more questions. But there is one last thing. The Lauber grave was disinterred over the weekend and the girl—the original Bonnie—was identified. It made it a lot easier for us that you remembered her last name. We checked with Missing Persons in San Diego and got dental records from her parents. You'll be relieved to know that she'll be given a proper burial, so to speak. The body will be sent down to San Diego. The coroner's office reported that except for a little dehydration in the lips the family could have a funeral with an open casket—she looked just like she was sleeping. I guess her family wants her cremated, though."

Good, thought Theresa. That body would never be comfortable in a coffin again. *Goodbye, old voice, released at last.*

"What about Lowell, the dealer?" she asked.

"All we had to go on was his first name, so I wasn't sure how far we'd get. But we got hold of the books at the funeral home and it turns out that this guy was listed as a partner in the Ballard Mortuary. Lowell Morino. When we checked on his residence, we knew we were going to have a little problem locating him. Apparently he's taken a vacation, his housekeeper didn't know just when he'd be back. The FBI traced his passport. My guess is he's on the beach right now—somewhere in Rio. Definitely beyond our reach."

Theresa shook her head. "At least Bonnie went home," she muttered.

"What?" asked Jardine.

"Nothing, I'm just relieved it's all over, that's all."

The lieutenant turned to leave through the double glass doors, but facing her again, he said solemnly, "Thank you, Theresa. I have to say you've given me a new appreciation for my mind."

"Why do you say that?"

"I've decided maybe I'm psychic." He smiled. "I think my intuitions about this case were pretty damn good. But would you ever be willing to give me some lessons?"

"Get out of here." She pushed him gently through the doors into the cool shade of Elizabeth's house.

Elizabeth insisted they walk at sunset along the beach that evening so that Theresa would continue to work through her residual fears about orange light on the water, fire at the line between sea and sky. Sarene and Camille walked slightly ahead of Elizabeth and Theresa, Sarene dragging a long stalk of kelp, drawing a design in the sand as she went.

"I wonder if I passed?" Theresa said to Elizabeth over the lulling roar of the ocean. "I mean, my test, as you called it. My initiation."

"What do you think?" asked the old woman. She curved her palm around the tip of the Camel she held in her lips, sprung a flame off a plastic lighter.

"Well, I'm alive," said Theresa.

"There you have it."

"But I don't feel any wiser, Elizabeth. Somehow, I imagined that if I ever passed an initiation ceremony, I'd feel totally clear. You know, I'd be a little *Bodhisattva*, enlightened. A goddess or something."

Elizabeth laughed. "Most people do die before they're sainted, Theresa. You're damn lucky you are alive. In the end survival always seems ordinary, though. At least, that's what my healed clients tell me. But I think you're a bit smarter. You know that you have to trust your first impulse, don't you? Not go questioning and doubting and asking for validation all the time. Your body won't lie to you. You've got to go with your own wild intelligence—even when it comes to your teachers. Maybe especially then. I think that you'd have been a lot better off if you'd never come to me for advice in the first place."

"I'd have been better off if I'd gone to Taos the day I saw you."

"That's not true," she said. "Many others might have died if you'd not stayed. You were courageous, Theresa."

"I was? I wasn't just stupid?"

"There you go again," said Elizabeth. Her white hair sailed back in the wind, and though her face was deeply lined, she looked quite young. Ageless, thought Theresa.

"I learned something from you, my dear," Elizabeth went on. "You put yourself at great personal risk because of what you believed was true. Your psychic gifts affected an entire city, didn't they? You pushed beyond the confines of mere personal will. Your mind is wider now. I always thought that your psychic work would eventually be planetary in some way."

Theresa blushed. "L.A. isn't exactly the planet," she scoffed.

"No, it's just that you know now that you can influence a whole community with your vision. You're not confined to individuals."

"Like how?"

Elizabeth shrugged. "I would not possibly presume to say, Theresa. I think you will be teaching me in that regard."

Up ahead, Sarene had picked up a shell from the sand and was holding it up for her mother to examine. Elizabeth joined them, the two women bent over the child's cupped hands. Theresa looked over their silhouettes at the sun, the actual sun. Not dreamed or imagined, not a future burning or some broken past. Theresa stood at the water's edge quietly watching it, whole and round, descend into the wide gray sea.